THE KINGDOM

ALSO BY JO NESBØ
AVAILABLE FROM RANDOM HOUSE LARGE PRINT

Knife

The Thirst

The Son

THE KINGDOM

Jo Nesbø

Translated from the Norwegian
by Robert Ferguson

RANDOM HOUSE
LARGE PRINT

Translation copyright © 2020 by Robert Ferguson

All rights reserved.
Published in the United States of America by Random House Large Print in association with Alfred A. Knopf, a division of Penguin Random House LLC, New York. Originally published in Norway as **Kongeriket** by H. Aschehoug & Co, Oslo, in 2020. Copyright © 2020 by Jo Nesbø. Published in agreement with the Salomonsson Agency. This translation was originally published in hardcover by Harvill Secker, an imprint of Vintage, a division of Penguin Random House Ltd., London, in 2020.

Cover photograph by ilikestudio / Shutterstock
Cover design by Michael J. Windsor

The Library of Congress has established a Cataloging-in-Publication record for this title.

ISBN: 978-0-593-33915-2

www.penguinrandomhouse.com/large-print-format-books

FIRST LARGE PRINT EDITION

Printed in the United States of America

10 9 8 7 6 5 4 3 2 1

This Large Print edition published in accord with the standards of the N.A.V.H.

THE KINGDOM

PROLOGUE

IT WAS THE DAY DOG died.

I was sixteen, Carl fifteen.

A few days earlier Dad had shown us the hunting knife I killed him with. It had a broad blade that glinted in the sun and was grooved on the sides. Dad had explained that the grooves were there to channel the blood away when you dismembered your prey. Even that was enough to turn Carl pale, and Dad asked if he was thinking of getting car-sick again. I think that was why Carl swore he was going to shoot something, anything at all, and dismember it – cut it up into tiny little fucking pieces, if that was what had to be done.

'Then I'll roast it and we'll eat it,' he said as we

1

stood outside the barn, me with my head bent over the engine of Dad's Cadillac DeVille. 'Him, Mum, you and me. OK?'

'OK,' I said as I turned the distributor cap to locate the ignition point.

'Dog can have some too,' he said. 'There'll be enough for everyone.'

'Sure there will,' I said.

Dad always said he'd named Dog Dog because at the time he couldn't think of anything else. But I think he loved that name. It was like himself. Never said more than was strictly necessary, and so American he had to be Norwegian. And he loved that animal. I've a feeling he valued that dog's company more than that of any human being.

Our mountain farm maybe doesn't have much, but it's got views and it's got outlying land, enough for Dad to refer to it as his kingdom. And day after day, from my position permanently bent over that Cadillac, I could see Carl head off out with Dad's dog, Dad's rifle and Dad's knife. Could see them turn into dots against the bare mountainside. But I never heard any shooting. And when he returned to the farm Carl always said he hadn't seen any game birds, and I kept my mouth shut, even if I had seen one small covey of grouse after another taking off from the mountainside, showing me roughly whereabouts Carl and Dog were.

And then one day, finally, I heard a shot.

I jumped so hard my head struck the underside

of the bonnet. Wiped the oil from my fingers and looked towards the heather-clad mountainside as the sound of that shot rolled outwards, like thunder, over the village down below by Lake Brudal. Ten minutes later Carl came running, slowing down when he was so close he knew he could be seen by Mum or Dad in the farmhouse. Dog wasn't with him. He didn't have his rifle either. I had already half guessed what had happened and went out to meet him. When he saw me he turned and began slowly walking back the way he had come. When I caught up with him I saw that his cheeks were wet with tears.

'I tried,' he sobbed. 'They flew up straight in front of us, there were so many of them and I took aim, but I just couldn't do it. And then I wanted you all to hear that at least I'd tried, so I lowered the rifle and pulled the trigger. Once the birds were gone I looked down and there was Dog, lying there.'

'Dead?' I asked.

'No,' said Carl, and now he began really crying. 'But he . . . he will die. He's bleeding from his mouth and both his eyes are shattered. He's just lying there on the ground whimpering and shaking.'

'Run,' I said.

We ran, and after a few minutes we saw something moving in the heather. It was a tail. Dog's tail. He smelled us coming. We stood over him. His eyes looked like two egg yolks pulled to shreds.

'He's done for,' I said. Not because I'm an expert vet like every cowboy in every Western movie seems to be, but because even if by some miracle Dog should survive, a life as a blind hunting dog didn't seem as if it would be worth living. 'You've got to shoot him.'

'Me?' exclaimed Carl, as though he couldn't believe that I was actually suggesting that he, Carl, take something's life.

I looked at him. At my kid brother. 'Give me the knife,' I said.

He handed me Dad's hunting knife.

I placed one hand on Dog's head and he licked my wrist. I grabbed him by the skin on the back of his neck and with my other hand slit his throat. But I was cautious, nothing happened, Dog just jerked. Not until the third attempt did I manage to cut through properly, and then it was like what happens when you make the hole too low in the juice carton, the blood came pouring out as if it had been just waiting for the chance to get free.

'There,' I said and dropped the knife in the heather. Saw the blood in the grooves and wondered if any of it had splashed onto my face, because I could feel something warm running down my cheek.

'You're crying,' said Carl.

'Don't tell Dad.'

'That you were crying?'

'That you couldn't bring yourself to . . . couldn't put him down. We say that I decided it had to be done, but you did it. OK?'

Carl nodded. 'OK.'

I slung the dog's corpse over my shoulder. It was

heavier than I expected and kept sliding about. Carl offered to carry it, but I saw the relief in his eyes when I said no.

I placed Dog on the ramp in front of the barn, went into the house and fetched Dad. On the way back I gave him the explanation we'd agreed on. He said nothing, just squatted down beside his dog, nodding as though this was something that he had in some way or other been expecting, like it was his own fault. Then he stood up, took the rifle from Carl and Dog's body under his arm.

'Come on,' he said, and walked up the ramp to the hayloft.

He lay Dog on a bed of hay and this time he knelt, bowed his head and said something – it sounded like one of those American psalms he knew. I looked at my father, a man I'd been looking at every day of my short life, but never seen like this before. Sort of falling apart.

When he turned towards us he was still pale, but his lip wasn't trembling any longer and his gaze was once again calm and decisive.

'Now it's our turn,' he said.

And it was. Even though Dad had never hit either one of us, Carl standing next to me seemed to shrink. Dad stroked the barrel of the rifle.

'Which one of you was it who . . .' He looked for the words, stroking and stroking that rifle. 'Who cut up my dog?'

Carl was blinking uncontrollably, like someone ter-rified out of his wits. Opened his mouth.

'It was Carl,' I said. 'I was the one who said it had to be done, but that he was the one who had to do it.'

'Oh really?' Dad's gaze went from me to Carl and then back again. 'You know what? My heart is weep-ing. It's weeping, and I have only one consolation. And you know what that is?'

We stood silent. The idea wasn't to answer when Dad asked something like that.

'It's that I have two sons who have, today, shown themselves to be men. Who have shown responsibil-ity and taken decisions. The agonies of choice – do you know what that means? When it's the choos-ing that chokes you up, not the choice you end up making. When you realise that no matter what you choose, you're going to lie awake nights and torment yourself, asking if the choice you made was the right one. You could have run from this, but you faced the hard choice head-on. Let Dog live and suffer, or let Dog die and be his killer. It takes courage not to turn away when you find yourself confronted with a choice like that.'

He reached out his big hands. One straight ahead that landed on my shoulder, the other a little higher up on Carl's. And his voice had taken on a vibrato Pastor Armand would have been proud of as he continued.

'It is the ability not to take the path of least resis-tance but the path of highest morality that separates humans from animals.' He had tears in his eyes again.

'I stand here a broken man. But, boys, I am so very proud of you.'

It was not only the most powerful but also the most sustained speech I had ever heard from my father. Carl began to whimper and damned if I didn't have a pretty big lump in my throat as well.

'Now let's go in and tell your mother.'

We dreaded it. Mum who had to take a long walk every time Dad was going to slaughter a goat, and came back red-eyed. On our way to the house Dad held me back a bit, until we were some distance behind Carl.

'Before she hears this version, best you give your hands a more thorough wash,' he said.

I looked up, ready for whatever else might be coming, but in his face I saw only mildness and a weary resignation. Then he stroked the back of my head. As far as I could remember he had never done that before. And he never did it again.

'You and me, we're alike, Roy. We're tougher than people like Mum and Carl. So we have to look after them. Always. Understand?'

'Yes.'

'We're family. We've got each other and nobody else. Friends, sweethearts, neighbours, the locals, the state. All that's an illusion, it's not worth a candle the day something really matters. Then it's us against them, Roy. Us against absolutely everybody else. OK?'

'OK.'

PART ONE

1

I HEARD HIM BEFORE I saw him.

Carl was back. I don't know why I thought of Dog, it was almost twenty years ago. Maybe I suspected the reason for this sudden and unannounced home-coming was the same as it was back then. The same as it always was. That he needed his big brother's help. I was standing out in the yard and looked at my watch. Two thirty. He'd sent a text message, that was all. Said they'd probably arrive by two. But my little brother's always been an optimist, always promised more than he could deliver. I looked out over the landscape. The little bit of it that showed above the cloud cover below me. The slope on the other side of the valley looked like it was floating in a sea of grey. Already the vegetation up here on the heights had a touch of autumnal red. Above me the sky was heavenly blue and as clear as the gaze of a pure young girl. The air was good and cold, it nipped at my lungs if I breathed in too quickly. I felt as though I was completely alone, had the whole world to myself. Well, a world that was just Mount Ararat with a farm on it. Tourists sometimes drove up the twisting road from the village to enjoy the view, and sooner or later they would always end up in our yard here. They usually asked if I still ran the smallholding. The reason these idiots referred to it as a smallholding was probably that they thought a proper farm would have to be like one of those you get down on the lowlands, with vast fields, oversized barns and enormous and splendid farmhouses. They had never seen what a storm in the mountains could do to a roof that was a bit too large or tried to start a fire in a room that was a little too big with a gale thirty degrees below blowing through the wall. They didn't know the difference between cultivated land and wilderness, that a mountain farm is grazing for animals and can be a wilderness kingdom many times the size of the flashy, corn-yellow fields of a lowland farmer.

For fifteen years I had been living here alone, but now that was over. A V8 engine growled and snarled somewhere down below the cloud cover. Sounded so close it had to have passed the corner at Japansvingen halfway up the climb. The driver put his foot down, took his foot off, rounded a hairpin bend, foot down again. Closer and closer. You could tell he'd navigated those bends before. And now that I could hear the nuances in the sound of the engine, the deep sighs when he changed gear, that deep bass note that's unique to a Cadillac in low gear, I knew it was a DeVille. Same as the great black beast our dad had driven. Of course.

And there was the aggressive jut of the grille of a DeVille, rounding Geitesvingen. Black, but more recent; I guessed an '85 model. The accompaniment the same though.

The car drove right up to me and the window on the driver's side slid down. I hoped it didn't show, but my heart was pounding like a piston. How many letters, text messages and emails and phone calls had we exchanged in all these years? Not many. And yet: had even a single day passed when I didn't think about Carl? Probably not. But missing him was better than dealing with Carl-trouble. The first thing I noticed was that he looked older.

'Excuse me, my good man, but does this farm belong to the famous Opgard brothers?'

And then he grinned. Gave me that warm, wide irresistible smile, and it was as though time was wiped from his face, as well as the calendar which told me it had been fifteen years since last time. But there was also something quizzical about his face, as though he were testing the waters. I didn't want to laugh. Not yet. But I couldn't help it.

The car door opened. He spread his arms wide and I leaned into his embrace. Something tells me it should have been the other way round. That it was me – the big brother – who should have been inviting the embrace. But somewhere along the line the division of roles between me and Carl had become unclear. He had grown bigger than me, both physically and as a person, and – at least when we were in the company of others – now he was the one conducting the orchestra. I closed my eyes, trembling, took a quavering breath, breathed in the smell of autumn, of Cadillac and kid brother. He was wearing some kind of 'male fragrance', as they call it.

The passenger door had opened.

Carl let go of me and walked me round the enormous front end of the car to where she stood, facing the valley.

'It's really lovely here,' she said. She was thin and slightly built, but her voice was deep. Her accent was obvious, and although she got the intonation wrong, at least the sentence was Norwegian. I wondered if it was something she had been rehearsing on the drive up, something she had made up her mind to say whether she meant it or not. Something that would make me like her, whether I wanted to or not. Then she turned towards me and smiled. The first thing I noticed was that her face was white. Not pale, but white like snow that reflects light in such a way as to make it difficult to see the contours in it. The second was the eyelid of one of her eyes. It drooped, like a half-drawn blind. As though half of her was very sleepy. But the other half looked wide awake.

A lively brown eye peering out at me from beneath a short crop of flaming red hair. She was wearing a simple black coat with no sidecut and there was no indication of shape beneath it either, just a black, high-necked sweater sticking up above the collar. The general first impression was of a scrawny little kid photographed in black and white and the hair coloured in afterwards.

Carl always had a way with girls, so in all honesty I was a bit surprised. It wasn't that she wasn't sweet, because she actually was, but she wasn't a **smasher,** as people round here say. She carried on smiling, and since the teeth could hardly be distinguished from the skin it meant they were white too. Carl had white teeth too, always did have, unlike me. He used to joke and say it was because his were bleached by daylight because he smiled so much more. Maybe that was what they had fallen for in each other, the white teeth. Mirror images. Because even though Carl was tall and broad, fair and blue-eyed, I could see the likeness at once. Something life-enhancing, as people call it. Something optimistic that is prepared to see the best in people. Themselves as well as others. Well, maybe; of course, I didn't know the girl yet.

'This is—' Carl began.

'Shannon Alleyne,' she interrupted, reaching out a hand so small that it felt like taking hold of a chicken's foot.

'Opgard,' Carl added proudly.

Shannon Alleyne Opgard wanted to hold hands longer than me. I saw Carl in that too. Some are in more of a hurry to be liked than others.

'Jet-lagged?' I asked, and regretted it, feeling like an idiot for asking. Not because I didn't know what jet lag was, but because Carl knew that I had never crossed even a single time zone and that whatever the answer was it wouldn't mean a lot to me.

Carl shook his head. 'We landed two days ago. Had to wait for the car – it came by boat.'

I nodded, glanced at the registration plates. MC. Monaco. Exotic, but not exotic enough for me to ask for it if the car was to be re-registered. On the walls of the office at the service station I had obsolete plates from French Equatorial Africa, Burma, Basutoland, British Honduras and Johor. The standard was high.

Shannon looked from Carl to me and then back again. Smiled. I don't know why, maybe she was happy to see Carl and his big brother – his only close relative – laughing together. That the slight tension was gone now. That he – that **they** were welcome home.

'Why don't you show Shannon round the house while I get the suitcases?' said Carl, and opened the **trunk,** as Dad used to call it.

'Probably take us about the same time,' I murmured to Shannon as she followed me.

We walked round to the north side of the house, where the main entrance was. Why Dad hadn't had the door open straight onto the yard and the road

16

I really don't know. Maybe because he liked to see all his land each day when he stepped outside. Or because it mattered more to have the sun warm the kitchen than the corridor. We crossed the threshold and I opened one of the three doors in the corridor.

'The kitchen,' I said, noticing the smell of rancid fat. Had it been there the whole time?

'How lovely,' she lied. OK, so I'd tidied up and even washed it, but you couldn't exactly say it was **lovely.** Wide-eyed – and maybe slightly anxious – her gaze followed the pipe that led from the wood stove through a hole sawn in the ceiling to the upper floor. Precision carpentry, that's what Dad had called it, the way the circular pipe had safety clearance through the timbers on its way up. If that was true then it was – along with the two equally circular holes in the outside toilet – the only example of it on the farm. I turned the light switch on and off to show her that at least we had our own electricity.

'Coffee?' I asked and turned on the tap.

'Thanks, but maybe later.'

At least she'd mastered her Norwegian courtesies.

'Carl will,' I said and opened the kitchen cupboard. Fished and fumbled about until I found the coffee pot. I'd actually even bought some old-fashioned coarse ground coffee for the first time in . . . well, ages. I managed just fine myself with freeze-dried and noticed as I held the pot under the tap that from sheer habit I'd turned on the hot tap. Felt myself getting a little hot around the ears myself. But anyway, who says there's something **sad** about making powdered coffee with water from the hot tap? Coffee's coffee. Water's water.

I put the pot on the hot plate, turned on the oven and took the two paces over to the door to one of the two rooms that sandwiched the kitchen. The one facing west was the dining room, which was closed in winter since it acted as a buffer against the wind from the west, and we ate all our meals in the kitchen. Facing east was the living room with its bookcases, TV and its own wood stove. On the south side Dad had allowed the house's only extravagance, a covered glass terrace, which he called **the porch** and Mum 'the winter garden', even though it was of course closed off in the winter and solidly barricaded behind wooden shutters. In summer Dad would sit there and suck on his Berry's tobacco and drink a Budweiser or two – another couple of extravagances. He had to travel to town to buy his pale American beer, and the silvery-green boxes of Berry's moist snuff were sent over the pond from a relative in America. Dad explained to me early on that unlike the Swedish crap American moist snuff goes through a fermentation process that you can taste. 'Like bourbon,' said Dad, who claimed that Norwegians only used that Swedish crap because they didn't know any better. Well, at least I knew better, and when I began using it was Berry's I used. Carl and I used to count up the empty bottles Dad lined up along the windowsill. We knew that if he drank more than four he could get tearful, and no one wants to see his dad tearful. Thinking back now, that might be why I seldom if ever drank more than one or two beers. I didn't want to get tearful. Carl was a happy drunk, so he had less need to set these kinds of limits.

All this was going through my mind while we traipsed around and I showed Shannon the biggest bedroom, the one Dad referred to, in English, as **the master bedroom.**

'Fantastic,' she said.

I showed her the new bathroom, which wasn't new any more, but at least it was the newest thing in the house. She probably wouldn't have believed me if I'd told her we grew up without one. That we washed downstairs in the kitchen, with water heated up on the stove. That the bathroom came after the car accident. If what Carl had written was true, that she was from Barbados, from a family that could afford to send her to college in Canada, then it would naturally be difficult for her to imagine sharing the grey water with your brother while the two of you stood there shivering over the bowl in the middle of winter. While Dad, paradoxically enough, had had a Cadillac DeVille parked out there in the yard, because a proper car, that was definitely something we should have.

The door to the boys' room had obviously swollen and I had to wiggle the latch a bit to get it open. A breath of stale air and memories wafted over us, like the smell of old clothes you'd forgotten you owned from a wardrobe. Along one of the walls stood a desk

19

with two chairs next to each other; along the opposite wall a bunk bed. The stovepipe from the hole in the floor down to the kitchen was at one end of it.

'This was Carl's and my room,' I said.

Shannon nodded at the bunk bed 'Who was on top?'

'Me,' I said. 'The oldest.' I drew my finger through a layer of dust on the back of one of the chairs. 'I'll move in here today. So you two can have the big bedroom.'

She looked at me in alarm. 'But, Roy, of course we don't want to . . .'

I focused my gaze on her one open eye. Isn't that a little strange, to have brown eyes when you have red hair and skin as white as snow? 'There are two of you and only one of me so it's no problem, OK?'

She gazed round the room again. 'Thanks,' she said.

I led her into Mum and Dad's room. I'd aired it thoroughly. Regardless of what people smell like, I don't like to breathe in their smells. Excepting Carl's. Carl smelled – if not exactly good – at least **right.** He smelled of me. Of **us.** When Carl was ill in the winter – like he always was – I snuggled up to him. His smell was always right, even though his skin was covered with the dried sweat of fever, or his breath smelled of sick. I inhaled Carl and shivered in close to his glowing body, used the heat he was losing to warm my own carcass. One man's fever is another man's hotplate. Living up here makes you practical.

Shannon crossed to the window and looked out. She'd kept her coat tightly buttoned up. She probably

20

thought the house was cold. In September. It didn't bode well for the winter. I heard Carl come thudding up the narrow staircase with the cases.

'Carl says you aren't rich,' she said. 'But you and him own everything you can see from here.'

'That's right. But it's just outfield, all of it.'

'Outfield?'

'Wilderness,' said Carl, who stood in the doorway panting and smiling. 'Grazing for sheep and goats. There's not a lot you can cultivate up on a mountain farm. You can see for yourself, there aren't even many trees. But we'll get something done about the skyline here. Ain't that right, Roy?'

I nodded slowly. Slowly, the way I had seen the old farmers nodding slowly when I was just a lad and believed so many complex thoughts went on behind those wrinkled brows that it would just take too long and maybe be impossible to express them all using our simple village dialect. And they seemed to have a telepathic understanding of each other, those grown-up, nodding men, the way the slow nodding of one would be answered by the slow nodding of the other. Now I gave that same slow nod, though I hardly understood any more now than I did then.

Of course, I could have asked Carl about all this, but I probably wouldn't have got the answer. Answers yes, plenty of them, not **the answer.** Maybe I didn't need one either. I was just glad to have Carl back and had no intention of bothering him with the question right now: why the hell had he come back?

'Roy is so kind,' said Shannon. 'He's giving us this room.'

'Figured you didn't come back just so you could sleep in the boys' room,' I said.

Carl nodded. Slowly. 'Then this won't seem like much in return,' he said, holding up a large carton. I recognised it at once and took it from him. Berry's. American moist snuff.

'Dammit, it's good to see you again, brother,' said Carl, his voice choked. He came over to me and put his arms round me again. Gave me a real hug this time. I hugged him back. Could feel his body was softer. A little more padding there. The skin of his chin against mine a bit looser, I could feel the rasp of his beard even though he was clean-shaven. The woollen suit jacket felt like good quality, tightly knitted, and the shirt – he never wore a shirt before. Even the way he spoke was different, he talked the city talk him and me used sometimes when we were imitating Mum. But that was fine. He still smelled the same. He smelled of **Carl.** He stepped back and looked at me. Eyes that were as beautiful as a girl's glowing. What the hell, mine were glowing too.

'Coffee's boiling,' I said, my voice not too choked up, and headed for the stairs.

In bed that evening I lay listening to the sounds. Did the house maybe sound different now people were living here again? It didn't. It creaked, coughed and whistled same as always. I listened out too for sounds from **the master bedroom.** The walls are thin, so even with the bathroom between the two bedrooms I could still hear voices. Were they talking about me? Was Shannon asking Carl if his big brother was always this quiet? If Carl thought Roy had enjoyed the chilli con carne she had made? If his silent brother really had liked the gift she had brought with her, which she'd had so much trouble getting hold of through relatives, a used licence plate from Barbados? Didn't his big brother like her? And Carl answering that Roy was like that with everybody, she should just give him time. And she said that maybe she thought Roy was jealous of her, that Roy was bound to feel she'd taken his brother from him, the brother that was all he had. And Carl laughing, stroking her cheek and telling her not to worry about things like that after just one day, that everything would work out. And she buried her head in his shoulder and said she was sure he was right, but anyway she was glad Carl wasn't like his brother. That it was strange how, in a land almost without crime, people go around scowling as though in constant fear of being robbed.

Or maybe they were getting it on.

In Mum and Dad's bed.

'Who was on top?' I should ask at breakfast in the morning. 'The oldest?' And see those gaping faces. Head out into the clear morning air, get into the car, release the handbrake, feel the steering wheel lock, see Geitesvingen coming up.

23

A long, lovely sad note coming from outside. The plover. The mountain's lonesome bird, skinny and serious. A bird that accompanies you when you're out walking, looking out for you, but always at a safe distance. As though too afraid to make a friend, and yet still needing someone to listen when it sings of its loneliness.

2

I GOT TO THE SERVICE station at five thirty, half an hour earlier than usual on a Monday. Egil was behind the counter. He looked tired.

'Morning, chief,' he said in a flat monotone. Egil was like a plover, he only had the one note.

'Good morning. Busy night?'

'No,' he said, without seeming to realise it was, as people say, a rhetorical question. That I knew it was never busy once the flow of cabin visitors heading back to the city had eased off on Sunday night. That I was asking because the area out round the pumps hadn't been tidied and cleaned. The rule at other all-night stations is that night-duty attendants working alone don't leave the building, but I hate mess and

25

with the boy racer gang in their custom cars using the place as a combination fast-food shop, hangout for smokers and a lovers' lane there's always a lot of paper, butt ends and, yeah, even the odd used condom. Since the frankfurters, the cigarettes and the blobs all come from the station I don't want to be driving my boy racer customers away, they're welcome to sit in their cars and watch the world drive by. Instead I get my night guys to clean up when they get the chance. I'd pinned a notice up in the staff toilet that stares you straight in the face every time you sit on the throne: 'DO WHAT HAS TO BE DONE. EVERYTHING DEPENDS ON YOU. DO IT NOW.' Egil probably thought it was something to do with having a shit. I'd also mentioned this about cleaning up and taking responsibility so many times you would think Egil would get the little joke about a busy night. But then again, Egil wasn't just tired, he was a simple lad of twenty who'd been the butt of jokes so many times in his life that it didn't bother him any more. If you want to get by with the minimum of effort then pretending to understand less than you do is not the stupidest tactic to employ. So maybe Egil wasn't so dumb after all.

'You're early, chief.'

A bit too early for you to have cleaned up around the pumps so I would think the place had been **shipshape** the whole night, I thought.

'Couldn't sleep,' I said. Crossed to the till and punched in the till-shift command. That ended the night and

I heard the printer in the office start grinding away. 'Go home and get some sleep.'

'Thanks.'

I went into the office and began looking through the takings while the paper was still being spewed out. It looked good. Another busy Sunday. Maybe our main road isn't the busiest in the country, but with thirty-five kilometres to the next service station in both directions we'd become a bit of an oasis for motorists, especially those with young families, on their way home from the cabin. I'd installed a couple of tables and benches by the birch grove with a view across Lake Budal where they could sit with their burgers and buns and Cokes. Sold almost three hundred buns yesterday. I had less of a guilty conscience about the CO_2 emissions than all the gluten intolerance I was causing the world. I let my eye run down the page and noted the number of frankfurters Egil had thrown away. Fair enough, but there were – as usual – a few too many compared to the sales figures. He'd changed now and was on his way out the door.

'Egil?'

He stiffened and stopped. 'Yeah?'

'Looks like someone's had fun winding the drying paper round pump number 2.'

'I'll fix it, chief.' He smiled and went out.

I sighed. It isn't easy to find good workers in a little village like this. The clever ones head for Oslo or Bergen to study, the hard workers to Notodden, Skien or Kongsberg to earn money. If I fired him he'd be straight on the dole, and he wouldn't be eating any fewer sausages, the only difference being he'd be standing on the other side of the counter and paying for them. They say obesity is mostly a small-town problem, and it's obvious how easy it is to start comfort eating when you're working at a service station, and everybody who calls in is heading someplace else, to somewhere you tell yourself has to be better than this, in cars you'll never be able to afford, with girls you wouldn't even dare to talk to unless it was at the village hop and you were pissed. But soon I would have to have a word with Egil. Head office wasn't interested in the likes of him, only in the bottom line. It's fair enough. In 1969 there were 700,000 cars and more than 4,000 service stations in Norway. Forty-five years on the number of cars had almost quadrupled, but the number of service stations more than halved. It was tough for them and tough for us. I kept abreast of the statistics and knew that in Sweden and Denmark over half the surviving service stations were already automated and unmanned. The widespread pattern of settlements here in Norway means we aren't there yet, but it's obvious that even here, petrol pump attendants are a dying breed. In actual fact, we're already extinct. When was the last time you saw one of us putting petrol in a car? We're too busy flogging frankfurters, colas, beach balls, barbecue charcoal, windscreen cleaner and bottled water that's no different from what comes out the tap but comes in by plane and costs more than

28

the videos we've got on offer. But I'm not complaining. When the service station chain showed an interest in the car repair workshop I had taken over at the age of twenty-three, it wasn't because of the two petrol pumps I had out on the forecourt or because the place was doing well financially, but on account of the location. They said they were impressed at how I had held out for so long; local car repair shops had disappeared from the map a long time ago, and they offered me the job of station boss along with a bit of small change for the property. I could maybe have got a little bit more, but we Opgards don't haggle. Still not thirty, I felt as though I was already finished. I used the small change to have the bathroom built on the farm so I could move out of the bachelor's bedsit I'd made at the repair shop. There was plenty of room on the site so the chain built a service station next door to the repair shop, which they left up, and modernised the old car-wash.

The door banged shut behind Egil and I recalled that head office had agreed to the automatic sliding doors I had requested. The head of sales who visited every fourteen days was all smiles and bad jokes. Now and then he'd lay a hand on my shoulder and say, as though it were confidential, that they were satisfied. Naturally they were satisfied. They read the bottom line and saw that we were putting up a good and profitable fight against extinction. Despite the fact that the forecourt around the pumps when Egil was on night shift weren't always spic and span.

29

Quarter to six. I stood brushing the buns that had de-frosted and risen during the night and it got me think-ing about the good years when I was down in the grease pit and oiling the cars. Working hard. Knowing that my reward awaited me, assignations up at the mountain cabin, the secret no one must find out. I saw a tractor approaching the car wash. Knew that once the farmer finished washing the monster I would need to wash and hose down the floor. As head of the place I had full re-sponsibility for the hiring and firing, the bookkeeping, the pep talks with staff and all the rest of it; but guess what takes up most of a service station boss's time? Cleaning up. With baking buns a good number two.

I listened to the silence. Although it's actually never silent – there's a steady, rushing symphony of sounds that doesn't stop until the weekend is over, the cabin folk are back home, and we start closing the place up at night again. There are coffee machines, sausage cookers, freezers, soft-drinks coolers. They each have their own sound, but the most distinctive is the bread warmer we put the hamburger rolls in. It cackles in a warmer way, almost like a well-oiled motor if you close your eyes and dream back in time a little. Last time the head of sales was here he suggested I consider playing low back-ground music in the shop. Said that research showed how the right sounds could stimulate both the desire to spend money and the appetite. I nodded slowly but said nothing. I like the silence. Soon the door will open. Probably a tradesman, it's generally tradesmen who want petrol or coffee before seven.

I watched the farmer filling up his tractor with the duty-free truck diesel. I knew a splash of that was going to end up in the tank of his own car once he got home, but that was a matter between him and the police, I really didn't care one way or the other.

My gaze moved on past the pumps, across the road, the cycle and footpath, and landed on one of the wooden houses typical of the village, three floors, built just after the war, a veranda facing out across Lake Budal, window dirty with road dust, a large poster nailed to the wall advertising haircuts and a solarium in a way that probably gave passers-by the impression that the cutting and the sunbathing went on **simultaneously,** as people say. Something done in the living room of the people who lived there. I'd never seen anyone other than locals going in there, and everyone in the village knew where Grete Smitt lived, so the actual purpose of the poster was unclear. Now I saw Grete standing by the side of the road, freezing in her Crocs and T-shirt, taking a good look left and right before crossing over to our side.

It was only six months ago that a driver from Oslo who claimed he never saw the fifty kilometres an hour speed-limit sign had mown down our Norwegian teacher a little further along the road. There are advantages and disadvantages to running a service station in a village. The advantages are that the locals do their shopping here and that the speed limit of fifty means out-of-town cars can turn into the station on impulse. When I had the repair shop we also contributed to the local economy because any out-of-town customers who needed bigger repair jobs would eat at the cafe and spend the night at one of the camping cabins down by the lakeside. The disadvantage is that it's only a question of time before you'll lose the traffic. Motorists want straight roads and speed limits of ninety, they don't want to be crawling through every little village they pass on the way to their destinations. Plans for a new main road that bypassed Os had been ready for a long time, but so far we had been saved by our geography; it had quite simply been too costly for the transport authorities to drive a tunnel through the mountain. But there will be a tunnel, as surely as the sun will blow our solar system to pieces in two billion years' time, and it'll come a lot sooner than that. Ending up in the back of beyond would of course mean the end for all of us who made a living from the through traffic; but for the rest of the village too, the shock waves would be pretty similar to when the sun says goodbye. The farmers would still milk their cows and raise what crops they could up here on the heights, but what would everyone else do without the main road? Cut each other's hair and tan themselves to a crisp?

The door opened. When we were growing up Grete had been a washed-out grey colour, with flat, dull hair. Now she was still that same grey but with a perm that made her look truly scary, in my opinion. Of course, being pretty isn't a human right, but the Creator really did skimp on Grete. Back, neck, knees, everything was sort of crooked; even her enormous, crooked nose looked out of place, as though it had been imposed on her narrow face by force. But if the Creator had been prodigal with her nose then He'd been correspondingly mean with the rest of her. Eyebrows, eyelashes, breasts, hips, cheeks – Grete actually had none of these. The lips were thin and resembled earthworms. In her youth she had coated these meaty-coloured worms with a thick layer of bright red lipstick, and it did actually suit her. But then suddenly she stopped wearing make-up. It must have been around the time Carl left town.

OK, so it's possible others didn't see Grete Smitt like I did. Maybe she was attractive in her own way, and what I saw when I looked at what was on the outside was coloured by what I knew about the inside. And I'm not saying Grete Smitt was actually evil, I'm sure there's some psychiatric diagnosis or other that gives a more flattering definition, as people say.

'It's sharp today,' said Grete. By **it** she presumably meant the north wind. When it came sweeping down through the valley it always carried with it the smell of glacier and a reminder of summer's evanescence. Grete had grown up in the village, but using a word like **it** was probably something she had from her parents, who had come here from the north, ran the camping site until it went bust and then lived on social security after both of them had been diagnosed with a rare form of peripheral neuropathy as a result of diabetes. Apparently it makes you feel as though you're walking on splintered glass. Grete's neighbour told me neuropathy isn't contagious in any way, so this must have been a statistical miracle. But statistical miracles happen all the time, and now both parents lived on the top floor, directly above the poster advertising 'Grete's Hair and Sun Salon', although you didn't see them often.

'Carl back?'

'Yes,' I answered, even though I knew it wasn't a Yes/No question. It was a statement with a question mark attached asking for further information. I had no intention of providing that. Grete's relationship with Carl wasn't healthy. 'What can I get you?'

'I thought he was doing so well in Canada.'

'Sometimes people get the urge to travel home even when things are going well.'

'I hear the property market out there is very unpredictable.'

'Yes, it either goes up very quickly or not quite so quickly. Coffee? Custard bun?'

'Wonder what it is that brings a big shot from Toronto back to our little village.'

'The people,' I said.

'Maybe,' she said, studying my poker face. 'But then he's brought a Cuban with him, I hear?'

Now it might have been easy to feel pity for Grete. Parents on social security, a meteorite crater for a nose, no customers, no eyebrows, no husband, no Carl and apparently no desire for anyone else. But then there was that hidden reef of evil you didn't notice was there until after you'd seen people scraping up against it. Maybe it was Newton's law about every action having a corresponding reaction, that all the pain she suffered had to be passed on in turn to others. If Carl hadn't screwed her beneath a tree when he was young and been drinking at a party, maybe she wouldn't have turned out that way. Or then again, maybe she would.

'A **Cuban,**' I said, wiping down the counter. 'Sounds like a cigar.'

'Yeah, doesn't it?' she said and leaned across the counter as though we were sharing forbidden confidences. 'Brown, nice to puff on and . . . and . . .'

Easy to light up, my mind instinctively added, even though what I wanted most was to stuff a custard bun into her mouth to stop the rubbish.

'. . . very smelly,' she finally concluded. That earthworm mouth of hers grinned; she seemed pleased with her analogy, as people say.

'Only she isn't from Cuba,' I said. 'She's from Barbados.'

'Yeah yeah,' said Grete. 'Thai, Russian, whatever, a skivvy, I expect.'

I lost it. Couldn't hide any more how much she was provoking me. 'Excuse me? What did you just say?'

'That she's pretty, I expect.' Grete grinned triumphantly.

'What do you want, Grete?'

Grete scanned the shelves behind me. 'Mum needs new batteries for her remote.'

I doubted that, since her mother had called in and bought batteries two days earlier, picking up her sore feet as though the floor was molten lava. I handed the batteries to Grete and rang it up.

'Shannon,' said Grete as she fumbled her card through the terminal. 'I saw the pictures on Instagram. Is there something wrong with her?'

'Not that I've noticed,' I said.

'Come on, you're not that white if you come from Barbados. And what's the matter with her eye?'

'That remote control should go like the clappers now.'

Grete pulled out her card and slipped it back into her purse. 'See you later, Roy.'

I nodded slowly. Of course we'd see each other later. That goes for everything and everyone in this village. But she was trying to tell me something more, so that's why I nodded as though I got it, and hoped she wouldn't bother me with the rest of it.

The door slid shut behind her, but not completely, even though I'd tightened the mechanism. It really was time for a new one. Automatic.

By nine one of the other employees had arrived and I was able to go out and clean up after the tractor. As expected there were huge clumps of clay and dirt on the floor. I had some ready-mixed Fritz heavy-duty cleaner that got rid of most of it and hosed it down, thinking about back when we were teenagers and thought our lives could be turned upside down every single day, and about how our lives **were** turned upside down every single day, when I felt a prickling between my shoulder blades. Like the heat from one of those red laser beams when the SWAT team has caught you red-handed. So that's why I wasn't startled when I heard the low coughing behind me. I turned.

'Been mud wrestling in here?' said the sheriff, cigarette twitching between his thin lips.

'Tractor,' I said.

He nodded. 'So your brother's back?'

Kurt Olsen the sheriff was a thin, bony-cheeked man with a trailer-trash moustache, always with a roll-up in his mouth, tight jeans and the snakeskin boots his father used to wear. In fact Kurt seemed to look more and more like Sigmund Olsen, the old sheriff, who had had long fair hair too, and always made me think of Dennis Hopper in **Easy Rider.** Kurt Olsen was bow-legged the way certain footballers are, and in his day had been captain of the local team that played in the 4th division. Solid technique, sound tactical sense, could run for the whole ninety minutes even though he smoked like two factories. Everyone said Kurt should have been playing in a higher division. But that would have meant moving to a larger place with the risk of ending up on the bench, and why sacrifice local hero status for that? 'Carl arrived yesterday,' I confirmed. 'How did you know?'

'This,' he said, unfurling a poster and holding it up.

I cut off the jet. FOLLOW THE DREAM! was the headline. And below: OS SPA AND MOUNTAIN HOTEL. I read on. The sheriff gave me plenty of time. We were about the same age, so maybe he knew that the class teacher had described me as **mildly dyslexic.** When the teacher informed my parents of this he mentioned at the same time that dyslexia is often an inherited condition. At this my father had flared up and asked was he insinuating the boy was a bastard? But then Mum reminded him of one of his cousins in Oslo, Olav, who was dyslexic and for whom things hadn't turned out too well. When Carl heard about the meeting he had offered to be my **reading mentor,** as he put it. And I know he meant it, that he would gladly have given his time to the task. But I said no. Who wants his kid brother as his teacher? Instead my teacher turned out to be my secret lover, and my school a summer farm cabin high up in the mountains. But that was many years later.

The poster was an invitation to a meeting of investors at Årtun Village Hall. All welcome, it said. Coffee and waffles would be served, and attendance was without further obligation. I got the picture even before I reached the name and signature at the bottom. Here it was. The reason Carl had come home.

There was a title after the name. Carl Abel Opgard. Master of Business. No less.

I didn't know what to think, only that it smelled like trouble already.

'This is on all the bus stops and lamp posts along the main road,' said the sheriff.

So the sheriff wasn't the only one. Carl had obviously been up early too.

The sheriff rolled the poster up again. 'Doing so without permission is an infringement of Paragraph 33 of the Highways Act. Can you ask him to take the posters down?'

'Why not ask him yourself?'

'I don't have his phone number and . . .' He wedged the poster under his arm, hooked his thumbs into the belt of his tight Levi's and nodded in the direction of north. 'Save me the trip if you do. Will you?'

I nodded slowly, looking up in the direction of where the sheriff wanted to save himself a trip. You couldn't see Opgard from the service station, could just about glimpse the bend at Geitesvingen, and a grey area at the top of the precipice. The house lay out of sight above and behind it, where the land flattened out. But today I saw something there. Something red. And then I knew what it was. A Norwegian flag. Damned if Carl hadn't hoisted the flag on a Monday. Wasn't that what the king did, as a signal that he was home? I almost started laughing.

'He can apply for permission,' the sheriff said and looked at his watch. 'And then we'll see about it.'

'OK then.'

'Right.' Kurt Olsen raised two fingers to the cowboy hat he should have been wearing.

We both knew it would take a day for the posters to come down, and by then the job would be done. Those who hadn't seen the invitation would have heard about it.

I moved away and turned on the hose pipe again.

But it was still there, that heat between the shoulder blades. The way it had been all these years. Kurt Olsen's suspicion that slowly and surely etched its way through the clothing, through the skin and onto the flesh, stopping short only when it came up against solid bone. Against willpower and stubbornness. Against a lack of proof and hard facts.

'What's that there?' I heard Kurt Olsen say.

I turned, acted surprised at still finding him there. He nodded towards the metal grid in the floor where the water gushed down. At the bits that lay there without being washed away.

'Huh?' I said.

The sheriff squatted down. 'There's blood coming out of them,' he said. 'This is flesh.'

'Must be,' I said.

He glanced up at me. All that remained of his cigarette was the glowing tip.

'Moose,' I said. 'Run over. Got caught in the front mesh. They come here to wash the mess away.'

'I thought you just said it was a tractor, Roy.'

'I guess it's from a car last night,' I said. 'I can ask Egil, if there's anything you want to . . .' The sheriff jumped back as I directed the stream of water onto the lump of flesh so that it was pulled clear of the mesh and floated out across the cement floor.

'. . . **investigate.**' Kurt Olsen's eyes flashed. He wiped off the thighs of his trousers, even though they were dry. I don't know if he used the word deliberately, it was the same word he had used back then.

40

Investigate. That of course this would have to be investigated. I didn't dislike Kurt Olsen. He was an OK guy just doing his job. But I had very definitely disliked his **investigating,** and I doubt whether he'd have dragged these posters along with him if the name Opgard hadn't been on them.

When I got back to the station shop two teenage girls were standing there. One was Julie who had taken over behind the counter after Egil. The other girl, the customer, was standing with her back to me. Her head was bowed, she was waiting and gave no indication she was about to turn even though the door had opened. All the same I thought I recognised the Moe girl, the roofer's daughter. Natalie. I saw her now and then with the boy racer gang outside. Where Julie was open, the bubbly type, as people say, there was something sensitive and at the same time something closed off about Natalie Moe's expressionless face, as though she thought that any feelings she showed would be either mocked or ridiculed. That's the age she was at. Although, surely she was at high school by now? Whatever, I had got the picture, picked up on the shame and had it confirmed when Julie greeted me at the same time as she nodded towards the shelf with the morning-after pills. Julie's only seventeen, so she's not allowed to sell tobacco and medicines.

I stepped behind the counter, resolved to get the Moe girl's embarrassment over as quickly as possible.

41

'EllaOne?' I asked and placed the little white box on the counter in front of her.

'Uh?' said Natalie Moe.

'Your morning-after pill,' said Julie mercilessly.

I entered it on the till with my own card, so that it would look as though some presumably responsible adult person had made the purchase. The Moe girl left.

'She's having it off with Trond-Bertil,' said Julie and snapped her bubblegum. 'He's over thirty, got a wife and kids.'

'She's young then,' I said.

'Young for what?' Julie looked at me. It was strange, she wasn't a big girl, but everything about her seemed big. The curly hair, the hands, the heavy breasts beneath the broad shoulders. The mouth almost vulgar. And the eyes. Those enormous blue peepers that looked me straight in the eye. 'To be having it off with someone over thirty?'

'Young to be making sensible decisions all the time,' I said. 'Maybe she'll learn.'

Julie snorted. 'That's not why it's called a morning-after pill. And just because a girl is young doesn't mean she doesn't know what she wants.'

'I'm sure you're probably right about that.'

'But when we put on an innocent face like that one there, then you men all think poor little girl. Just the way we want you to think.' She laughed. 'You're so simple.'

I slipped on a pair of plastic gloves and began to butter some baguettes. 'Is there a secret society?' I asked.

'Eh?'

'All you women, you think you know how other women think. Do you tell each other how it works, so that you've got like a complete internal overview? Because when it comes to other men, all I know is that I don't know shit. That anything is possible. That at the most forty per cent of what I think I know about a man turns out to be right.' I added the salami and the egg, delivered ready-sliced to the door. 'And it's us who are supposed to be **simple.** So all I can do is congratulate you on having one hundred per cent insight into the other half of the human race.'

Julie didn't answer. I saw her swallow. Must have been the lack of sleep last night that made me use heavy artillery like that against a teenage high-school dropout. The kind of girl who gets into all the wrong things too early and none of the right things. Although that could change. She had **attitude,** as Dad used to say, rebellious, but still, more in need of encouragement than resistance. Needing both of course, but mostly encouragement.

'So you're beginning to get the hang of how to change tyres,' I said.

Despite still being September, it had snowed on the cabins highest up the mountain. And even though we didn't sell tyres or advertise a tyre-changing service we still got city folk coming in with their SUVs begging for help. Men as well as women. They simply don't know how to carry out the most basic tasks. They'll be dead before the end of the week the day a

43

solar storm knocks out all the electrical equipment in the world.

Julie smiled. She looked almost **too** happy. Changeable weather in there.

'City folk think the roads are slippery now,' Julie said. 'Imagine when it gets really cold, minus twenty, thirty.'

'Then the roads'll be less slippery,' I said.

She looked quizzically at me.

'Ice is slippier when it's closer to melting point,' I said. 'Slippiest of all when it's exactly seven degrees below. That's the temperature they try to keep the ice in ice-hockey stadiums. What we slip on isn't an invisible thin coating of water on account of the pressure and friction, the way people used to think, but gas that's formed by loose molecules at those temperatures.'

'How come you know all this stuff, Roy?' She gave me a look of undeserved admiration.

That, of course, made me feel like one of those idiots I can't stand myself, always showing off with random and superficial snippets of knowledge.

'It's the kind of stuff you can read in what we sell,' I said, pointing to the magazine racks where **Popular Science** was stacked next to magazines about cars, boats, hunting and fishing, **True Crime** and – at the insistence of the head of sales – a couple of fashion magazines.

But Julie wasn't going to let me down from my pedestal that easily.

44

'Thirty's not that old if you ask me. At least it's better than twenty-year-olds who think they're grown up just because they've passed their driving test.'

'I'm over thirty, Julie.'

'Are you? Then how old's your brother?'

'Thirty-five.'

'He was in buying petrol yesterday,' she said.

'You weren't working.'

'I was here with some of my friends sitting in Knerten's car. It was him said it was your brother. Know what my friends said? They said your brother was a DILF.'

I didn't reply.

'But you know what? If you ask me, you're more of a DILF.'

I gave her a warning glare. She just grinned. Straightened up almost unnoticeably and drew her broad shoulders back. 'DILF stands for—'

'Thank you, but I think I know what it stands for. You gonna handle the Asko delivery?'

An Asko truck had pulled into the station. Soda water and sweets.

Julie looked at me with a deeply practised I'm-bored-to-death look. She blew a bubble gum balloon that burst. Tossed her head and marched out.

3

'HERE?' I ASKED IN DISBELIEF, looking across our outfields.

'Here,' said Carl.

Rocks with heather. Wind-blasted bare mountain-side. Fantastic view of course, with blue mountain tops in all directions and the sun glinting on the water down there. But all the same. 'You're going to have to build a road up here. Water. Sewage. Electricity.'

'Right.' Carl laughed.

'Carry out maintenance on something that's on a . . . on a fucking **mountain top.**'

'It's unique, right?'

'And lovely,' said Shannon. She was standing behind

us with her arms folded, shivering in her black coat. 'It'll be lovely.'

I'd come home early from the station and of course the first thing I did was confront Carl about those posters.

'Without saying a single fucking word to me?' I said. 'Have you any idea how many questions I've had today?'

'How many? Did they seem positive?' The keen way Carl asked made me understand he really didn't care a damn about how I felt about being trampled over and ignored.

'But for chrissakes,' I said, 'why didn't you tell me this was what you were coming back for?'

'Because I didn't want you to hear just half the story, Roy.' Carl laid an arm around my shoulder, gave me that warm damn smile. 'Didn't want you wandering about up here thinking up all kinds of objections. Because you're a born sceptic, and you know it. So now let's go and have dinner and I'll tell you the whole story. OK?'

And yes, my mood improved slightly, if for no other reason than that for the first time since Mum and Dad there was a meal cooked and ready on the table when I came home from work. After we'd eaten our fill Carl had shown me the drawings for the hotel. It looked like an igloo on the moon. The only difference being that on this moon a couple of reindeer wandered by. Those reindeer and some moss were all the architect had provided of exterior staffage, apart from that it looked pretty sterile and modernist. The funny thing was that I liked it, but that was probably because I saw something that resembled a service station on Mars and not a hotel where people could relax and enjoy themselves. I mean, surely people want places like that to have a bit more warmth and class, a bit more of Norwegian national romance about them, rose-painted panels, turf roofs, like the palace of some fairy-tale king or whatever.

Then we'd walked the short kilometre from the house to the proposed building site, with the evening sun glowing in the heather and on the polished granite of the peaks.

'See how it moulds itself into the landscape,' said Carl as he drew in the air the hotel we had been looking at in the dining room. 'The landscape and the function are what matter, not people's expectations of what a mountain hotel should look like. This is a hotel that will change people's ideas about architecture, not just hum along with them.'

'OK then,' I answered, no doubt sounding as sceptical as I thought there was every reason to be.

Carl explained the hotel would be 11,000 square metres and have two hundred rooms. It could be up and running within two years of the first shovel of dirt being shifted. Or the first explosive detonated – there wasn't a lot of earth up here. Carl's 'pessimistic estimate' was that it would cost four hundred million.

'How do you propose to get hold of four hundred—'

'The bank.'

'Os Savings Bank?'

'No, no.' He laughed. 'They're too small for this. A city bank. DnB.'

'And why would they loan you four hundred mil for this . . . ?' I didn't actually **say** lunacy, but it was pretty obvious what I was thinking.

'Because we're not going to start a limited company. We're going to start an SL.'

'SL?'

'A Shared Liability company. People in the village don't have a lot of cash. What they do have are the farms and the land they live on. With an SL they don't need to put up a single krone to come along for the ride. And everyone who's in, the great and the small, has the same share and makes the same profit. They can all just sit back and let their property do the work for them. The bankers will be drooling at the mouth for the chance to finance this whole thing because they've never been offered better security than a whole bloody village!'

I scratched my head. 'You mean, if the whole thing goes to hell, then—'

'Then each investor is liable only for his own share. If there are a hundred of us, and the company goes bankrupt with a debt of a hundred thousand, then all you're liable for, you and the rest of the investors, is a thousand kroner each. Even if some of the investors can't manage the thousand, that's not your problem, it's the creditors' problem.'

'Jesus.'

'Beautiful, isn't it? So the more that are involved, the less the individual risk. But of course that also means the less they earn when this thing really takes off.'

It was a lot to take on board. A type of company where you don't have to lay out a single krone and just rake it in, if everything goes according to plan. And if it all goes to hell, the only thing you're liable for is your own share.

'OK,' I said, trying to figure out where the catch might be. 'So why invite people to an investors' meeting when they aren't going to be investing anything?'

'Because "investor" sounds a lot more impressive than just "participant". Don't you think?' Carl hooked his thumbs into his belt and put on a funny voice: **'I ain't just a farmer, I'm a hotel investor, don't you know.'** He laughed loudly. 'It's pure psychology. When half the village has signed up the rest won't be able to stand the thought of their neighbours buying themselves Audis and calling themselves hotel owners and not being a part of it themselves. Better to risk losing a few kroner, so long as your neighbour does the same.'

I nodded slowly. He'd probably got the psychology about right there.

'The project is solid. The tricky bit is to get the train rolling.' Carl kicked at the ground beneath us. 'Get the first few to commit, people who can show the others they think the project's attractive enough to want to be a part of. If we manage that, then everyone will want to climb on board and then the thing will be rolling along under its own steam.'

'OK. And how are you going to persuade the first to come on board?'

'When I can't even manage to convince my own brother, you mean?' He smiled that fine, open smile with the slightly sad eyes. 'One'll do,' said Carl before I could respond.

'And that one is . . . ?'

'The bellwether. Aas.'

Of course. The old council chairman. Mari's father. He'd been calling meetings to order for more than twenty years, run this solidly Labour commune with a firm hand through good times and bad until one day he'd decided that was enough. Aas had to be over seventy by now and busied himself mostly at home on the farm, although now and then he would write something in the local newspaper, the **Os Daily,** and people read what he wrote. And even those who didn't agree with Aas to begin with would start looking at things in a new light. Light shed through the old chairman's way with words, his wisdom and his un-deniable knack of always making the right decisions. People really did believe that the plans for a national highway bypassing the village would never have seen the light of day if Aas had still been chairman, that he would have explained to them how this would ruin everything, deprive the village of the extra income the through-traffic brought them, wipe an entire local community off the map and turn it into a deserted

51

ghost town with just a few subsidised farmers close to retiring age still clinging on. And someone had suggested that Aas – and not the current chairman – lead a delegation to the capital to talk some sense into the transport minister.

I spat. Which, for your information, is the opposite of the good ole boy's slow nodding of the head and means that you do **not** agree.

'So you think Aas is just dying to risk his farm and his land on a spa hotel high up on top of the bare mountain? That he wants to put his fate in the hands of the guy who cheated on his daughter and then ran off abroad?'

Carl shook his head. 'You don't get it. Aas liked me, Roy. I wasn't just his future son-in-law, I was the son he never had.'

'**Everybody** liked you, Carl. But when you screw her best friend . . .'

Carl gave me a warning look and I lowered my voice and checked that Shannon – who was squatting in the heather and studying something – was out of earshot.

'. . . then you slip a few places down the hit parade.'

'Aas never knew about what happened between me and Grete,' said Carl. 'All he knows is that his daughter dumped me.'

'Oh?' I said in disbelief. And then a little less disbelieving once I thought about it. Mari – always very conscious of appearances – had naturally preferred the official version of her break-up with the village

52

heart-throb, this being that she had dumped him, the unspoken assumption being that she was aiming higher than the mountain farm boy Opgard.

'Straight after Mari broke up with me, I was summoned by Aas, and he told me how disappointed he was,' said Carl. 'He wondered if me and Mari couldn't make up again somehow. Told me how him and his wife had been through some rough patches too, but they'd stuck it out now for over forty years. I said I would like that too, but right now I needed to get away for a while. He said he understood and gave me a few suggestions. My exam results at school were good, Mari had told him, and maybe he could arrange for a scholarship to a university in the States.'

'Minnesota? Was that Aas?'

'He had some contacts with the Norwegian–American Society there.'

'You never mentioned that.'

Carl shrugged. 'I was embarrassed. I'd been unfaithful to his daughter and now I was letting him help me in all good faith. But I think he had his reasons, he probably hoped I'd return with a university degree and win back the princess and half the kingdom, like the boy in the fairy story.'

'So now you want him to help you again?'

'Not me,' said Carl. 'The village.'

'Naturally. The village. And exactly when was it you started having these heart-warming thoughts about the village?'

'And just exactly when did you become so cold-hearted and cynical?'

I smiled. I could have told him the date and the hour.

Carl took a deep breath. 'Something happens to you when you're sitting on the other side of the world and wondering who you **really** are. Where you come from. What context you belong to. Who your people are.'

'So you've discovered that these are your people?' I nodded in the direction of the village a thousand metres beneath us.

'For good and ill, yes. It's like an inheritance you can't give away. It comes back to you, whether you want it to or not.'

'Is that why you've dropped your accent? You turning against your own culture?'

'No way. This is Mum's culture.'

'She talked city talk because she spent so long working as a housekeeper, not because it was her own dialect.'

'Then put it this way: our heritage is her adaptability. There are a lot of Norwegians in Minnesota, and I was taken more seriously, especially by potential investors, when I spoke **naicely.**' He said it through his nose, the way Mum spoke, and with an exaggeratedly posh accent. We laughed.

'I'll be back talking in the old way soon enough,' said Carl. 'I'm from Os. But even more from Opgard. My real people, Roy — above all, that's **you.** If the national highway is routed round the village and nothing else comes along that turns the village into a place to come to then your service station—'

'It isn't **my** station, Carl, I just work there. I can run a service station anywhere, the company has five hundred of them, so you've no need to be rescuing me.'

'I owe you.'

'I said, I don't need anything—'

'Oh yes, you need something. What you really fucking need is to own your own service station.'

I shut my mouth. OK, so he'd hit the nail on the head there. He was my brother, after all. No one knew me better.

'And with this project you'll raise the capital you need, Roy. To buy a station here, or wherever.'

I'd been saving up. Saving every damn krone I didn't need for food and electricity to warm up the king-size pizzas when I didn't eat my dinner at the station, for petrol for the old Volvo, and to keep the house in a reasonable state of repair. I'd talked to head office about possibly taking over the station, signing a franchise contract. And they weren't completely negative about it when they realised the main road and all the traffic with it would soon be gone. But the price hadn't fallen as much as I had hoped it would, which was, paradoxically enough, my own fault, since we were quite simply doing too well.

'Supposing I **did** go along with this SL thing . . .'

'Yes!' he yelled. Typical Carl, celebrating as though I was already in.

I shook my head irritably. 'It'll still be two years before your hotel is up and running. Plus another two years minimum before it starts earning money. If it doesn't all go to shit, that is. Whatever, if in the course of the next decade I can buy the service station and need a quick loan, the bank will say "no, you're in debt up to your chimney pot with this here SL project".'

Carl couldn't even be bothered to pick me up on my embarrassingly obvious bullshit. SL or no SL, no bank would give a loan for the purchase of a service station that would be slap bang in the middle of nowhere the way things were shaping up.

'You're going to be part of this hotel project, Roy. And what's more, you'll have the money for your station even before we start building the hotel.'

I looked at him. 'What d'you mean?'

'The SL has to buy the land the hotel is going to be built on. And who owns that?'

'You and me,' I said. 'So what? You don't get rich selling a few acres of bare mountainside.'

'That depends who sets the price,' said Carl.

I'm not usually reckoned to be slow when it comes to logic and practical thinking, but even so it took a few seconds before it dawned on me.

'You mean . . .'

'I mean that I'm responsible for the description of the project, yes. And that means that it's me who defines the items in the budget that I'm going to present at the investors' meeting. Of course I won't lie about the value of the land, but let's say we set it at twenty million—'

'Twenty million!' I slapped the heather with my hand in exasperation. 'For **this**?'

'—then that is relatively speaking such a small sum in comparison with the four hundred million total that it'll be a small matter to split the price of the property and spread it out over the other items. Item 1, the road and surrounding area; item 2, the parking space; item 3, the actual building site . . .'

'And what if someone asks the price per acre?'

'Then of course we tell them. We're not thieves.'

'If we're not thieves then what . . . ?' We? How had he suddenly managed to get **me** into this? Well, OK, this was no time to be splitting hairs. 'What are we then?'

'We're business people who are playing the game.'

'Playing? These are villagers, people without a clue, Carl.'

'Country bumpkins you mean? Yes, well, we should know, we're from round here.' He spat. 'Like when Dad bought the Cadillac. That sure bothered people, you bet it did.'

He gave a crooked smile.

'This project is going to push up land prices here for everybody, Roy. Once the hotel is financed we roll out stage two. The ski lifts, cabins and lodges. That's where the real money is. So why should we sell at a giveaway price now, when we know prices are guaranteed to go through the ceiling? Especially when **we** are

57

the ones who made it happen. We're not tricking any-one, Roy, there's just no need for us to shout it from the rooftops that the Opgard brothers are scooping in the first millions. So . . .' He looked at me. 'You want the money for the station, or don't you?'

I chewed it over.

'Think about it while I take a leak,' said Carl.

He turned and walked up to the top of the knoll, probably thinking he'd be sheltered on the other side.

So Carl had given me the time it takes to empty a bladder to decide whether I wanted to sell the property that had been in our family's possession for four gen-erations. For a price that under other circumstances would be considered highway robbery. I didn't need to think. I don't give a fuck about generations, at least not as far as this family is concerned, and we're talk-ing about a wilderness that has no sentimental value whatever nor any other type of value either, unless someone suddenly discovers a rare metal. And if Carl was right and the millions we were about to scoop up were just the icing on a cake that every participant in the village would have a share in in due course, that was fine by me. Twenty million. Ten for me. You could get a bloody nice service station for ten million. Top class, good location, not an øre in debt. Fully automated car wash. Separate restaurant.

'Roy?'

I turned. Hadn't heard Shannon approaching be-cause of the wind. She looked up at me.

'I think it's sick,' she said.

For a moment I thought she was referring to herself, she looked so windblown and cold standing there, her big brown eyes looking up from under the old knitted hat I used to wear as a kid. Then I realised she was cupping her hands round something. She opened them.

It was a little bird. Black hood on a white head, light brown throat. Colours so pale it had to be a male. It looked lifeless.

'A dotterel,' I said.

'It was just lying there,' she said, and pointed to a hollow in the heather where I saw an egg. 'I nearly stepped on it.'

I squatted down and felt the egg.

'Yes, the dotterel will stay sitting on the eggs and let itself be trodden on rather than sacrifice the eggs.'

'I thought birds here hatched in the spring – they do in Canada.'

'Yes, but this egg never hatched because it's dead. He obviously didn't realise, poor thing.'

'He?'

'The male dotterel does the brooding and looks after the chicks.' I stood up and stroked the bird in Shannon's hands on the breast. Felt its quick pulse beneath my fingertip. 'He's playing dead. To distract us from the egg.'

Shannon looked round. 'Where are they? And where is the female?'

'The female is probably somewhere having it off with another male.'

'Having it away?'

'You know, mating. Having sex.'

She gave me a sceptical look. 'Do birds have sex outside the mating season?'

'I'm kidding, but we can always hope so,' I said. 'Anyway, it's called polyandry.'

She stroked the bird's back. 'A male that sacrifices everything for the children, who keeps the family together even when the mother's unfaithful. That really is something rare.'

'That's not actually what polyandry means,' I said. 'It's—'

'—a form of a marriage in which the woman takes several husbands,' she said.

'Oh?' I said.

'Yes. You get it in a number of places in the world. Especially in India and Tibet.'

'Jesus. Why . . .' I was about to ask **do you know that?,** but then changed it to 'do they do that?'

'Usually it's brothers who marry the woman, and the reason is so as not to break up the family home.'

'I didn't know that.'

She put her head on one side. 'Maybe you know more about birds than people?'

I didn't answer. Then she laughed and threw the bird up high into the air. It spread its wings and flew straight ahead, away from us. I followed its flight until suddenly I detected a movement at the edge of my vision. My first thought was that it was a snake. I turned and saw the dark form winding its way towards us down the rocky slope. Lifted my gaze and saw Carl was standing there up at the top, looking out like some statue of Christ over Rio and still pissing. I stepped aside, coughed, and Shannon saw the stream of urine and did the same. It continued to wind its way on downwards towards the village.

'What do you think of us selling the land up here for twenty million kroner?' I asked.

'Sounds like a lot. Where do you think the nest might be?'

'That's two and a half million American dollars. We're going to build a house with two hundred beds in it.'

She smiled, turned and began walking back the way we had come. 'That's a lot. But the dotterel was here first.'

The power went just before bedtime.

I was sitting in the kitchen looking over printouts of the most recent accounts. Working out how head office would discount future profits and price the station in the event of a sale. I had worked out that with ten million I would not only manage to buy a ten-year franchise but the whole shooting match, buildings and land included. Then I would **really** own my own station.

I stood up and looked down over the village. No light down there either. Good, so that meant the problem wasn't up here. I took a couple of paces in the direction of the living-room door, opened it and peered out into the pitch darkness.

'Hello,' I called out experimentally.

'Hi,' came the response in unison from Carl and Shannon.

I fumbled my way to Mum's rocking chair. Sat down. The rockers creaked against the floor planking. Shannon giggled. They'd had a drink.

'Sorry about this,' I said. 'It isn't us, it's . . . them.'

'Doesn't bother me,' said Shannon. 'When I was a kid there were power cuts all the time.'

I said into the darkness: 'Is it poor, Barbados?'

'No,' said Shannon. 'It's one of the richest Caribbean islands. But where I grew up there were so many people **cable hooking** . . . what do you call that in Norwegian?'

'Actually I don't think we have a word for it,' said Carl.

'They stole electricity by connecting up to the mains. And that made the whole net unstable. I got used to the idea. You know, that everything can disappear, at any time.'

Something told me she wasn't just talking about electricity. About home and family, maybe? She hadn't given up until she'd found the dotterel's nest, and then she'd stuck a twig in the ground so we wouldn't tread on it the next time.

'Tell us about it,' I said.

For a few moments the silence in the darkness was complete.

Then she gave a low laugh, as though excusing herself. 'Why don't you tell us instead, Roy?'

What surprised me was that even though she never got the wrong Norwegian word or made a mistake in the syntax, her accent still made you think of her as a foreigner. Or maybe it was that meal she'd made. That **mofongo,** some Caribbean dish.

'Yeah, let Roy tell us, he's good at telling stories in the dark. He used to do it for me when I couldn't get to sleep.'

When you couldn't get to sleep because you were **crying,** I thought. When I climbed down into your bed, after it was over, and put my arms around you, felt your skin so warm against mine, and told you not to think about it, just think about the story I'm telling you and let sleep come. And at the same moment as I was thinking that I realised that it wasn't the accent or the **mofongo,** it was the fact that she was here, in the dark, with me and Carl. In the dark in our house, the dark that belonged to him and me and no one else.

4

CARL WAS ALREADY AT THE door, waiting to greet the guests. We heard the first cars struggling up the track towards Geitesvingen, change down, then down again. Shannon gave me a quizzical look when I poured more of the strong stuff into her punchbowl.

'They like it to taste more moonshine than fruit,' I said and peered out of the kitchen window.

A Passat stopped in front of the house and six people tumbled out of the five-seater. It was always the same thing; they travelled up in a gang and the women drove. I don't know why guys think they have priority when it comes to drinking parties like this, or why the girls volunteer to drive even before they're asked, but that's the way it is. The lads who came along because they were single or because someone had to stay home and look after the kids did a round of rock paper scissors to decide who drove. When Carl and I were growing up, people drove when they were drunk. Take Dad. But people don't drink and drive any more. They still beat their wives, but no way would they drink and drive.

There was a banner in the living room with HOMECOMING on it. I thought it was a bit strange because I thought the point of that American custom was that it was family and friends and not the homecoming person himself who was supposed to arrange the party. But Shannon just laughed and said if no one else was going to do it then you had to do it yourself.

'Let me do the punch,' said Shannon, who had come up to me as I stood and ladled the mixture of home brew and fruit cocktail into the glasses I'd put out. She was wearing the same outfit as when she arrived, black polo-neck sweater and black trousers. I mean, probably another set of clothes but that looked exactly the same. I don't know much about clothes, but something told me that hers were of the discreet and exclusive type.

'Thanks, but I'm quite capable,' I said.

'No,' said the little lady and shoved me aside. 'Off you go and talk to old friends, while I'll go round with the glasses and get to know everyone a bit better.'

'OK,' I said. I didn't bother to explain to her that they were Carl's friends, that I didn't have friends. But anyway, it was nice to see them all give Carl a hug in the doorway, slap him on the back as though he'd got something stuck in his throat, grin and say some laddish thing they'd worked out on the drive up, a little bit high, a bit shy and ready for a drink.

Me they shook hands with.

Of all things, this was perhaps the biggest difference between my brother and me. These were people whom Carl hadn't seen for fifteen years, but they'd seen me every other day at the service station, year in and year out. And yet still they felt as though he was the one they knew, not me. Standing there and watching him now, how he relished the warmth and nearness of our friends, things which I had never enjoyed – did I envy him? Well, I guess we all want to be loved. But would I change places? Would I be willing to let people get as close as Carl did? It didn't seem to cost him anything. But for me the price would have been too high.

'Hi, Roy. Not often we see you with a beer.' It was Mari Aas. She was looking good. Mari always looked good, even when she was wheeling her twins around when they had gripe. And I know how much that annoyed the women in town who had been hoping they might finally get to see little Miss Perfect having a hard time of it like the rest of us mere mortals. The girl who had everything. Because as well as the silver spoon in her mouth she was born with, and a brain that got her top marks at school, and the respect that came with her surname Aas, she had the looks to match it all. From her mother Mari Aas inherited the dark glow in her skin and feminine curves, and from her father the blonde hair and the cold, blue, vulpine eyes. And maybe it was those eyes, her sharp tongue and air of superiority and coolness that had kept the boys at an oddly respectful distance.

'Funny we don't run into each other more often,' said Mari. 'So how are you, really?'

That **really** was a signal that she didn't want the standard just-fine-thanks answer, but that she cared, she wanted to know. And I think she really meant it. By nature Mari was friendly and helpful towards people. But still she gave this impression of looking down on you. Of course that might be on account of the fact that she was 180cm tall, but I do remember one time when the three of us were in the car driving home after a dance – me driving, Carl drunk, Mari angry and pissed off – and her saying, 'Carl, I can't have a boyfriend who drags me down to the level of everyone else in this town, you do see that?'

But even if she wasn't happy about the level, it was obvious that it was here she wanted to be. Though she'd been even smarter than Carl at school, she didn't have the same drive as him, that burning desire to head on out and **be** somebody. Maybe because she was already up there, floating around on the surface in the sunshine. So it was mostly about staying there. Maybe that was why – after it was over with Carl – she'd just taken a short course in political science – or **posh**litical science as the locals called it – and then come straight back home with

67

Dan Krane and an engagement ring. And while he started work as editor of the local Labour Party newspaper, she was apparently still working away on a final paper she was clearly never going to finish.

'Doing OK,' I said. 'Did you come alone?'

'Dan wanted to look after the boys.'

I nodded. Knew that the grandparents next door would have been delighted to help out with the babysitting but that Dan had insisted. I'd seen his expressionless, ascetic face at the service station when he pumped up the tyres on the costly-looking bike he was going to use in the Birken long-distance race. Pretended he didn't know who I was but his animosity was palpable, simply because I shared a lot of DNA with the guy who'd slept with the woman who was now his lawful wedded wife. Oh no, Dan probably didn't entertain any burning desire to come up and celebrate the return of a home-town boy who was also his wife's ex.

'Have you met Shannon?' I said.

'No,' said Mari, scanning the already packed room where we'd shoved all the furniture to one side and everyone was standing. 'But Carl is so fixated on looks she's bound to be so pretty you can't mistake her.'

From the way she said this it was obvious what she thought of all talk about appearances. When Mari gave the speech on behalf of the school-leavers for her year the headmaster had introduced her by saying that she 'wasn't only intelligent but also a striking beauty'. Mari had started her speech by saying:

'Thank you, headmaster. I wanted to say a few words of thanks for all you've done for us these past three years, but I didn't know quite how to express myself, so let's just say that you have been remarkably lucky in your appearance.' The laughter had been isolated, the line delivered with a little too much venom, and as the daughter of the chairman it wasn't really clear whether she'd been kicking upwards or downwards.

'You must be Mari.'

Mari looked round before she looked down. And there, three heads below her, Shannon's white face and white smile smiling up at us. 'Punch?'

Mari raised an eyebrow. Looked as though she thought this slight-built figure had challenged her to a boxing match until Shannon lifted the tray higher.

'Thanks,' said Mari. 'But no thanks.'

'Oh no. You lost at rock paper scissors?'

Mari looked blankly at her.

I coughed. 'I told Shannon about the custom of driving and the—'

'Oh that,' Mari interrupted with a thin smile. 'No, my husband and I don't drink.'

'Aha!' said Shannon. 'Because you're alcoholics or because it's not good for your health?'

I saw Mari's face stiffen. 'We aren't alcoholics, but on a worldwide basis alcohol kills more people annually than wars, murders and drugs put together.'

'Yes, and thank goodness for that,' said Shannon, smiling. 'That there aren't more wars, murders and drugs, I mean.'

'What I'm trying to say is that alcohol isn't necessary,' said Mari.

'I'm sure it isn't,' said Shannon. 'But at least it's got the people who've come here tonight talking a bit more than when they arrived. Did you drive up?'

'Of course,' said Mari. 'Don't the women drive where you come from?'

'Sure they do, but only on the left.'

Mari gave me an uncertain look, as though asking if there was some joke here she didn't get.

I coughed. 'They drive on the left in Barbados.'

Shannon laughed loudly, and Mari smiled tolerantly as at a child's embarrassing little joke.

'You must have put a lot of time and effort into learning your husband's language. Did you never consider him learning your language instead?'

'That's a good question, Mari; but English is the language of Barbados. And of course, I want to know what you're all saying behind my back.' Shannon laughed again.

I don't always understand what women are saying when they talk, but even I could see that this was a catfight, and my only job was to stay well out of the way.

'Anyway I prefer Norwegian before English. English has the worst written language in the world.'

'Prefer Norwegian **to** English, you mean?'

'The idea behind the Arabic alphabet is that the symbols reflect the sounds. So when for example you write an **a** in Norwegian, German, Spanish, Italian

70

and so on, then it's pronounced **a**. But in English a written **a** can be anything at all. **Car, care, cat, call. ABC.** And the anarchy just goes on. As early as the eighteenth century Ephraim Chambers was of the opinion that English orthography is more chaotic than that of any other known language. While I found out that without knowing even a single word of Norwegian I was able to read aloud from Sigrid Undset – Carl understood every word!' Shannon laughed and looked at me. 'Norwegian ought to be the world language, not English!'

'Hmm, maybe,' said Mari. 'But if you're serious about sexual equality then you shouldn't be reading Sigrid Undset. She was a reactionary anti-feminist.'

'Well, I'm inclined to think of Undset more as a sort of early **second-wave** feminist, like Erica Jong. Thanks for the advice about what not to read, but I also try to read writers with some of whose viewing points I don't agree.'

'**Viewpoints,**' corrected Mari. 'I see you spend a lot of time thinking about language and literature, Shannon. You'd probably be better off talking to Rita Willumsen, or our doctor, Stanley Spind.'

'Instead of . . . ?'

Mari gave a thin smile. 'Or perhaps you should think about doing something useful with your knowledge of Norwegian. Like looking for a job? Contributing to the community here in Os?'

'Fortunately I don't need to look for a job.'

'No, I'm sure you don't,' said Mari, and I could

see she was on the offensive again. That contemptuous, patronising look, the one Mari thought she kept so successfully hidden from the other villagers, was there in her eyes as she said: 'After all, you do have a . . . husband.'

I looked at Shannon. People had taken glasses from the tray as we stood there and she moved the ones that were left to restore the balance. 'I don't need to look for a job because I already have one. A job I can do from home.'

Mari looked surprised, and then almost disappointed. 'And that is?'

'I draw.'

Mari brightened up again. 'You draw,' she repeated in an exaggeratedly positive way, as though someone with a job like that would naturally need encouragement. 'You're an artist,' she announced with a pitying derision.

'I'm not too sure about that. On a good day maybe. What do you do, Mari?'

Mari suffered a moment's disorientation before she composed herself enough to say: 'I'm a political scientist.'

'Brilliant! And are they much in demand around here in Os?'

Mari gave the kind of quick smile people do when they feel a pain somewhere. 'Right now I'm a mother. To twins.'

'No! Really?' cried Shannon in enthusiastic disbelief.

'Yes. I wouldn't lie ab—'

'Pictures! Do you have any pictures?'

Mari gave a sideways look down at Shannon. Hesitated. Maybe those vulpine eyes thought for a moment about resisting. A scrawny little one-eyed fledgling of a woman; how dangerous could that be? Mari pulled out a phone. Tapped away. Held the picture up to Shannon who gave vent to one of those long-drawn-out **aahhhs** that are supposed to express how adorable something is, before handing me the tray with glasses so that she could take hold of Mari's phone, the better to feast her eyes on the twins.

'What d'you have to **do** to get two like that, Mari?'

I don't know if Shannon was just flattering her, but if she was, it was a brilliant bit of play-acting. Good enough anyway for Mari Aas to drop the hostile look on her face.

'Any more?' asked Shannon. 'Can I look?'

'Er, sure.'

'Can you serve the guests, Roy?' Shannon said, without taking her eyes off the screen.

I made a circuit with the tray, pushing my way between guests, but the glasses disappeared without my having to get involved in small talk. When the tray was empty I returned to the kitchen where it was just as crowded.

'Hi, Roy. I saw you had your little silver tin of tobacco out – can you spare me a wedge?'

It was Erik Nerell. He stood leaning against the fridge with a beer in his hand. Erik pumped iron and his head was so small on his thick, muscular neck you could hardly see the join; it looked like a tree trunk that just grew out the top of his T-shirt. On top of it all was a yellow crew cut, tight as a bundle of uncooked spaghetti, with shoulders sloping down the sides towards two biceps that always looked as if they'd just been inflated. And who knows, maybe they had been. He'd been a paratrooper, and now he ran what was actually the village's only real bar, Fritt Fall. It had been a cafeteria and he'd taken the place over and turned it into a bar with a disco, karaoke, bingo every Monday and quiz every Wednesday.

I fished the tin of Berry's snuff out of my pocket and handed it to him. He stuffed a wedge under his upper lip.

'Just want to see what it tastes like,' he said. 'I've never seen anyone else using American snuff. Where d'you get hold of it?'

I shrugged. 'Here and there. Get people who are going out there to bring some back.'

'That's a neat tin,' he said as he handed it back. 'Ever been in the States yourself?'

'Never.'

'Something else I've always wondered about,' he said. 'How come you put the snuff inside your **lower** lip?'

'The American way,' I said in English. 'That's the way Dad did it. He always used to say only Swedes put it under the upper lip, and everyone knows how the Swedes chickened out during the war.'

Erik Nerell laughed, his upper lip bulging. 'Nice bit of stuff your brother's picked up.'

I didn't answer.

'It's almost freaky how good her Norwegian is.'

'You've spoken to her?'

'Just asking if she danced.'

'You asked if she **danced**? Why?'

Erik shrugged. 'Because she looks like a ballerina. **Tiny dancer,** right? And then she's from Barbados. Calypsos and that . . . what d'you call it again? Soca!'

There must have been something in the look on my face that made him laugh.

'Take it easy, Roy, she was cool with it, said she'd teach it to us later on tonight. You ever seen soca? Fucking sexy stuff.'

'OK,' I said, and thought that was probably pretty good advice. Take it easy.

Erik took a swig from his bottle of beer and belched discreetly into his hand. I guess that's what living with a woman does to you. 'Know if there are a lot of rock-falls in Huken at the moment?' he said.

'Dunno,' I said. 'Why d'you ask?'

'Has nobody told you?'

'Told me what?' I felt a chill, like cold air wafting through the rotting window putty.

'The sheriff wants us to check the wall with a drone and if it looks OK we're going to rappel down to the wreck. A few years ago I'd've done it like a shot, but now, what with Thea sitting at home with a bun in the oven, things look a bit different.'

No, not just a breath of cold air. An injection, a hypo dispensing ice-cold water. The wreck. The Cadillac.

It had been lying there for eighteen years. I shook my head. 'Well, it probably looks OK, but then I do hear stones falling. It happens all the time.'

Erik gave me a sort of calculating look. I don't know whether it was the danger of the falling stones or my own trustworthiness he was wondering about. Maybe it was both. He must have heard the story of what happened when they were going to recover Mum's and Dad's bodies from Huken. Two men from the mountain rescue team climbed down there and when they started hoisting up the stretchers with the bodies, the stretchers banged against the rock face, but no stones came loose. The accident happened as the men were on the way back up themselves. A rock dislodged by the person on the rope struck the man below securing it and crushed his shoulder joint. Me and Carl had been standing on Geitesvingen, behind the ambulance, the rescue crew and the sheriff, and what I remember most clearly are the screams through the cold, still evening air of the climber who was out of sight. They were tossed back and forth between the rock faces down there. Slow and controlled, almost as if they were measuring the pain, like the raven's calm cry of alarm.

'Hey, come on, speech!' exclaimed Erik.

I heard Carl's voice coming from the living room and saw people pushing their way in. I found somewhere to stand in the doorway. Even though Carl was a head taller than most people he'd still clambered up onto a chair.

'My dear, dear friends,' his voice boomed. 'It's just so fucking great to see you all again. Fifteen years . . .' He let it hang there for us to savour. 'Most of you have been seeing each other every day, so you haven't noticed the gradual changes, that we've actually got older. So let me just make one thing very clear, that when it comes to you guys . . .' He took a breath, looked round with his cheeky, teasing smile. 'I seem to be wearing a lot better than you.'

Laughter and loud protests.

'Oh yes, oh yes!' Carl shouted. 'And it's even more remarkable when you realise I'm the only guy here who had any looks to lose.'

More laughter, whistles and jeers. Someone tried to pull him down off the chair.

'But,' said Carl, as someone helped him stay steady on the chair, 'when it comes to the ladies, it's the other way round. You look a **lot** better now than you did back then.'

Cheers and applause from the women.

A man's voice: 'Watch it now, Carl!'

I turned and looked for Mari. It was automatic, I had never got out of the habit. Shannon was sitting on the worktop in the kitchen to get a better view. Her back arched. Erik Nerell was standing by the fridge studying her. I left the room and headed up the stairs to the boys' room, closed the door and lay down on the upper bunk. Heard Carl's voice in through the kitchen and up through the hole around the stovepipe. I couldn't hear every word, but I got the gist of it. I heard my own name, and then a pause.

A man's voice: 'He'll be in the bog.' Laughter.

Shannon's name. Heard her deep, masculine tone. A sparrow with the song of an owl. A few words, then polite and restrained applause.

I took a swig of beer, stared at the roof. Closed my eyes.

When I opened them again, it was quieter. And I realised I had slept through the party, that the last of the guests were leaving. Engines starting, revving up. The chatter of gravel beneath tyres. Red lights on the curtains as they braked heading into Geitesvingen.

And then the silence was almost complete. A few padding footsteps and low voices coming from the kitchen. Adult voices in normal, everyday conversation, about small, practical matters. The sounds I had fallen asleep to as a child. Safe sounds. A safety you think will last because it feels so right, so good, so unchanging.

I had dreamed. About a car that for an instant floats off into the air and looks as if it's heading on into outer space. But then gravity and the real world get hold of it, and slowly the heavier front end, with the engine, starts to dip downwards. Into the darkness. Into Huken. There's a scream. It's not Dad's. And not Mum's. And not the climber's. It's my scream.

I hear Shannon giggle and whisper 'No!' outside my door, and then Carl's drunken 'Roy just thinks it's cosy. Now I'm going to show you what it was like for us.'

I stiffened, even though I probably realised he wouldn't do it. Show her what it was **really** like for us.

The door opened.

'You asleep, bro?' I felt Carl's boozy breath against my face.

'Yes,' I answered.

'Let's go,' whispered Shannon, but I felt the bed shake as Carl lay down on the lower bunk and pulled her down with him.

'We missed you at the party,' said Carl.

'Sorry,' I said. 'I needed a little timeout and then fell asleep.'

'Takes some doing to sleep through the racket from that **rånergjengen.**'

'Yeah,' I answered.

'What's a **rånergjengen**?' asked Shannon.

'A boy racer gang. Noisy bastards with simple pleasures,' sniggered Carl. 'Burning up tyres in their souped-up cars and sleepers.' I heard him take a swig from a bottle down there. 'But the ones who were here tonight, their old ladies don't let them do it any more. The ones who keep the tradition going are the kids who hang out at Roy's station.'

'So then a **råne** is a what?' asked Shannon

'It means a pig.' I said. 'A male pig. Hot and dangerous.'

'Does it **have** to be dangerous?'

'Well, you can castrate it. Then it becomes a **galte.**'

'**Galte,**' she echoed.

'So strictly speaking, what we had up here tonight wasn't actually a **rånegjeng** but a **galtegjeng.**' Carl chuckled. 'Married, settled, castrated, but obviously still capable of reproducing.'

'**Galtegjeng.** And some of them drive American cars, which you call Amcars.' I could see how every Norwegian word we said went straight into that linguist's brain of hers.

'Shannon loves American cars,' Carl went on. 'She was driving her own Buick from the age of eleven. Ouch!'

I heard Shannon's whispered protest from below.

'Buick,' I said. 'Not bad.'

'He's lying, I didn't **drive,**' said Shannon. 'My grandma let me hold the steering wheel of this rusty old car she inherited from my great-uncle Leo. He was killed in Cuba, fighting with Castro against Batista. The car and Leo both came back from Havana in pieces, and Grandma put the car back together by herself.'

Carl laughed. 'But Leo she couldn't put back together?'

'What type of Buick was it?' I asked.

'A Roadmaster '54,' said Shannon. 'When I was at university in Bridgetown, Grandma drove me there in that car every single day.'

I must have been tired, or else still groggy from the punch and the beer, because I almost said that those vintage Buick Roadmasters were the most beautiful cars ever in my view.

'Shame you slept through the whole party, Roy,' said Shannon.

'Oh, he doesn't mind,' said Carl. 'See, Roy doesn't really like people. Apart from me, that is.'

'Is it true you saved his life, Roy?' asked Shannon.

'No,' I said.

'Oh yes!' said Carl. 'That time we bought the second-hand diving gear from Willumsen and didn't have enough money to pay for the course, so we tested it out without knowing a fucking thing about it.'

'It was my fault,' I said. 'I was the one who said it was just simple, practical logic.'

'Says he. Of course, he managed it all right,' said Carl. 'And when it was my turn I got water inside the mask, I panicked and spat out the mouthpiece. If it hadn't been for Roy . . .'

'No, no, I just leaned over the side of the boat and pulled you to the surface,' I said.

'That same evening I sold my share in the diving equipment. Never wanted to set eyes on it again. How much did you give for it? Hundred, was it?'

I could feel the corners of my lips widening. 'All I remember is that for once I thought I got a good price from you.'

'It was a hundred too much!' cried Shannon. 'Did you ever do anything in return for your big brother?'

'No,' said Carl. 'Roy's a far better brother than I am.'

Shannon gave a sudden laugh and the bunk beds swayed; I think he must have been tickling her.

'Is that true?' Shannon hiccupped.

There was no answer, and I realised it was me she was asking.

'No,' I said. 'He's lying.'

'Is he? How did he help you then?'

'He corrected my homework for me.'

'No I did not!' protested Carl.

'The nights before I had to hand in my essays he used to get up from where you are now, sneak over to my satchel, take my exercise book out to the toilet and correct all the misspellings. Then put the book back and crept back into his bed again. Never said a word about it.'

'That happened maybe once!' said Carl.

'Every time,' I said. 'And I never said anything about it either.'

'Why not?' Shannon's whisper had the same dark quality as the darkness in the room.

'I couldn't have people knowing that I quite happily let my kid brother sort things out for me,' I said. 'But on the other hand I needed a pass mark in Norwegian.'

'Twice,' said Carl. 'Maybe three times.'

We lay in silence. Shared the silence. I heard the sound of Carl's breathing, so familiar it was like hearing my own. Now there was a third person breathing in the room, and I felt a stab of jealousy. That it wasn't me lying down there with my arms around him. There was a chill cry; it sounded like it came from the outfields. Or from Huken.

I heard muttering from the bunk below.

'She's asking what kind of animal that was,' said Carl. 'A raven, wasn't it?'

'That's right,' I said and waited. The raven – at least

the one that lived up here – usually called twice, but this time not.

'Does it mean danger?' asked Shannon.

'Could be,' I said. 'Or it's answering another raven, one we can't hear, that's half a dozen kilometres away.'

'Do they have different calls?'

'Yes,' I said. 'There's a different call if you get too close to the nest. The females call most. Sometimes a whole choir at it for no reason you can figure out.'

Carl chuckled. I love that sound. It spread warmth, goodness. 'Roy knows more about birds than anything else. Apart from cars maybe. And service stations.'

'But not about people,' said Shannon. From the way she said it you couldn't tell if it was a question or a statement.

'Precisely,' said Carl. 'So instead he gives people bird names. Dad was the mountain lark, Mum the wheatear. Uncle Bernard was the bunting because he was training to be a priest before he became a car mechanic, and the reed bunting has a white collar.'

Shannon laughed. 'And what were you, darling?'

'I was . . . what was I again?'

'The meadow pipit,' I said quietly.

'I presume the meadow pipit is handsome, strong and intelligent then,' chuckled Shannon.

'Maybe,' I said.

'It was because it flies higher than all the others,' said Carl. 'And on top of that it's a big-mouthed big head that practises . . . what d'you call it again?'

'Fluktspill,' I said.

'**Fluktspill,**' Shannon said. 'That's a nice word. What does it mean?'

I sighed as though it was a lot of bother for me to explain everything. 'It's a sort of winnowing display. Once it's flown as high as it can it starts to sing, so that everyone can see how high up it is. Then it floats down with wings outstretched, showing off all the tricks and acrobatics it can do.'

'Carl to a P!' cried Shannon.

'To a T,' said Carl.

'To a T,' she repeated.

'But even though the meadow pipit likes to show off, it's not an unprincipled con man,' I said. 'In fact, it's pretty easy to trick. That's what makes it a favourite when the cuckoo's looking for someone else's nest to lay eggs in.'

'Poor Carl!' said Shannon, and I heard a big wet kiss. 'Roy, what kind of bird would you say I was?'

I thought about it. 'I don't know.'

'Come on,' said Carl.

'I don't know. Hummingbird? I only really know mountain birds.'

'I don't want to be a hummingbird!' Shannon protested. 'They're too small and they like sweet stuff. Can't I be like the one I found. The dotterel?'

I thought of the dotterel's white face. Dark eyes. The cap that almost looks like a crew cut.

'OK,' I said. 'You're the dotterel.'

'And you, Roy, what are you?'

'Me? I'm not anything.'

'Everybody's something. Come on.'

I didn't respond.

'Roy's the storyteller who tells us who we are,' said Carl. 'So that makes him everyone and no one. He's the mountain bird that has no name.'

'The solitary mountain bird with no name,' she said. 'What kind of song does a nameless male like you sing to attract a mate?'

Carl laughed. 'Sorry, Roy, but this one here won't stop until you've revealed your entire life to her.'

'Fine,' I said. 'A characteristic of the male mountain bird is that he doesn't sing for the female. He thinks it's a load of flash nonsense and anyway up here in the mountains there are no trees for him to sit in and sing. So what he does instead is build a nest to impress her.'

'Hotels?' she asked. 'Or service stations?'

'Looks like hotels work best,' I said.

They both laughed.

'Now let's give the mountain thrush up there a bit of rest,' said Carl.

They climbed out of the bunk.

'Goodnight,' said Carl and stroked my head.

The door closed behind them and I lay there listening.

He remembered. That once, a long time ago, I'd told him I was the mountain thrush, the ring ouzel. A shy and cautious bird that hides away among the rocks. He'd said there was no need for me to do that, there was nothing out there to be afraid of. And I had answered that I knew that, but that I was still afraid anyway.

I slept. Dreamed the same dream, as though it had just been paused and was waiting for me. When I woke to the scream of the climber getting hit by the rock I realised it was Shannon screaming. She screamed again. And again. Carl was fucking her well. Good for them. But of course, hard to sleep through a racket like that. I listened for a bit, thought she'd reached her climax, but it didn't stop, so I put a pillow over my head. After a while I took it away again. It was quiet in there now. They were probably sleeping, but I couldn't get back to sleep. Tossed and turned and the bed creaked as I thought about what Erik Nerell had said about the sheriff wanting to send climbers down into Huken to check the Cadillac.

And finally it came.

The raven's second call.

And I knew that this time it warned of danger. Not some immediate danger, but a fate that was out there, waiting somewhere. That had been waiting a long time now. Patient. Never forgetting. Trouble.

PART TWO

5

CARL. HE'S THERE IN ALMOST all my childhood memories. Carl in the lower bunk. Carl whom I crept in beside in January, when the thermometer dropped to minus fifteen, or when the other situation demanded it in some way. Carl, my kid brother, with whom I quarrelled until he sobbed with anger and lashed out at me, and with the same result every time: I got him down easily, sat astride him so his arms were pinioned, pinched his nose. When he stopped struggling and just sobbed I could feel how his weakness and his giving up irritated me. Until at last he gave me that helpless kid brother look, and I got a lump in my throat, let him up and put an arm around him and promised him something or other. But the lump in the throat and the guilty conscience were still there long after Carl had dried his tears. Once Dad had seen us fighting. He hadn't said a word, just let us get on with it, the way those of us who live up on the mountain let nature take its brutal course without interfering, unless our own goats were involved. It ended with me and Carl sitting on the sofa, me with my arm round him, both of us tearful. He just shook his head in exasperation and left the room.

And I remember when I was twelve years old and Carl eleven, when my uncle Bernard turned fifty. He did something that, from Mum and Dad's reaction, we realised was something really big time; he invited everyone to the city – the **big** city – to celebrate at the Grand Hotel. Mum said it had a swimming pool, and Carl and I were just crazy with excitement. And when we got there, it turned out there was no swimming pool, never had been, and I was pretty pissed off. But it didn't seem to bother Carl that much, and when one of the people working there offered to show the eleven-year-old around the hotel I saw the bulge in Carl's jacket pocket where he'd stuffed his swimming trunks. When he got back he went on about all the incredible things he'd seen, said the hotel was a bloody palace, and that one day he was going to build himself a fucking palace just like it. He said. Minus the swearing. And in the years that followed he always swore he'd had a swim in the pool at the Grand Hotel that evening.

I think that was something Carl and Mum had in

common, that the dream could top the reality, the packaging beat the contents. If things weren't exactly like you wanted them to be, then you just reimagined them until they were, and remained more or less blind to things that shouldn't have been there. For example, Mum always used the English word 'hall' to refer to the passageway in our house that stank of dung and stables. The **haaall** – that was how she said it. She'd worked as a maid and housekeeper for a shipping family from when she was a teenager and liked things to sound English and upper class.

Dad was the opposite. He called a stable shovel a shite shovel, and he wanted everything around him to be, sound and feel American. And not big-city American but Midwest American, like Minnesota, where he had lived from the age of four until he was twelve, with the father whom we had never met. America was and remained the promised land for Dad, along with Cadillacs, the Methodist Church and **the pursuit of happiness,** always expressed in English. Originally he had wanted to name me Calvin, after the American president Calvin Coolidge. A Republican, naturally. Unlike his more charismatic predecessor Warren Harding – who had left in his wake a trail of scandals that all began with a **c:** chicks, cards, corruption and cocaine – Calvin was a hard-working man, serious, slow, taciturn and gruff, a man who, according to my father, hadn't rushed things but climbed the career ladder one rung at a time. But Mum had protested, so they compromised on Roy, with Calvin as a middle name.

Carl had been given the middle name Abel, after Secretary of State Abel Parker Upshur, an intelligent and charming man, according to Dad, as well as a man who dreamed big. So big that he arranged the annexation of Texas to the USA in 1845 and in so doing made it in one night a much bigger country. As part of the deal Abel accepted that Texas could continue with slavery. But under the circumstances that was, according to Dad, a mere detail.

It could be that Carl and I matched pretty well the two we were named for. No one in the village – apart from maybe the old chairman Aas – knew anything about the original Calvin and Abel. They just said that I was most like Dad, and Carl most like Mum. But people down in Os don't know what they're talking about, they just talk.

I was ten years old the time Dad came driving home in a Cadillac DeVille. Willum Willumsen at Willumsen's Used Car and Breaker's Yard had boasted about this beautiful specimen the owner had imported from the USA but found he couldn't afford the import duty and had had to sell. In other words the car, a 1979 model, had done nothing but drive along dead straight highways through bone-dry Nevada deserts, so no rust to worry about there. Dad probably nodded his head slowly. He hadn't a clue about cars, and my own interest still lay in the future. He made the deal without even haggling over the price, and after it had to be taken back to the repair shop less than two weeks later it was obvious it had as many pirated parts and faults as any of those wrecks you see balanced on breeze blocks on the streets of Havana. In the end the repairs set him back more than the car had. The locals laughed themselves silly about it and said that was what you get for not knowing the first thing about cars, one up for Willumsen, that wily old horse-trader. But I got a new toy. No, it was more than that, it was an education. A gadget in a thousand mechanical pieces, from which I learned that if you just took the time to understand the construction, and used your brain and your fingers then it was actually possible to mend things.

I started spending more time at Uncle Bernard's car repair shop. He allowed me to 'help him out', as he put it, though to begin with I was more of a hindrance than a help. And Dad taught me to box. Around that time Carl is a little hazy for me. This was before he shot up. At first it looked as though I was going to be the taller of us, and for a while back then he had some terrible pimples. He did well at school, but he was quiet, had few friends, and kept himself to himself most of the time. And once he started at secondary school and I was spending more and more time at the repair shop it was often bedtime before we saw each other.

I remember one evening talking about how much I was looking forward to turning eighteen, coming of age, getting a driving licence, and Ma shed a little tear and asked if the only thing I thought about was jumping into the car and getting away from Opgard.

And of course, looking back, it's easy to say that would have been best. But things had already started falling apart, and I couldn't just run off. I had to fix them. Repair them. Anyway: where would I go?

Then came the day Mum and Dad died, and Carl is back in all of those memory-pictures. I was almost eighteen, him not yet seventeen. Him and me sit watching as the Cadillac heads away from the yard and down in the direction of Geitesvingen. Even now it's still like a film I can watch and discover new details in every time.

Two tons of machinery from the General Motors factory, rolling along and gradually gathering speed. Now it's so far away from me I can no longer hear the gravel crunch beneath the tyres. Silence, silence and the red rear lights. I can feel my heart beating, the speed increasing there too. Another twenty metres to Geitesvingen. The Highways Maintenance Department had been on the point of erecting a crash barrier when the council discovered that the last hundred metres up to the farm were private road and Opgard's responsibility. Ten metres to go. The brake lights – like two bars, two hyphens running between the lid of the boot and the shiny bumper bar – lit up for a moment. Then they were gone. Everything was gone.

6

'NOW LET'S SEE, ROY. YOU were standing outside the house on the evening of the accident at half past . . .' Sheriff Sigmund Olsen sat with his head bent as he looked through the documents. His thick mane of blond hair made me think of the mop in the gym at school. The hair hanging down was the same length at the front, the sides and the back. He had one of those thick walrus moustaches too, probably had the mop and the moustache ever since the seventies. Because he could. There wasn't a trace of baldness on his bent head. '. . . seven. And you saw your parents go over the edge?'

I nodded.

'And you say you saw the brake lights go on?'

'Yes.'

'You're sure it wasn't just the rear lights? You know they're both red?'

'The brake lights are brighter.'

He looked up at me quickly.

'You'll soon be eighteen, right?'

I nodded again. Maybe it was in his papers, maybe he remembered I'd been a class ahead of his son Kurt at junior school.

'Secondary school?'

'I work at my uncle's car repair shop.'

The sheriff bent over the desk again. 'Good, then you'll understand why we think it's odd we didn't find any skid marks. And even if the blood test shows your Dad had had a drink, it was hardly enough for him to forget about the bend, or put his foot down on the wrong pedal, or fall asleep at the wheel.'

I said nothing. He'd dispensed with three possible explanations in one blow. And I didn't have a fourth to offer.

'Carl told us you were going to visit your uncle Bernard Opgard at the hospital. That's who you work for?'

'Yes.'

'But we've talked to Bernard, and he says he never heard about any planned visit. Did your parents usually make unannounced visits?'

'No,' I said. 'And not announced ones either.'

The sheriff nodded slowly. Again he studied his

papers. Seemed like that's what he was most comfort-able doing. 'Was your father depressed, do you think?'

'No,' I said.

'You sure? Other people we've talked to thought he seemed very down.'

'You want me to say he was depressed?'

Olsen raised his eyes again. 'Now what do you mean by that, Roy?'

'That maybe that would make the case simpler. If you can say he killed himself and my mum.'

'Why do you think that makes it simpler?'

'No one liked him.'

'That's not true, Roy.'

I shrugged. 'OK then, I'm sure he was depressed. He spent a lot of time alone. Sat most of the time inside the house and didn't talk much there either. Drank beer. That's what depressed people do.'

'People who suffer from depression can be very clever at hiding it.' Sheriff Olsen's gaze worked to hold mine, and once he'd managed it, he had a job keeping it steady. 'Did your father ever say anything about . . . about not liking being alive?'

Not liking being alive. Once he'd said the words, it was as though Sigmund Olsen had got over the worst of it. His gaze rested calmly on me.

'Who the hell likes being alive?' I asked.

For a moment Olsen looked shocked. He put his head on one side and his long hippy hair dangled down on his shoulder. Maybe it **was** a mop. I knew that hidden behind the desk he had an enormous belt buckle with a white buffalo skull on it and a pair of snakeskin boots. We dress ourselves in death.

'Why live if you don't like it, Roy?'

'Isn't it obvious?'

'Is it?'

'Because being dead may be even worse.'

My eighteenth birthday was just around the corner, but according to the stupid rules Carl and I still needed a guardian. The county governor appointed my uncle Bernard as our guardian. Two women from the social services in Notodden came and checked Uncle Bernard's set-up and evidently found everything adequate. Bernard showed them the bedroom we had been given and promised to have regular discussions with the school about how Carl was doing.

Once the social services women had gone I asked Uncle Bernard if it was OK if Carl and I spent a couple of nights up at Opgard, there was so much damn noise from the main road outside the bedroom window down here in the village.

Bernard said it was OK and gave us a big pot of **lapskaus** to take with us.

And after that we never moved back down again, although officially our address was with Uncle Bernard. That didn't mean he didn't look out for us, and the money he got from the state as guardian he gave straight to us.

A couple of years later, quite a while after what I

began to think of as the Fritz night, Uncle Bernard was admitted to hospital again. It turned out the cancer had spread. I sat sobbing beside his bed as he told me.

'You know there's not long to go when the vultures move into your house without asking,' he said.

Meaning his daughter and her husband.

Uncle Bernard always said she'd never done him any harm, he just didn't like her much, but I knew who he was thinking of when he explained to me what a wrecker was. People who lit fake flares for ships in the night, and plundered them once they'd run aground.

She visited him at the hospital twice. Once to find out how long he had left, and the second time to pick up the key to the house.

Uncle Bernard lay a hand on my shoulder and told one of those old soppy Volkswagen jokes, probably trying to make me laugh.

'You're going to die!' I shouted out. I was pretty angry.

'You too,' he said. 'And this is the right order for dying in. Right?'

'But how can you lie here and tell jokes?'

'Well,' he said, 'when you're up to your neck in shit, the thing to remember is to keep your head up.'

And then I just couldn't help laughing anyway.

'I've got a last request,' he said.

'A smoke?'

'That too. The other is that you take the theory exam as a working apprentice this autumn.'

'Already? Don't I need five years' practical?'

'You've **got** five years' practical. With all the over-time you've put in.'

'But that doesn't count—'

'It counts for **me.** I would never let an unqualified mechanic take the theory exam, you know that. But you're the best mechanic I've got. So for that reason there's documentation in that envelope on the table there that says you've worked for me for five years. Never mind the dates on it. Is that clear?'

'Clear as muck,' I said.

It was a joke we shared. A mechanic who worked for Uncle Bernard didn't understand the expression but used it all the time, and Bernard never corrected him. That was the last time I heard Uncle Bernard laugh.

By the time I had passed the theory exam, and the practical exam a few months later, Uncle Bernard was already in a coma. And after his daughter told the doctors to turn off the life-support machine that was keeping him alive, in effect it was me, a lad of twenty-one, who ran the car repair shop. All the same it came as a shock . . . no, that's too strong, it came as a **surprise** when his will was read out and it turned out Uncle Bernard had left the business to me.

His daughter protested, naturally, claiming that during the hours when I'd been sitting with her poor father I'd been manipulating him. I said I couldn't be bothered arguing, that Uncle Bernard hadn't given me the repair shop to make me rich but so that it would stay in the family. So if she wanted, I'd buy the place from her at her asking price, that way at least his wishes would be respected. So she named her price. I told her that we Opgard people never haggled, but that the price was more than I could afford, and that it was way out of proportion to the income from the repair shop.

She put the business on the open market, got no buyers though she lowered the price again and again, and in the end came back to me. I paid what I'd offered in the beginning, she signed the contract and marched furiously out of the workshop as though she was the one who had been cheated.

I ran the business as best I could. Which isn't saying much, since I didn't have the experience or the market trend with me. But didn't do too badly either, since the other repair shops in the area began closing down and the work came to me. Enough of it for me to keep Markus on part-time. But when I sat down in the evenings and went through the accounts with Carl – who was doing a business course and knew the difference between debit and credit – it was obvious that the two petrol pumps out front of the greasing station were bringing in more than the repair shop.

'The Public Roads Administration people were here checking,' I said. 'If I'm to keep my licence we need to upgrade the equipment.'

'How much?' asked Carl.

'Two hundred thousand. Maybe more.'

'You're not going to get that here.'

'I know that. So what do we do?'

I said 'we' because the workshop was keeping us both. And asked Carl, even though I knew the answer, because I preferred it to be him who said it out loud.

'Sell the repair shop and keep the pumps,' said Carl.

I rubbed the back of my neck where Grete Smitt had used the shaver and felt the prickling of the stubble on my fingertips. A **crew cut,** she called it. Not the fashion, but a classic, meaning that when I looked at photos ten years from now I wouldn't squirm with embarrassment. Afterwards people said that I looked more like my father than ever, the very image of him, and I hated it, because I knew they were right.

'I know you prefer fixing cars to filling them,' said Carl after a long silence, during which I neither nodded nor spat.

'That's OK. There's less and less fixing to do anyway,' I said. 'They don't make cars like they used to anyway, and most of the jobs we get an idiot could do. You don't need a **feeling** for the job nowadays.' I was twenty-one and sounded like a sixty-year-old.

The following day Willum Willumsen came up and looked over the repair shop. Willumsen was a naturally fat man. In the first place, the proportions required it, so much for the stomach, so much for the thighs and chin, for the whole thing to balance out and make the complete man. In the second, he walked, talked and gesticulated like a fat man, though I'm not sure exactly how to explain that. But OK, let me try: Willumsen waddled around with his feet splayed out, like a duck. He spoke in a loud and uninhibited voice, and illustrated what he was saying with expansive gestures and grimaces. In sum: Willumsen took up a lot of room. And in the third place: he smoked cigars. Unless your name is Clint Eastwood, you **can't** be fat and hope to be taken seriously as a cigar smoker. Even Winston Churchill and Orson Welles would have had a hard time doing that. Willumsen sold used cars and stripped those he couldn't fool anyone into buying. Now and then I bought parts from him. He sold other second-hand stuff as well, and rumour had it that if you were trying to get rid of stolen goods then Willumsen might be the man to approach. Same thing if you needed a quick loan but didn't enjoy the confidence of your bank. But God help you if you didn't make the payments on time. Then he had a Danish enforcer come up from Jutland with a pair of pliers and other tools of the trade that would soon persuade you to pay what you owed even if it meant robbing your own mother. As it happens no one had ever actually seen this enforcer, but the rumour had really taken off in our imaginations as young kids when we one day saw a white Jaguar E-Type with Danish plates parked outside Willumsen's Used Car and Breaker's Yard. The Danish enforcer's white car. That was all we needed.

Willumsen went through all the gear, the tools, anything that could be screwed down or taken apart before making his offer.

'That's not much,' I said. 'You know enough about the business to know that this is all top-quality gear.'

'You said it yourself, Roy. The equipment needs to be upgraded to keep the accreditation.'

'But you won't be running an authorised repair shop, Willumsen. All you'll be doing is just enough repairs so those wrecks you sell will keep running for a week after you've sold them.'

Willumsen gave a hearty laugh. 'I'm not pricing the stuff on what it's worth to you, Roy Opgard, I'm pricing it on what it's **not** worth to you.'

I was learning something new every day.

'On one condition,' I said. 'You take Markus as part of the deal.'

'Part of the deal as the troll that comes with the barn? Come on, that Markus is more of a troll than a mechanic.'

'That's the deal, Willumsen.'

'Really don't know if I can use a little troll like Markus, Roy. National insurance. Social outlays.'

'Yeah yeah, I know all that. But Markus will make certain the cars you sell aren't actually a danger to traffic. Which is more than you do.'

Willumsen plucked at the lowest of his chins and looked as if he was working out the cost. He looked at me with one of his big octopus eyes and then offered an even lower price.

I couldn't stand it any more. Said OK and Willumsen straight away held out his hand, probably to make sure I wouldn't change my mind. I looked at those five spread, small grey-white fingers, like a latex glove filled with water. Shuddered as I took it.

'I'll be over tomorrow to pick it all up,' said Willumsen.

Willumsen sacked Markus after three months, in the middle of his trial period so he didn't have to give Markus paid notice. He told Markus it was because he'd been turning up late, been given a warning, and then turned up late again.

'And is that right?' I had asked Markus when he came to me looking for a job at what was now my one-man service station, the place where I was spending twelve hours every working day.

'Yes,' said Markus. 'Ten minutes in September. And four minutes in November.'

So with that there were three guys living off two petrol pumps. I'd installed a dispensing machine with soft drinks and snacks in the old repair shop, but for the locals the Co-op was nearer and had more choice.

'It's not going to work,' said Carl, pointing to the balance sheet we had drawn up together.

'Further up the valley they're selling cabins on three new sites,' I said. 'Just wait for the winter – we'll have all the new cabin owners driving past here.'

Carl sighed. 'You're a hell of an obstinate bugger.'

One day an SUV pulled up in the forecourt. Two guys got out and wandered off round the repair shop building and the car wash as though looking for something.

'If you're looking for the toilet, it's in here,' I called out.

They walked over to me, each gave me his card, from which I learned that they were from what was definitely the biggest chain of service stations in the country, and asked if we could have that talk. I asked 'What talk?', and then realised Carl must have been in touch with them. They said they were impressed by how much I had got out of so little, and explained how much I could get with just a little bit more.

'Franchise agreement,' they said. 'Ten years.'

They had also heard about the massive investment in new cabins further up the valley and the traffic prognosis for our main road.

'What did you say to them?' asked Carl excitedly when I got home.

'I said thanks,' I answered, and slumped down at the kitchen table. Carl had heated up some meatballs.

'**Thanks?**' said Carl. 'As in . . .' He read my face as I tucked in. 'As in **no** thanks? What the fuck, Roy!'

'They wanted to buy everything,' I said. 'The buildings, the land. Lots of money, of course, but I guess I like owning it. Must be the farmer in me.'

'But for chrissakes, it's all we can do just to keep our heads above water here.'

'You should've told me they were coming.'

'You would have said no even before hearing what they had to say.'

'That's probably true.'

Carl groaned and put his head in his hands. Stayed

like that for a while. Sighed. 'You're right,' he said. 'I shouldn't get involved. Sorry. I was only trying to help.'

'I know that. Thanks.'

He opened the fingers of one hand and looked at me through one eye. 'So you got nothing out of the visit at all?'

'Sure did.'

'Oh yeah?'

'They had a long drive back, so they had to fill up the tank.'

7

EVEN THOUGH DAD HAD TAUGHT me a bit of boxing, I don't really know if I was that good a fighter.

There was a dance at Årtun. Same band as usual, all in tight-fitting white suits, playing hits from Sweden. The vocalist, a skinny guy everyone called Rod because his ambition was to sound like Rod Stewart and score as many girls, got things going, howling away in a mixture of Norwegian and Swedish that made him sound like Armand, the travelling preacher who passed through the village now and then preaching about the great wave of awakening that was breaking over the land, and how it was good, because the Day of Judgement was nigh. If he'd been in Årtun that evening the preacher would have realised there was quite a bit of work still to do. People of all ages and both sexes, off their heads on home brew that would have been confiscated if they tried to take it inside, staggering around on the grass in front of the village hall, couples propping each other up as Rod sang about those **golden-brown eyes.** Until they too had had enough and spilled out onto the grass for another swig or else to copulate among the birch trees, puke or take a crap. Some didn't even bother to head for the trees. People talked about the time our very own Rod invited a diehard female fan up onstage to join him in singing one of the band's own compositions, 'Are You Thinking of Me Tonight'. It was so like Eric Clapton's 'Wonderful Tonight' that it was a miracle he was able to keep a straight face. After two verses he got the guitarist to play an extra-long solo, disappeared into the wings with the girl and the microphone, and when it was time for the third verse it came somewhat breathlessly from offstage. Halfway through the verse Rod came strutting out again, alone this time, winked at a couple of girls in front of the stage and, noticing the horrified looks on their faces, glanced down and saw the smeared blood on his white trousers. He sang the last verse, put the microphone back in the stand, and with a sigh and a smile and a 'well well well . . .' counted in the next number.

Long, light summer nights. As a rule the fighting didn't start before ten o'clock. Two boys, and the cause was almost always a girl. A girl somebody had spoken to, or danced with a bit too often, or a bit too closely.

Maybe the story started way before that particular Saturday evening at Årtun, but it was now, fuelled by alcohol and urged on by spectators, that the thing came to a head. Sometimes the girl was just a handy excuse for boys who wanted to fight, and there were plenty of those. Guys who thought they were good at fighting and maybe not much else, and who used the dances at Årtun as their stage.

And of course there were other times when the jealousy was real. This was usually the case whenever Carl was involved, though he himself was never the one who started a fight. The new Carl was too disarming for that, too charming, and too little of a benchmark for the hard cases to bother with. Those who attacked Carl did so in the heat of the moment. Sometimes Carl hadn't even done anything, just made the girls laugh, been a bit more romantic than their own beaux could manage, had some girl's eyes meet his own blue gaze but done nothing about it. Because Carl had a girlfriend, the council chairman's daughter no less. He shouldn't have been a threat, but things probably looked different through the fog of whisky, and they wanted to teach the silver-tongued lover boy a lesson. They started swinging, got even more provoked by Carl's genuine and almost patronising surprise when the first punch landed, and wound up even more by the way he wouldn't defend himself.

Which is where I came in.

I think my talent lay more in **disarming** people, in stopping them from doing damage, the same way you disarm bombs. I'm practical. I understand how things function. Maybe that's why. Understood the centre of gravity, mass, speed, stuff like that. So I did what was necessary to stop those who were trying to beat up my little brother. What was **necessary,** no more and no less. But of course, **more** was sometimes necessary. A nose broken, the occasional rib, and at least one jaw. That was an out-of-town guy who had punched Carl hard on the nose.

I was there quick. I remember the bleeding knuckles, the blood on my shirtsleeves, and someone saying: 'That's enough now, Roy.'

But no, it wasn't enough. One more punch of that bloody face below me. One more punch and the problem would be permanently solved.

'The sheriff's coming, Roy.'

I lean down and whisper into the ear with blood running down both sides of it.

'You don't touch my brother again, understand?'

A glassy-eyed stare, emptied by drink and pain, is fastened on me, but staring inwards. I raise my arm. The head below me nods. I stand up, dust off my clothes, walk over to the Volvo 240 with its engine running and the driver's door open. Carl is already stretched out in the back seat.

'Don't get any blood on my fucking seat covers,' I say as I release the clutch and accelerate so hard bits of the lawn fly up in the air around us.

'Roy,' says a groggy voice once we're through the first few corners on the drive up the mountain.

111

'No,' I said. 'I won't say anything to Mari.'

'That's not it.'

'You gonna be sick?'

'No. I want to tell you something.'

'Why not try instead to—'

'I love you, bro.'

'Carl, don't—'

'Yes! I'm a fool and an idiot, but you, you don't let that bother you, you come along and you **bail me out** every time.' Tearful now. 'Roy, listen . . . you're all I've got.'

I look at the bloodied fist holding the wheel. I'm wide awake and the blood is pounding pleasurably through my body. I could have hit him one last time. The guy on the ground beneath me was just a jealous nobody, a loser, it really wouldn't have been necessary. But Jesus, how I had **wanted** to.

It turned out that the guy whose jaw I broke had a reputation for turning up at parties where people didn't know how good he was at fighting, provoking someone and then giving them a good kicking. After I heard about the jaw I was expecting a summons, but it never came. Or rather, I heard the guy had gone to the sheriff, and the sheriff advised him to drop it since Carl had suffered a broken rib, which was actually not true. Afterwards I realised that jaw had been a good investment. It gave me a reputation, so that it was often enough for me just to square up to someone if Carl got in trouble and they would back off.

'Shit,' Carl snuffles, choked up and drunk, as we

lie in our beds afterwards. 'I'm just a peaceful guy. Make the girls laugh. But the guys get all pissed off, and then you come along and sort it all out for your brother, and I've made you a lot of new enemies. Shit.' He snuffled again. 'Sorry.' He hits the planks under my mattress. 'You hear? I'm sorry.'

'They're idiots,' I say. 'Go to sleep now.'

'Sorry!'

'I said **sleep.**'

'Yeah yeah, OK. But, Roy . . .'

'Mm.'

'Thanks. Thanks for . . . for . . .'

'Just shut up, all right?'

'. . . for being my brother. Goodnight.'

Silence. Then, the steady breathing of the one in the bunk bed below me. Safe. Nothing is as good as the sound of a little brother who is safe.

But at the party that led to Carl leaving town, and leaving me, not a single blow was struck. Carl had been drunk, Rod had been hoarse, and Mari had gone home. Had he and Mari quarrelled? Maybe. Mari being the chairman's daughter it was probably not surprising she was more concerned with appearances than Carl was, but she was maybe tired of Carl always drinking too much at parties. Or perhaps Mari had to get up early, go to church with her parents, or study for her exams. No, she wasn't that prim and proper. Decent yes, but not prim and proper. She just didn't like looking out for Carl when he was pissed, and gave that job instead to her best friend Grete, who was a little too happy to do it. You would need to be pretty short-sighted not to see that Grete was in love with Carl, but of course it was quite possible Mari hadn't noticed, and she certainly never saw what was coming. That Grete – having supported Carl out on the dance floor as Rod ended the evening as usual with 'Love Me Tender' – had dragged Carl up into the birch trees. They'd had it away standing up against a tree trunk. He hadn't really known what was going on, he said, and only woke up at the sound of her down jacket scraping up and down against the bark. A sound that abruptly ceased when the cloth gave way and feathers like miniature angels were floating in the air around them. That's how he referred to them. As **miniature angels.** In the silence he realised that Grete herself hadn't made a single sound, either because she didn't want to break the spell or because she wasn't getting too much out of it. So that's when he stopped.

'I said I'd buy her a new jacket,' said Carl from the lower bunk next morning. 'But she said it was OK, she could repair it. Then I asked . . .' Carl groaned. His boozy breath hung in the air. 'I asked if she wanted me to help her with the sewing.'

I had laughed until I was crying in the top bunk and heard him pull the duvet over his head. Leaned out:

'So what you gonna do now, Don Juan?'

'Don't know,' from beneath the duvet.

'Anyone see you?'

No one had seen them. At any rate, a week passed and we hadn't heard any village gossip about Grete and Carl. Neither had Mari, apparently. It was beginning to look as though Carl was **home free.**

Until later in the day when Grete came visiting. Carl and me were sitting in the winter garden and saw her coming round Geitesvingen on her bicycle.

'Shit,' said Carl.

'She's probably looking for her climbing jacket,' I said. 'Meaning you.'

Carl pleaded with me and in the end I went out and said Carl had a terrible cold. Very contagious. Grete had stared at me, almost like she was taking aim, along her enormous sweaty, shiny nose. Then she'd turned and left. Back at the bike she'd put on the down jacket she had fastened to the carrier. The stitches were like a scar running down the back of it.

She came back the following day. Carl opened the door and before he could say anything she told him she loved him. And he replied that it was a mistake. That he'd done something really stupid. That he regretted it.

The next day Mari phoned and said Grete had told her everything and that she couldn't be with some-one who was unfaithful to her. Carl told me after-wards that Mari had cried, but otherwise been calm, and that he couldn't figure it out. Not that Mari had broken up with him, but that Grete had told her what had happened up in the birch trees. He could under-stand that Grete was pissed off with him, about the jacket and everything. Revenge. Fair enough. But to lose the only friend she had into the bargain, wasn't that like shooting yourself in the foot, as people say?

I didn't have much to say about that, but thought of that story Uncle Bernard had told about the wreckers, those people in the old days of sailing ships who gave false signals to sailors and lured them onto under-water reefs so that they could plunder the wrecks. That was when I began to think of Grete as an underwater reef. Lying there, invisible, just waiting for the chance to rip open a hull. In a way I felt sorry for her, caught up in the passion of her own feelings, but she had betrayed Mari every bit as much as Carl had. I sensed something in that woman that Carl hadn't seen. A hidden wickedness. That the pain you get from ruining things for yourself is less than the joy it brings to drag others down with you. The psychology of mass shootings in schools. The difference here being that this particular school shooter was still alive. Or at least still existing. To burn people up. Cut off their hair.

A few weeks later Mari suddenly moved from Os to the city. Although she claimed that had been the plan all along, to go there to study.

And a few weeks after that – just as unexpectedly – Carl revealed that he had been granted a scholar-ship to study finance and business administration in Minnesota, USA.

'Well, it's obvious, you can't turn that down,' I said and swallowed.

'I guess maybe I can't,' he said, as though doubtful. But of course, he couldn't fool me, I realised he had made up his mind a long time ago.

The next few days were busy. I had plenty to keep me going at the service station, and he was fully pre-occupied getting ready to leave, so we didn't have much time to talk it over. I took him to the airport, a drive of several hours, but strangely enough we didn't talk much about it then either. It poured with rain and the sound of the windscreen wipers camouflaged the silence.

When we stopped outside the Departures entrance and I turned off the engine I had to cough to get my voice going again. 'Are you coming back?'

'What? Of course,' he lied with a warm, beaming smile and put his arms around me.

The rain kept on all the way back to Os.

It was dark by the time I parked in the yard and went back to the ghosts inside the house.

8

CARL WAS HOME AGAIN. IT was Friday evening and I was alone at the service station. Alone with my thoughts, as people say.

When Carl left for the USA I had thought that of course it was to make use of his good exam results from school and his talents, and to get out of this dump, broaden his horizons. I had also thought that it was as much about getting away from the memories, the shadows that lay so heavy and oppressive over Opgard. Only now, now that he was back, did it occur to me that it might have had something to do with Mari Aas.

She'd dumped Carl because he'd had it away with her best friend, but wasn't there just the faintest possibility that it had given her the chance to get out too? She was aiming higher, after all, than a country boy, an Opgard. Her choice of husband seemed to confirm that. Mari and Dan Krane had met each other at university in Oslo. Both were active members of the Labour Party, and he came from an extremely comfortable home in the city's west end. Dan got the job as editor of the **Os Daily.** He and Mari had two kids now and extended their place until it was bigger than the main house where Mari's parents lived. She'd silenced that gleefully malicious gossip about her apparently not being good enough for Carl Opgard. She'd had her revenge, and more besides.

Whereas Carl's problem remained: how to regain his lost sense of honour and his local prestige? Was that what the homecoming was all about? To show off his trophy wife, his Cadillac, to build a hotel bigger than anyone around here had ever seen?

Because it really was an insane and almost desperate project. In the first place because of his insistence that the hotel be built above the treeline, which meant several kilometres of road had to be built. Solely so that it wouldn't be a lie when they advertised it as a 'mountaintop hotel', the way other hotels below the treeline so blithely did. And in the second place: who heads for the mountains to sit in a steam-bath and bathe in piss-warm water? Isn't that the kind of thing people in the cities and towns down below do?

119

And in the third place: he would never manage to persuade a handful of farmers to risk their farms and land for a castle in the air – how the hell do you do that in a place where scepticism towards anything new from the outside – unless it's a Ford car or a Schwarzenegger film – is something you ingest with your mother's milk, as people say?

And finally there was, of course, the question of his motives. Carl said it was to build a spa and mountaintop hotel resort that would put the village on the map and rescue it from a slow and silent death.

But wouldn't people here see through that? Realise that what he really wanted was to put himself – Carl Opgard – on a pedestal? Because that's why people like Carl return home, people who have made it out in the big wide world, while back in their old home town they're still just the randy bastard who got dumped by the chairman's daughter and ran off. There's nothing like being acknowledged in your own home town, the place where you think everyone misunderstood you, and at the same time the place where you are understood in such a consuming and liberating way. 'I know you,' as they would say, half threatening, half comforting, meaning that they know who you really are. That you can't always hide behind lies and appearances.

My gaze traced the main road in towards the square. Transparency. That's the curse and the glory of all little villages. Sooner or later, everything will be revealed. Everything. That was a risk Carl was willing to take for the chance of getting his statue in the square, the sort of posterity that is usually reserved for chairmen, preachers and dance-band singers.

My thoughts were interrupted as the door opened and Julie came in.

'Are **you** working nights now?' she asked loudly, rolling her eyes, overdoing the surprise. Chewed hard on her gum, swaying from one foot to the other. She was dressed up a bit, short jacket on top of a tight-fitting T-shirt, arms folded, more make-up than she usually wore. She hadn't expected me to be there, and it made her self-conscious to realise I was seeing her in this particular role – a babe, out on a Friday night with her boy racer crowd. It was all OK by me, evidently not so OK for her.

'Egil's not well,' I said.

'Then you should ring one of the others,' she said. 'Me for example. You're not supposed to be the one who—'

'Short notice,' I said. 'It's OK. What can I get you, Julie?'

'Nothing,' she said, adding a full stop by bursting a gum bubble. 'Just called in to say hi to Egil.'

'OK, I'll give him the message, tell him you were here.'

She looked at me, chewed. Her eyes were glazed. She'd regained her composure, superficially at least, and now she was Julie the tough girl again.

'What did you used to do Friday nights when you were kids, Roy?' She slurred her words slightly and it occurred to me she'd had a drop out in one of the cars.

'Dance,' I said.

She opened her eyes wide. 'You danced?'

'That's one way of describing it.'

Outside a car engine revved. Like the growling of some nocturnal beast of prey. Or a mating call. Julie glanced over her shoulder towards the door with a look of pretended irritation. Then she turned her back to the till, put her hands onto the counter behind her so that the short jacket rode up, took a breath and jumped, sliding her arse up onto the counter.

'Did you get a lot of girls, Roy?'

'No,' I said, and checked the security cameras by the pumps. When I tell people that every weekend at least one motorist a day fills up with petrol and drives off without paying they're shocked and say those cabin owners are a bunch of thieves. I say on the contrary, it's because the cabin owners are rich and don't think about money. That nine times out of ten when we send reminders to the address we get from the number plates they pay up in full and with a note of genuine apology saying that they quite simply forgot. Because they had never, like Dad, Carl and me, stood and watched the counters while filling up a Cadillac, seen those hundreds of kroner flashing by and along with them all the other things they could have bought with the money: CDs, a new pair of trousers, that road trip across the USA their father had always talked about.

'Why not?' said Julie. 'I mean, you're really hot, you know?' She giggled.

'Probably wasn't back then, I guess,' I said.

'And what about now? How come you don't have a girlfriend?'

'I did have,' I said as I finished washing off the food trays. Business had been good, but now the weekend visitors were all up at their cabins and we wouldn't be seeing them again until they headed home. 'Got married when we were nineteen. But she drowned on our honeymoon.'

'Eh?' exclaimed Julie, even though she knew I was making it up.

'Tumbled overboard from my sailing boat in the Pacific. Bit too much champagne probably. Gurgled that she loved me and then down she went.'

'Didn't you dive in after her?'

'A sailing boat like that moves faster than you can swim. We would both have drowned.'

'But all the same. You did love her.'

'Yes, so I threw her a lifebuoy.'

'Oh well, that's all right then.' Julie sat leaning forward, the palms of her hands on the counter. 'But could you still go on living, after you lost her?'

'It's amazing what we can manage without, Julie. Just wait and see.'

'No,' she said tonelessly. 'I'm not going to wait and see. I'm going to get everything I want.'

'OK. And what do you want?'

The question came automatically. Lazy and unfocused,

I had just batted the ball back across the net. I could have bitten off my tongue when I saw that veiled gaze fasten on mine, and that flushed grin.

'Then I guess you watch a lot of porn. Since your dream girl drowned. Seeing she was nineteen, do you search for Nineteen? With big boobs?'

I took too long to come back at her, and realised of course that she took this to mean she'd hit the nail on the head. It left me fumbling even more for my words. The conversation had already left the rails. She was seventeen, I was the boss she had persuaded herself she wanted, and now here she was a little tipsy, a bit too bold, playing a game she thought she could control because it worked with the boys sitting out there in their cars waiting for her. I could have said all this to her and salvaged my own pride, but that would have been kicking a champagne-tipsy teenager off my sailing boat. So instead I looked for the lifebuoy, hers and mine.

The lifebuoy arrived in the form of the door opening. Julie at once slid down from the counter.

A man stood in the doorway. I couldn't immediately place him, but no car had pulled in to the forecourt so he had to be a local. His back was stooped, and the hollow cheeks gave his face the shape of an hourglass. A few wisps of hair across his otherwise bald head.

He stopped there in the doorway. Stared at me, looked as though most of all he wanted to turn and leave. Maybe it was somebody I'd once beaten up on the grass outside Årtun, somebody I'd made my mark

on, somebody who hadn't forgotten. He crossed hesitantly to the rack of CDs. Flipped through them,
now and then glancing over at us.

'Who's that?' I whispered.

'Natalie Moe's dad,' whispered Julie.

The roofer. Of course. He'd changed. Looked a bit
reduced, as people say. Maybe he was sick. He reminded me of my uncle Bernard, near the end.

Moe approached us and put a CD on the counter.
Roger Whittaker's Greatest Hits. Bargain-basement
price. He looked a little sheepish, as though he wasn't
proud of his own taste.

'Thirty kroner,' I said. 'Card or . . .'

'Cash,' Moe said. 'Isn't Egil working today?'

'Not well,' I said. 'Anything else I can get you?'

Moe hesitated. 'No,' he said, took his change,
picked up the CD and left.

'Jesus,' said Julie and pulled herself up onto the
counter again.

'Jesus what?'

'Didn't you see? He pretended not to know me.'

'All I noticed was that he seemed stressed, and
it sounded like he wished it had been Egil here.
Whatever it was he wanted to buy from him.'

'What do you mean?'

'No one leaves their house and comes here on a
Friday night because all of a sudden the most important thing in the world is to hear Roger Whittaker. It
wasn't the choice of music he was embarrassed about,
he just chose the cheapest one.'

'Then he probably wanted condoms and chickened out.' She laughed. She made it sound as though she'd been there herself. 'He's probably having a fling with someone. It's in the family.'

'Give over,' I said.

'Or else some antidepressants because he's gone bankrupt. Didn't you see him staring at the pills on the shelf behind you?'

'You mean he thinks we might have something stronger than headache pills? I didn't know he'd gone bankrupt.'

'Jesus, Roy, I mean, you don't talk to people, so of course they don't tell you anything, either.'

'Maybe so. Aren't you off out to celebrate your youth this evening?'

'Youth!' she snorted, and went on sitting. Looked like she was racking her brain for an excuse to stay. A gum bubble oozed out in front of her face. Burst like a starting pistol. 'Simon says the hotel looks like a factory. He says no one will invest in it.'

Simon Nergard was Julie's uncle. I knew for sure I'd left my mark on him. He was a rough type, in the year above me, and he'd taken boxing lessons, even fought a couple of bouts in town. Carl danced with a girl Simon fancied, and that was enough. A crowd had gathered round where Simon was holding Carl by the scruff of his neck when I arrived and asked what the trouble was. I'd wrapped a scarf around my fist and swung at him as he opened his mouth to answer. Felt the soft pressure of teeth giving way.

126

Simon staggered, spat blood and stared at me, amazed rather than afraid. Guys that train for martial arts think there are rules, so that's why they lose. But give Simon his due, he didn't give up. He started skipping about in front of me, fists raised in a guard in front of his chin. I kicked him in the knee, and he stopped the skipping. I kicked him in the thigh and saw his eyes widen with shock at the effect. He'd probably never considered what happens when muscles as big as that start to bleed internally. He couldn't move any more, just stood there and waited to be slaughtered, like a platoon surrounded but determined to fight to the last man. But I didn't even leave him the dubious honour of a getting a real thrashing. Instead I turned my back, looked at my watch and – as though I had an appointment and plenty of time left to keep it – sauntered off. The crowd urged Simon to get after me, they didn't know what I knew, that Simon wasn't capable of taking a single step. So instead they began shouting at him, mocking and ridiculing him, and that, and not those two, overly white teeth the dentist put in, that was the mark I left on Simon that night.

'So your uncle thinks he's seen the drawings?'

'He knows someone who works at the bank in town who's seen them. He says it looks like a cellulose factory.'

'Cellulose,' I said. 'Above the treeline. That's interesting.'

'Eh?'

Outside an engine roared and another one responded.

'The testosterone boys are calling you,' I said. 'Watch the carbon emissions drop once you go out and join them.'

Julie groaned. 'They're so childish, Roy.'

'Then go home instead and listen to this,' I said and handed her one of the five copies of J. J. Cale's **Naturally** which I'd finally had to remove from the CD rack. I'd ordered them specially, convinced that people in the village were bound to go for Cale's sub-dued blues and minimalist guitar solos. But Julie was right, I didn't talk to people, didn't know them. She took the CD, slipped sulkily down off the counter and walked towards the door, gave me the finger at the same time as she wiggled her arse in outrageous invitation, with all the cold and calculating innocence only a seventeen-year-old can muster.

A thought struck me – not quite sure why – that in fact it was probably slightly less innocent than the sixteen-year-old she'd been when she first started working here. What the fuck was the matter with me? I'd never thought of Julie that way before, not ever. Or had I? No. It must have been when she put her arms out behind her to hoist herself up onto the counter, the way her jacket fell open, out past her breasts, with the nipples pressing, clearly visible through the bra and the T-shirt. But for chrissakes, the girl had had big boobs since she was thirteen years old and I'd never given them a second thought, so what was this now? I wasn't a tit man or hot for teenage

128

girls either, I never searched for either big boobs or nineteen.

And that wasn't the only mystery.

There was that shameful expression on the face. Not Julie's, when she thought I'd caught her out in her Friday version with the boy racer crowd. No. The roofer's face. Moe's gaze flitting about like a moth. Trying to avoid mine. Julie said it had been dancing over the shelves behind me. I turned and scanned them. A suspicion crossed my mind, I dismissed it at once. But it returned, like that white dot tennis ball thing Carl and I played with that time when the village got its first and only slot machine, next to the ice-cream dispenser at the coffee bar. Dad used to drive us there, we'd wait in line, and he'd have a look on his face as though he'd taken us to Disneyland.

I had seen that shame before. At home. In a mirror. I recognised it. It couldn't be more profound. Not just because the sin committed was so despicable and unforgivable, but because it would be committed again. Despite the fact that your mirror swears to you this is the last time, it happens, over and over again. Shame at the act, but more than that, shame at one's own weakness, at doing what you don't want to do. If it was something that you wanted to do, then at least you could lay the blame on the pure, unadulterated evil of your own nature.

9

SATURDAY MORNING. MARKUS HAD TAKEN over at the station, and I drove up the hill in second gear. Stopped in front of the house and revved the engine to let them know I was back.

Carl and Shannon were sitting in the kitchen, studying the plans for the hotel and discussing the presentation.

'According to Simon Nergard no one's going to invest,' I said with a yawn, leaning against the door jamb. 'He heard that from a bank guy who's seen the plans.'

'And I have talked to at least a dozen people who love the plans,' said Carl.

'Here in the village?'

'In Toronto. People who know what they're talking about.'

I shrugged. 'The people you have to convince don't live in Toronto and they don't know what they're talking about. Good luck. I'm off to bed.'

'Jo Aas has agreed to a meeting with me today,' said Carl.

I stopped. 'Really?'

'Yes. I asked Mari at the party if she could set it up.'

'Excellent. Was that why you invited her?'

'Partly. And I wanted her and Shannon to meet. If we're going to be living here then best if those two don't have to walk around scowling at each other. And you know what?' He rested a hand on Shannon's shoulder. 'I think my girl melted the ice queen.'

'Melted?' said Shannon and rolled her eyes. 'Sweetie, that woman hates me. Am I right, Roy?'

'Hmm,' I said. 'A bit less than she would otherwise have done had you not pulled that trick with the picture of the twins.'

For the first time since coming in I looked directly at Shannon. She was wearing a large white dressing gown and her hair was still wet from the shower. She hadn't displayed so much skin before, always the black pullovers and trousers, but now I could see that the skin on her slender legs and in the neck of the dressing gown was as white and unblemished as her face. The wet hair was darker and less glossy, almost a rust red, and I discovered something I hadn't noticed before, the scattering of pale freckles around

131

her nose. She smiled, but there was something in her expression, something wounded. Had Carl said the wrong thing? Had I said the wrong thing? Of course it could have been that I more than hinted that she had been cynical in pretending to find the twins so fantastic, but something told me she wouldn't have a problem admitting that kind of cynicism. That a girl like Shannon did what she had to without asking anyone's pardon.

'Shannon says she wants to cook us something Norwegian this evening,' said Carl. 'I thought—'

'I've got to work tonight too,' I said. 'Someone's off sick.'

'Oh?' Carl raised an eyebrow. 'Don't you have five other people who could cover for him?'

'No one can manage it,' I said. 'It's the weekend, and short notice.' Spread my arms as though to say such is the fate of the boss of a service station, got to cover for everybody. I could see Carl didn't believe me for a moment. That's the problem with brothers, they pick up every bloody false note, but what the hell else could I say? That I wasn't getting any sleep because of all their screwing?

'I'm going to get some shut-eye.'

I was woken by a noise. It wasn't that it was particularly loud, but in the first place, there aren't that many sounds up here in the mountains, and in the second, it didn't belong up here, which was probably the reason my brain hadn't filtered it out.

It was a kind of hissing hum, somewhere between a wasp and a lawnmower.

I looked out the window. Got up, dressed quickly, hurried down the steps and then walked slowly over towards Geitesvingen.

Sheriff Kurt Olsen was there with Erik Nerell and a guy who was holding a remote control with antennae. They were all looking up at the thing that had woken me, a white drone about the size of a dinner plate that was hovering a metre above their heads.

'OK,' I said, and they became aware of my presence. 'Are you looking for posters for the investors' meeting?'

'Good morning, Roy,' said the sheriff without touching the ciggy that bounced around in time to his words.

'This is a private road, you know.' I was buckling my belt, which I had forgotten in my hurry. 'So that's all right then, isn't it?'

'Well, there's private, and then there's private.'

'Oh yeah?' I said, and then realised I had better calm down. That if I wasn't careful I was going to get too wound up. 'If it was a public road then the traffic authorities might have coughed up for a safety barrier, don't you think?'

'True enough, Roy. But the whole area round here is a designated wilderness, so it's all public right of way.'

'I'm talking about the posters, not whether or not you've got the right to be standing where you are, sheriff. I've just got off a night shift, so if you were

133

planning to wake me up with that drone you might have warned me.'

'Might have done,' said Sheriff Olsen. 'But we didn't want to disturb anyone, Roy. This won't take long, just a few pictures. If we decide it's safe enough for us to come back and lower people down there, then of course we'll let you know in advance.' He looked at me. Not coldly, just observing me, as though he was taking snapshots of me, like the drone, which by now disappeared beneath the edge of the ridge and was snapping away for dear life down there in Huken. I nodded, tried to keep my face expressionless.

'I'm sorry,' Olsen went on. 'I know this business is . . . sensitive.' He lingered over the word, like a priest. 'I should have warned you, I didn't remember how close to the house the ridge was. What can I say? You can be glad your taxpayer's money is being used to establish exactly how the accident really did happen. That's something we all want to know.'

All? I roared inwardly. You, don't you mean? It's that same old damned imperative, Kurt Olsen, you want to sort out something your father couldn't sort out.

'Fine,' I said instead. 'And you're right, it's a sensitive matter. Carl and I know the big picture of what happened, so our focus has been more on trying to forget than on getting to the bottom of every little detail.' Calm down. Like that, yeah. Like that.

'Naturally,' said Olsen.

The drone appeared over the edge again. Stopped, just hovering in the air, nagging at the ears. Then it navigated in towards us, and landed in the hand of the guy with the remote control, like those trained falcons I'd seen on YouTube landing on their owner's glove. It was unpleasant, like something from a science-fiction film set in a Big Brother Sees You fascist state, and you know that the guy with the drone has bundles of electric cable running under his skin.

'That was a quick trip,' said the sheriff, dropping his cigarette to the ground and stepping on it.

'The thin air is a drain on the batteries,' said the drone guy.

'But did it get any pictures?'

The drone guy touched the screen of his phone and we huddled round him.

Lacking light and sound the video imagery was grainy. Or maybe there was sound recording and it was just that silent down there. The wreck of Dad's Cadillac DeVille looked like a beetle that had landed on its back and died there, legs helplessly flailing in the air until a passer-by inadvertently trod on it. The rusting and partly overgrown chassis and wheels facing upwards were undamaged, but the front and rear of the coupé were crimped flat as though they'd been through Willumsen's car-crusher. Maybe because of the stillness and darkness down there the pictures reminded me of a documentary film I had seen about divers going down to the **Titanic.** Maybe it was the sight of the Cadillac, another wreck with beautiful lines from a vanished age, another narrative of sudden death turned into a tragedy and related so often that in my imagination and the imagination of others it had, with the years, come to seem like something that had to be there, that it was written in the stars. The physical and metaphorically spectacular, the presumed invincibility of the machine exposed as it plummeted to the depth. Presentations of how it must have been, the fear of the passengers as it dawns on them that here it is now: death. Not just any old death, not a lived life gradually breaking down, but an unannounced and sudden departure, the murderous coincidences. I shuddered.

'Quite a few loose boulders on the slope,' Erik Nerell remarked.

'They could have fallen down there a thousand years ago, or a hundred,' said Kurt Olsen 'There's none on top of the car. And I don't see any marks or dents in the chassis either, so for all we know not a single bloody rock has fallen down there since the one that hit the climber.'

'He's not climbing any more,' said Nerell as he peered at the screen. 'His arm just dangles by his side and it's only half the size it used to be. He's been on painkillers for years. Doses big enough to knock a horse out.'

'At least he's still alive,' Olsen interrupted impatiently. His face was flushed. When he said 'alive', did he mean, unlike those who had been sitting in the Cadillac? No, it was just something he came out with. And yet there was something else there. Was it the old sheriff he was talking about? Sigmund Olsen, his own father?

'Most of what falls down into this chute is bound to hit the car,' said Olsen and pointed to the screen. 'And yet it's overgrown with moss. Not a mark on it. That tells us its history. History is something we can learn from. Lines that can be traced backwards can be traced forwards too.'

'Until you get a rock on your shoulder,' I said. 'Or your head.'

I saw Erik Nerell nodding slowly as he scratched his chin. Olsen flushed even more.

'As I said, we hear loose rocks down in Huken all the time.' I was looking directly at Olsen, but my words were obviously directed at Erik Nerell. He was the one who was about to become a father. He was the one responsible for an expert assessment of whether or not it was justifiable to send a crew down there to investigate the wreck. Clearly Olsen couldn't ignore his advice without losing his job should something happen. 'Maybe the rocks don't hit the wreck directly,' I said. 'But they land beside it. Presumably that's where your people will be standing?'

I didn't need to hear Olsen's reply. Out of the corner of my eye I could see that particular battle had already been won.

I stood on Geitesvingen as the sound of their cars faded. Watched a raven glide by, waited until everything was silent once again.

Shannon, dressed as usual in black, was leaning against the worktop when I came in. Again it struck me that despite an outfit that accentuated the almost

137

boyish skinniness of her body, there was something distinctively feminine about her. Her small hands warmed themselves around a steaming cup with the string of a tea bag dangling over the rim.

'Who was that?' she asked.

'The sheriff. He wants to examine the wreckage. He thinks he needs to find out why Dad went over the edge into Huken.'

'And doesn't he?'

I shrugged. 'I saw it all. He didn't brake until it was too late. You have to brake in time.'

'You have to brake in time,' she repeated with a slow, farmer's nod of the head. Looked like she was already picking up our body language too. It made me think of those science-fiction films again.

'Carl said it's not possible to retrieve the wreckage. Does it bother you having it there?'

'Apart from the pollution aspect? No.'

'No?' She lifted the mug with both hands again, took a sip of tea. 'Why not?'

'If they'd died in the double bed we wouldn't have thrown that out either.'

She smiled. 'Is that being sentimental or being unsentimental?'

I smiled too. Hardly noticed that lazy eyelid of hers any more. Or maybe it didn't hang as low as it did when she arrived and was still tired from all the travelling.

'I think the practical circumstances dictate more of our emotional lives than we realise,' I said. 'Even though novels are about unattainable love, nine out of ten fall in love with someone they know they can have.'

'You sure?'

'Eight out of ten,' I said.

I stood beside her and noticed that she watched me as I used the yellow measuring spoon to spoon the coffee powder into the pot.

'Practical in death and love,' I said. 'That's the way it is when things are tight the way they are for the people round here. It's probably not normal for you.'

'Why should it not be normal?'

'Barbados is a wealthy island, you said. You drove a Buick, went to university. Moved to Toronto.'

She seemed to hesitate for a moment before replying. 'It's called social mobility.'

'Are you saying you grew up poor?'

'Yes and no.' She took a deep breath. 'I'm a redleg.'

'Redleg?'

'You've probably heard of the lower-class whites in the Appalachian mountains in the USA. What people call hillbillies?'

'**Deliverance.** Banjos and incest.'

'That's the stereotype, yes. Unfortunately some of it's accurate, just as it is with the redlegs, the lower-class whites in Barbados. The redlegs are the descendants of the Irish and the Scots who came to the island in the seventeenth century, a lot of them transported convicts, same as in Australia. In practice they were slaves, and it was they who made up the workforce

139

until Barbados began to import slaves from Africa. But once slavery was abolished and the descendants of the Africans began to move up in society, most of the white redlegs got left behind. Most of us live in our own shanty town. **Rønner,** I think that's what you say in Norwegian. We're a society on the outside of society, stuck in a poverty trap. Zero education, alcoholism, incest, sickness. The redlegs in St John on Barbados rarely own anything, apart from the few who have farms and small shops serving the wealthier blacks. Other redlegs live off the state, financed by the black and brown Bajanere. Know how you can recognise us? The teeth. If we have any then they're usually brown from . . . **decay**?' she concluded, using the English word.

'**Råte,**' I supplied in Norwegian. 'But your teeth are . . .'

'I had a mother who made sure I got proper food and brushed my teeth every day. She was determined that I should have a better life. When she died, my grandmother took over the job.'

'Jesus.' I couldn't think of anything else to say.

She blew on her tea. 'If nothing else, we redlegs are proof that it's not just the blacks and Latinos who never manage to escape the poverty trap.'

'At least you got out.'

'Yes, and I'm racist enough to believe that it was my African genes that got me out.'

'You? African?'

'My mother and grandmother were both Afro-

Bajanere.' She laughed when she saw my incredulous expression. 'My hair and skin are from an Irish redleg who drank himself to death before I was three years old.' She shrugged her narrow shoulders. 'Even though both my grandmother and my mother lived in St John and were married respectively to an Irishman and a Scot, I was never reckoned to be a proper redleg. Partly because we owned a little land, but especially after I matriculated at the University of the West Indies in Bridgetown. I wasn't just the first from my family to go to university, I was the first in the whole neighbourhood.'

I looked at Shannon. It was the longest speech I'd heard her make about herself since she came here. Maybe the reason was simple: I hadn't asked for her story. Or at least not since that time she and Carl were in the bunk beneath me, and she said she'd rather hear me talk. Maybe she wanted to check me out first. And now she had.

I coughed. 'Must have been quite something to make a choice like that.'

Shannon shook her head. 'It was my grandmother's decision. She got the whole family, uncles and aunts and all, to spill my school fees.'

'**Split** your school fees.'

'Split my school fees, and later on for my studies in Toronto. The reason my grandmother drove me back and forth to the university was that we couldn't afford for me to live in the city. One lecturer told me I was an example of the new social mobility in Barbados.

I told him that even after four hundred years redlegs were still sloshing about in social cement, and I have my family to thank, not social reformers. I'm a redleg girl who owes everything to her family, and I always will be. So even though I've lived better in Toronto, Opgard is still luxury to me. You understand?'

I nodded. 'What happened to the Buick?'

She looked at me as if to check I wasn't trying to be funny. 'Not "what happened to your grandmother"?'

'She's alive and doing well,' I said.

'How d'you know that?'

'Your voice when you talk about her. It's steady.'

'So, car mechanic **and** psychologist?'

'Car mechanic,' I said. 'The Buick's gone, am I right?'

'By mistake my grandmother left the gear lever in drive when she parked outside our house. It rolled off an incline and was smashed to pieces in the rubbish dump below. I cried for days. Did you hear that in my voice when I was talking about it?'

'I did. A Buick Roadmaster 1954. I can understand that.'

She dipped her head from one side to the other as though she was studying me from several angles, as though I were a bloody Rubik's cube.

'Cars and beauty,' she said, almost to herself. 'You know, last night I dreamed about a book I read a long time ago. I'm sure it was because of that wreck down in Huken. **Crash,** it was called. J. G. Ballard. About people getting turned on by car crashes. By the crashes, and the injuries. Their own and others'. Did you ever see the film?'

I tried to think.

'David Cronenberg,' she said, trying to help me out.

I shook my head.

She hesitated. As though regretting she had started a conversation about something that couldn't possibly interest a guy who worked at a service station.

'I prefer books to films,' I said to help her out. 'But that's one I haven't read.'

'In the book there's a description of a blind corner on Mulholland Drive where cars drive over the edge at night and fall down the cliff into a wilderness. It's too expensive to salvage the cars so a sort of car cemetery has built up down there which gets higher every year. In time there won't be any drop there at all, anyone driving over the edge will be saved by the mountain of wrecks.'

I nodded slowly. 'Saved by a car wreck. Maybe I should read it. Or see the film.'

'Actually I prefer the film,' she said. 'The book is a first-person narrative and that makes it perverse in a way that's subjective and . . .' She stopped. 'How do you say **intrusive** in Norwegian?'

'Sorry, we'll need to ask Carl for that,' I said.

'He's gone to have a word with Jo Aas.'

I looked at the kitchen table. The plans were still lying there, and Carl hadn't taken his laptop with him either. Perhaps he thought he had a better chance of convincing Aas that the village needed a spa hotel if he didn't swamp him with material.

'**Påtrengende?**' I suggested.

'Thanks,' she said. 'The film isn't as **påtrengende.** As a rule the camera is more objective than the pen. And Cronenberg managed to get hold of the essence of it.'

'Which is?'

A sort of spark flared in her good eye, and her voice became animated now she realised I was genuinely interested.

'The beauty of a thing spoiled,' she said. 'The partially destroyed Greek statue is extra beautiful because from what isn't damaged we can see how beautiful it could have been, should have been, must have been.' She pressed the palms of her hands against the worktop as though about to hoist herself up onto it, sit there with her back arched the way she had at the party. **Tiny dancer.** Christ.

'Interesting,' I said. 'I should try to get back to sleep.'

The spark in her eye went off like an indicator.

'What about your coffee?' she said, and I could hear the disappointment in her voice. Now that she'd finally got someone to talk to. They probably talk to each other all the time over there in Barbados.

'I need another couple of hours, I can feel it,' I said, turned off the hot plate and pulled the pan off the heat.

'Of course,' she said, and took her hands off the worktop.

I lay in bed for half an hour. Tried to sleep, to think of nothing. Heard the tapping of the laptop keyboard up through the hole, the rustle of paper. Not a chance.

I repeated the ritual. Got up, dressed, hurried out. Called out 'See you!' before the door slammed shut behind me. It must have sounded as though I was running from something.

10

'OH, HI,' SAID EGIL AS he opened the door. He looked ashamed. Must have been because he knew I could hear the sounds of a war game and the excited voices of his pals from the living room. 'Yeah, actually I'm better now,' he said quickly. 'I can work tonight.'

'Take as long as you need to get well,' I said. 'That's not why I came.'

He seemed to be searching his conscience to find out what that might possibly be. Clearly there were a couple of things to choose between.

'What does Moe come in to buy?' I asked.

'Moe?' Egil said it as though he'd never heard the name.

'The roofer,' I said. 'He asked after you.'

Egil smiled, but there was fear in his eyes.

'What does he come in for?' I repeated, as though I thought Egil might have forgotten the question.

'Nothing special,' said Egil.

'Tell me anyway.'

'Hard to remember.'

'But he pays cash?'

'Yes.'

'If you can remember that then you can remember what it is he buys. Come on.'

Egil stared at me. And in that sheep-like gaze I saw a prayer for permission to confess.

I sighed. 'This is something that's been eating away at you, Egil.'

'Eh?'

'He's got something on you, is that it? Is he threatening you in some way?'

'Moe? No.'

'Then why are you covering up for him?'

Egil stood there blinking. Behind him, in the living room, a war was raging. I saw chaos behind that desperate look.

'He . . . he . . .'

I really didn't have the patience for this, but for added effect I lowered my voice. 'Now don't make anything up, Egil.'

The boy's Adam's apple bobbed up and down like a lift and he'd taken a half-step back into the hallway, looked almost ready to slam the door shut in panic, but then stopped. Maybe he saw something in my eyes, something his brain connected to what he'd heard about guys getting their lights punched out in Årtun. And he gave in.

'He let me keep the change for whatever it was he bought.'

I nodded. Naturally I had told Egil when he started working for me that we don't accept tips, that if the customer insisted then we punch the amount into the till and leave the money out for the times when one of us made a mistake and handed over too much change. Usually that would be Egil, but he might have forgotten, and right now I wasn't about to tell him; what I wanted was to have my suspicions confirmed.

'And what did he buy?'

'We didn't do anything illegal,' said Egil.

I didn't bother to tell him that him using the imperfect like that told me he understood that whatever arrangement he might have had with Moe was as of now over, and was therefore unlikely to have been legit. I waited.

'EllaOne,' said Egil.

So that was it. The morning-after pill.

'How often?' I asked.

'Once a week,' said Egil.

'Did he ask you not to tell anyone?'

Egil nodded. He was pale. Pale and stupid, but not mentally defective, as people call it. I mean, they change the words like they change dirty underwear, so probably they call it something else now, but anyway: Egil had probably managed to put two and two together, even if Moe had gambled he wouldn't. I saw it now, that he wasn't just ashamed of himself, he was totally mortified. There's no heavier punishment than that. And I say that as someone who's drunk cup after cup of that bitter stuff. Someone who knows that there's nothing a judge could do that would add to that shame.

'Then let's say you're sick today and good tomorrow,' I said. 'OK?'

'Yes,' he said, at the second time of trying to get sound into his voice.

I didn't hear the door close behind me. He was probably still standing there watching me. Wondering what was going to happen now.

I entered Grete Smitt's hair salon. It was like emerging from a time machine that had landed in the USA straight after the war. There was an enormous and much patched red leather barber's chair in one corner. According to Grete, Louis Armstrong had once sat in it. The other corner housed a salon hairdryer from the 1950s, one of those helmets on a stand that the old biddies sit under while reading magazines and gossiping in old American movies, though it always makes me think of Jonathan Pryce and the lobotomy scene in **Brazil.** Grete uses that helmet for something she calls a **shampoo and set,** which is when you first wash the hair with a special shampoo, put in the curlers and then dry the hair slowly by sticking your head up inside this helmet, preferably with a headscarf so you don't touch any of the elements which in her fifties version look like the glowing insides of a toaster. According to Grete, a **shampoo and set** was now retro-hip and on its way back in again. The thing is, here in Os it had probably never really been away in the first place. Anyway, if you ask me, Grete herself was probably the most frequent user of that helmet, to maintain those rat-brown permed curls that hung from her head.

Pictures of old American film stars hung on the walls. The only thing that wasn't American must have been that famous pair of salon scissors Grete used, a stainless-steel affair which she told anyone who would listen was a Japanese Niigata 1000 that cost fifteen thousand kroner and came with a lifetime guarantee.

Grete looked up, but the Niigata went on cutting.

'Olsen,' I said.

'Hi, Roy. He's sunning himself.'

'I know that, I saw his car. Where's the sun?' I watched as the Japanese superscissors snipped dangerously close to the customer's earlobe.

'I don't think he wants to be disturbed . . .'

'In there?' I pointed towards the other door in the room. There was a poster on it showing a sun-bronzed and desperately smiling girl in a bikini.

'He'll be finished in . . .' She glanced down at a remote control on the table next to her. 'Fourteen minutes. Can't you wait outside?'

'Could do. But even men can manage to do two things at once if all that's involved are sunning yourself and speaking.' I nodded to the lady in the barber's chair who was staring at me in the mirror, and opened the door.

It was like entering a lousy horror film. The room was in darkness apart from a bluish light that seeped out from the crack along the side of a Dracula's coffin, one of two sunbeds that were all the room contained, apart from a chair over the back of which hung Kurt Olsen's jeans and his light leather jacket. A threatening, juddering sound came from the lamps inside, heightening the sense that something terrible was about to happen.

I pulled the chair up to the side of the sunbed. Heard music buzzing from a couple of earphones. For a moment I thought it was Roger Whittaker and that this really **was** a horror film, before recognising John Denver's 'Take Me Home, Country Roads'.

'I've come to warn you,' I said.

I heard movement from inside, something hit the lid of the coffin so it shook and there was a low cursing. The buzzing of the music stopped.

'It's about a possible case of sexual assault,' I said.

'Oh yeah?' Olsen's voice sounded as if he was talking inside a tin can, and I couldn't tell if he recognised my voice on the outside.

'A person having sexual relations with someone in his own immediate family,' I said.

'Go on.'

I stopped. Maybe because it suddenly struck me that the situation had bizarre similarities to the Catholic confessional. Apart from the fact that it wasn't me who was the sinner. Not this time.

'Moe – the roofer – is buying morning-after pills once a week. As you know, he has a teenage daughter. She bought morning-after pills the other day.'

I waited as I left it up to Sheriff Olsen to reach the obvious conclusion.

'Why once a week, and why here?' he asked. 'Why not bulk-buy in town? Or put the girl on the contraceptive pill?'

'Because he thinks that every time is the last time,' I said. 'He thinks he can manage to stop.'

I heard the clicking of a lighter from inside the sun-bed. 'How do you know that?'

I searched for the right way to answer as the cigarette smoke seeped out of Dracula's coffin, dissipated in the blue light and vanished into the darkness. Felt the same urge as Egil had felt: to confess. To drive over the edge. To fall.

'We all like to believe that we'll be a better person tomorrow,' I said.

'It isn't easy to keep something like that quiet in a village like this for any length of time,' said Olsen. 'I've never heard anyone suspect Moe of anything.'

'He's gone bankrupt,' I said. 'Hangs around at home with nothing to do.'

'But he's still a teetotaller,' said Olsen, showing that at least he was following my train of thought. 'Not everyone starts fucking his own daughter when things begin to go a little wrong for him.'

'Or purchase morning-after pills once a week,' I said.

'Maybe it's because he doesn't want his wife to get pregnant again. Or maybe the daughter's having it away with some lad and Moe is just a concerned father.' I heard Olsen take a drag on his cigarette in there. 'He doesn't want her on anything more permanent, because then he's worried she might start having it away all the time with whoever. Moe's a Pentecostal, you know.'

'I didn't know that, but that doesn't exactly diminish the possibility of a little incest.'

I sensed a reaction beneath the coffin lid when I used the i-word.

'If you're going to make a serious accusation like that you should have a bit more to go on than the person in question buying contraception,' said Olsen. 'Do you?'

What could I say? That I had seen the shame in his eyes? A shame so powerful that for me it was stronger proof than anything?

'So now you know,' I said. 'I suggest you have a chat with the daughter.'

Maybe I should have dropped the 'suggest'. Maybe I should have known it sounded as though I was telling Olsen how to do his job. On the other hand, maybe I knew all this and went ahead and did it anyway. Whatever, Olsen's voice went up a semitone and a decibel.

'And I suggest you leave this to us, although I can

tell you straight off we'll probably go on prioritising more pressing cases.' His tone of voice left room for my name at the end of his sentence, but he left it there. Churning through his brain was probably the thought that if I later turned out to be right and the sheriff's office had done nothing then it would be easier for him if he could claim the tip-off that came in was anonymous. Anyway, I fell for it.

'And what pressing cases might that be?' I asked, and could have bitten my tongue off.

'None of your business. In the meantime I suggest you keep this small-town gossip to yourself. We don't need that type of hysteria here.'

I had to swallow and before I could say anything else John Denver was back.

I stood up and went back into the salon. Grete and her customer had moved to the washbasin where they were rinsing her hair and chatting away. I thought they always washed your hair **before** they cut it, but this here was clearly something different, some sort of chemical warfare was being waged against the hair, at any rate there were several tubes on the rim of the basin and they were too busy to notice me. I picked up the remote that was next to the door. Looked like Olsen had ten minutes to go. I pressed an upward-pointing arrow until the display showed twenty. Pressed the key above FACIAL TANNER and a display appeared showing a scale with one dot. Three taps on the arrow and it was on maximum. Those of us who work in the service industries know how important it is for people to feel they're getting value – and plenty of it – for their money.

As I passed Grete and the customer I picked up the words: '. . . jealous now, because of course he was in love with his little brother.'

Grete's face stiffened when she noticed me, but I merely nodded and pretended not to have heard.

Out in the fresh air I thought how this was like a fucking repeat. Everything had happened before. Everything would happen again. And with the same result.

11

NOT EVEN THE VILLAGE'S ANNUAL fete ever attracted such a crowd. We'd placed six hundred chairs in the main function room at the village hall and still some people had to stand. I turned in my seat and looked towards the back of the hall, pretending to be looking out for someone. Everyone was there. Mari with her husband Dan Krane, who was scanning the place himself with his journalist's eye. Willum Willumsen the used-car dealer with his tall, elegant wife Rita, who towered a full head above him even when they were seated. The new chairman Voss Gilbert, who also refereed Os Football Club's home games, not that it seemed to do any good. Erik Nerell with his very pregnant wife Thea. Sheriff Kurt Olsen too, his scorched face glowing like a red lantern. His hate-filled gaze met mine. Grete Smitt had brought along Mr and Mrs Smitt, I could just see them shuffling speedily across the car park on their way in. Natalie Moe was sitting between her parents. I tried to catch her father's eye, but he had already looked away. Maybe because he suspected I knew. Or maybe because he knew that everyone knew that his roofing business had gone bust and that if he invested in the hotel project it would be an insult to every one of his creditors in the village. But he could probably get away with just turning up at the meeting. Most of those present had probably come out of curiosity, not out of any desire to invest. Yes, Jo Aas the old council chairman hadn't seen the place so packed since the seventies, when Preacher Armand was making the rounds. Aas was standing at the podium looking out at the gathering. Tall, and thin and skinny as a flagpole. His upward-arching birch-white eyebrows seemed to reach higher and higher with each passing year.

'There was a time when entertainment such as talking in tongues and the healing of the sick and lame was every bit as popular as the films on show at the village cinema,' said Aas. 'And what's more it was free.'

The laughter duly came.

'Now you haven't come here to listen to me, but to one of our own homecoming sons, Carl Abel Opgard. I don't know whether his sermon will bring salvation and life everlasting to the village, you'll have to make up your own minds about that. I have agreed to introduce this young man and his project because this village, at this moment in time, in the situation in which we find ourselves, should welcome any and every fresh initiative. We **need** new thinking. We need commitment. But we also need old thinking. The thinking that has stood the test of time, and has enabled us to go on living out here in these barren but beautiful villages. And so I ask you to listen with a mind both open and fair to a young man who has proved that a simple farm boy from these parts can also succeed in the big wide world. Carl, the stage is yours!'

Thunderous applause, though it was noticeably muted by the time Carl reached the podium and was probably more for Aas than him. Carl was wearing a suit and tie, but he'd taken off the jacket and rolled up his sleeves. He'd modelled the outfit at home, asked for our opinions. Shannon wondered why he wouldn't wear the jacket, and I explained it was because Carl had seen American presidential candidates trying to be folksy when addressing factory workers on the campaign trail.

'They wear windjammers and baseball caps,' said Shannon.

'It's a question of finding just the right balance,' said Carl. 'We don't want to seem stuffy and pompous, we're from round here, after all, where people drive tractors and walk around in rubber boots. But at the same time we need to appear serious and professional. You don't turn up for a confirmation here not wearing a tie, and if you do it's obvious you don't get it. That I **have** a jacket, but have taken it off, is a way of signalling that I respect the task ahead and take it seriously, at the same time as I'm keen, fired up, ready to get cracking.'

'Not scared to get your hands dirty,' I said.

'Exactly,' said Carl.

On the way out to the car Shannon had whispered to me with a chuckle in her voice: 'You know what, I thought the expression was **to get dirt under your nails.** Is that completely wrong?'

'Depends what you were trying to say,' I answered.

'What I'd like to say,' said Carl, resting both hands on the podium, '. . . **before** I start speaking about the adventure I'm inviting you all to join me on, is that simply standing here on this stage in front of so many old friends and faces is really quite something for me. It's really quite moving.'

I noticed the air of cautious expectation. Carl had been well liked. At least by those whose ladies hadn't liked him a little too well. And certainly Carl as he was when he had left town. But was he still Carl? The lively mischief-maker and fun guy with the bright smile, the kind, thoughtful boy with a friendly word for everyone, men and women alike, children as well as adults. Or had he turned into what he described himself as on the invitation: a Master of Business? A mountain bird able to fly at heights where others couldn't breathe? Canada. Property magnate. An exotic and educated wife from the Caribbean sitting there a little too well made up. Would a normal girl from around these parts be too dull for him now?

'Wonderful and moving,' Carl said once again. 'Because now, finally, I get a taste of what it must have been like to stand here and be . . .' An artful pause as he looked out over the gathering and adjusted his tie. '. . . Rod.'

A brief moment. And then came the laughter.

Carl's white smile. Sure now, sure that he had them. He rested his long arms along the sides of the podium as though he owned it.

'Fairy tales usually begin with **Once upon a time,** but this fairy tale hasn't been written yet. But when the time comes for it to be written, it will begin **Once upon a time there was a village that had a meeting at Årtun village hall where they talked about a hotel they were going to build.** And we are talking about **this** hotel . . .'

He tapped on the remote. The plans appeared on the giant screen behind him. There was a gasp, but I could see that Carl had expected a bigger gasp. Saw it because he's my brother. Or more accurately: a more positive gasp. Because as I said: I think that in general people prefer the comfort of hearth and home to an igloo on the moon. On the other hand, it had undeniably a certain elegance. There was something about the proportions and the lines, there was a universal beauty about them, like that of an ice crystal, a white-topped breaker, or a pristine mountain face. Or even a service station.

Carl could see that he had a job to do to convince the gathering. I could see him regrouping, as people say. Mobilising himself. Gathering himself for the next assault. He went through the plans and explained what was what. The spa section, the gym, the pool, the kids' playroom, the different classes of hotel room, the reception and lobby, the restaurant. Stressing that everything here would be top of the range, that their main target group was going to be guests with high expectations. In other words: people with fat wallets. The hotel's name would be the same as the village. The Os Spa and Mountain Hotel. A name that would be promoted across all media platforms. The village's name would become a byword for quality, he said. Something exclusive. But not **excluding.** It should be possible for a family on a normal income to spend a weekend here. But it would have to be something they saved up for, something they looked forward to. The village name should be associated with joy. Carl smiled, showed them a little of that joy. It seemed to me that he was beginning to get the crowd on board. I'd even say that the gathering was starting to show signs of enthusiasm, and that's not something you get every day around these parts. All the same, the next gasp wasn't until people heard the total cost.

Four hundred million.

A gasp. The temperature in the room plummeted.

Carl had expected the gasp. But, as I saw from his expression, not quite such a big one.

He began speaking faster, afraid now that he was losing them. Said that for landowners in the area the rise in property prices because of the hotel and the cabin developments by itself would be enough to make investment profitable. The same went for those who ran shops and service businesses, as the hotel and the cabins would bring with them a stream of paying customers. Because these were people who had money, and liked to spend it. In fact, taken separately, the village would probably profit more from this than the hotel itself.

He paused for a few moments. People sat silent and unmoving. Everything seemed to be in the balance. From where I sat in the fifth row I saw something move. Like a flagpole in a stiff wind. It was Aas, sitting in the front row. His white head towering above the others. He nodded. Nodded slowly. Everyone saw it.

And then Carl played his ace.

'But the precondition of all this is that the hotel is built, and that it opens for business. That people are willing to make the necessary effort. That **certain people** are willing to accept a degree of risk and finance this project. For the good of the others. Of **everyone** in the village.'

On average the people round here are less educated than those in the cities. They aren't as quick to get the point in clever films and urbane sitcoms. But they get the **subtext.** Because the ideal in Os is not to say more than is necessary, people have a developed understanding of what remains unexpressed.

And what remained unexpressed here was that if you didn't join the ranks of the **certain people** who invested in the project, then that made you one of **the others.** Those who would profit from the secondary benefits, without having contributed themselves.

I saw more slow nodding. It seemed to spread.

But then a man raised his voice. Willumsen, the man who had sold Dad the Cadillac.

'If this is such a good investment, Carl,' said Willumsen, 'why do you need all of us? Why not keep the whole cake for yourself? Or as much of it as you can handle alone and get a couple of other big shots to cover the rest?'

'Because,' said Carl, 'I'm not a big shot. And not too many of you are either. I could have taken a bigger share, sure, and I'll happily take what's left over if the investment isn't fully covered. But my vision when I came home with this project was that **everyone** should have the chance to take part, not just those with money to spare. That's why I'm seeing this as an SL company. Shared Responsibilty. It means that none of you need to put anything up front at all to become part-owners of this hotel. Not one single øre!' Carl pounded the podium.

Pause. Silence. I could feel what they were thinking. **What kind of fucking hocus pocus is that? Is this Preacher Armand all over again?**

Then Carl read them the Good News gospel. About how you can own without paying. And as the Master of Business spoke, they listened.

'That means,' he said, 'that the more who invest, the less the risk at the individual level. If everyone signs up, none of us risks any more than what we might pay for a car. At least, not if we bought it second-hand from Willumsen here.'

Laughter. Even some applause from the back of the hall. Everyone knew the story of the car sale, and right at that moment no one seems to have been thinking about what happened to that car later. A smiling Carl pointed to someone with a raised hand.

A man stood up. Tall, as tall as Carl. I could see that it was only now Carl recognised him. Maybe he regretted inviting the guy to speak. Simon Nergard opened a mouth in which two teeth were noticeably whiter than the others. I could be wrong, but it seemed to me I could still hear a whistling from his nostrils when he spoke, from the bone that didn't mend right.

'Since this hotel is going to be on land you and your brother own . . .' He took his time, let it hang for a moment.

'Yes?' said Carl in a loud, firm voice. Probably no one else besides me noticed it was a bit **too** loud and firm.

'. . . it would be interesting to know how much you intend to ask for it.'

'Ask for it?' Carl scanned the gathering with his eyes. His head didn't move. The place was silent again. It sounded undeniably – and it was probably not just me that thought it – as though Carl was playing for time. Simon at least had heard it, because when he spoke next there was almost a note of triumph in his voice.

'Perhaps the Master of Business will understand better if I say **what price,**' he said.

Scattered laughter. An expectant silence. People had raised their heads, like animals at the watering hole that see the lion approaching, although still a safe distance away.

Carl smiled. He bent over the documents in front of him and his shoulders shook as though he were laughing at a comradely kick in the shins from an old pal. Sorted his papers into a neat pile and seemed to be taking a break as he worked out how best to formulate his answer. I felt it, and from a quick look round realised that so did everyone else. That this was it. The moment of decision. I saw a straight back straighten further still two rows in front of me. Shannon. Looking up at the podium I saw Carl's gaze fastened on me. I read something into it. An apology. He had lost. Screwed up. Screwed things up for the family. Both of us knew it. He wouldn't be getting his hotel. And I wouldn't be getting my service station.

'We don't want anything for it,' said Carl. 'Roy and I are **donating** the land.'

At first I thought I had heard wrong, and I could see Simon thought the same. But then I heard the murmuring that spread through the hall, and realised that people had heard the same as me. Someone started to clap.

'No, no,' said Carl, holding up his hands. 'We've still got a long way to go. What we need now is for enough people to sign a preliminary document of intention to join, so that when we apply to the council for permission they can see this is a serious project. Thank you!'

The applause swelled. It grew and it grew. Soon everyone was clapping. Apart from Simon. And maybe Willumsen. And me.

'I had to!' said Carl. 'It was the make-or-break moment. Couldn't you tell?'

He followed me half running back out to the car. I opened the car door and got behind the wheel. It was Carl who had suggested we drive to the meeting in my grey-and-white Volvo 240 rather than his flashing dollar sign of a car. I turned the ignition, put my foot down and slipped the clutch even before he'd closed the passenger door.

'For fuck's sake, Roy!'

'For fuck's sake what?' I yelled and adjusted the mirror. Saw Årtun disappearing behind us. Saw Shannon's silent, frightened face in the rear seat. 'You promised! You said you'd tell them what the land cost if they asked, you prick.'

'Oh, give me a break, Roy! You felt the mood as well. Don't lie, I could see it on you. You know that if I had said **well, yes, now that you ask, Simon, Roy and I are actually asking forty million for that lump of rock,** that would have been end of story.

And there's no way you would have got the money for your station.'

'You lied!'

'I lied, yes. So you've still got the chance to get your own service station.'

'What fucking chance?' I put my foot down, felt the grunt of the tyres as they bit down into the gravel as I spun the wheel and we skidded out onto the main road. The tyres squealed before the rubber sucked down onto the asphalt and from the back seat came a little squeal too. 'The one in ten years' time when the hotel has started to give some returns?' I spat as I floored the pedal. 'The point is you lied, Carl! You lied and you gave them 320 acres of my . . . **my** land – for nothing!'

'Not ten years, jughead. You'll get your chance in a year at the most.'

In our vocabulary jughead was not far off a term of endearment, and I realised he was asking for a truce.

'Yes, one year and then what?'

'And then the plots of land for the cabins come up for sale.'

'Plots of land for the cabins?' I punched the steering wheel. 'Jesus Christ, forget the cabins, Carl! Haven't you heard? The council has voted to stop any more cabin developments.'

'They have?'

'There's no money for the council in cabins, only expenses.'

'Is that right?'

'Cabin owners pay taxes where they live, and when they're only here for an average of six weekends a year they don't leave enough money to cover what those fucking cabins cost the community. Water, sewage, collecting the rubbish, clearing the snow. Cabin owners fill up with petrol, they buy hamburgers from me, and that's good for the station and a few of the other businesses, but for the council it's a drop in the ocean.'

'I really didn't know that.'

I glanced over at him. He grinned back at me, the prick. Of course he knew.

'What we do with the council,' said Carl, 'is we sell them warm beds. As opposed to cold beds.'

'Come again?'

'Cabins are cold beds, empty nine weekends in ten. Hotels are warm beds. Filled every night all year round with people who spend money without costing the council anything. Warm beds are the wet dream of every local council, Roy. Never mind what the regulations say – they chuck planning permissions at you. That's the way it is in Canada and that's the way it is here. It isn't the hotel that's going to make the big bucks for you and me. It's when we get permission to sell cabin plots. And we will, because we'll offer the council a thirty–seventy deal.'

'Thirty–seventy?'

'We offer them thirty per cent warm beds in exchange for building permission for seventy per cent cold beds.'

I eased off on the speed. 'And you think they'll go for it?'

'Normally they'll only accept a deal the other way round. With seventy per cent warm. But think of the council meeting next week where they'll also be discussing the consequences of the rerouting of the main road and I present this project and we offer them a hotel that the entire village has voted for this evening. And they glance over at the spectators' benches and there sits Abraham Lincoln and he's nodding his head, this is good stuff.'

Lincoln was the nickname Dad had given Jo Aas. And yes, I could see it. They would give Carl exactly what he was asking for.

I glanced in the mirror. 'What do you think?'

'What do I think? I think you drive like a pig in heat.'

Our eyes met and we began to laugh. Soon all three of us were laughing, me so hard that Carl had to put a hand on the wheel to steer for me. I took the wheel back again, changed down and turned along the gravel lane and the hairpin bends that led up to our farm.

'Look,' said Shannon.

And we looked.

A car with a blue flashing light in the middle of the road. We slowed down and the headlights picked out Kurt Olsen. He was lounging against the bonnet of his Land Rover with arms folded. I didn't stop until my bumper almost touched his knees, but he didn't move a muscle. He walked up to the side of the car and I wound down the window.

'Breathalyser test,' he said and shone a torch beam straight into my face. 'Get out of the car.'

'Out?' I asked, shading my face with one hand. 'Can't I just blow into the bag sitting here?'

'Out,' he said. Hard, calm and cold.

I looked at Carl. He nodded twice. The first time to tell me to do what Olsen said, the second that, yes, he would hold the fort from here on in.

I climbed out.

'You see that?' said Olsen and shone his torch on a more or less straight furrow in the gravel. I realised he had made it with the heel of his cowboy boot. 'I want you to walk along that.'

'You're joking, right?'

'No, I don't make jokes, Roy Calvin Opgard. Start here. Go ahead.'

I did as he said. Just to get it over with.

'Uh-oh, careful, carefully now,' said Olsen. 'And again, slowly. Think of it as a line. Put your foot down on the line every time.'

'What sort of line?' I asked as I set off again.

'The type you suspend across a gulch. For example a ravine with rocks so loose that people who claim to know about such things write, in a report, that they advise against any investigation of the location. One false step along that line, Roy, and down you go.'

I don't know whether it was having to parade along like a fucking male model or the flickering light

170

from his torch, but it had actually become extremely bloody difficult to keep my balance.

'You know I don't drink,' I said. 'So what is this?'

'You don't drink, no. It means your brother can drink for two. Which makes me think that you're the one to watch out for. People who are always sober are hiding something, don't you think? They're afraid they'll reveal their secrets if they get drunk. So they stay away from people, and parties.'

'If you're turning over stones, Olsen, turn over Moe the roofer. Have you done that yet?'

'Put a sock in it, Roy. I know you're trying to distract me.' His voice was starting to lose its controlled calm.

'You think trying to stop sexual abuse is a distraction? You think breathalysing teetotallers is a better use of your time?'

'Oops, you stepped over the edge there,' said Olsen.

I looked down. 'Fucking well didn't.'

'Look there, see?' He shone the torch on a footprint outside the line. It was the print of a cowboy boot. 'You better come with me.'

'Fucking hell, Olsen, get out the fucking breathalyser!'

'Someone buggered it up. Pressed the wrong keys and ruined it,' he said. 'You failed the balancing test and so that's what we're going to have to rely on. As you know, we have a comfortable cell at the sheriff's office where you can wait until the doctor arrives to take a blood sample.'

I gave him a look of such disbelieving astonishment

that he pushed the torch up under his chin and shouted 'Boo!', and then gave a ghostly chuckle.

'Careful with that light,' I said. 'Looks like you've had enough radiation to be going on with.'

He didn't seem particularly pissed off. Still laughing, he uncoupled the handcuffs from his belt.

'Turn around, Roy.'

PART THREE

12

I HEARD IT THROUGH THE stovepipe hole late one evening. I was sixteen years old, and had almost fallen asleep to the steady sound of conversation down there in the kitchen. Even though she didn't have much to say, she was the one who did the talking. Dad said mostly yes and no, apart from the few occasions when he stopped her and told her clearly and concisely how things were, how things should be done, or not done as the case might be. This almost always happened without him raising his voice, but afterwards, as a rule, she kept quiet for a while. Before starting to talk calmly about something else, as though the subject of their previous conversation had never been raised. I know it sounds strange, but I never really got to know my mum. Maybe because I didn't understand her, or because I wasn't interested enough, or because she was so self-effacing next to Dad that she simply disappeared for me. Of course it's strange that the person you've been most intimate with, who gave life to you, whom you spent every day with for eighteen years, can remain someone whose thoughts and feelings are a complete mystery to you. Was she happy? What were her dreams? Why was she able to talk with Dad, and a bit with Carl, but almost never with me? Did she have as little understanding of me as I did of her? On only one occasion did I catch a glimpse of what lay behind Mum in the kitchen, Mum in the cowshed, Mum who mended clothes and told us to do as our father said, and that was that evening at the Grand when Uncle Bernard turned fifty. After the meal in the rococo room the grown-ups jived to the music of a trio of fat men in white jackets, and while Carl was shown around the hotel I sat at the table and saw that Mum was watching the dancers with a look on her face I'd never seen before, dreamy and half smiling, her gaze slightly veiled. And for the first time in my life it struck me that my mother might be pretty, **pretty,** as she sat there humming in a red dress that matched the drink in front of her. I had never seen Mum drinking except on Christmas Eve, and then only the one glass of aquavit, and she had an unfamiliar warmth in her voice when she asked Dad if he wanted to dance. He shook his head, but smiled at her, maybe he saw the same thing as me.

176

Then a man a bit younger than Dad came up and asked Mum for a dance. Dad sipped his beer, nodded and smiled at the man, as though he felt proud. I didn't want to, but my gaze followed Mum out onto the dance floor. I just hoped it wasn't going to be too embarrassing. I saw her saying a few words to the man, he nodded, and they began. First Mum danced quite close to him, then closer, then further away, she danced quick, then slow. She really could dance, and I had never had the faintest idea. But there was something else too. The way she looked at this stranger. The half-closed eyes and that fixed half-smile, like a cat playing with a mouse it intends to make a meal out of, only just not quite yet. Then I noticed Dad beside me getting restless. And suddenly it struck me that it wasn't the man who was the stranger, it was her, the woman I called Mum.

Then it was over and she sat down with us again. Later that evening, after Carl had fallen asleep beside me in the hotel room we shared, I heard voices in the corridor. I recognised Mum's, it was unusually loud and piercing. I got up and opened the door just a fraction, enough to see across to the doorway of their room. Dad said something, Mum raised her hand and hit him. Dad touched his cheek and said something in a calm, low voice. She raised the other hand and struck him again. Then she grabbed the key from him, unlocked the door and disappeared into the room. Dad stayed where he was, hunched over slightly, rubbing his cheek and looking in the direction of the door where I was standing in the dark. He looked sad and lonely, almost, maybe like a kid that's lost his teddy bear. I don't know if he realised the door was ajar, all I know is that on that evening I got an insight into something to do with Mum and Dad. Something I didn't quite understand. Something I wasn't sure I wanted to know any more about. And next day, driving back home to Os, everything was just as it had always been. Mum talked to Dad, a quiet, even flow of everyday talk, with him saying yes, and sometimes no, or else having a coughing fit, at which she kept quiet for a while.

The reason I listened with particular interest that evening all those years ago was that it was my dad who, after a long pause, began to speak. And it sounded like it was something he had been wondering how best to say. Also he kept his voice even lower than usual. Almost whispering. Now of course my parents knew we could hear them up through the stovepipe hole to our bedroom; what they didn't realise was how **well** we could hear them. The hole was one thing, but it was the pipe itself that did the trick, amplifying the sound so much that it was like sitting down there between them. Carl and I had agreed there was no point in making them aware of this.

'Sigmund Olsen mentioned it today,' he said.

'Oh?'

'He's had what he referred to as a "warning report" from one of Carl's teachers.'

'And?'

'She told him that on two occasions she's seen blood on the back of Carl's trousers, and when she asked Carl what had happened, he offered her what she called a "fairly unlikely explanation".'

'And that was?' Mum had lowered her voice too by now.

'Olsen wouldn't give any details, he just wanted to pass on the message that the sheriff's office wanted to talk to Carl. Apparently they have to inform the parents when they interrogate someone under sixteen.'

I felt like a bucket of ice-cold water had been emptied over my head.

'Olsen said we could be present if Carl wanted, and that Carl isn't legally obliged to talk to them. Just so we know.'

'What did you say?' my mum whispered.

'That of course my son wouldn't refuse to talk to the police, but that I would like to talk to him first myself, and so it would be useful to know what kind of unlikely explanation Carl had given his teacher.'

'And what did the sheriff say to that?'

'He thought about it. Said he knows Carl of course because he's in the same class as his own lad, what's his name?'

'Kurt.'

'Kurt, yes. So he knows that Carl is an honest and upright lad, and he says that personally he believes Carl's explanation. He says the teacher is straight

179

out of teacher training college and nowadays they're indoctrinated to be on the lookout for things like this, so that means they see it everywhere.'

'But of course they do, for chrissakes. What did he say Carl told the teacher?'

'Carl said he'd sat on the pile of planks behind the barn and sat right down on a nail that was sticking out.'

I waited for Mum's next question: **Twice?** It never came. Did she know? Had she guessed? I swallowed.

'Oh my God, Raymond,' was all she said.

'That pile of planks should have been shifted a long time ago,' he said. 'I'm thinking I'll get it done tomorrow. Then we'll have a word with Carl. We can't have him hurting himself like that and not telling us. Rusty nails – that can mean blood poisoning and God knows what else.'

'We'd better talk to him. And tell Roy to keep an eye out for his little brother.'

'That won't be necessary, it's all Roy ever does. Actually I think it might even be a bit unhealthy, the way he looks out for him all the time.'

'Unhealthy?'

'They're like a married couple.'

Pause. Now here it comes, I thought.

'Carl has to learn to stand on his own two feet,' said Dad. 'I've been thinking, it's about time the boys each had a room of their own.'

'But we don't have the space.'

'Come on, Margit. You know we can't afford the bathroom you want between the bedrooms, but moving a couple of walls around for an extra bed-room won't cost all that much. I can have it done in two or three weeks.'

'You think so?'

'I'll start this weekend.'

Obviously the decision had been taken long before he aired this idea of a separation to Mum. What Carl and I might think was irrelevant. I bunched my fist and bit back my curses. I hated him, hated him. I trusted Carl to keep his mouth shut, but that wouldn't be enough. The sheriff. The school. Mum. Dad. It was out of control, too many people who knew something, saw something and suddenly understood everything. Soon the tidal wave of shame would wash over us, dragging us all down with it. The shame, the shame, the shame. It was unendurable. **None of us** would be able to endure it.

13

Carl and I never called it that, but that was the name I gave it in my own head.

It was a blisteringly hot autumn day. I was twenty years old. Two years had passed since the Cadillac with Mum and Dad inside had gone down into Huken.

'Feeling a little better now?' asked Sigmund Olsen and swung the rod above his head. The line flew out, the reel made a clattering sound, descending in pitch, like some kind of bird I'd never heard before.

I didn't answer, just followed the spinner with my eye as it glinted momentarily in the sunlight before disappearing beneath the surface of the water, so far from the boat we were sitting in I couldn't hear if it made a splash. I wanted to ask why you had to cast the spinner so far away when you could just as well move the boat over to where you wanted it to go. Maybe it has something to do with the fact that it looks more like a living fish if it's swimming more or less horizontal when you reel it in. I don't know the first thing about fishing and don't plan to find out either, so I kept my mouth shut.

'Because even though it doesn't always seem that way, it's actually true what people say, that time heals all wounds,' the sheriff said as he brushed his mop of hair off his sunglasses. 'A few of them anyway,' he added.

I had no answer to that.

'How's Bernard?' he asked.

'Doing fine,' I said, there being no way I could know then he only had months left to live.

'I hear you and your brother are mostly living up at Opgard and not so much at Bernard's, like the child-care people said?'

I had no answer to that either.

'Well, anyway, you're old enough now for that not to matter any more, so I'm not going to make a fuss about it. Carl's still at school, isn't he?'

'That's right,' I said.

'And he's doing all right?'

'Yes.' What else could I say? It wasn't a porky. Carl said he still thought about Mum a lot, and he could spend entire days and evenings alone in the winter garden where he sat to do his homework and read over and over again the two American novels Dad had brought back to Norway with him, **An American Tragedy** and **The Great Gatsby.** I never saw him reading any other proper novels, but he loved those two, especially **An American Tragedy,** and some evenings he would sit and read to me from it and translate the difficult words.

Once he claimed to have heard Mum and Dad screaming from Huken, but I told him it was only ravens. I felt uneasy when he said he had nightmares about the two of us ending up in prison. But gradually things calmed down. He was still pale and thin, but he ate well, and he was shooting up, pretty soon he was a head taller than me.

So, incredibly enough, things had fallen into place. Calmed down. I could hardly believe it. The end of the world had come and gone, and we had survived. A fair few of us anyway. Were the ones who perished what Dad used to call **collateral damage**? Unintentional fatalities, but necessary when there's a war to be won? I don't know. I don't even know if the war was won. There was certainly a ceasefire, and if a ceasefire lasts long enough it's easy to confuse it with peace. That's what things felt like the day before the Fritz night.

'I used to bring Kurt along,' said Olsen. 'But I don't think he's all that interested in fishing.'

'Never,' I said, as though I found the thought incredible.

'Tell the truth, I don't think he's that interested in

anything I do. What about you, Roy? You gonna be a car mechanic?'

I didn't know why he'd taken me out on Lake Budal in that dinghy of his. Maybe he thought it would get me to relax. Say something I hadn't said when I was being interrogated. Or maybe it was simply that as sheriff he felt a certain responsibility and wanted to have a talk, find out how things were going.

'Yes, why not?' I said.

'Yes, because you've always liked tinkering about with things,' he said. 'Right now all Kurt's interested in is girls. Always some new one he's off out to meet. What about you and Carl? Any girls on the radar for you two?'

He let his question drift while I peered into the darkness beneath the surface of the water, trying to spot the spinner.

'I don't think you've ever had a girlfriend, have you?'

I shrugged. There's a difference between asking a twenty-year-old if he has a girlfriend and if he's **ever** had a girlfriend. And Sigmund Olsen knew that. Have to wonder how old he was when he styled that moptop of his. Guess it must have worked for him anyway.

'Haven't seen anything that takes my fancy,' I said. 'No point having a girlfriend just to say you have.'

'Of course not,' said Olsen. 'And some people don't even want girls at all. To each his own.'

'Yes,' I said. If only he knew how true that was. But no one did. Only Carl.

185

'So long as no one else gets hurt,' said Olsen.

'Sure.' I wondered what we were actually talking about and how long this fishing trip was going to last. I had a car at the repair shop that was supposed to be ready by tomorrow and we were a bit too far from land for my taste. Lake Budal was big and it was deep. For a joke Dad called it **the great unknown** because it was the nearest thing we had to a sea. At school we'd learned that wind and inflow and outflow of three rivers created horizontal currents in Lake Budal, but the really scary thing was that the differences in temperature in the water – especially in the spring – brewed up strong vertical currents. I don't know if they were enough to suck you down into the depths if you were so keen you went for a swim in March, but we sat wide-eyed in class and imagined they were. Maybe that's the reason I'd never really felt comfortable either in the lake or on it. When Carl and I tested out that diving equipment we did it in one of the smaller mountain lakes where there were no currents and where we could swim ashore if the boat went over.

'Do you remember when we had a chat just after your parents died, and me saying that a lot of people hide the fact that they're suffering from depression?' Olsen reeled in the dripping line.

'Yes,' I said.

'You do? Good memory. Well, I've had a taste of what it's like to be depressed myself.'

'Have you?' I said, a note of surprise in my voice

186

since I supposed that was what he was expecting to hear.

'Even been on medication for it.' He looked at me and smiled. 'It's gotta be OK to admit that when even prime ministers do it. Anyway, it was a long time ago now.'

'Blimey.'

'But I've never thought of taking my own life,' he said. 'Know what it would take for me to do that? For me to just end it all and leave a wife and two kids behind?'

I swallowed. Something told me the ceasefire was in danger.

'Shame,' he said. 'What d'you think, Roy?'

'Dunno.'

'You don't?'

'No.' I gave a dry-nosed snuffle. 'What are you actually fishing for here?' I held his gaze for a couple of seconds before nodding at the water. 'Cod and flounder, coalfish and salmon?'

He did something with the reel, locked it I think, and wedged the rod between the bottom of the boat and one of those things you sit on. Took off his sunglasses. Hoisted up his dungarees by the belt. There was a mobile phone in a leather holder dangling from it. Every once in a while he'd check it. He fixed his eyes on me.

'Your parents were conservative people,' he said. 'Strict Christians.'

'Not so sure about that,' I said.

'They were members of the Methodist Church.'

'That was mostly just something my dad brought with him from the USA.'

'Your parents were not exactly tolerant of homosexuality'

'Mum didn't really have any problem with it, but my dad was dead against it. Unless they were Americans and standing for election as Republicans.' I wasn't kidding, just repeating word for word what Dad had said himself, without mentioning that later he added Japanese soldiers to his shortlist, since they were – as he put it – worthy opponents. He said that as though he'd fought in the war himself. What Dad admired was the ritual of hara-kiri. He obviously believed it was something all Japanese soldiers did whenever the situation called for it. 'See what a small population can achieve once they've realised there's no option to fail,' Dad said to me once as I sat and watched him polishing his hunting knife. 'Once they've understood that whoever fails has to sever himself from the body of society, like a cancer.' I could have told Olsen that. But why should I?

Olsen coughed. 'What's your own attitude towards homosexuality?'

'My attitude? What's to have an attitude about? What attitude should you have towards people with brown hair?'

Olsen took hold of the rod again and went on turning the reel. It struck me then that you move your hand in the same way when you want to encourage people to go on talking, to **expand** on things, as people say. But I kept my mouth shut.

'Let me be direct, Roy. Are you gay?'

I don't know why he switched from talking about 'homosexuality' to talking about being 'gay'. Maybe he thought it was less liable to cause offence. I saw the lure glint down in the water, a muted and slightly protracted flash, as though light travels more slowly through water. 'Are you coming on to me, Olsen?'

He probably hadn't seen that coming. He stopped reeling and jerked the rod up, staring at me in horror. 'Eh? Fucking hell, no. I . . .'

Just then the spinner broke the surface of the water, floating over the gunwale like a flying fish. It did a circuit of our heads before heading back towards the rod, landing softly on the back of Olsen's head. The mop was clearly even thicker than it looked, because he didn't even seem to have noticed it.

'If I am gay,' I said, 'I haven't come out the closet yet, otherwise you and everybody else in the village would have known within fifteen minutes. So that must mean I prefer the closet. The other possibility is that I'm not gay.'

At first Olsen looked surprised. Then he seemed to be chewing over the logic of it.

'I am the sheriff, Roy. I knew your father, and I can never get that suicide to add up. At least, not that he would take your mother with him.'

'That's because it wasn't a suicide,' I said in a low voice, at the same time screaming the words

189

inside my head. 'I keep saying, he didn't make the corner.'

'Maybe.' Olsen rubbed his chin.

He had something or other, the fucking cuckoo.

'I spoke to Anna Olaussen a couple of days ago,' he said. 'You know, she used to be the nursing sister at the surgery. She's in a care home now, got Alzheimer's. She's my wife's cousin, so we called in to see her. While my wife was out getting some water for the flowers Anna said to me that there was one thing she had always regretted. That she had never broken her vow of confidentiality and told me about it when your brother Carl had been to the surgery and she had seen that he had anal ecchymosis. It means he had lacerations. Your brother didn't want to tell her how it happened, but there aren't that many options. On the other hand, Anna thought he seemed so calm about it when he said no, he hadn't had sexual relations with a man, that she thought maybe it didn't involve rape. That it may have been consensual. Because Carl was so . . .' Olsen stared out over the water. The spinner dangling from the back of his head. '. . . well, such a pretty boy.'

He turned to me again.

'Anna didn't tell me, but she did alert your mother and father, she said. And two days after she did so, your father drove the car over the edge and into Huken.'

I averted my eyes from his penetrating gaze. Saw a seagull skimming low over the calm water, looking for prey.

'As I say, Anna has dementia, and everything she says you have to take with a pinch of salt. But I related it to a warning note from the school a few years earlier, from a teacher who had twice noticed that Carl had blood on the seat of his trousers.'

'Nails,' I said in a low voice.

'Missed that?'

'Nails!'

My voice floated over the strangely still surface of the water towards land. It struck the rock face and came bouncing back twice . . . **ails** . . . **ails.** Everything comes back at you, I thought.

'I had hoped you might be able to help me shed light on why your father and mother didn't want to live any more, Roy.'

'It was an accident,' I said. 'Can we go back now?'

'Roy, you must understand; I can't just let this go. It'll all come out sooner or later, so the best thing for you now is to tell me exactly what was going on between you and Carl. There's no need to worry it'll be used against you, because this isn't an official interrogation in any judicial sense. It's just you and me on a fishing trip. I'll make it as easy as I can for everybody involved, and if you cooperate I'll make sure any potential punishment is as lenient as possible. Because the way things are looking at the moment, this was going on while Carl was still underage. That means that you, being a year older, risk—'

'Listen,' I interrupted, my throat so tight my voice sounded as though it was coming up through a stovepipe, 'I've a car that needs repairing, and it looks like you're not going to get a bite today, sheriff.'

Olsen looked at me for a long time, as though he wanted me to believe he could read me like an open book, as people say. Then he nodded, moved to lay the rod down in the boat and cursed as the hook bit and stretched his sunburnt neck below his mop of hair. He detached the hook with two fingers, and I saw a single drop of blood that quivered on the skin, but didn't run anywhere. Olsen started the outboard motor, and five minutes later we pulled the dinghy up into the boathouse below their cabin. From there we drove to the village in Olsen's Peugeot and he dropped me off at the repair shop. It was a bloody quiet fifteen-minute drive.

I had only been working on the Corolla for half an hour and was about to change the steering box when I heard the phone ringing in the car wash. A few moments later Uncle Bernard's voice:

'Roy, it's for you. It's Carl.'

I dropped what I had in my hand. Carl didn't call me at the repair shop. In our house we never rang anywhere unless there was a crisis.

'What is it?' I shouted above the sound of Bernard's hosepipe, the note rising and falling all according to where the jet was hitting the car.

'It's Sheriff Olsen,' said Carl. His voice was shaking.

I understood it really was a crisis and steeled myself. Had that bastard already gone public with his suspicions that it was me, the big brother, who was Carl's shirtlifter?

'He's disappeared,' said Carl.

'Disappeared?' I laughed. 'Rubbish. I saw him three-quarters of an hour ago.'

'I mean it. And I think he's dead.'

I squeezed the phone hard. 'What d'you mean, you **think** he's dead?'

'I mean I don't know. Like I said, he's disappeared. But I can just feel it, Roy. I'm pretty sure he's dead.'

Three thoughts struck me in quick succession. The first was that Carl had lost it completely. He didn't sound even remotely pissed, and although he was a bit soft he wasn't the oversensitive type who actually **saw** things. The second was that it would be almost absurdly convenient if Sheriff Sigmund Olsen had disappeared from the surface of the earth just when that was what I needed most. The third was that this was a repeat, this was Dog all over again. I had no choice. By betraying my little brother I had incurred a debt I was going to have to go on paying until I died. This was just another instalment falling due.

14

'THINGS CHANGED AFTER DAD DISAPPEARED,'
said Kurt Olsen as he placed a cup of coffee on the
table in front of me. 'It's not like I was fated to be
a policeman.'

He sat down, brushed the blond quiff aside and
started rolling a cigarette. We were sitting in a room
that functioned as a cell but was obviously used for
storing stuff too. Folders and documents were piled
on the floor along the walls. Maybe the idea was that
people held in custody could while away the time
checking their own records and anybody else's too
while they sat here.

'But then things do look a bit different once your
father's gone, don't they?'

I took a swig of coffee. He'd pulled me in here for a test that he knew as well as me wouldn't show any blood alcohol content. Now he was offering a truce. OK by me.

'You sort of grow up overnight,' said Kurt. 'Because you have to. And you begin to understand something about the responsibility he had, and how you did everything you could to make his job more difficult for him. You ignored all his advice, dismissed what he thought and said, did all you could to be as unlike him as you could. Maybe because there's something inside telling you that's how you're going to end up. As a copy of your father. Because we go round in circles. The only place we're going is back where we came from. Everyone's like that. I know you were interested in mountain birds. Carl brought some feathers to school that he'd got off you. We teased him about it.' Kurt smiled as though at a fond memory. 'Take these birds, Roy, they move about all over the place. Migrate, I think it's called. But they never go anywhere their forefathers haven't been before them. The same habitats and mating sites at the same damned times. Free as a bird? We're kidding ourselves. It's just something we like to believe. And we move around inside the same damned circle. We're caged birds, but the cage is so big and the bars so thin we don't see it.'

He glanced over at me as though seeing if his monologue had had any effect. I considered giving the slow nod, but didn't.

'And it's the same for you and me too, Roy. Big

circles and little circles. The big circle is me taking over the sheriff's office after my father. The little is that he had this one unsolved case he kept going back to, and I've got mine too. Mine is my own father's disappearance. There are similarities, don't you think? Two despairing or depressed men taking their own lives.'

I shrugged and tried to look uninterested. Shit, was that all this was about – the disappearance of Sheriff Sigmund Olsen?

'The difference being that, in my father's case, there's no body, and no exact location,' said Kurt. 'Only the lake.'

'The great unknown,' I said, nodding slowly.

Kurt looked sharply at me. And then he too began to nod, in time to my own nodding, so that for a moment we were like two synchronised oil pumps.

'And since the fact of the matter is that you were the next to last person to see my father alive, and your brother the last, I've got a few questions.'

'I guess that's something we all have,' I said and took another swig of coffee. 'But I've told you in detail about that fishing trip with your father – I'm sure you have a transcript of it here.' I nodded towards the papers piled up against the wall. 'And anyway, I'm here to take a blood alcohol test, aren't I?'

'Absolutely,' said Kurt Olsen. He was done rolling his cigarette and put it away in his tobacco pouch. 'So this isn't an official interview. No notes will be taken, and there are no witnesses to anything that might be said here.'

Just like that fishing trip, I thought.

'What I'm quite specifically interested in is finding out what happened after my father dropped you off at the car repair shop at six o'clock, for you to work on a car.'

I took a deep breath. 'Quite specifically? I changed the steering box and the bearings on a Toyota Corolla. I think it was a 1989 model.'

Kurt's eyes stiffened, the truce was obviously under threat. I made a strategic withdrawal.

'Your father drove up to the farm and talked to Carl. After he left Carl phoned me because the power was down and he couldn't work out why. The generator is old and we've had a few earth faults. He's not exactly a handyman so I drove up and fixed it. It took a few hours because it was getting dark, so it was late by the time I got back to the workshop.'

'According to the transcript you got back there at eleven o'clock.'

'Sounds about right. It was a long time ago.'

'And a witness thinks he saw my father driving through the village at nine o'clock. But it was already dark and the person concerned can't be sure.'

'All right.'

'The question is: what was my father doing between six thirty, when he left the farm, according to Carl, and nine o'clock?'

'There's your riddle.'

He stared at me. 'Any theories?'

I gave him a look of surprise. 'Me? No.'

I heard a car pull up outside. Must be the doctor. Kurt glanced at his watch. I was guessing he'd told him to take his time.

'By the way, how did things work out with that car?' Kurt asked casually.

'Car?'

'The Toyota Corolla.'

'OK, I suppppose.'

'I've checked the interviews and who owned old Toyotas. You're right, it was an '89 model. Turns out Willumsen wanted it repaired before selling it on. Just enough so it would start, I'm guessing.'

'Sounds about right,' I said.

'Only it didn't.'

'Eh?' I exclaimed.

'I talked to Willumsen yesterday. He remembered Bernard promising that you would have the car drive-able. He remembers it clearly because the customer came a hundred kilometres to test-drive it and the repairs hadn't been fixed the way you promised they would be.'

'Oh yeah?' I narrowed my eyes, trying to look like a man peering into the mists and darkness of the past. 'Then I was probably delayed by the time it took me to find and fix that earth fault.'

'Well, you certainly spent long enough on it.'

'I did?'

'I spoke to Grete Smitt day before yesterday. It's amazing what everyday little trivia people remember when they can relate it to a special event, such as their sheriff being reported missing. She recalls waking up at five in the morning, looking out the window and seeing there was a light on in the workshop, and that your car was parked there.'

'When you make a promise to a customer, you do everything you can to keep that promise,' I said. 'Even if you don't succeed, it's still a good rule of life.'

Kurt Olsen glowered at me as though I'd just told a particularly offensive joke.

'Yeah yeah,' I said breezily. 'So what's happening about sending the guys down into Huken?'

'We'll have to see.'

'Nerell advises against it?'

'We'll have to see,' Olsen said again.

The door opened. It was the doctor, Stanley Spind, the doctor who'd been an intern here and afterwards come back to work full-time, a guy from the Bible Belt. He was in his thirties, a friendly and outgoing man whose clothes and hair were artfully unkempt in an I-just-threw-these-on-and-they-seem-to-match-anyway sort of way and an I-didn't-comb-my-hair-this-is-just-how-it-is fashion. His body was an odd mixture of firmness and softness, as though he'd bought the muscles somewhere. People said he was gay, and that he had a lover in Kongsberg with a wife and kids.

'Ready for your blood test?' he asked, ferociously rolling his 'r's'.

'Looks like it,' said Kurt Olsen without taking his eyes off me.

I left with Stanley after he'd taken the blood sample.

From the moment the doctor had entered the room Kurt Olsen had stopped talking about the case, confirming what he'd said earlier, that at this stage the investigation was still a purely private matter. Kurt gave me only the slightest nod of his head as we left.

'I was at Årtun,' said Stanley as we inhaled the fine, sharp evening air in the square outside the sheriff's office. It was in the same featureless 1980s building that also housed the local authority offices. 'Your brother certainly got everybody all fired up. So now maybe we'll be getting a spa hotel?'

'It's got to go through the council first.'

'If they say yes then I definitely want in.'

I nodded.

'Can I drive you somewhere?' asked Stanley.

'No thanks, I'll call Carl.'

'Are you sure? It's not too far out of my way.' He might have held my gaze a fraction of a second too long. Or else, what's just as likely, I'm a little paranoid.

I shook my head.

'Another time,' he said and opened his car door. He'd obviously stopped locking his car after moving here, the way city people often do. They have the romantic idea that people in country villages don't do that. They're wrong. We lock our houses, boathouses and we definitely lock our cars. I watched the rear lights of his car disappearing as I took out my phone and set off on foot to meet Carl. When the Cadillac

200

pulled up on the hard shoulder in front of me twenty minutes later, however, Shannon was at the wheel. She explained that Carl had broken out the champagne after they got home. And since he'd drunk most if it and she'd only had a taste, she'd persuaded him to let her drive.

'You two celebrating that I was in jail?' I asked.

'He said he knew you would say that, and I was to say that he was celebrating that you were definitely going to be released. He's good at finding reasons to celebrate.'

'True,' I said. 'I envy him that too.' I realised that the **too** was open to misunderstanding and was about to explain. Tell her that when I stressed **envy,** the **too** bit meant both that it was true **and** that I envied him his ability to **compartmentalise,** as people say. So, not **too** in the sense that there was something **else** that I **also** envied him for. But then I've always had a tendency to complicate things.

'You think,' said Shannon.

'Not much,' I said.

She smiled. The wheel seemed enormous between her small hands.

'Can you see properly?' I asked, nodding towards the darkness that the cones of light swept away in front of us.

'It's called **ptosis,**' she said. 'It's Greek for "to fall". In my case it's congenital. You can train your eye so there's less chance of developing amblyopia, what people call "lazy eye". I'm not lazy. I see everything.'

'Good,' I said.

She changed down approaching the first hairpin bend. 'For example I can see it's a problem for you, to you it seems as if I've taken Carl away from you.' She accelerated and a spray of gravel rattled under the wheel arch. For a moment I wondered whether to pretend I hadn't heard what she'd just said. But I had the definite feeling that if I did, she'd just repeat it.

I turned towards her.

'Thanks,' she said, before I could get a word out.

'Thanks?'

'Thanks for everything you're giving up. Thank you for being a wise and good man. I know how much you and Carl mean to each other. Besides being a complete stranger who's married your brother I've pushed my way into your physical domain. I've quite literally taken over the place where you used to sleep. You should hate me.'

'Well,' I said, and took a deep breath. It had already been a very long day. 'I'm not exactly known for being a good man. The real problem is that unfortunately there's very little about you to hate.'

'I've talked to a couple of the people who work for you.'

'You have?' I asked, genuinely surprised.

'This is a very small place,' said Shannon. 'I probably speak to people a bit more than you do. And you're wrong. You **are** thought of as a good man.'

I snorted. 'Then you haven't talked to anyone whose teeth I've knocked out.'

'Maybe not. But even that was something you did to protect your brother.'

'I don't think you should expect too much of me,' I said. 'I'll only let you down.'

'I think I know already what to expect of you,' she said. 'The advantage of having a lazy eye is that people reveal themselves to you, they think you're not listening properly.'

'So you think you know all there is to know about Carl, is that what you're saying?'

She smiled. 'Love is blind, is that what you're saying?'

'In Norwegian we say love **makes** you blind.'

'Aha.' She gave a low laugh. 'But that's even more precise than my English **love is blind.** Which people use in the completely wrong way anyway.'

'They do?'

'They use it to mean that we see only the good side of people we love. But actually it refers to the fact that Cupid wears a blindfold when he shoots his arrows. Meaning that the arrows strike at random, and it isn't us who chooses who to fall in love with.'

'But is that right? At random?'

'Are we still talking about Carl and me?'

'For example.'

'Well, maybe not at random, but falling in love isn't always a voluntary thing.'

'I'm really not so sure that we mountain people are as practical in matters of love and death as you seem to think we are.'

The headlights strafed the wall of the house as the

car climbed the final incline. A face, ghostly white in the light, its eyes black holes, stared out at us from behind the living-room window.

She stopped, shoved the gearstick into P, turned off the lights and the engine.

Silence descends so quickly up here when you turn off the only source of sound. Like a sudden roar. I remained in my seat. So did Shannon.

'How much do you know?' I asked. 'About us. About this family?'

'Pretty much everything, I think,' she said. 'As a condition of marrying and coming here I told him he would have to tell me absolutely everything. Including the bad stuff. Especially the bad stuff. And anything he didn't tell me I've seen for myself since I came here.' Shannon pointed to her half-drawn eyelid.

'And you . . .' I swallowed. 'You feel you can live with the **you know what**?'

'I grew up on a street where brothers fucked sisters. Fathers raped daughters. Sons repeated the sins of the fathers and became parricides. But life goes on.'

I nodded slowly, and not ironically, as I pulled out my tin of snuff. 'Guess it does. But it seems a lot to put up with.'

'Yes,' said Shannon. 'It is. But everyone has something. And it was a long time ago. People change, I truly believe that.'

I sat there and wondered why it was I had imagined that this was the worst thing that could happen – that some outsider found out – when it just didn't feel that way. And the answer was obvious. Shannon Alleyne Opgard wasn't an outsider.

'Family,' I said as I wedged tobacco in below my upper lip. 'That means a lot to you, doesn't it?'

'Everything,' she replied without hesitation.

'Does love of family make you blind too?'

'What do you mean?'

'In the kitchen, when you talked about Barbados, I thought you said you believed that people's loyalty is attached more to family and feelings than principles. More than political views and people's ideas in general of right and wrong. Did I get that right?'

'Yes. Family is the only principle. And right and wrong proceed from that. Everything else is secondary.'

'Is it?'

She peered out through the windscreen at our little house. 'We had a professor of ethics in Bridgetown. He told us that Justitia, who symbolises the rule of law, holds a pair of scales and a sword in her hands that stand for justice and punishment, and that she wears a blindfold, like Cupid. The usual interpretation is that this means all people are equal in the eyes of the law. That the law doesn't take sides, doesn't concern itself with family and love, only the law.'

She turned and looked at me, her snow-white face glowing in the dark interior of the car.

'But with a blindfold you can see neither the scales nor where your sword strikes. He told us that in Greek mythology, blindfolded eyes meant only the inner eye was used, the eye that found the answer within. Where the wise and blind see only what they love, and what's on the outside has no meaning.'

I nodded slowly. 'We – you, me and Carl – are family?'

'We're not blood, but we are family.'

'Good,' I said. 'Then as a family member you can join Carl and me when we have our councils of war, instead of just listening to the stovepipe.'

'The stovepipe?'

'A turn of phrase.'

Carl had walked round from the front door and was now heading towards us across the gravel.

'And why council of war?' asked Shannon.

'Because this is war,' I said.

I looked at her. Both eyes flashed like a battle-ready Athena. God, how beautiful she was.

And then I told her about the Fritz night.

15

I SPOKE INTO THE PHONE hoping Uncle Bernard couldn't hear me over the sound of the hosepipe.

'Carl, what d'you mean, you're certain he's dead?'

'He must have fallen a long way. And I can't hear anything from down there. But I can't be sure, he's disappeared.'

'Disappeared where?'

'Down Huken, of course. He's gone, even when I lean over the edge I can't see him.'

'Carl, stay right where you are. Don't say a word to anyone, don't touch anything, don't do anything, OK?'

'How quickly can you—'

'Fifteen minutes. OK?'

I hung up, left the car wash and looked up towards

Geitesvingen. You can't see the track itself where it's hewn into the mountain, but if someone's driving there you can see the top half of the car. If a person is standing on the edge of the drop and wearing brightly coloured clothing you can see them on a clear day, but now the sun was too low.

'I've got to go home and sort something out,' I called out.

Uncle Bernard twisted the mouthpiece on the hose and cut off the stream.

'What's up?'

'Earthing problem.'

'Oh yeah? Is it that urgent?'

'Carl's got to have power tonight,' I said. 'Some school stuff he has to finish. I'll come back down afterwards.'

'I see. Well, I'll be off in half an hour, but you've got your own keys.'

I got into the Volvo and drove. Kept to the speed limit, even though the chances of being stopped were low, considering that the village's only lawman was lying at the bottom of a ravine.

Carl was standing on Geitesvingen when I arrived. I parked in front of the house, turned off the engine, pulled on the handbrake.

'Heard anything?' I asked, nodding in the direction of Huken.

Carl shook his head. He was quiet, and there was a wild look in his eyes. I'd never seen him like that before. His hair was sticking up all over the place, as though he'd been rubbing his head with his hands. His pupils were dilated, as though he were in shock. He probably **was** in shock, the poor bastard.

'What happened?'

Carl sat down in the middle of the bend, the way the goats often do. Bowed his head and hid his face in his hands. He cast a long, troll-like shadow across the gravel.

'He came up here,' he stammered. 'He said you and him had been out fishing, and he started asking a lot of questions, and I . . .' He clammed up.

'Sigmund Olsen came here,' I prompted, sitting down beside him. 'He probably said I'd told him things and asked if you could confirm that I had messed about with you when you were underage.'

'Yes!' yelled Carl.

'Shush!' I said.

'He said the best thing would be for us both to confess and get it over with as quickly as possible. The alternative was for him to use the evidence he had in a long, painful and very public court case. I said you'd never touched me, not like that, not . . .' Carl spoke and gestured to the ground, as though I wasn't even there. 'He said it wasn't uncommon for the victim to sympathise with the attacker in situations like this, that they took part of the responsibility themselves for what had taken place, especially if it had been going on for some time.'

And I thought that, well, Sheriff Olsen had got that just about right.

A sob broke from Carl's lips. 'Then he told me that Anna at the surgery had told Mum and Dad what we were doing just two days before they went over into Huken. Olsen said Dad knew it was bound to come out one day and that he, like the conservative Christian he was, couldn't live with the shame.'

And took Mum along with him, I thought. Instead of the two sodomites in the boys' room.

'I tried to tell him no, that wasn't right, it was an accident. A pure accident, but he wouldn't listen, on he went. Said Dad's blood alcohol level was minimal and no one drives right off a corner like that when they're sober. And then I got desperate, I realised he was really going to go ahead with it . . .'

'Yep,' I said, flicking away a sharp stone I was sitting on. 'Olsen just wants to **clear up** his big fucking case.'

'But what about us, Roy? Will we go to jail?'

I grinned. Jail? Yeah, maybe so. I hadn't even thought much about it. Because I knew that if the whole truth came out it was the shame I couldn't live with, not the being in jail. Because if they, the others, the village found out, it wouldn't just be the shame I had to deal with alone in the dark for so many years. The whole disgraceful, treacherous business would be exposed, condemned, ridiculed. The Opgard family would be humiliated. Maybe it's an aberration of the personality, as people say, but Dad had understood the logic behind hara-kiri, and I did too. That death is the only way out for someone broken down by shame. On the other hand, you don't want to die unless you have to.

'We don't have much time,' I said. 'What happened?'

'I was desperate,' said Carl and glanced up at me the way he did when he was about to confess something. 'So I said I knew it was an accident, that I could prove it.'

'You said **what**?'

'I had to say **something,** Roy! So I said one of the tyres had punctured, that that's why they went over the edge. I mean, no one had checked anything at all on the car, they'd just winched up the bodies, that climber got hit by a loose boulder and after that no one dared go down there again. I said it wasn't so surprising they never noticed the puncture, you can't tell if a tyre's got a puncture when the car's on its back with the wheels sticking up in the air, but I said a couple of weeks ago I'd got a pair of binoculars and climbed down over the edge where there's a couple of solid rocks you can hold on to and lean out so you can see the car. I said I saw how the left front tyre was noticeably a bit shrivelled, and that the puncture must have happened **before** the car went over the edge, because the undercarriage is completely undamaged, the car did a half somersault through thin air and landed on its roof, full stop.'

'And Olsen bought that?'

'No. He wanted to see for himself.'

I could see where this was going. 'So you fetched the binoculars, and . . .'

'He climbed right out to the very edge, and . . .' Carl let the breath burst from his lungs and continued, his eyes closed. 'I heard the sound of stones loosening, a scream. Then he was gone.'

Gone, I thought, but not completely gone.

'Don't you believe me?'

I looked down into the abyss. A memory from when I was twelve, from my uncle Bernard's fiftieth birthday gathering at the Grand Hotel, flickered through my mind. 'You realise what this is going to look like?' I said. 'The sheriff comes up here to interview you in connection with a serious criminal investigation, and he ends up dead down there. If he is dead.'

Carl nodded slowly. Of course he realised. That was why he had called me instead of the mountain rescue team, or the doctor.

I stood up and dusted myself off. 'Fetch the rope from the barn,' I said. 'The long one.'

I fastened one end of the rope to the tow hitch of the car up by the house and the other round my waist. Then I began to walk down towards Geitesvingen with the rope uncoiling. I counted a hundred paces before it was taut. I was ten metres from the edge of the drop.

'Now!' I shouted. 'And remember: slowly!'

Carl gave me a thumbs up through the window of the Volvo and began to reverse.

The trick was to keep the rope taut, I'd explained to him, and now there was no way back. I lay into the rope and headed towards the drop as though I was in a hurry to get us both down there. The edge was the worst. My body protested, it wasn't as sure as my mind was that this would be OK and made me hesitant. The rope slackened because Carl didn't notice that I'd stopped at the edge. I shouted to him to drive forward a bit, but he didn't hear me. So I turned my back to Huken, took a step backwards and fell. It can't have been more than a metre, but when the rope tightened round my waist it squeezed the breath out of me and I forgot to straighten my legs so that I hit the rock face with my knees and forehead as I was thrown inwards. I swore, managed to brace the soles of my shoes against the wall, and started to climb down the vertical stone wall. Looked up at the sky above me which was now pale blue and translucent and breaking up, already I could see a couple of stars. I could no longer hear the car, in fact there was complete silence. Maybe it was the silence, the stars and dangling weightless like that attached to a car that made me feel like an astronaut, floating in space and connected to a space capsule. I thought of Major Tom in Bowie's song. For a moment I wished it could go on like that, and even end like that, that I could just float away.

And then the wall came to an end, I touched solid ground and watched the rope coiling like a cobra on the ground in front of me. Two, three coils and then the rope stopped. I followed it with my eyes to the top. Saw a tiny cloud of exhaust smoke. Carl must have stopped at the very edge. The rope had just been long enough and no more.

I turned. I was standing on a scree of large and small stones that time had chewed loose from the walls surrounding me on all sides and deposited at the bottom. The drop down from Geitesvingen was vertical, but the walls of the sharp, lower pillars sloped slightly, so that the square of evening sky above me was larger than the roughly hundred square metres of rocky ground I was standing on. Nothing grew down here in this place that never saw so much as a glint of sunlight and had no smell either. Just rock. Space and rock.

The spaceship, Dad's black Cadillac DeVille, lay the way I had imagined it would that time the mountain rescue guys described the scene down here.

The car was lying on its roof with its wheels in the air. The rear part of the coupé was squashed flat, with the front so little damaged you might even have supposed it possible for the passengers sitting there to have survived. Mum and Dad had been found outside the car; they'd been thrown through the windscreen when the front end hit the ground. The fact that they hadn't been wearing seat belts strengthened the suicide theory, even though I had explained that Dad was against seat belts on principle. Not because he didn't see the point, but because it was a mandatory requirement made by what he called the 'nanny state'. The only reason Sheriff Olsen thought he'd seen Dad using the belt several times when driving in the village was that Dad would wear one when he thought the law was around, because he hated getting fined even more than he hated the nanny state.

A raven stood on Sheriff Olsen's stomach watching me cautiously, claws clutched around the big belt buckle with the buffalo skull. Olsen had landed in such a way that the lower half of his body lay across the back end of the chassis, with the rest of him hanging over the side and out of view from where I was standing. The raven's head swivelled, following me as I made my way round the car. Broken glass crunched beneath my feet, and I had to use my hands to get past a couple of enormous loose boulders. The upper part of Olsen's body hung down in front of the licence plate and the boot. The unusual ninety-degree angle at which his back was broken made him look like a scarecrow, a figure with no joints, straw stuffed inside clothes, with a mop hanging from its head, dripping with blood onto the stones below with a low, soft smacking sound. Hanging there with his hands in the air – that's to say, towards the ground – as though trying to signal that he was giving up. Because as Dad always said: 'If you're dead then you've lost.' Olsen was as dead as a dodo. And he smelled.

I took a step closer, and the raven screeched at me without moving. It probably saw me as a kind of Arctic skua, that's a sneaky type of seabird that lives by stealing food from other birds. I picked up a stone and threw it at the raven and it flew off with two shrieks, the one hate-filled and aimed at me, the other an expression of his own regret.

Darkness was already swelling out from the mountainside and I had to work fast.

Had to think through how we were going to get Olsen's body up the rock face using just one rope and with a minimum risk of the body getting caught on something or sliding out of the rope. Because the human body is like a bloody Houdini. If you tie the rope around the chest, the arms and shoulders squeeze themselves together and the body slips out that way. Tie it to the belt buckle or round the waist and drag the body up like a trussed shrimp and at some point the centre of gravity will move and the body tip upside down and slip out of the rope or out of his trousers. I decided that the simplest thing would be to make a slip knot and tie it round his neck. The centre of gravity would be so low that he couldn't tip in any direction and with the head and shoulders clearing the way there was less chance of him getting caught on something. And of course you might well ask yourself how come I knew how to tie a knot that's usually only learned by people who intend to hang themselves.

I worked systematically, concentrating entirely on the practical aspects. I'm good at that. I knew that these were images that would come back again – Olsen as a gaping figurehead mounted on the stern of a black spaceship – but that would be another time, another place.

It was dark by the time I called up to Carl that the package was ready. I had to call him three times, he had Whitney Houston on the car's CD player and the sound of her singing 'I will always love you' was echoing across the mountains. He started the engine and I heard him riding the clutch to keep it going slowly enough. The rope tightened and I held round the body, helped it over to the rock face where I let go. Stood below and watched as it rose to the heavens like an angel with neck outstretched. Slowly it was swallowed up by the dark until all I could hear was the scraping sound of the body against the rock. Then a brief swishing noise through the dark and the crack of something hard hitting the ground just a few metres away from me. Shit, the body must have dislodged some rocks, and there could be more. I took shelter in the only place there was shelter. Crawled in through the windscreen of the Cadillac. Sat there and looked at the dials on the instrument panel, tried to read them upside down. Thought of what came next. How to deal with the next part of the plan. The practical details, everything that had to be done right, other options if something went wrong with plan A. It must have been this simple act of thinking that made me feel calmer. The situation was crazy, of course. I was trying to cover up the fact that a man was dead, and that settled me down. Or maybe it wasn't these practical thoughts but the smell. The smell of the leather seats, impregnated with Dad's sweat, Mum's cigarettes and perfume, and Carl's vomit from the time we drove to the city in the newly purchased Cadillac and he got carsick and puked over the seats even before we'd navigated all the hairpin bends on the way down to the village. Mum put out her cigarette, wound down the window and took a wad of tobacco from Dad's silvery snuffbox. But Carl carried on puking as we drove out of the village, so suddenly and without any warning that he never had time to open the sick bag and the coupé stank like a fucking gas chamber even with all the windows open. Carl had lain down in the back seat with his head in my lap, closed his eyes and everything had calmed down. After Mum had wiped up the sick she'd handed us the bag of biscuits, and Dad had sung 'Love Me Tender' at half speed and with double vibrato. Looking back on it I recalled it as the best trip we ever had.

The rest happened quickly.

Carl tossed the rope down, I tied myself in, called up that I was ready and I made my way up the rock face the same way I had come down, like a film shown backwards. I couldn't see what I was standing on, but nothing came loose. If I hadn't just nearly been hit on the head I would have said the mountain was quite safe.

Olsen was laid out on Geitesvingen, in the light from the Volvo's headlamps. There weren't many visible signs of external damage to the body. His mane of hair was soaked in blood, one hand looked as though it had been crushed, and he had livid markings on his neck from the slip knot. I don't know whether it was discolouring from the rope, or if a fresh corpse can haemorrhage. But of course, there was a broken spine in there, and enough internal injuries for a pathologist to be able to determine that the cause of death was not exactly hanging. And not drowning either.

I stuck my hand into one of Olsen's wet back pockets, fished out his car keys, and in the other found the bunch of keys he had used when he locked the boathouse.

'Go and fetch Dad's hunting knife,' I said.

'Eh?'

'It's hanging in the entrance hall, next to the shotgun. Get a move on.'

While Carl ran back to the house I took out the snow shovel any mountain dweller has in the back of the car all year round, scooped up the gravel where Olsen had been dragged and tossed it down into Huken, vanishing without a sound.

'Here,' said Carl, panting.

He handed me the knife, the one with the grooves in the blade that I had used to finish off Dog.

And now, as then, Carl was standing behind me and looking away as I used the knife. I grabbed hold of Olsen's mop of hair, holding his head the same way I had held Dog, put the point of the blade in his forehead, forced it through the skin until it hit bone, then cut an angled circle down and around the head, directly above the ear and the knotty clump of bone at the top of the neck, the point of the blade all the time following the line of the cranium. Dad had shown me how you flay a fox, but this was different. This was scalping.

'Move, Carl, you're blocking the light.'

I heard Carl turn towards me, yawn and walk round to the other side of the car.

As I worked away at loosening the bottom of the head from the scalp I heard Whitney Houston start singing again, about how she would never, absolutely bloody **never,** stop loving you.

We spread rubbish bags along the floor of my Volvo, pulled off Sigmund Olsen's snakeskin boots and loaded the mangled corpse into the boot. Then I sat behind the wheel of Olsen's Peugeot, glanced in the mirror and adjusted the scalp. Even with that mop of fair hair on my head I didn't look like Sigmund Olsen, but when I put on his sunglasses the illusion was good enough to fool anyone seeing me from outside, in the dark, who would be hardly likely to suppose that it **wasn't** the sheriff driving his own car.

I drove slowly, but not too slowly, through the village. No need to blow the horn or attract attention in some other way. A couple of people out walking and I saw their heads automatically turn and knew their brains would register the sheriff's car and half consciously wonder where he was off to, at any rate he was heading out along the lakeside. Maybe in their half-asleep farmers' brains they figured he was off to his cabin, if they knew where that was.

When I arrived at the cabin I drove down to the boathouse and turned off the engine but left the keys in the ignition. Switched off the headlights, not because anyone else lived within view but because you never know. If someone who knew Sigmund Olsen drove by and saw lights they might decide to drop in to say hello. I wiped off the steering wheel, the gear-stick, the door handles. Looked at my watch. Carl had been told to drive my Volvo to the workshop, park outside so that it was clearly visible, open the place with the keys I had given him and turn on the lights so that it looked as though I was at work. Leave Olsen's body where it was, in the boot of the car. Wait twenty minutes or so, check first there was no one walking down the road when he pulled out from the workshop, and then join me at the cabin.

I unlocked the boathouse and dragged out the dinghy. It rumbled as it glided over the track of horizontal timbers until at last the lake received the boat with what sounded like a sigh of relief. I dried the snakeskin boots with a cloth, dropped Sigmund Olsen's bunch of keys into the right boot, tossed both boots into the dinghy and pushed it out onto the water. Stood there and watched as it glided out towards **the great unknown** and felt almost proud of myself. The business with the boots was a touch of genius, as people say. I mean, when they find an empty boat with just keys and a pair of boots, what else can you say? And aren't the boots in themselves a kind of suicide note, an announcement that your wanderings on this earth are over? Yours sincerely, the depressed sheriff. You might almost say it was beautiful if it wasn't so fucking idiotic. Fall a hundred metres down a gulley right in front of someone you're investigating. Completely fucking unbelievable. In fact, I was far from sure I believed it myself. And as I stood there thinking all this, the idiocy just got more idiotic as the boat started drifting back towards the shore. I shoved it again, harder this time, but the same thing happened again, and a minute later the keel was rubbing against the lakeside stones again. I couldn't figure it out. From what I remembered our teacher saying about Budalvannet's horizontal currents, the wind direction and outflow, the boat should have been drifting away from me. Maybe we were in a backwater where everything circled round and came back in an eternal recurrence. That must be it. The boat needed to be further from the shore before it met the outflow currents and the Kjetterelva River down in the south, so that the area where Olsen could potentially have jumped overboard was so big that it was no surprise his body was never found. I stepped on board, started the motor and chugged along for a bit, turning it off again while it was still gliding away from the shore. Wiped the rudder clean, but only that. If it occurred to them to check the boat for fingerprints, it would be more suspicious if they did **not** find some of mine – after all, I'd been on board earlier the same day. I glanced over at the shore. Two hundred metres. Should be able to manage that.

I considered climbing over the side of the boat and into the water but then realised this would stop the boat's forward motion so instead I stepped up onto the thwart and dived. The shock of the cold water felt surprisingly like a liberation as my overheated brain suddenly cooled down for a few moments. Then I started to swim. Swimming with clothes on was more difficult than I had expected and my movements awkward. I thought of my teacher's vertical currents, and it seemed as though I could feel them, pulling me down, and I had to remind myself it was autumn, not spring, as I parted the water in a long, clumsy breaststroke. I had no landmarks to guide me, so perhaps I should have left the headlights on after all. I remembered being taught that the legs are stronger than the arms and kicked and kicked away for all I was worth.

And then, suddenly and without any warning, I was caught.

I went under, swallowed water, rose to the surface again, splashing out wildly to get free of whatever it was that had attacked me. It wasn't the current, it was . . . something else. Something that wouldn't let go of my hand, I could feel teeth or at least jaws clamped around my wrist. I went under again, but at least this time managed to keep my mouth closed. I pressed my fingertips together, narrowed my hand and jerked it towards me. I was free. Back up on the surface I gasped for air. There, a metre in front of me in the dark, I saw something light floating on the water. Cork. I had swum into a seine net.

I calmed my breathing, and when a car with headlights on full beam drove past along the main highway I saw the outline of Olsen's boathouse. The rest of the swim was uneventful, as people say. Apart from the fact that when I crawled ashore I realised it wasn't Olsen's boathouse I had seen, but possibly the owner of the seine net. I hadn't gone far out, but it just shows how easy it is to lose your way completely. My shoes squelching, I made my way through a stand of trees towards the highway, and from there back to Olsen's cabin.

I sat hiding behind a tree when Carl eventually arrived in the Volvo.

'You're soaking wet!' he exclaimed, as though this was the most surprising thing he'd experienced all evening.

'I've got dry clothes at the workshop,' I tried to say, but my teeth were chattering like a two-stroke East German Wartburg 353. 'Drive.'

Fifteen minutes later I was dry and wearing two pairs of overalls, one on top of the other, and my body was still shivering. We backed the Volvo into the workshop, closed the door and got the body out of the boot and onto the floor, where we sat him on his back in an X position. I looked at him. Something seemed to be missing from him, something he had had during our fishing trip. Maybe it was that mop of hair. Or the boots. Or was it something else? I don't believe in souls, but there was definitely something, something that had made Olsen Olsen.

I drove the Volvo out again and parked it in a clearly visible spot outside the workshop. The task that lay ahead of us was a purely practical, technical business, something for which we needed neither luck nor inspiration but only the correct tools. And if there was something we had here, it was tools. There's no need for me to go into detail about what we used where, only to say that we first removed Olsen's belt and then cut off his clothes, and after that all his bodily parts. Or rather, I did. Carl was carsick again. I went through Olsen's pockets and removed everything metal; coins, belt and buckle, and the Zippo lighter. I'd chuck them into the lake when I got the chance. Then I loaded all the body parts and the mane of hair in the scoop of the tractor Uncle Bernard used for clearing snow in winter. When I was done I fetched six metal drums of Fritz heavy-duty workshop cleaner.

'What's that?' asked Carl.

'Something we use when we clean out the car wash,' I said. 'It gets rid of everything, diesel, asphalt, it even dissolves plaster. We dilute it, five litres of water per decilitre of this. Which is to say, if you don't dilute it then it will get rid of absolutely **everything.**'

'You **know** that?'

'Uncle Bernard told me. Or in his exact words: "Get it on your finger and if you don't wash it off immediately, you can say goodbye to that finger."'

I told him that to lighten the atmosphere a bit, but

Carl couldn't even raise a smile. As though all of this was **my** fault. I didn't pursue the thought, because I knew that it would end up with me thinking that it really **was** my fault, that it always had been.

'Anyway,' I said, 'I guess that's the reason it comes in metal drums and not plastic.'

We taped rags over our mouths and noses, removed the stoppers from the drums and emptied them into the scoop, one after another, until the grey-white liquid had completely covered Sigmund Olsen's dismembered body.

Then we waited.

Nothing happened.

'Shouldn't we turn off the light?' Carl asked from behind his cleaning cloth. 'Someone might come in to say hello.'

'Nope,' I said. 'They can see that's my car outside, not Uncle Bernard's. And I'm not exactly—'

'Yeah yeah,' Carl interrupted, so there was no need for me to go on. **Not exactly the kind of guy people stop by to have a chat with.**

Another few minutes passed. I tried to keep still so the overalls were in minimal contact with my crown jewels, as people say. I don't really know what I had imagined would happen in the scoop, but whatever it was it didn't. Was the Fritz overhyped?

'Maybe we should bury him instead?' said Carl, coughing.

I shook my head. 'Too many dogs, badgers and foxes round here, they'd dig him up.'

It was true, foxes in the cemetery had dug holes all the way into the Bonaker family grave.

'Hey, Roy?'

'Mmm?'

'If Olsen had still been alive when you got down there in Huken . . .'

I knew he was going to ask me that, and I wished he wouldn't.

'. . . what would you have done?'

'That depends,' I said, trying to resist the temptation to scratch my balls, because I'd realised I was wearing Uncle Bernard's overalls on the inside.

'Like with Dog?' Carl asked.

I thought about it.

'If he'd survived then at least he'd have been able to tell people it was an accident,' I said.

Carl nodded. Moved his weight from one foot to the other. 'But when I said that Olsen just, that's not quite—'

'Shh,' I said.

There was a low, sizzling sound, like an egg in a frying pan. We peered into the scoop. The grey-white was now whiter, you could no longer see the body parts, and bubbles were floating on the surface.

'Check it out,' I said. 'Fritz is playing.'

'So what happened after that?' asked Shannon. 'Did the whole body dissolve?'

'Yep,' I said.

'But not that night,' said Carl. 'Not the bones.'

227

'So then what did you do?'

I took a deep breath. The moon had risen over the mountain ridge and peered down on the three of us sitting on the bonnet of the Cadillac on Geitesvingen. An unusually warm breeze was blowing in from the south-east, a foehn wind that I liked to imagine had come all the way from Thailand and those other countries down there I've never been to and never will.

'We waited until just before daylight,' I said. 'Then we drove the tractor over to the car wash and emptied the scoop. A few bones and fleshy fibres got caught on the grate so we chucked them back into the scoop and doused them with more Fritz. Then we parked the tractor at the back of the workshop and raised the scoop to its top position.' I illustrated this by raising both hands over my head. 'In case any passers-by might be tempted to take a look inside. Two days later I emptied it into the car wash too.'

'What about Uncle Bernard?' asked Shannon. 'Didn't he ask questions?'

I shrugged. 'He wondered why I'd moved the tractor and I told him I'd had three calls from people who wanted their cars repaired at the same time, so we needed the room. That none of the three showed up was weird, of course, but it does happen. He was more bothered that I hadn't managed to finish work on Willumsen's Toyota.'

'Well, you'd been too busy,' said Carl. 'Anyway, like

228

everyone else, he was more concerned by the fact that the sheriff had drowned himself. They'd found his boat with the boots in and were searching for the body – but I told you all this already.'

'Yes, but not in such detail,' said Shannon.

'I guess Roy remembers it better than me.'

'And that was it?' asked Shannon. 'You were the last people to see him alive; weren't you questioned?'

'Oh yes,' I said. 'A short conversation with the sheriff from the neighbouring district. We told him the truth, which was that Olsen asked us how we were doing after the accident, because he was such a considerate man. Although, actually, I said he **is** a considerate man, acting as though I was presuming he was still alive, even though everyone realised he must have drowned himself. A witness who owned a cabin out that way thought he'd heard Olsen's car arrive after dark, the boat starting, and shortly afterwards something that might have been a splash. He had a quick look himself, in the lake in front of the boathouse. But without . . . finding anything.'

'They weren't surprised they never found the body?' said Shannon.

I shook my head. 'People seem to think that bodies in the sea always turn up sooner or later. Float to the surface, wash ashore, get spotted by someone. Those are the exceptions. As a rule they're gone forever.'

'So what might his son know that we don't know he knows?' Shannon – who was sitting on the bonnet between us – turned, first to me, then to Carl.

'Probably nothing,' said Carl. 'There are no loose ends. At least nothing that hasn't been washed away by the rain and the frost and the passage of time. I think it's just that he's the same as his father, he's got this one unsolved case in particular he can't let go of. For his father it was the Cadillac down there, and for Kurt it's his own father disappearing without leaving any message. So he starts looking for answers that don't exist. Am I right, Roy?'

'Maybe, although I haven't noticed him sniffing around this case before, so why start now?'

'Maybe because I've come home,' said Carl. 'The last person to see his dad. The guy he was once in the same class with, a nobody from Opgard farm but it says in the local paper that he's done well in Canada and now he thinks he's going to come back and rescue the village. Put it this way, I'm big game, and he's the hunter. But he's got no ammunition, just a gut feeling that there's something that doesn't add up about his father driving away after a meeting with me and vanishing straight away. So when I come back home it starts him thinking again. The years have passed, he's got a distance on things now, his head is cool, he can think more clearly. He starts guessing. If his father didn't end up in the lake, then where did he end up? In Huken, he thinks.'

'Maybe,' I said. 'But he's on to something. There's a reason he's so determined to get down there. And sooner or later he will.'

'Didn't you say Erik Nerell would be telling him not to, because of the risk from loose rocks?' asked Carl.

'Yes, but when I asked Olsen about that he said **we'll see** in a cocky sort of way. I think he's thought of another way to do it, but what's even more important is: what the fuck is he looking for?'

'He thinks the body is in the perfect hiding place,' said Shannon, her eyes closed, her face turned to the moon as though she were sunbathing. 'He thinks we've put it in the boot of the wreck down there.'

I studied her from the side. Something about the moonlight on her face made it impossible to take your eyes off her. Did something like that happen to Erik Nerell when he was ogling her at the party? No, all he saw was a woman he wouldn't mind having it away with. What I saw was . . . well, what did I see? A bird unlike any other I had ever seen in the mountains. Shannon Alleyne Opgard belonged to the Sylviidae family. Like Shannon, they are small, some smaller even than the hummingbird, and they're quick to pick up the songs of other species which they immediately imitate. They're highly adaptable, some even change their feathers and colouring to merge better with their surroundings when the dangers of winter approach. When Shannon included herself, when she said in that very natural way that **we** had put the body there, it seemed so completely right. She had adapted to the new territory she found herself in without feeling that she had had to renounce anything. She had called me brother without even hesitating or trying the word out first. Because now we were her family.

'Exactly!' said Carl. It was a word he had picked up and obviously fallen in love with while he'd been away. 'And if Kurt believes that, then we ought to make it easy for him to get down there and see for himself how wrong he is, so that gets that out the way. We've got a business proposal that needs financing, we need the whole village behind us. We can't afford to have any kind of suspicion hanging over us.'

'Maybe,' I said, and scratched my cheek. Not because it was itching, but now and then that kind of distraction can make you think something you haven't thought before, and that was the feeling I got then. That there was something here that hadn't occurred to me. 'But I really wish I knew exactly what he was going to be looking for down there.'

'Ask him?' suggested Carl.

I shook my head. 'When Kurt Olsen and Erik Nerell were here, Kurt lied and made out it was about the accident, not about his father. So there's no way Kurt Olsen's going to show us his hand.'

We sat in silence. The bonnet beneath had gone cold.

'Maybe this Erik has seen his cards,' said Shannon. 'Maybe he could tell us.'

We looked at her. Her eyes were still closed.

'Why would he do that?' I asked.

'Because it'll be better for him than if he doesn't tell us.'

'Oh yeah?'

She turned to me, opened her eyes and smiled. Her moist teeth shone in the moonlight. Of course I didn't know what she had in mind, but I did know that she was like my father and followed the law of nature that says family comes first. Before right and wrong. Before the rest of all mankind. That it's always us against the rest.

16

NEXT DAY THE WIND HAD SHIFTED.

When I got up and went downstairs to the kitchen, Shannon was standing beside the wood stove with her arms folded and wearing one of my old woollen sweaters. It looked comically oversized on her, and it occurred to me she must have run out of her own polo-neck 'artist's' pullovers.

'Good morning,' she said. Her lips were pale.

'You're up early.' I nodded towards the sheets of paper on the kitchen table. 'How's the drawing going?'

'So-so,' she said, took two paces forward and picked them up before I could take a look. 'But doing mediocre work is better than lying in bed and not being able to sleep.' She put the paper into a folder and went back to the stove again. 'Tell me, is this normal?'

'Normal?'

'For the time of year.'

'The temperature? Yes.'

'But yesterday . . .'

'. . . was normal too,' I said, crossing to the window and peering up at the sky. 'I mean, it's normal for it to change so quickly. Up here in the mountains.'

She nodded. Seemed to have got used to that one word 'mountain' as being the explanation for most things. I noticed the coffee pot halfway over the hotplate.

'Fresh and good,' she said.

I poured myself a cup, looked at her, but she shook her head.

'I've been thinking about Erik Nerell,' she said. 'He's got a girlfriend who's pregnant, right?'

'Yes,' I said, and drank. Good. That is, objectively speaking I knew it wasn't good, but it was exactly how I liked it. Unless we shared the same taste in coffee, she must have been watching as I made mine. 'I don't think there's any pressing need to get anything out of him right now.'

'Oh?' she said.

'Looks like snow on the way.'

'Snow?' She looked at me in disbelief. 'In September?'

'If we're lucky.'

She nodded slowly. An intelligent girl who didn't need to ask why. Whatever the hell Kurt Olsen was thinking of doing down in Huken, snow would make

the job of getting down there safely and possibly finding something much more difficult.

'But it could disappear again,' she said. 'Things
change so quickly here . . .' She gave me a sleepy
smile. 'Up here in the mountains.'

I chuckled. 'I thought it could get cold in
Toronto too?'

'In the house where we lived you didn't notice the
cold until you went outside.'

'It gets better,' I said. 'Days like this are the worst,
when the wind blows from the north and the first
frost is on the bare ground. It gets milder when the
winter comes and there's more snow. It takes a few
days after we start having a fire before the heat pen-
etrates the walls.'

'So until then,' she said – and now I could see she
was shivering – 'we just freeze?'

I smiled and put my mug of coffee on the worktop.
'I'll help you get warm,' I said, and walked towards
her. Her eyes met mine, she gave a start and crossed her
arms even more firmly across her narrow chest, a
blush spreading like tongues of fire across her white
cheeks. I bent down in front of her, opened the door
of the wood stove and saw that, sure enough, the
fire was going out because the logs were too big and
there were too many of them. I pulled the largest out
with my hand, put it on the base plate in front of
the stove where it lay smouldering, used the bellows
and by the time I closed the door again the fire was
burning brightly.

Carl came in as I stood up. He was half dressed, hair sticking up all over the place. He was holding his phone in his hand and grinning broadly.

'The order of business for the council meeting's been announced. We're number one on the agenda.'

At the station I told Markus to put the lightweight snow shovels on display, along with the ice scrapers and the bottles of antifreeze I'd ordered in a couple of weeks ago.

I read the **Os Daily,** which had dedicated most of its front page to the council elections due next year, but at least there was a reference to something inside about the investors' meeting at Årtun. And there we had a whole page, with a few lines of text and two big pictures. One showed the packed meeting hall, the other Carl posing with a grin and one arm around the shoulder of the former chairman Jo Aas, who looked slightly nonplussed, like a man taken by surprise. Dan Krane's editorial mentioned the new spa hotel, but it was hard to tell whether he was for or against. Or rather, it wasn't hard to see that deep down he wanted to trash the entire business, as when he quoted an un-named source who referred to it as the 'spa-nic hotel', something people were clinging to in hopes of saving the village. I guessed that source was Krane himself, but he was obviously in a dilemma. If he was too positive it would seem as though he was using the local paper to back his own father-in-law. Too negative and people might accuse him of wanting to get one over

237

on his wife's former boyfriend. Being a journalist on a local paper is a tough balancing act, I guess.

At nine o'clock a light drizzle started falling. I could see it was falling as snow up on Geitesvingen.

At eleven o'clock it started falling as snow in the village too.

At twelve o'clock the head of sales walked in through the door.

'Ready for all eventualities as usual,' he grinned, once I had finished serving a customer who headed out with one of my shovels in his hand.

'We live in Norway,' I said.

'We've got an offer for you,' he said, and I supposed it was yet another sales campaign he was about to force onto us. Nothing at all wrong with the campaigns, eight out of ten of them work well, so the people at head office know their business. But sometimes those countrywide special offers of a parasol and volleyball or some exotic type of Spanish sausage with a Pepsi Max are a little bit too generalised. Local knowledge of local needs and likes matters too.

'You're going to get a call from one of the bosses,' said the head of sales.

'Oh?'

'One of the bigger stations down in Sørlandet is struggling a bit. Good location with modern facilities, but the station boss hasn't managed to get things moving down there. He doesn't follow up on the campaigns, doesn't report when and how he should, his staff aren't motivated, and . . . well, you know. They need someone who can turn it round. It's not part of my job, I'm just giving you a heads-up since I'm the one who suggested they have a word with you.' He spread his arms as if to say it was nothing, from which I realised he was expecting an expansive display of gratitude.

'Thanks,' I said.

He smiled, waiting. Maybe he thought I owed it to him to tell him what my answer would be.

'That's pretty sudden,' I said. 'I'll hear what they have to say and give it some thought.'

'You'll give it **some** thought?' The head of sales laughed. 'This is something you should be giving a **lot** of thought to. An offer like this doesn't just mean more money, Roy, it's a chance to show what you can do on the big stage.'

If he was trying to get me take the job so he would look like some kind of small-town **kingmaker** he'd made a bad choice of metaphor, as people say. But of course, he wasn't to know that the mere thought of appearing on any stage, big or small, was enough to make my palms sweat.

'There will be thinking,' I said. 'How about a cheeseburger campaign? What d'you think?'

At one o'clock Julie came in.

There was no one in the station and she came straight up and kissed me on the cheek. Deliberately, kept her lips soft, left them there a little too long. I don't know what perfume she had on, only that there was too much of it.

'Yes, and?' I said as she let me go and looked up at me.

'Just had to try out my new lipstick,' she said, wiping my cheek. 'I'm meeting Alex after work.'

'Granada-Alex? You're checking how much lipstick is left after a kiss?

'No, how much feeling you lose in the lips with lipstick. Like you men and condoms, more or less, right?'

I didn't answer. This was a conversation I didn't want to be having.

'Alex is actually quite sweet,' said Julie. She put her head on one side and studied me. 'Maybe we'll do more than just kiss.'

'Lucky Alex,' I said as I pulled on my jacket. 'You going to be all right alone?'

'Alone?' I saw the disappointment in her face. 'Aren't we going to—'

'Sure, and I'll be back in an hour at most. OK?'

The disappointment vanished. Then a wrinkle appeared in her forehead. 'The shops are closed. Is it a woman?'

I smiled. 'Call if there's anything.'

I drove through the village and then turned in along Lake Budal. The snow was gone the moment it hit the road and the fields down here, but I could see it lying higher up on the hills. I looked at my watch. The chances of finding an unemployed roofer at home and on his own at one o'clock on a normal working day should be pretty high. I yawned. Had slept badly.

Lain awake listening out for sounds from their bedroom. There were none, which made it almost worse, since it made me listen out even more intently, made me feel tense.

Driving up to the roofer's I noticed there was at least a hundred metres of cultivated land between his white house and the nearest neighbour.

Anton Moe had probably heard and seen the car coming. He opened the door seconds after I rang the bell, his wispy hair blowing about in the wind. He looked at me quizzically.

'Can I come in?' I asked.

Moe hesitated, maybe thinking up some excuse to say no, then stepped aside to let me in.

'Keep your shoes on,' he said.

We sat down opposite each other at the kitchen table. On the wall above were a couple of framed embroideries with verses from the Bible and a cross. He could see that I had noticed the full pot of coffee standing on the worktop.

'Some coffee?'

'No thanks.'

'If you're looking for people to invest in your brother's hotel I can save you the bother. Not much cash flowing here at the moment.' Moe smiled sheepishly.

'It's about your daughter.'

'Oh yeah?'

I looked at a little hammer lying on the windowsill. 'She's sixteen years old and she attends Årtun secondary school, right?'

'That's right.'

There was an inscription on the hammer. **Roofer of the Year 2017.**

'I want her to move away and start at Notodden secondary,' I said.

Moe looked at me in amazement. 'Why is that?'

'The courses they offer there are more oriented to the future.'

He looked at me. 'What exactly do you mean, Opgard?'

'I mean that that's what you should say to Natalie when you tell her why you're sending her there, that the courses are more oriented towards the future.'

'Notodden? It's two hours' drive away.'

His face showed nothing, but I guess it was dawning on him. 'It's good of you to concern yourself with Natalie's welfare, Opgard, but I think Årtun is fine. She's in her second year there already. Notodden is a big place, and bad things can happen in big places, you know.'

I coughed. 'What I mean is, Notodden is best for all concerned.'

'All?'

I took a deep breath. 'Your daughter can go to bed each night without worrying about whether her father will be coming in to fuck her. You can go to bed without degrading your daughter, your family and yourself night after night, so that at some point in the future you might perhaps all be able to forget about it and pretend it never happened.'

Anton Moe stared at me, his face blazing, his eyes looking as though they were about to explode. 'What are you talking about, Opgard? Are you drunk?'

'I'm talking about shame,' I said. 'The sum total of shame in your family. Because everyone knows and no one's done anything, everyone thinks part of the blame is on them, that it's all lost already so there's nothing to lose by allowing it to continue. Because when all is lost, one thing at least remains. The family. Each other.'

'You're sick, man!' He had raised his voice, and yet it sounded thinner and diminished. He stood up. 'I think you better leave now, Opgard.'

I stayed seated. 'I can go into your daughter's bedroom, pull off the sheet and hand it over to the sheriff to check for sperm stains and whether they're yours. You won't be able to stop me, but I'm guessing that won't matter, because your daughter won't help the police by being a witness against you, she'll want to help her father. Always, no matter what. So the only way to put a stop to this is . . .' I paused, looked up, caught his eyes. 'Because we all want to put a stop to this, don't we?'

He didn't respond, just stood staring at me, a cold, dead look in his eyes.

'This is another way; I'll kill you if Natalie doesn't move to Notodden. She'll spend her weekends there and you will not visit her. Her mother, yes, but not you. Not one single visit. When Natalie is at home for Christmas you will invite your own parents or your in-laws to celebrate and stay with you.' I smoothed my hand over a crease in the gingham check cloth on the table. 'Questions?'

A fly buzzed and buzzed against the windowpane.

'How would you propose killing me?'

'By smiting you, I was thinking. That's probably appropriately . . .' I smacked my lips. **Mind games.** '. . . appropriately biblical?'

'Well, you certainly had a reputation for hitting people.'

'Are we agreed, Moe?'

'You see that Bible verse up there, Opgard?' He pointed to one of the embroideries above us and I spelled my way through its convoluted lettering. **The lord is my shepherd. I shall not want.**

I heard a soft thump and howled as the pain ran up my arm from my right hand. Moe was holding the Roofer of the Year hammer aloft ready to bring it down again and I just about managed to withdraw my left hand before the hammer struck the table. My right hand was so painful that I felt dizzy as I rose, but I used my speed to throw a left uppercut. I struck his chin, but with the table between us the angle was too great for me to get enough power in the blow. He swung the hammer at my head and I ducked and stepped away. He came rushing towards me, the table legs scraped and chairs went flying. I feinted, he fell for it and my left fist met his nose. He howled, swung the hammer again. He might have been Roofer of the Year back in 2017, but he messed up this time. I moved in close to his body while he was still off balance and used my left to deliver three quick punches to his right kidney. I heard him gasp with pain and when I followed up by lifting my foot and bringing it down hard on his knee I felt something snap and give and I knew that he was finished. He collapsed to the floor, then whipped round on the grey linoleum and fastened his arms around my legs. I tried to stay upright by holding on to the cooker with my right hand, but realised Moe's hammer must have damaged something there, I couldn't get a purchase. I fell onto my back and moments later Moe was on top of me, his knees holding my arms and the handle of the hammer pressed across my larynx. In vain I gasped for air, could feel myself blacking out. His head was right next to mine and he hissed into my ear:

'Who do you think you are, coming into my house, threatening me and mine? I'll tell you who you are, you filthy mountaintop heathen.'

He gave a low laugh and leaned forward so that the weight of his body pressed the last of the air out of my lungs and I felt the onset of a delicious dizziness, like the moment before you fall asleep in the back seat, entangled in the soft, sleeping body of your little brother, you see stars in the sky through the rear window and your parents are talking and laughing in low voices in front of you. And you let go, let yourself tumble backwards into yourself. I could feel coffee and cigarette breath on my face, and spittle.

'You're a bow-legged, dyslexic, goat-fucking queer,' Moe hissed.

Like that, I thought. That's the way he talks to her.

I tensed my stomach muscles, made a bridge of my back, tensed again and then swung. Hit something, usually it would be the nose, but whatever it was, it was enough to relieve the pressure on my larynx for a moment and I was able to drag enough air into my lungs to fill the rest of my musculature with oxygen. I jerked my left hand free of his knee and hit him hard in the ear. He lost his balance, I tipped him off me and hit out again with my left. And again. And again.

By the time I was done a little stream of blood was running from Moe's nose as he crouched there in a foetal position on the linoleum. The blood stopped as it reached the seat of one of the upended chairs.

I leaned over him, and I don't know whether he heard me, but anyway I whispered it into his bloodied ear:

'I am not fucking bow-legged.'

'The bad news is that the inner joint is probably shattered,' said Stanley Spind from behind his desk. 'The good news is that your blood alcohol test from the other day gave a reading of zero.'

'Shattered?' I said and looked down at my middle finger. It was sticking out at a strange angle and had swollen to twice its normal size. The skin was split, and where it wasn't it had assumed a darkly livid colour that made me think of the plague. 'You sure?'

'Yes. But I'll write you a referral so you can have it X-rayed at the hospital in town.'

'Why should I, if you're so sure?'

Stanley shrugged. 'You'll probably need an operation.'

'And if I don't . . . ?'

'Then I can guarantee you'll never be able to move that finger again.'

'And with the operation?'

'In all probability you'll never be able to move that finger again.'

I looked at the finger. Not good. But obviously much worse if I'd still been working as a mechanic.

'Thanks,' I said and stood up.

'Wait, we're not finished,' said Stanley, moving his roller chair over to a bench with a paper sheet covering it. 'Sit here. That finger is out of position, we need to repone it.'

'What does that mean?'

'Straighten it.'

'Sounds painful.'

'You'll have a local anaesthetic.'

'Still sounds painful.'

Stanley gave a crooked smile.

'On a scale of one to ten?' I asked.

'A stiff eight,' said Stanley.

I smiled back at him.

After he'd given me the injection he told me it would take a few minutes for the injection to take effect. We sat in silence, something which he seemed more comfortable with than me. The silence went on building until it became deafening, and finally I pointed to the headphones on his desk and asked what he liked to listen to.

'Audio books,' he said. 'Anything by Chuck Palahniuk. Have you seen **Fight Club**?'

'No. What's so good about him?'

'I didn't say he was that good.' Stanley smiled. 'But he thinks like me. And manages to express it. Are you ready?'

'Palahniuk,' I repeated and held out my hand. His gaze met mine.

'Just for the record, I don't buy that explanation about slipping on the fresh snow and trying to break your fall,' said Stanley.

'OK,' I said.

I could feel him place a warm hand around my finger. And there was me hoping it would be completely anaesthetised.

'And speaking of **Fight Club,**' he said as he started pulling, 'it looks to me as though you've come straight from a club meeting.'

A stiff eight was no exaggeration.

On my way out of the surgery I passed Mari Aas in the waiting room.

'Hi, Roy,' she said. She was smiling that superior smile of hers, but I could see she was blushing. This business of using a person's name when you say hello was something she and Carl had started doing when they were going out together. Carl had read about a research project which concluded that people's positive response increased by forty per cent without their realising it when researchers used their names in addressing them. I hadn't been part of that research project.

'Hi,' I said, keeping my hand behind my back. 'Early for snow.' See, that's the way you say hello to someone else from your village.

Back in the car I wondered how I was going to turn on the ignition without using the bandaged and throbbing finger, and why Mari had blushed back there in the surgery. Was there something wrong with her she was ashamed of? Or was she ashamed of the fact that there was anything at all wrong with her? Because Mari wasn't a blusher. When she and Carl were together, I was the one who blushed if she appeared unexpectedly in front of me. Although actually, yes, I had seen her blush a couple of times. Once was after Carl had bought a necklace for her birthday. Even though it wasn't flashy, Mari knew Carl was completely penniless and forced him to admit that he had stolen two hundred kroner from the drawer in Uncle Bernard's desk. I knew about it of course, and when Uncle Bernard complimented Mari on her nice necklace, I'd seen Mari blush so fiercely I was afraid she might burst a blood vessel. Maybe she was the same as me in that regard, that stuff like that – a minor theft, a trivial rejection – you never get over. They're like lumps in the body that get encapsulated but can still ache on cold days, and some nights suddenly begin to throb. You can be a hundred years old and still feel the blush of shame washing up into your cheeks.

Julie said she felt sorry for me, that Dr Spind should have given me some stronger painkiller, and that business about Alex was just something she'd made up, she wasn't really meeting anyone and certainly not going to let anyone kiss her. I only half listened. My hand was throbbing and I should have gone home, but I knew that all I could expect there was more pain.

Julie leaned into me as she studied my bandaged finger with a concerned expression on her face. I could feel her soft chest against my upper arm and sweet, bubblegum breath on my face. Her mouth was so close to my ear that her chewing sounds were like a cow grazing in a bog.

'You didn't start to feel just a little jealous?' she whispered with all the sly innocence of which a seventeen-year-old is capable.

'Start to?' I said. 'Listen, I've been jealous since I was five years old.'

She laughed as though I was joking, and I forced a smile to confirm that I was.

17

MAYBE I'D BEEN JEALOUS OF Carl since the day
of his birth. Maybe even before that, maybe when I
saw my mother tenderly stroking her swollen stomach and saying that a brother was on the way. But I
was five years old the first time I can remember being
confronted by jealousy, when someone gave a name
to this painful, jabbing sensation. 'Don't be jealous of
your little brother.' I think it was Mum who said that,
with Carl sitting on her lap. He'd been sitting there a
long time. Mum said later that Carl was given more
love because he needed more love. Maybe so, but she
didn't say the other thing she could have said, that
Carl was easier to love.

And I was the one who loved him most of all.

That's why I was jealous not just of the unconditional love people around him showed him, but also of those Carl showed love for. Like Dog.

Like the boy whose family rented a cabin here one summer, who was as good-looking as Carl, and whom Carl hung out with morning, noon and night, while I counted the days until the summer was over.

Like Mari.

During the first months they were together I used to fantasise about Mari having an accident, and that I was the one who had to comfort Carl. I don't know exactly when it was that jealousy turned into love, or if it ever did, maybe the two feelings existed side by side, but at any rate it was love that drowned everything else out. It was like some terrible sickness. I couldn't eat, sleep or concentrate on a normal conversation.

I both dreaded and longed for her visits to see Carl, blushed when she gave me a hug or suddenly spoke to me without any warning or looked at me. Naturally I felt deeply ashamed of my feelings, of not being able to let go of them and being grateful for any small crumbs, of sitting in the same room as them, trying to justify my presence by pretending to be what I wasn't, such as amusing, or interesting. In the end I found my role. It was to be the silent one, the one who listened, who laughed at Carl's jokes or nodded slowly at something Mari had read, or heard her father, the chairman, say. I drove them to parties where Carl got drunk and Mari did what she could to make sure he behaved. When Mari asked if I thought it was boring always to be sober I said it was fine, I liked driving cars better than drinking alcohol, and sometimes Carl needed two to look out for him, right? She smiled and didn't ask me again. I think she understood. I think everyone understood. Everyone but Carl.

'Of course Roy must come with us!' he would say whenever there was talk of going skiing, or a party in town at the weekend, or riding Aas's old nags. He didn't give a reason, his happy, open face was argument enough. It said that the world was a good place, with only good people living in it, and everyone should be happy just to be there.

Naturally, I never made a move, as people say. I wasn't stupid enough to think that Mari saw in me anything other than a rather silent but self-sacrificing big brother who was always ready to help them out.

But then one Saturday evening at the village hall Grete came over and told me Mari was in love with me. Carl was in bed at home with the flu I'd had the week before, so I had no driving duties and I'd drunk some of the home brew Erik Nerell always brought with him. Grete was drunk too, and it was dancing in her eyes, that evil witch's dance. And I knew she was just shit-stirring, trying to fuck things up a bit, because I knew her and I'd seen the way she looked at Carl. All the same, it was like when Armand the preacher in his dance-band Swedish accent boomed out that our redeemer liveth, and there is life after death. If someone says something that is clearly unlikely but that you desperately want to hear, there's a small part of you – the weak part – that chooses to believe it.

I saw Mari standing over by the entrance. She was talking to a boy, not someone from the village, because boys from round here were too afraid of Mari to come on to her. Not because she was Carl's girl, but because they knew she was smarter than them, looked down on them, and that when she spurned them it would be very obvious, and in front of everyone, since everyone in Årtun kept half an eye on anything the daughter of the council chairman did.

But it was OK for me, Carl's brother, to approach her. OK for me and her at least.

'Hi, Roy.' She smiled. 'This is Otto. He's studying political science in Oslo. He thinks I should do the same.'

I looked at Otto. He lifted a beer bottle to his lips and was looking off in another direction, probably not wanting me to join the conversation, wanting me to get lost as quickly as possible. I had to struggle not to thump the bottom of his bottle. I concentrated on Mari. I wet my lips.

'Shall we dance?'

She looked at me in mildly amused surprise. 'But you don't dance, Roy.'

I shrugged. 'I can learn.' I was obviously drunker than I had thought.

Mari laughed loudly and shook her head. 'Not from me. I need a dancing teacher myself.'

'I can help there,' said Otto. 'I actually teach swing in my spare time.'

'Yes please!' said Mari. She gave him that radiant smile she could turn on just like that, the one that made you feel like you were the only other person in the world. 'As long as you're not afraid of people laughing.'

Otto smiled. 'Oh, I don't think it'll look that bad,' he said, putting his beer bottle down on the step and making me wish I'd shoved it into his mouth when I had the chance.

'Now that's what I call a brave man,' said Mari, laying a hand on his shoulder. 'Is that OK with you, Roy?'

'Yeah, sure,' I said, looking round for a wall I could butt my head against.

'So **two** brave men then,' said Mari, putting her other hand on my shoulder. 'Teacher and pupil, I'm going to enjoy seeing the two of you on the dance floor together.'

And with that she left, and it was a couple of seconds before I understood what had happened. This Otto guy and me were left standing there looking at each other.

'Would you rather fight?' I asked.

'Of course,' he said. He rolled his eyes, picked up his beer bottle and moved off.

Fair enough, I was too drunk anyway, but the headache and hangover guilt when I woke up next morning were worse than any beating Otto could have given me. Carl coughed and laughed and coughed again when I told him what had happened, leaving out the bit about what Grete had said.

'You are absolutely the fucking tops! You'll even **dance** to keep those other jerks away from your brother's girl.'

I grunted. 'Only with Mari, not with that Otto guy.'

'All the same, let me give you a big kiss!'

I pushed him off. 'No thanks – don't want flu again.'

I didn't have an especially guilty conscience about not telling Carl how I felt about Mari. Mostly I was amazed he hadn't realised it himself. I could have told him everything. I could have, and he would have understood. At any rate **said** he understood. Put his head on one side, given me a thoughtful look and said things like that happen, things like that pass. I knew that, and that was why I kept my mouth shut and waited for it to pass. I never asked Mari to dance again, neither metaphorically nor literally.

But Mari asked me.

It happened a few months after Grete had told Mari about her and Carl having it away, and Mari had dumped Carl. Carl had gone to Minnesota to study, and I was living alone on the farm. One day there was a knock on the door. It was Mari. She gave me a hug, pushing her breasts against my chest, wouldn't let me go and asked if I wanted to sleep with her. 'Will you sleep with me?' were the words she whispered in my ear. And then added 'Roy'. Hardly because of the research that shows that using a person's name puts them in a more receptive frame of mind, but more to emphasise that it was me, Roy, she meant.

'I know you want to,' she said when she noticed my hesitation. 'I've known it all along, Roy.'

'No,' I said. 'You're mistaken.'

'Don't lie,' she said, slipping her hand down between us.

I pulled myself away from her. Of course I knew why she'd come. Even though she was the one who had broken with Carl, she was the one who felt scorned. Maybe she didn't even really want to break up but felt she had no choice. Because of course Mari Aas, the chairman's daughter, couldn't live with the fact that the son of a mountain farmer had been unfaithful to her, not when Grete had made sure half the village knew about it. But just to send Carl packing, as people say, wasn't enough. The balance had to be restored. The fact that two months had passed indicated that she'd reached her decision reluctantly. In other words, if we went to bed together now it wouldn't be a case of me exploiting a woman in a vulnerable situation after a break-up; she would be the one exploiting a brother who had just been abandoned by the person he loved most of all.

'Come on,' she said. 'Let me help you.'

I shook my head. 'It isn't you, Mari.'

She stopped in the middle of the floor and stared at me in disbelief. 'So then it's true?'

'What's true?'

'What people say.'

'Damned if I know what they say.'

'That you're not interested in girls. That the only things on your mind are . . .' She paused. Pretended to be looking for the right words. And then Mari Aas found them: '. . . are cars and birds,' she said.

'I mean that the problem isn't you, Mari. It's Carl. I just don't think it would be right.'

'Correct. It wouldn't be.'

Now I saw it too, that condescending contempt people down in the village thought she viewed them with. But there was something else, as though she knew something she wasn't supposed to know. What had Carl said?

'Better find some other way to take your revenge,' I said. 'Ask Grete for advice. She's good on stuff like that.'

And then Mari blushed, and this time she really was lost for words. She marched out and got into her car, gravel flying behind her as she sped down towards Geitesvingen.

When I saw her in town a few days later she blushed again and pretended not to see me. It happened several times – in a village like ours it's impossible not to bump into people. But time passed, Mari went to Oslo and studied political science, and when she came back we were able to speak to each other almost like before. Almost. Because we had lost each other. She knew what I knew, that, for her, this was like a cancerous lump inside her body: not that I had rejected her, but that I had **seen** her. Seen her naked. Naked and ugly.

As for cancerous lumps of my own, there was probably still one there with Mari's name on, but it had stopped growing. I'd waited out that crush. It's funny, but I stopped being in love with Mari at almost exactly the same time it was over between her and Carl.

18

TWO DAYS AFTER MY VISIT to Moe the roofer, head office called and offered me the station down in Sørlandet. They sounded disappointed when I said no thanks. They asked for a reason, so I gave them one. I said the station I was running faced some interesting challenges now that the main highway was being rerouted, and that I looked forward to getting to grips with them. They sounded impressed and said it was a pity, they really believed I was the man they needed down there.

Later that day Kurt Olsen called in at the station.

He stood, legs apart, in front of the counter, drew his index finger and thumb over his **Easy Rider** moustache and waited until I had finished serving a customer and the shop was empty.

'Anton Moe has reported you for grievous bodily harm.'

'That's a cute choice of phrase,' I said.

'Maybe,' said Olsen. 'He told me about the accusations you made, and I've had a chat with Natalie. She confirms that her father has never touched her.'

'What did you expect? That she'd say yes, since you ask, my father is actually screwing me?'

'If it was a question of rape, then I don't doubt—'

'Jesus, I never said it was rape. Not technically. But it's rape all the same, you must surely see that.'

'No.'

'Maybe she thinks she didn't resist enough, that she should have known it was wrong, even if she was only young when it started.'

'Steady on now, you don't know—'

'Listen: kids think everything their parents do is right, OK, but she remembers too that she was told to keep it secret. So perhaps some part of her understood that it wasn't right? And because she's been party to the secrecy, because loyalty to the family comes before loyalty to God and the sheriff, she takes some of the blame herself. When she turns sixteen maybe it makes the burden easier to bear if she persuades herself that she was a willing participant.'

Olsen stroked his moustache. 'Sounds like you've

just done a course in social studies and been living over at Moe's while you did it.'

I didn't answer.

He sighed. 'I can't force a sixteen-year-old to give evidence against her father, you must realise that. On the other hand she's old enough to take responsibility for whatever she says.'

'So what you're saying is, you choose to look the other way because it could be consensual and the girl is no longer legally a minor?'

'No!' Kurt Olsen looked round to make certain we were still alone and lowered his voice again. 'Incest in the direct line of descent is punishable by law, regardless. Moe risks six years in jail even if the girl was thirty and it was all a hundred per cent consensual; but how can I prove anything when no one talks? All that happens if I arrest the father is a scandal that will ruin the lives of all those involved. There would be a massive investment of resources in something that wouldn't lead to a conviction. Plus the village name would be dragged through the mud in the national newspapers.'

You forgot to add that you personally would end up with a very black mark against your name, I thought. But when I looked at Olsen I could see that the despair in his face and voice were genuine.

'So what can you do?' he sighed, opening his arms wide.

'Make sure the girl gets away from her father,' I said. 'By moving to Notodden, for example.'

He turned his gaze away from mine. Fastened it on the newspaper stand, as though there was something of interest there. Nodded slowly.

'In any case, he's lodged a complaint against you, and I need to do something about it, you realise that? The maximum penalty is four years.'

'Four years?'

'His jaw is broken in two places and he risks permanently impaired hearing in one ear.'

'Then he's still got one left. Whisper to him in his good ear that if he drops the summons then at least this business with his daughter won't become public knowledge. I know, and you know, and he knows that the only reason he's taking out this summons is that if he didn't it would look like there was something in what I accuse him of.'

'I understand your logic, Roy, but as the sheriff I can't turn a blind eye to the fact that you've incapacitated another man.'

I shrugged. 'Self-defence. He attacked me with the hammer before I even touched him.'

Olsen gave a short laugh that never reached his eyes. 'And how are you going to get me to believe that? That a Pentecostalist who's never been in trouble before attacks Roy Calvin Opgard, a guy known throughout the village as someone who likes nothing better than a punch-up?'

'By using your head and your eyes.' I placed my hands flat on the counter.

He stared. 'And?'

'I am right-handed. Everyone I've ever had a fight with will tell you, I knocked them out with my right. How come there isn't a scrap of skin on the knuckles of my left, while my right is completely untouched apart from that finger? Explain to Moe how this whole thing is going to look, not just his daughter but the grievous bodily harm, when it emerges that he was the one who attacked me.'

Olsen stroked his moustache intently. Gave a nod. 'I'll have a word with him.'

'Thank you.'

He raised his head and fixed me with his gaze. I saw a flash of anger there. As though with my thank you I was making fun of him. That he wasn't doing it for my sake but his own. Maybe for Natalie's and the village's too, but at any rate, not for me.

'The snow won't last long,' he said.

'No?' I said casually.

'The forecast is for mild weather next week.'

The council meeting started at five o'clock. Before he left, Carl, Shannon and I ate a meal of mountain trout with potatoes, cucumber salad and sour cream which I served in the dining room.

'You're a good cook,' said Shannon as she cleared the table.

'Thanks, but that's actually about as simple as it gets,' I said, listening to the throb of the Cadillac's engine as it faded away.

We sat in the living room where I served our coffees.

'The hotel is first up on the agenda,' I said with a glance at the clock. 'So he'll probably be in action pretty soon. We'll just have to cross our fingers and hope he manages to **klare brasene.**'

'**Klare brasene?**' said Shannon.

'You haven't heard that phrase? It means overcome the difficulties.'

'What are **braser?**'

'No idea. Something maritime. Not my scene.'

'We must have some wine.' Shannon went out to the kitchen and returned with two glasses and a bottle of sparkling wine that Carl had kept in the fridge to cool.

'So, Roy, what **is** your scene?'

'My scene?' I said, watching as she opened the bottle. 'I want my own service station and . . . well, I guess that's actually about it.'

'Wife? Kids?'

'If that's what happens then OK.'

'Why have you never had a girlfriend?'

I shrugged. 'I guess I just don't have what it takes.'

'You mean you don't think you're attractive? Is that what you're saying?'

'I was sort of half joking, but yes.'

'Well then, let me tell you that's not true, Roy. I'm not saying that because I feel sorry for you, but because it's a fact.'

'A fact?' I took the glass she offered me. 'Aren't things like that subjective?'

'Some things are subjective. And the sum attractiveness

of a man is probably more in the eye of the woman doing the looking than is the case the other way round.'

'You think that's unfair?'

'The man is maybe freer because less importance is attached to his appearance, but then more importance is attached to his social status. When women complain about being judged on their looks, men ought to complain about the pressures of status.'

'And if you possess neither beauty nor social status?'

Shannon had kicked off her shoes and drawn her feet up onto the chair. She took a long drink of wine. Seemed to be enjoying herself.

'Just like beauty, status is measured using differing weights and differing scales,' she said. 'A dirt-poor painter who's a genius might have a whole harem of women. Women are attracted to resourceful men, men who stand out from the crowd. If you possess neither beauty nor status then you have to compensate by having charm, or strength of character, humour or some other quality.'

I laughed. 'And that's where I score, is that what you think?'

'Yes,' she said simply. 'Cheers.'

'Cheers and thanksafuckingmillion,' I said and raised my glass. The tiny bubbles fizzed and whispered something to me, though I couldn't hear what they were saying.

'You're welcome.'

'So with Carl, what was it you fell for? The looks,

the status or the charm?' I said, noticing to my surprise that my glass was almost empty.

'The insecurity,' she said. 'The kindness. That's where Carl's beauty lies.'

I raised my right hand to wag a warning index finger but being unable to bend the bandaged middle finger had to use my left instead. 'You can't advance that kind of Darwinian theory of reproduction and at the same time claim to be an exception to it. Insecurity and kindness won't do.'

She smiled and replenished our glasses. 'You're right, of course, but that's what it **felt** like. I know my rational animal brain must have been looking for someone to father my offspring, but what my scatterbrained humanity saw and fell in love with was this vulnerable beauty of a man.'

I shook my head. 'Appearance, status or other compensatory qualities?'

'Let me see,' said Shannon, holding up her glass to the light from the table lamp. 'Appearance.'

I said nothing but nodded and thought of Carl and Grete in the woods. The ominous rubbing of her jacket before it tore. There was another sound there too. A squishing sound. Like a cow in a bog. A soft breast. Julie. I forced the thought away.

'Of course beauty isn't an absolute quality,' said Shannon. 'It's what we, each of us as individuals, say it is. Beauty is always in a context, it's in relation to our previous experiences, everything we've

267

sensed, learned and put together. People in countries all over the world have a tendency to think their own national anthem just happens to be the best in the world, that their mothers are the best cooks, that the most beautiful girl in town is also the most beautiful on the planet, and so on. The first time you come across music that's new and strange you won't like it. That's to say, if it's **really** strange. When people claim to like or even **love** music that's completely new to them, it's because they like the idea of the exotic, it's stimulating, and what's more it gives them the feeling of possessing a sensitivity and a cosmic understanding that is superior to their neighbour's. But what they really like is what they unconsciously recognise. In the course of time that which was once new becomes a part of their experiential basis, and the conditionally learned, the indoctrination into what is lovely and what is beautiful, a part of their aesthetic sense. Early in the twentieth century American films began teaching people all over the world to find beauty in white film stars. And in time black too. Over the last fifty years Asian films have done the same for their stars. Although it's like music, their beauty has to be something the public recognise, an Asian mustn't be too Asiatic, but have a similarity to an established idea of beauty, an ideal which is still white. Seen from that perspective, the word **sense** when used of aesthetics is, at best, imprecise. We are born with vision and hearing, but in aesthetics we all start from a clean sheet. We—'

She stopped abruptly. Smiled fleetingly and raised the wine glass to her lips, as though realising she was lecturing to an audience that was probably not interested. We sat a while in silence. I coughed.

'I read somewhere that everyone, even the most isolated tribes, like symmetry in a face. Doesn't that suggest that some things are congenital?'

Shannon looked at me. A smile glided across her face and she leaned forward in her chair.

'Maybe. On the other hand, the rules governing symmetry are so simple and strict that it's not surprising we share the taste for it all over the world. The same way belief in a higher power is something that's easy to turn to, which makes it universal but not congenital.'

'So if I was to say that I think you're pretty?' The words just slipped out of me.

At first she looked surprised, then she pointed to her droopy eye, and when she spoke now her voice wasn't warm and dark, but had a harsh, metallic ring to it. 'Then it's either a lie or you've failed to comprehend the most elementary principles behind the idea of beauty.'

I realised I had crossed some kind of line. 'So then there are principles?' I said, trying get back over on the right side again.

She gave me a look as though trying to decide whether to let me get away with it or not. 'Symmetry,' she said at last. 'The golden ratio. Shapes that imitate nature. Complementary colours. Harmonising notes.'

I nodded, relieved that the conversation was back

on the rails again but knowing I'd have a hard time forgiving myself for that slip.

'Or in architecture, where you have functional shapes,' she went on. 'Which are actually the same as shapes that imitate nature. The hexagonal cells in a beehive. The beaver's regulatory dam. The fox's network of tunnels. The woodpecker's hole of a nest which becomes a home for other birds. None of these are built to be beautiful, and yet they are. A house that's good to live in is beautiful. It's actually as simple as that.'

'How about a service station?'

'That can also be beautiful, provided its function is something we regard as praiseworthy.'

'So then a gallows . . . ?'

Shannon smiled. '. . . can be beautiful as long as the death penalty is regarded as necessary.'

'Wouldn't you have to hate the condemned person to think like that?'

Shannon licked her lips, as though testing the notion. 'I think it would be enough to find it necessary.'

'But a Cadillac is beautiful,' I said, pouring more wine. 'Even though compared with modern cars its shape isn't especially functional.'

'It has lines that imitate nature, it looks as if it was built to fly like an eagle, bare its teeth like a hyena, glide through the water like a shark. It looks as though it's aerodynamic and has room for a rocket engine that could launch us into outer space.'

'But the form lies about the function, and we know it. But we still find it beautiful.'

'Well, even atheists can find churches beautiful. But believers probably find them even more beautiful because they're associated with everlasting life, the same way the female body affects a man who wants to pass on his own genes. Without his being aware of it a man's desire for a female body will be slightly less if he knows that she is not fertile.'

'You think so?'

'We can test it out.'

'How?'

She smiled weakly. 'I've got endometriosis.'

'What's that?'

'It's a condition in which cells similar to those in the layer of tissue that normally covers the inside of the uterus grow outside it. It means I'm unlikely ever to have children. You agree that an awareness of something lacking in the content makes the exterior a little less attractive?'

I looked at her. 'No.'

She smiled. 'That's your superficial, conscious self answering. Let your unconscious chew over the information for a while.'

Maybe it was the wine that coloured her usually snow-white cheeks. I was on the point of answering when she interrupted with a peal of laughter.

'Anyway, you're my brother-in-law so not very suitable as a guinea pig.'

I nodded. Then I got up and crossed to the CD player. Put on J. J. Cale's **Naturally.**

We listened to the album in silence, and when it

was over, Shannon asked me to play the whole thing again from the start.

The door opened in the middle of 'Don't Go to Strangers' and there on the threshold stood Carl. He had a serious, resigned look on his face. He nodded in the direction of the bottle of sparkling wine.

'Why did you open that?' he asked in a subdued voice.

'Because we knew you would persuade the council that what this place needs is a hotel,' said Shannon, raising her glass. 'That they'll allow you to build as many cabins as you ask for. We're celebrating in advance.'

'Do I look as though that's what happened?' he said, staring gloomily at us.

'What you look like is a very bad actor,' said Shannon. She took a drink. 'Get yourself a glass, sweetie.'

Carl's mask dropped. He gave a loud laugh and came towards us with his arms outspread. 'Only one vote against. They loved it!'

A halo of enthusiasm seemed to hover over Carl as he drank up most of what was left of the sparkling wine and gave a vivid description of events at the meeting.

'They lapped it up, every word. Know what one of them said? "One of our mantras in the Left Party is that everything can be done better; but today, he said, nothing could have been done better." They agreed to the zoning plans on the spot, so now we have our cabins.' He pointed to the window. 'After the meeting Willumsen came over to me, said he'd been sitting on the public bench and congratulated me not just for making me and my family rich but for turning the farmland of every villager into nothing less than an oilfield. He said how much he regretted he didn't own even more of the mountain than he did, and on the spot he offered us three million for our land.'

'And what did you say?' I asked.

'That maybe that was double what the land was worth yesterday, but that now the price had gone up tenfold. No, fifty-fold! Cheers!'

Shannon and I raised our empty glasses.

'What about the hotel?' asked Shannon.

'They loved it. **Loved** it. The changes they asked for were minimal.'

'Changes?' The light brow over her right eye rose.

'They thought it was a bit . . . sterile, I think the word was. They want a bit more Norwegian local colour. Nothing to worry about.'

'Local colour? Meaning what?'

'Details. They want turfed roofs, some lafted timber here and there. Two big trolls carved in wood on each side of the entrance. Stupid things like that.'

'And?'

Carl shrugged. 'And I said yes. **It's no big deal,**' he added in English.

'You **what**?'

'Listen, darling, it's psychology. They need to feel they're in control, that they aren't just a bunch of peasants being ridden roughshod over by some loud-mouth who's just come back from abroad, under-stand? So we have to give them **something.** I acted as though these concessions were going to cost us, so now they think they've pushed it as far as they can and they won't be asking for anything else.'

'No compromises,' said Shannon. 'You promised.' Her staring eye flashed.

'Relax, darling. In a month's time, when we turn over the first shovelful of earth, we're going to be the ones in the driving seat, and then we'll give them some practical explanation of why we can't use this kitschy stuff after all. Until then we let them think they'll get what they want.'

'The way you let everyone think they'll get what they want?'

There was a chill in her voice that I had never heard before.

Carl wriggled in his chair. 'Darling, this is a time for celebrating, not—'

Shannon stood up suddenly. Marched out.

'What was all that about?' I asked as the front door slammed.

Carl sighed. 'It's her hotel.'

'Hers?'

'She designed it.'

'**She** designed it? Not an architect?'

'Shannon **is** an architect, Roy.'

'She is?'

'Best in Toronto if you ask me. But she has her own

274

style and her own opinions, and unfortunately she's a bit of a Howard Roark.'

'A bit of a who?'

'He's an architect who blew his own work up because it wasn't built exactly the way he drew it. Shannon's going to make trouble about every little detail. If she'd been a bit more flexible she would have been not only the best but also the most in-demand architect in Toronto.'

'Not that it matters all that fucking much but why the hell did you never say it was her who designed the hotel?'

Carl sighed. 'The drawings are signed with the name of her firm. I figured that was enough. When the project leader allows his young, foreign wife to design the place then people are automatically going to suspect the project lacks professionality. Of course, everything'll be fine once they see her track record, but my thinking was, we could do without all that fuss until the investors and the council were on board. Shannon agreed.'

'OK, but why did neither of you tell **me**?'

Carl opened his arms wide. 'So you wouldn't have to go round and tell lies as well. What I mean is, it's not lies, the name of her company is there, but . . . well, you understand.'

'Not so many loose ends? Fewer loose cannons?'

'For fuck's sake, Roy.' He fixed me with his sorrowing, beautiful eyes. 'I'm juggling a million balls in the air here. I'm just trying to keep the distractions to a minimum.'

I sucked my teeth. It's something I must have started doing recently. Dad did it and it used to annoy me. 'OK,' I said.

'Good.'

'Speaking of balls in the air and distractions, I met Mari at the surgery the other day. She blushed when she saw me.'

'Oh yeah?'

'As if she was ashamed of something.'

'Such as?'

'I don't know. But after all that stuff involving you and Grete and you going to the States, she tried to get her revenge on you.'

'What did she do?'

I took a deep breath. 'She came on to me.'

'To you?' Carl laughed uproariously. 'And you complain about me not keeping the family informed?'

'That's what she wanted, for you to find out. And get hurt.'

Carl shook his head. Putting on a local accent he said: 'Never underestimate a woman scorned. Did you go for it?'

'No,' I said. 'When I saw that deep blush of shame it struck me that she'd never got her revenge, and that Mari Aas is not the type to forget, that that business is still inside her like some kind of encapsulated cyst. So I think you better watch out for her.'

'You think she's planning something?'

'Or she's already done it, something so extreme

that she feels ashamed when she sees a member of our family.'

Carl rubbed his chin. 'Like something for example that could affect our project?'

'She might have arranged something that's going to screw things up for you. I'm just saying.'

'And you base this on the fact that you saw her blush as you happened to be passing by?'

'I realise it sounds idiotic,' I said. 'But Mari isn't the type to blush, we know that. She's a self-assured lady and there's almost nothing that embarrasses her. But she's also a moralist. Remember that necklace you bought for her with money you nicked from Uncle Bernard?'

Carl nodded.

'That's what she looked like. As though she'd been party to something she knew was wrong, and it was too late to regret it.'

'Got it,' said Carl. 'I'll watch out for her.'

I went to bed early. Through the floor I could hear Carl and Shannon in the living room. Not the words, just the quarrelling. And then they fell silent. Footsteps on the stairs, the bedroom door closing. And then fucking.

I pressed the pillow over my ears and sang J. J. Cale's 'Don't Go to Strangers' inside my head.

19

THE SNOW HAD MELTED.

I stood at the kitchen window and looked out.

'Where's Carl?' I asked.

'Talking to the contractors,' said Shannon, who was sitting on the worktop behind me reading the **Os Daily.** 'They're probably on site.'

'Shouldn't the architect be there too?'

She shrugged. 'He wanted to handle it alone, he said.'

'What does the paper say?'

'That the council has opened the floodgates. That Os will turn into a holiday camp for rich city folk, and we'll be the servants. That we would be better off building refugee camps for people who really need us.'

'Jesus, is that Dan Krane saying that?'

'It's something sent in by a reader, but they've given it plenty of prominence and there's a reference to it on the front page.'

'What's Krane's editorial about?'

'A story about a Pastor Armand. Revivalist meetings and miracle cures. That one week after he left Os with his collecting box full the people he cured were back in their wheelchairs again.'

I laughed and studied the sky above Ottertind, the mountain at the southern end of Lake Budal. It was full of contradictory signs and revealed little about the kind of weather we could expect. 'So Krane doesn't dare to criticise Carl directly,' I said. 'But he gives plenty of space to those who do.'

'Well, anyway it doesn't sound as if we have much to fear from that quarter,' said Shannon.

'Maybe not from there.' I turned to her. 'If you still think you can find out what Kurt Olsen's looking for, I think now might be a good time.'

Fritt Fall was the type of bar that defines itself by the size of its market. Which in this case meant satisfying everyone's demands. A long counter with stools for the thirsty beer drinkers, small round tables for the diners, a little dance floor with disco lights for people looking for action, a billiard table with holes in the cloth for the restless, and betting slips, coupons and a TV screen showing races for the hopeful. Who the black rooster that sometimes strutted between the tables was for I don't know, but it didn't bother anyone, no one bothered it, and it would neither take orders for beer nor respond when called by its name, Giovanni. But Giovanni would certainly be missed when he died and would – according to Erik Nerell – be dished up to the regulars as a slightly tough but agreeable coq au vin.

Shannon and I entered the bar at three o'clock. I saw no sign of Giovanni, just two men staring at the TV screen where horses with flowing manes were swarming round a gravel track. We sat at one of the window tables and as agreed I took out Shannon's laptop, placed it on the table between us, stood up and walked to the bar from where Erik Nerell had been watching us since we came in, while pretending to read the **Os Daily.**

'Two coffees,' I said.

'OK.' He put a cup under the tap of a black Thermos and pressed the top.

'What's happening?' I said.

He gave me a funny look. I nodded at his newspaper.

'Oh, here,' he said. 'No. Well, actually . . .' He changed the cups over. 'No.'

Shannon had turned the laptop on by the time I returned with the coffees. I sat down beside her. The screensaver was a rather sombre-looking, rectangular and to my eyes quite ordinary-looking skyscraper which, she had explained to me, was a masterpiece, the IBM building in Chicago. She said it was designed by someone called Mies.

I looked around. 'OK. How do you want to do this?'

280

'You and I just make small talk while we're drinking our coffee. Which by the way is disgusting, but I'm not going to pull a face because he's looking at us.'

'Erik?'

'Yes. And those two over by the TV as well. Once you've finished your coffee, take over the laptop and act as if you're very preoccupied by something there, use the keyboard a bit. Don't look up and leave the rest to me.'

'OK,' I said and took a swig of coffee. She was right, it was chemically revolting, plain hot water would have tasted better. 'I googled endometriosis. It says if the old way doesn't work, you can try artificial insemination. Have you two thought about that?'

She opened one eye wide, looked furious.

'You're the one who said small talk,' I said.

'That isn't small talk,' she said in a low hiss. 'That's big talk.'

'I could talk about service stations if you prefer,' I said with a shrug. 'Or the comical and humiliating problems that arise when the middle finger on your right hand is stiff.'

She smiled. Her mood changed like the weather over the 2,000-metre mark, but to be enfolded in that smile was like slipping into a warm bath.

'I do want children,' she said. 'It's what I want most of all. Not with my brain, of course, but my heart.'

She looked over my shoulder in the direction of Erik. Smiled as though her look had been returned.

What if Erik didn't know what Kurt was looking for? I wasn't so sure any more that this was a good idea.

'What about you?' she asked.

'Me?'

'Kids.'

'Oh Jesus, yes. Indeed. I just . . .'

'Yes?'

'I don't know if I'd be much good as a dad.'

'You **know** you would be, Roy.'

'Well, it would have to be with a mother who could be everything I'm not at least. And who understood how much time running a service station takes.'

'The day you become a dad maybe you'll stop thinking the world is made up of nothing but service stations.'

'Or skyscrapers in anodised aluminium.'

She smiled. 'It's time.'

Our eyes met for a moment, then I pulled the computer over, opened a Word document and started to write. I just let the words come, concentrating only on spelling them correctly. After I'd been doing that for a while I heard her get up and walk across the floor. I didn't have to look to know that she gave her hips an extra sway. That fucking **soca swing.** I had my back to the counter, heard the legs of a bar stool scrape and knew she'd sat down and was chatting to Erik Nerell and that his gaze was riveted on her just the way it had been at the homecoming party. As I sat there deep in my spelling exercises someone slumped down in the chair on the other side of the table. For a moment I thought it was Shannon, back already with her mission unaccomplished, and felt a strangely paradoxical relief. But it wasn't Shannon.

'Hi,' said Grete.

The first thing I noticed was that her perm was now blonde.

'Hi,' I said, trying to convey in that monosyllabic way that I was extremely bloody busy.

'Well, well, pretty and flirty,' said Grete.

My gaze automatically followed hers.

Shannon and Erik were leaning towards each other across the short end of the bar, so that we saw them in profile. Shannon laughed at something, smiled, and I saw Erik enjoying that same warm bath I had just been sitting in. And maybe it was only because Grete had primed me with that 'pretty', but now I actually **saw** it. That Shannon Alleyne Opgard was not just pretty, she was beautiful. There was something in the way she simultaneously absorbed and reflected the light. And I could not take my fucking eyes off her. Not until I heard Grete's voice again.

'Uh-oh.'

I turned to her. She was no longer looking at Shannon but at me.

'What?'

'Nothing,' she said, a sour little smile on those wormlike lips of hers. 'Where's Carl today?'

'At the hotel site I should think.'

Grete shook her head, and I tried not to think how she could know.

'Then I've no idea. Talking with the partners maybe.'

'That's probably more like it,' she said, looking as though she was wondering whether or not to say more.

'Didn't know you were a Fritt Fall regular,' I said to change the subject.

She held up a handful of coupons she must have picked up from the table below the TV on her way in. 'For Dad,' she said. 'Even though he says he's thinking of backing the hotel instead of the horses. The principle's the same, according to him. Minimum outlay with the possibility of a big profit. Has he got that right?'

'No outlay,' I said. 'Possibility of some profit, yes. But also of a hefty bill. First he should check that he can afford a worst-case scenario.'

'Meaning what?'

'Meaning if it all goes to hell.'

'Oh, that.' She slipped the coupons into her bag. 'I think Carl does a better job of selling it than you, Roy.' She looked up at me and smiled. 'But then he always has done. Say hello from me. And watch out for that Barbie doll of his. Looks like she's trying to outdo him over there.'

I turned and looked at Shannon and Erik. Both had their phones out and were entering text. When I turned back again Grete was on her way out.

I looked at the screen. Started to read what I had written. Dammit. Had I completely lost my mind? I heard the scraping of the bar stool again and hurriedly dragged the document over to the rubbish.

'Done?' asked Shannon.

'Yup,' I said, closing the laptop and standing up.

'Well?' I said as we sat in the Volvo.

'I'm guessing it's going to happen tonight,' she said.

After driving Shannon back to the farm I headed back down to the station and relieved Markus who had asked if he could finish early.

'Any news?' I asked Julie.

'Nah,' she said and blew a gum bubble. 'Alex is pissed off. Calling me a prick teaser. And Natalie's going to move.'

'Move where?'

'To Notodden. I can understand that, nothing happens here.'

'Absolutely nothing,' I said and took a key from a drawer under the till. 'I'm just going over to the workshop, OK?'

I left the garage door locked and used the office door instead. Could smell from the stale air that it was a while since I'd been in. We took cars in here to change the tyres if it was too cold out, but the grease pit had hardly been used once the workshop closed. After Carl left and I was alone on the farm I'd rigged up a little hole-in-the-wall at the rear of the place with a bed, a TV and a hotplate. I lived there during the coldest months of the winter, when the road up and the farm were deep in snow and there seemed no point in heating the house for the few hours I was alone and not at the station. I closed the doors to the car wash and showered. Never been cleaner. Went back to the repair shop and checked the mattress. Dry. The hotplate working. Even the TV worked after a little initial hesitation.

I walked into the workshop.

Stood there where we had chopped the arms, legs and head of old Olsen. **I** had chopped. Carl couldn't stand to even watch, and that was fine, why should he? The tractor had remained outside with its scoop in the air for three days before I drove it into the car wash and emptied its contents and watched as they ran away smoothly through the sluice grid. Then I had hosed the scoop clean, and that was that. How did it feel to be standing back in the same place? Were there ghosts here? It was sixteen years ago. And I hadn't felt much that night, there just hadn't been room for it. And any ghosts there might be were down in Huken, not here.

'Roy,' said Julie when I returned, drawing the vowels out as though it was an extremely long name, 'do you have a dream place where you'd really like to go?' She flipped through a travel magazine and showed me a beach where a scantily clad young pair reclined in blistering sunshine.

'That would have to be Notodden, I guess,' I said.

She gawped at me. 'What's the furthest away place you've ever been?'

'I've not been anywhere,' I said.

'Oh come on.'

'I've been south. And north. But I've never been abroad.'

'Course you have!' She put her head on one side, studying me, and then added slightly less cockily. 'Hasn't everyone?'

'I've been to a few faraway places,' I said. 'But that was here.' I tapped my bandaged finger carefully on my forehead.

'What do you mean?' She smiled faintly. 'You mean like you've been mad?'

'I've dismembered human beings and shot defenceless dogs.'

'Sure, and you tossed a lifebelt to your wife when she was drunk on champagne and drowning.' Julie laughed. 'Why aren't boys of my own age as funny as you?'

'It takes a long time to be funny,' I said. 'Time and hard work.'

When I got back to the farm that evening Shannon was sitting in the winter garden wearing Carl's old quilted anorak, one of my hats and a woollen blanket over her lap.

'It's cold, but it's so nice here just after the sun goes down,' she said. 'In Barbados it happens so quickly, suddenly it's just dark. And in Toronto it's so flat and there are so many tower blocks that at some point the sun just vanishes. But here you can see everything happening in slow motion.'

'**Sakte kino** in Norwegian,' I told her.

'**Sakte kino?** Slow cinema?' She laughed. 'Yeah, I like that. Because so much happens to the light. The

287

light on the lake, the light on the mountain, the light **behind** the mountain. It's like a photographer has gone crazy with his lighting. I love Norwegian nature.' And added, with ironic, exaggerated sincerity, 'Wild, naked Norwegian nature.'

I sat down beside her with the cup of coffee I had brought from the kitchen. 'Carl?'

'He had to sweet-talk someone who's important for the project. A used-car salesman.'

'Willumsen,' I said. 'Anything else?'

'Anything else?'

'Anything else happened?'

'Such as what?'

Through a gap in the clouds the moon showed her pale face. Like an actor taking a peek at the audience from behind the curtain before the show begins. And in the reflected light falling on Shannon's face I could see now that that's exactly what she was: an actress who couldn't wait to get started.

'He held out until eight o'clock,' she said, pulling her hand out from under the blanket and handing me the phone. 'I told him I liked him, that I was bored here, and asked if he could send me some pictures. He asked what sort. I said I wanted Norwegian nature. Naked, wild Norwegian nature. Preferably in full bloom.'

'And he sent you this?' I looked at Erik Nerell's customised selfie. Dick pic was putting it mildly. He was lying naked in front of an open fireplace on what looked like a reindeer hide and with some kind of lotion that gave his flexed muscles a dull sheen. And in the middle of the picture, an exemplary erection.

No, the face wasn't visible, but there was more than enough for a pregnant girlfriend to recognise.

'He might claim to have misunderstood me,' said Shannon. 'But I find this incredibly offensive. And I think his father-in-law will too.'

'His father-in-law?' I said. 'Not his girlfriend?'

'I've given that some thought. Erik was a little too clever at knowing what to say. So I think he knows he can talk his way out of it with a pregnant girlfriend. Prostrate himself, beg for forgiveness, blah blah. A father-in-law, on the other hand . . .'

I chuckled. 'You really are wicked.'

'No,' she said seriously. 'I'm good. I love the ones I love and do what I have to in order to protect them. Even if that means doing bad things.'

I nodded. Something told me this wasn't necessarily the first time. I was on the point of saying something when I heard the low rumble of an eight-cylinder American. Cones of light, and then the Cadillac rounding Geitesvingen. We saw it park and Carl get out. He stood by the car, lifted his phone to his ear. Spoke quietly as he headed towards the house. I leaned back in my chair and switched on the light on the wall behind us. I saw Carl give a start when he caught sight of us. As though he were the one caught red-handed at something. But I was the one who didn't want to be caught red-handed hiding away in the dark with Shannon. I switched the light off again to show that we preferred it dark, that was all. And I knew as I did so that the decision I had made was the right one.

'I'm going to be moving down to the workshop,' I said in a low voice.

'What?' said Shannon, her voice also low. 'Why?'

'Give you two a bit more space.'

'Space? Space is all we've got. A whole house and a whole mountain for just three people. Can't you stay, Roy? For my sake?'

I tried to see her face, but the moon had hidden herself again, and that was all she said.

Carl came through the door of the living room and joined us.

'And with that the deadline for being part of Os Spa and Mountain Hotel SL is closed,' he said, and slumped down in one of the wickerwork chairs with an open beer in his hand. 'Four hundred and twenty participants – in effect that's everybody in the village who can afford it. The bank's ready and I've talked to the contractors. In principle we could get the diggers in there after the company meeting tomorrow.'

'To dig what?' I asked. 'It'll have to be dynamited first.'

'Sure, sure, it was just an image. I sort of look on the diggers as tanks that are going to move in and conquer this mountain.'

'Do like the Americans do and bomb it first,' I said. 'Extinguish all life. And **then** advance and conquer.'

I heard the scrape of his stubble against his collar as

he turned his head towards me in the dark. He was probably wondering if I meant a little bit more than what I was actually saying. Whatever that might be.

'Willum Willumsen and Jo Aas have agreed to sit on the board,' said Carl. 'On condition that the company votes for me as manager.'

'Sounds like you'll have complete control.'

'You could say that,' said Carl. 'The advantage of SL is that, unlike a limited company, the law doesn't require you to have a board, an accountant and all that kind of control stuff. We will have a board and an accountant because the bank demands it, but in practice it's possible for the manager to run the company like an enlightened despot, and that makes everything that much fucking easier.' There was a klunk from the beer bottle.

'Roy says he's moving,' said Shannon. 'To the workshop.'

'Nonsense,' said Carl.

'He says we need more space.'

'OK,' I said. 'Maybe I'm the one who needs space. Maybe all these years of living alone have turned me into a weirdo.'

'Then it should be me and Shannon that move,' said Carl.

'No,' I said. 'I'm happy there's more than one person living here. The **house** is happy too.'

'In that case three has to be even better than two,' said Carl, and I sensed he lay his hand in Shannon's lap. 'And who knows, one day we may even be four.'

For a couple of seconds there was complete silence, and then he sort of woke up again. 'Or not. What made me think of it was I just saw Erik and Gro out for an evening stroll. She's pretty big now.' Still no response. More chugging from the bottle. Carl belched. 'Why do the three of us spend so much time sitting in the dark when we talk?'

So our faces don't give anything away, I thought. 'I'll have that little chat with Erik tomorrow,' I said. 'And I'll move out in the evening.'

Carl sighed. 'Roy . . .'

I stood up. 'I'm off to bed now. You're fantastic people and I love you both, but I look forward to not having to see other people's faces when I get up in the morning.'

That night I slept like a stone.

20

ERIK NERELL LIVED OUT OF town. I had explained to Shannon that when we said 'out of town', we meant up along the shore of Lake Budal, towards where the water ran out into the Kjetterelva River. And since the lake was shaped like an upside-down V, with the village in the apex, so 'in town' and 'out of town' weren't compass directions but just a way of telling you which way to head from your starting point, since the main road followed the lake regardless. Aas, Moe the roofer and Willumsen lived 'in town', which was reckoned to be a touch better, because the fields were flatter and got more sun, whereas Olsen's cabin and the Nerell farm were out of town, on the shadowed side. The path up to Aas's cabin where Carl, Mari and a gang

293

of other youngsters used to sneak off to in our teen-age years and party to the break of day was also 'out of town'.

I was thinking about this a bit as I drove along.

I parked behind a Ford Cortina sleeper in front of the barn. Gro, Erik's partner, opened the door and as I asked for Erik I couldn't help wondering how those short arms had managed to extend out beyond that bulging stomach to reach the doorknob, that maybe she tackled the problem by approaching it from the side. Which was the way I had planned to approach this.

'He's working out,' she said, pointing towards the barn.

'Thanks,' I said. 'Not long to go now?'

She smiled. 'Yes.'

'But you and Erik still take your evening walk, I gather?'

'Got to exercise the old lady and the dog.' Gro laughed. 'But never more than three hundred metres from the house now.'

Erik neither saw nor heard me when I entered. He was lying on a bench and pumping iron, wheezing and panting with the bar across his chest and giving a roar when it was time to lift it. I waited until the bar was once more back on its rack before entering his field of vision. He pinched the buds out of his ears and I heard the descant from 'Start Me Up'.

'Roy,' he said. 'You're up early.'

'You're looking in good shape,' I said.

'Thanks.' He got up and pulled a fleece jacket over the sweaty T-shirt with a picture of the Hollywood Brats. His cousin, Casino Steel, had played keyboards in the band, and Erik always insisted that if the timing had been a bit better the Hollywood Brats would have been bigger than the Sex Pistols and the New York Dolls. He'd played us a couple of their songs and I remember thinking the problem wasn't just the timing. But I liked him for caring. In general, I actually quite liked Erik Nerell. But that wasn't the point.

'There's something we need to sort out,' I said. 'The picture you sent Shannon did not go down all that fucking well.'

Erik turned pale. He blinked three times.

'She came to me, didn't want to show it to Carl because she said he'd go ballistic. But that she was going to go to the sheriff. In legal terms, this here is actually flashing.'

'No no, wait a minute, she said—'

'She said something about pictures of nature. Whatever, I persuaded her not to report it, explained it would mean a whole lot of bother for all of us and be bloody traumatic for Gro.'

I saw the muscles of his jaw tighten at the mention of his partner's name.

'When Shannon learned that you were expecting a kid she said she'd show the picture to your father-in-law and let him be the one to decide what to do. And I'm afraid I have to tell you that Shannon is a very determined lady.'

Erik's mouth was still open, but nothing came out of it now.

'I came here because I want to help you. See if I can stop her. I really don't like a lot of fussing and fighting, you know that.'

'Yes,' said Erik, with an almost inaudible question mark at the end.

'For example I don't like it when people go rooting about on our property where Mum and Dad died. If they do then I really need to know what's going on.'

Erik blinked again. Like he was trying to signal with his eye that he understood. That I was looking to do a trade.

'Olsen's going to send people down into Huken anyway, isn't he?'

Erik nodded. 'He's ordered a safety suit from Germany. Like what bomb squads use. It means you're safe unless actual boulders fall on you. Plus you can move about in them.'

'What's he looking for?'

'All I know is that Olsen wants to get down there, Roy.'

'No. He's not the one going down there, you are. And that being so, he must have told you what to look for.'

'If I knew I wouldn't be allowed to tell anyone, Roy, you must understand that.'

'Of course,' I said. 'And you must understand that I don't feel I'm allowed to stop a lady who has been so outrageously offended as Shannon.'

Erik Nerell sat there on the bench and gave me a doleful dog-eyed stare. Shoulders sloping, hands in his lap. 'Start Me Up' was still buzzing from the ear-buds lying on the bench between his thighs.

'You tricked me,' he said. 'You and that cunt. It's down there, isn't it?'

'What's down there?'

'The old sheriff's mobile phone.'

I steered the Volvo with one hand while holding the phone in the other. 'Sigmund Olsen's mobile was still giving out signals until ten o'clock on the night he disappeared.'

'What are you talking about?' Carl grunted. He sounded like he had a hangover.

'A mobile phone that's turned on sends out a signal every half-hour, which is registered at the base stations that provide the phone with coverage. In other words, the base stations' records are a logbook of where the phone was and when.'

'And?'

'Kurt Olsen was in town not long ago and spoke to the phone company. He got hold of the records for the day his father disappeared.'

'They still have records from that far back?'

'Apparently. Sigmund Olsen's phone is registered at two base stations, indicating that he can't – or at least his phone can't – have been out at his cabin at the time when a witness says he heard a car stop there and a motorboat engine starting up. Because that was after dark. What the base stations show is that his phone was actually in an area that only covers our farm, Huken, Simon Nergard's farm and the woods between there and the village. And that doesn't square with what you told the police about Sigmund Olsen driving away from our farm at 6.30 p.m.'

'I didn't say where the sheriff drove to, only that he drove away from the farm.' Carl sounded wide awake and clear now. 'For all I know he might have stopped somewhere between our place and the village. And maybe that car and that boat the witness heard some-time after dark belonged to somebody else, after all there are other people besides Olsen who have cabins out there. Or maybe the witness is mistaken about the time – it wasn't exactly the kind of thing to stick in the memory.'

'Agreed,' I said as I saw I was approaching a tractor. 'But questions cropping up about the timeline aren't what worry me most. It's if Kurt finds the phone down there in Huken. Because according to Erik Nerell **that** is what Kurt wants to go down and look for there.'

'Ah shit. But can it be down there? Didn't you tidy up after him?'

'Yes,' I said. 'And none of his stuff got left behind. But you remember how it was getting dark when we dragged the body up, and I heard loose rocks falling and took cover inside the wreck?'

'Yeah?'

I crossed into the other lane. Saw the tractor was

much too close to the corner but did it anyway. Put my foot down and slipped in front of the tractor at the start of the corner, just in time to see the driver shaking his head in the rear-view mirror.

'It wasn't rocks falling, it was his phone. He had it in one of those holders that just clips onto the belt. And when he was dragged up the rock face it was pulled off and fell down, but of course in the dark I couldn't see that.'

'How can you be so sure about that?'

'Because when we were at the workshop dismembering the body, I pulled off his belt and cut off his clothes. Went through his pockets to remove anything metal before leaving the rest to Fritz. There were coins, the belt buckle and a lighter. But no mobile phone. It didn't even fucking occur to me, and I **knew** he had that stupid leather holder.'

Silence for a few moments at Carl's end. 'So what do we do?' he asked.

'We've got to go down into Huken again,' I said. 'Before Kurt does.'

'And when is that?'

'Kurt's safety suit arrived yesterday. Erik's meeting him to try it on at ten o'clock and then they're going straight to Huken.'

Carl's breathing crackled through the phone. 'Oh shit,' he said.

21

IT WAS AS THOUGH THE repeat, this second descent, was slower but at the same time quicker. Quicker, because we had solved the practical problems and actually remembered our solutions. Slower, because it had to happen fast because we didn't know when Kurt and his climbing crew would be here, and that gave me the same feeling as you get in those nightmares where someone's after you and you're trying to run fast but it's like you're running in water. Shannon was posted at the outer edge of Geitesvingen, from where she could see cars turning up off the highway.

Carl and I used the same rope as previously, meaning that Carl knew exactly how close to the edge he had to reverse the Volvo before I was down.

When at last I touched ground, my face to the rock face, I freed myself from the rope before turning round slowly. Seventeen years. But it was as though time had stood still down here. On account of the lower but partly overhanging wall on the south side the rain didn't fall straight down here, it came trickling down the higher, vertical wall from Geitesvingen and drained away through the rocks. That was probably why there was so remarkably little rust on the wrecked car and the tyres were still intact, though the rubber looked slightly rotten. Nor had any animal made its home in Dad's Cadillac and the seat coverings and panelling all seemed intact.

I looked at my watch. Ten thirty. Shit. Closed my eyes and tried to recall where I had heard that sound of something hitting the ground back then. No, it was too long ago. But, exposed only to the force of gravity, the phone should have fallen in a vertical line from the body. The plumb line. The simple law of physics that says anything that doesn't have a horizontal speed will fall straight down. I had consciously dismissed the thought back then, and I might just as well do the same thing now. I had a torch with me and started to search among the boulders close to the rock face where the rope was dangling. Since we had done everything in exact repetition, reversing the car along the same narrow track up there, I knew the phone must have fallen somewhere there. But there were hundreds of different places between the rocks where it could have slipped down and hidden itself.

And naturally it might also have ricocheted off the rocks and landed somewhere else entirely. One good thing was that, being in a leather case, bits of it were unlikely to be scattered all over the place. If, that is, I found the fucking thing.

I knew I had to be more systematic, not let myself get carried away by hunches about where it might have landed and start running round like those chickens Mum couldn't bear to keep hold of once Dad had chopped their heads off. I defined a square within which it was reasonable to assume the phone had to be and started in the upper left corner. On my knees I began the search, lifting the stones that weren't too heavy, and shining my torch into the spaces between those that were. In the spaces where I could neither see nor feel with my hand I used Carl's smartphone and selfie stick. Put the camera on video and turned on the flash.

After fifteen minutes I was in the middle of my square and had just poked the stick between two rocks the size of fridges when I heard Carl's voice from above.

'Roy . . .'

I knew of course what it was.

'Shannon's seen them coming!'

'Where?' I called back.

'They're starting up the mountain now.'

At the most we had three minutes. I withdrew the stick and played back the video. Jumped when I saw a pair of eyes in the dark. A fucking mouse. It turned away from the light and with a flick of the tail it was gone. And that was when I saw it. There were holes chewed in the black leather holder, but there was no doubting it, I had found Sheriff Olsen's phone.

I lay on my stomach and reached my arm in under the rocks but it wasn't long enough, my fingers scraped against granite or thin air. Shit! If I found it, they could find it. I had to move that fucking rock out of the way. I pressed my back against it, bent my knees, wedged my feet against the rock face and heaved. It didn't move.

'They're just taking the bend at Japansvingen,' called Carl.

I tried again. Felt the sweat break out on my forehead, my muscles and sinews straining to breaking point. Was that a slight movement in the rock? I heaved again and felt it, yes, there was movement. In my back. I yelled in pain. Jeeezus! Slumped down. Was I still able to move? Yes, dammit, it just hurt like fuck.

'Roy, they're—'

'When I say **drive** put your foot down and drive forward two metres!'

I jerked on the rope. I didn't have enough slack to twine it more than once around the rock, fastening it with what Dad called a bowline knot. I stood behind the rock, ready to push if the Volvo managed to lift the rock slightly.

'Drive!'

I heard the engine revving, and suddenly a hail

of small stones was falling over me. One struck me right on top of the head. But I could feel the rock moving and I pushed up against it like an American linebacker. The rock stood poised and swaying as gravel from the spinning tyres of the Volvo up there rained down. And then it toppled over, and a whiff of something like rotting bad breath rose up from the ground. I had a glimpse of insects scurrying away from the sudden light as I sank to my knees and took hold of the phone. At that same instant there was a loud noise. I looked up, just in time to see the frayed end of the rope shooting up the rock face as the rock began toppling back towards me. I leapt back and landed on my arse, shaking and out of breath, glaring at the rock that had returned to its place, like a jaw I had just escaped from.

Up there the Volvo had stopped, probably realising that the resistance had stopped. Instead now I heard another engine, the tractor-like rumble of a Land Rover climbing a steep incline. The sound carried well, they could still be a couple of turns away, but the end of the rope was now seven or eight metres away up the rock face.

'Back up!' I called as I loosened what was left of the rope around the rock, coiled it and squeezed it into my jacket pocket on top of Olsen's old phone.

The hanging end of the rope was closer now, but it was still almost three metres up, and I realised Carl had reversed all the way to the edge. With my good left hand I found a hold to climb up, and felt the whole rock move. I was the one who'd lied about all the loose rocks I said we heard falling here – but it was true, they **were** loose! Still I had no choice. I put my right hand on a ledge, and fortunately the pain in my back was so great I didn't even notice the throbbing middle finger. I managed to get my feet on top of the rock, my hand found a hold above it, and I moved my legs upward, my arse sticking out like a caterpillar until I straightened up and got hold of the rope with my right hand. And then what? I had to use the other hand to hold on with, and I couldn't be tying any knot with just one hand.

'Roy!' It was Shannon's voice. 'They're coming round the final bend.'

'Drive!' I shouted, grabbing onto the rope half a metre higher up at the same time as I managed to wind it one and a half times around my wrist. 'Drive! Drive!!' I heard the message being passed on up there, and as I felt the rope begin to pull me up I moved my left hand onto the rope, at the same time tensing my stomach muscles, raising my legs and planting my feet against the rock face. And then I ran straight to heaven. I'd told Carl to accelerate hard not because Olsen and his crew were approaching but because there is a limit to the number of seconds you can hang on to a rope using just your hands. And I like to tell myself that on that morning I set some kind of world record for the hundred metres vertical. And like the world's best sprinters, I don't think I breathed even once the whole way. I thought only of the drop growing below me, death that was ever more certain with every second that passed, every ten metres covered. And when I jerked up over the top of Geitesvingen I didn't let go but held on tight and let myself be dragged across the gravel for several metres before I felt it was safe to let go. Shannon helped me to my feet, we ran to the car and dived in. 'Drive to the back of the barn,' I said.

Just as we turned onto the muddy field I caught a glimpse of Olsen's Land Rover rounding the bend at Geitesvingen and hoped that he neither saw us nor the rope that twisted like an anaconda through the grass behind the Volvo.

I sat in the front passenger seat, fighting to catch my breath as Carl jumped out and started to coil the rope. Shannon ran to the corner of the barn and looked down at Geitesvingen.

'They've stopped down there,' she said. 'It looks like they've got a . . . what's a beekeeper in Norwegian?'

'**Birøkter,**' said Carl. 'They're probably worried there might be wasps down there.'

I laughed, and the shaking felt as though someone was sticking knives into my back.

'Carl,' I said quietly, 'why did you say you were at Willumsen's last night?'

'What?'

'Willumsen lives in town. Erik and his missus who you met last night live out of town'

Carl didn't reply. 'What do you think?' he finally asked.

'You want me to take a guess,' I said. 'So you can work out whether to confirm it instead of the truth?'

'OK,' said Carl, checking in the mirror that Shannon was still standing by the corner of the barn and watching Olsen and his crew. 'I could have told you I needed to take a drive just to think. And that would've been true enough. Our main contractor suddenly raised his estimate yesterday by fifteen per cent.'

'Really?'

'They've been up here. They're postponing the start because they say we didn't give them a proper description of the site conditions and how exposed to weather it is.'

'And what does the bank say to that?'

'They don't know. And now that I've sold this whole enterprise to the participants for four hundred million, I can't very well present them with a revised estimate of another sixty million before we've even started.'

'So what are you going to do?'

'I'm going to tell the chief contractor to go fuck himself and I'll make deals with the subcontractors myself. It means more work, I'll have to deal with carpenters, masons, electricians, the whole lot of them, and make sure everything's being done. But it'll be a lot cheaper than the chief contractor taking his ten or twenty per cent just for hiring a firm of electricians.'

'But that's not why you went out of town last night?'

Carl shook his head. 'I . . .'

He stopped as the door opened and Shannon sat in the back seat.

'They're getting ready to go down,' she said. 'It might take a while. What are you talking about?'

'Roy was asking where I was yesterday. And I was about to say I'd driven to Olsen's cabin. Went down to the boathouse. Tried to imagine everything Roy must have gone through that evening.' Carl took a deep breath. 'You faked a suicide and you almost got drowned, Roy. And all of it to save me. Don't you ever get tired, Roy?'

'Tired?'

'Of clearing up after me?'

'It wasn't your fault Olsen fell into Huken,' I said.

He looked at me. And I don't know if he could see what I was thinking about. About the plumb line law. About Sigmund Olsen landing on the back of the car, five metres away from the rock face. If that was what made him take a deep breath and start to speak: 'Roy, there's something you need to know about all that—'

'I know all I need to know,' I interrupted. 'And that is that I am your big brother.'

Carl nodded. He was smiling but seemed to be close to tears. 'Is it that simple, Roy?'

'Yes,' I said. 'It really is.'

22

WE WERE SITTING IN THE kitchen drinking coffee by the time they had finished down in Geitesvingen. I had fetched the binoculars and focused on the faces down there. It was three o'clock, they had been down there for almost four hours and I opened the window slightly so that we could hear as Kurt Olsen shouted something. Kurt's mouth – no cigarette for once – formed words that were unmistakable, and his flushed face was no longer entirely due to that overdose of UV radiation. Erik's body language expressed more indifference and probably the desire to get away from there. Perhaps he guessed that Olsen suspected something. The two men helping the sheriff and Nerell looked slightly confused. They probably knew little of the actual purpose of the operation since Olsen almost certainly knew enough about village gossip to keep things on a **need-to-know** basis, as people say.

Once Erik was out of that comical bomb-disposal suit, he and the other two got into Kurt's Land Rover, while Kurt himself remained standing with his head turned towards the house. Of course I realised that with the sunlight directly on the window he couldn't see us, but perhaps there had been a flash of light reflected from the binoculars. And maybe he'd noticed the fresh marks of spinning tyres and a rope in the gravel. And maybe I'm just paranoid. Anyway, he spat on the ground, got into the car and they drove off.

I went from room to room, packing my things. At least the things I figured I'd have a use for. And even though I wasn't going far and didn't exactly need to think hard about it I did so. Packed as though I'd never be coming back.

I was in the boys' room stuffing the duvet and my pillow into a big blue IKEA bag when I heard Shannon's voice behind me.

'Is it that simple?'

'Moving?' I asked without turning round.

'That you're his big brother. Is that why you always help him?'

'Why else?'

She came in and closed the door behind her. Leaned

against the wall, her arms crossed. 'When I was in second grade at primary school I pushed a friend of mine once. She banged her head on the asphalt. Shortly afterwards she started wearing glasses. She'd never complained about her sight before and I became convinced that it was my fault. I didn't say so, but I hoped she would push me so I would hit my head on the asphalt too. By the time we were in fifth grade she'd still not got a boyfriend and said it was because of the glasses, and I blamed myself for that too, and spent more time with her than I actually really wanted to. She wasn't very good at school and had to take the sixth grade again. I was certain it was because of that blow to the head. So I took sixth grade again with her.'

I stopped. 'You did what?'

'I skipped classes, never did my homework, and at the orals I deliberately gave wrong answers to the easiest questions.'

I opened the wardrobe and started packing folded T-shirts, socks and underwear in a bag. 'Did she end up OK?'

'Yes,' said Shannon. 'She stopped wearing glasses. And one day I surprised her with my boyfriend. She said how sorry she was and that she hoped one day I'd have the chance to break her heart the way she'd broken mine.'

I smiled as I packed the licence plate from Barbados into the bag. 'What's the moral of the story?'

'Sometimes feelings of guilt are wasted and no good to anyone involved.'

'You think I feel guilty about something?'

She put her head on one side. 'Do you?'

'And what might that be?'

'I don't know.'

'Me neither,' I said, zipping up the bag.

As I was about to open the door she put a hand on my chest. The touch made hot and cold run through me.

'I don't think Carl has told me everything, has he?'

'Everything about what?'

'About you two.'

'It's never possible to tell everything,' I said. 'About anyone.'

And then I was out the door.

Carl saw me off in Mum's **haaall** with a big, warm silent hug.

And then I was out the door.

I chucked the bag and the IKEA holdall into the back seat of the car, climbed in, beat my forehead against the steering wheel before turning on the ignition and accelerating off down towards Geitesvingen. And for an instant the possibility flashed through my mind. A permanent solution. And a pile of wrecked cars and corpses that just grew and grew.

Three days later I was standing on Os FC's home ground and almost regretting I had turned the steering wheel at all by Geitesvingen. It was pouring down, five degrees and 3–nil. Not that the score bothered me, I don't give a damn about football. But I had just realised that the other match, the one against Olsen and the past, the one I'd thought we'd won, wasn't even halfway played.

23

CARL PICKED ME UP IN the Cadillac.

'Thanks for coming along,' he said as he wandered around the workshop.

'Who are we playing?' I asked as I pulled on my wellingtons.

'Can't remember,' said Carl, who had stopped in front of the lathe. 'But it's apparently a game we must win if we're not to get relegated.'

'To which division?'

'What makes you think I know any more about football than you do?' He brushed his hand over the tools hanging on the wall, the ones Willumsen hadn't taken. 'Jesus Christ I've had some nightmares about this place.' Maybe he recalled some of them I had used for the dismemberment. 'That night, I puked up, didn't I?'

'A bit,' I said.

He chuckled. And I remembered something Uncle Bernard said. That in time all memories turn into good memories.

He took a plastic bottle down from the shelf. 'You still use that cleaning fluid?'

'Fritz heavy-duty workshop cleaner? Sure. But by law they're no longer allowed to make it so concentrated. EU rules. I'm ready.'

'Well then, let's go.' Carl smiled and twirled his flat cap. **'Heia Os, knus og mos, tygg og spytt en aprikos!** Remember that?'

I remembered, but the rest of the home supporters, about 150 shivering souls, seemed to have forgotten the chant from back then. Or else saw no reason to sing it since we were already 2–nil down after ten minutes.

'Remind me why we're here,' I said to Carl. We were standing at the bottom of the round seven-metre-wide and two-and-a-half-metre high stand that was built halfway along the western side of the AstroTurf pitch. As several posters made clear, the wooden stand had been sponsored by Os Sparebank. Everyone knew that it was Willumsen who had paid for the artificial grass that now lay atop the old cinder pitch. Willumsen claimed he'd bought it only slightly used from a top club in the east of the country, but in truth it was an old surface from the early days of artificial grass, from a time when teams rarely left the pitch without burn marks, twisted ankles and at least one torn ligament. And Willumsen had been offered it free on condition that he removed it himself so that it could be replaced by a newer pitch that was less of a health hazard.

The stand provided a degree of overview, but its most important function was to provide shelter from the westerly winds, and act as an unofficial VIP area for the village's more affluent citizens, who occupied the topmost of the seven rows. That was where the arbiter, the new chairman Voss Gilbert, stood. The manager of Os Sparebank, whose logo adorned the front of Os FC's blue shirts. Along with Willum Willumsen, who had managed to get Willumsen's Used Cars and Breaker's Yard squeezed in above the numbers on the back of the shirts.

'We're here to show our support for our local club,' said Carl.

'Then maybe we should start making a noise,' I said. 'We're being slaughtered here.'

'Today is just about showing we care,' said Carl. 'So next year when we support the club financially people will know the money comes from two real fans who've followed the club through thick and thin.'

I snorted. 'This is the first match I've been to in two years, and the first time you've been here in fifteen.'

'But we'll be at all three of the remaining home games this season.'

'Even if they're already relegated?'

'**Because** they're already relegated. We didn't

abandon them in the hour of their defeat, people notice things like that. And when they get the money, all the matches we never went to will be forgotten. By the way, from now on it's not "they" and "them", it's "we" and "us". The club and Opgard are a team.'

'Why?'

'Because the hotel needs all the goodwill it can get. We need to be regarded as supporters. This time next year the club's going to be buying a great new striker from Nigeria, and where it says "Os Sparebank" on the shirts it's going to say "Os Spa and Mountain Hotel".'

'You mean a professional player?'

'No, are you crazy? But I know someone who knows a Nigerian who works at the Radisson Hotel in Oslo who's played football. No idea how good he is but we'll offer him the same job at our hotel only at a better wage. Maybe that'll tempt him.'

'Yeah, why not?' I said. 'He can't be any worse than this lot.' Out on the pitch our left back had just chanced a sliding tackle in the rain. Alas, there was still plenty of friction in those bright green plastic tufts and he'd ended up tripping and landing on his belly five metres away from his man.

'And I'm going to want you to stand up there,' said Carl with a nod back towards the top row. I half turned. Voss Gilbert, the new chairman, was standing there, along with the bank manager and Willumsen. Carl had told me that Gilbert had agreed to dig the first shovelful of earth to mark the official start of the building process. Carl had already made deals with the most important contractors, and now it was about making a start before the first frost came, so the building process had been brought forward.

Turning, I caught sight of Kurt Olsen standing by the substitutes bench and talking to the manager of Os FC. I could see the manager looked uncomfortable, but he could hardly openly refuse to take advice from Os's old record goal scorer. Kurt Olsen spotted me, laid a hand on the manager's shoulders, gave him a last piece of advice and strode bow-legged up towards Carl and me.

'Didn't know the Opgard boys were interested in football,' he said.

Carl smiled. 'Hey, I remember the time you scored in the Cup against one of the big teams. Odd, was it?'

'Yes,' said Olsen. 'We lost 9–1.'

'Kurt!' called a voice behind us. 'You should be out there now, Kurt!'

Laughter. Cigarette in mouth Kurt Olsen grinned in the direction of the voice and nodded before turning his attention back to us. 'Anyway, I'm glad you're here, because there's something I want to ask you, Carl. And you're very welcome to listen in too, Roy. You want to do this here or on the way over to the hot-dog stand?'

Carl hesitated. 'A hot dog sounds like a good idea,' he said.

We made our way through the blustery wind and

rain towards the hot-dog stand behind one of the goal-posts. I'm guessing the other spectators were watching us. At that particular moment, with the team 2–nil down and that council resolution passed, Carl Opgard was probably more interesting than Os FC.

'It's about the timeline on the day my father disappeared,' said Kurt Olsen. 'You said he left Opgard at six o'clock. Is that right?'

'It's a long time ago now,' said Carl. 'But yes, if that's what it says in the report.'

'It is. But signals received by the base stations show that my father's phone was in the area around your farm until ten o'clock that evening. After that there's nothing. It could be that the battery ran out, someone removed the SIM card, or the phone was damaged. Or that the phone was buried so deeply the signals no longer carried. What it means is, we have to check the area around the farm with metal detectors. It means that nothing up there should be touched, and that starting date I've been hearing about will have to be postponed until further notice.'

'Wh-what?' stammered Carl. 'But . . .'

'But what?' Olsen stopped by the hot-dog stand, stroked his moustache and looked calmly at him.

'How long are we talking about?'

'Hmm.' Olsen stuck his lower lip out and looked as if he was calculating. 'It's a large area. Three weeks. Maybe four.'

Carl groaned. 'Jesus, Kurt, that's going to cost us a

fucking fortune. We've got contractors coming in at agreed times to do their work. And the frost—'

'I'm sorry,' said Olsen. 'But investigations into a suspicious death can't take your desire to turn a profit into consideration.'

'It isn't just my profit we're talking about,' said Carl, his voice shaking slightly. 'It's the whole village. And I think you'll find Jo Aas is of the same opinion.'

'The old chairman, you mean?' Kurt held up one finger to the lady at the hot-dog stand which obviously meant something since she grabbed the sausage tongs and plunged it down into the pan in front of her. 'I was talking earlier today to the new one, the one that actually **makes the decisions.** Voss Gilbert up there.' Olsen nodded in the direction of the stand. 'When Gilbert heard what I had to say about the matter he was most worried about news leaking out that the man behind the new hotel project was involved in a possible murder case.' The woman handed Olsen his hot dog on a piece of waxed sandwich paper. 'But he said that of course he had no authority to stop me.'

'And what are we going to say to the press?' I asked. 'When we announce that the start has been postponed?'

Kurt Olsen turned and stared at me. Chomped into his sausage which gave off a wet, flaccid sound. 'I really don't know,' he said, his mouth full of pig's intestines. 'But yes, it could well be that Dan Krane will think it's an interesting story. OK then, now I've got my answer about the timeline, and you've been informed that you can't start building, Carl. Better luck in the second half.'

Kurt Olsen raised two fingers to his imaginary Stetson and left.

Carl turned and looked at me.

Naturally, he looked at me.

We left the game with a quarter of an hour to go and the team losing 4–nil.

We drove straight to the workshop.

I'd been thinking.

There were certain things we had to do.

'Like that?' asked Carl. His voice echoed around the walls of the empty workshop.

I leaned over the turning lathe and inspected the result. Carl had used a gimlet to scrape the capital letters into the metal of Olsen's mobile phone. SIGMUND OLSEN, it read in clear script. Maybe a bit **too** clear.

'We better green it a bit,' I said and slipped the phone back into its leather case. Clipped it onto a thick piece of string that was lying about, swung it up and down a bit and checked that the clip held the phone in place. 'Come on.'

I pulled open the door to the metal wardrobe that stood in the corridor between the workshop and the office. And there it was.

'Jesus,' said Carl. 'Have you had it here all the time?'

'Well, apart from that one time we tried it out it was never used,' I said, and rocked the yellow oxygen tank and squeezed the slightly rotten wetsuit. The mask and snorkel were up on the shelf.

'I better ring Shannon and say I'm going to be late,' he said.

24

WHEN I RETURNED TO THE workshop that night
I was so cold I couldn't stop shivering. Carl had
handed me his hip flask in the car, to drive out the
cold as people say. I hung on to the hip flask when
Carl drove on home to Shannon, who I guessed was
lying in the warm double bed waiting for him. Too
bloody right I was jealous, I'd given up pretending
otherwise. But what was the use? I couldn't have it.
I didn't **want** to have it. I was like Moe the roofer,
fighting a hopeless battle against my own lust.
It was a fucking awful illness I thought I'd got rid
of, but now here it was again. I knew that distance
and forgetting were my only hope, but I knew no
one would be intervening here, no one would be

sending anyone to Notodden, it was a move I had to make myself.

I unlocked the car wash, attached the hose to a standpipe, turned up the hot tap, pulled off my clothes and stood in front of the scalding hot jet. And I don't know if it was the sudden rise in temperature, if it was the same physiological reaction as you get when men are hanged from the gallows, or whether the heat of the water was transformed in my head to the heat beneath the duvet in the double bed, and that I was the one lying there. But standing there with my eyes closed I felt two things at least. A sobbing in my throat. And a throbbing erection.

The hissing of the water must have drowned out the sound of the key turning in the door. I only heard it open at the same time as I opened my eyes. I saw the outline of her in the darkness outside the door and turned my back as quickly as I could.

'Oh, sorry!' I heard Julie call above the hissing of the water. 'I saw lights and the car wash is supposed to be closed, so—'

'OK!' I interrupted in a voice thick with whisky, unshed tears and shame.

I heard the door close behind me and stood there, my head bent. Looked down at myself. The excitement had passed, the erection was fading, there was only a heart beating in panic, as though I had just been exposed. As though now they all knew who he was and what he had done, that damned traitor, the coward, the murderer, the lecher. Naked, so fucking naked. But then my heart slowed down too. 'The good thing about losing everything is that you have nothing left to lose,' Uncle Bernard said to me when I went to see him in hospital after he'd been told he was going to die. 'And in a way that's a relief, Roy. Because then there's nothing else to fear.'

So then I can't have lost everything after all. Because I was still afraid.

I dried myself and pulled on my trousers. Turned to pick up my shoes.

Julie was sitting on a chair next to the door.

'Are you OK?' she asked.

'No,' I said. 'I've bust my finger.'

'Don't be silly,' she said. 'I saw you.'

'Well,' I said as I pulled on my shoes, 'since you saw me, it's a little hurtful of you to ask if everything's all right.'

'Stop being silly, I said. You were crying.'

'No. But it's not unusual to get water on your face when you're showering. You're not supposed to be working this evening.'

'I'm not. I was sitting in one of the cars and I needed to pee. I didn't want to go into the trees, so can I use yours?'

I hesitated. I could have suggested she use the station toilet, but we'd told the boy racers it was bad enough them using our parking space as a meeting place without having them running in and out of the station toilet. And now that she'd asked I couldn't exactly tell her to go behind a tree either.

I finished dressing and she padded after me through the workshop.

'Cosy,' she said after she'd finished in the toilet. She glanced round the walls of my room. 'Why is there a wet wetsuit hanging out there in the corridor?'

'For it to dry,' I said.

She pouted. 'Can I have a cup?' She crossed un-invited to the coffee maker, took a clean mug from the drying rack and filled it.

'They'll be waiting for you,' I warned her. 'Soon they'll start searching the woods.'

'No way,' she said, and sat down on the bed be-side me. 'I quarrelled with Alex, so I think they went home. What do you do here? Watch TV?'

'That kind of thing.'

'What's that?' She pointed to the licence plate I'd mounted on the wall above the kitchen alcove. I'd looked it up in my licence-plate book, **Vehicle Registration Plates of the World,** and found that the J stood for the parish of St John. Four numbers followed the letter. There was no flag or anything else to denote nationality, like the Monaco plates on the Cadillac. Maybe that was because Barbados was an island and the cars registered there would probably never cross an international border. I'd also googled **redlegs** and found out that St John was the parish in which most of them lived.

'It's a car registration plate from Johor,' I said. Finally my body was feeling warm. Warm and re-laxed. 'A former sultanate in Malaysia.'

'Shit,' she said in an awed tone that referred to the plate or the sultanate or me. Julie was sitting so close her arm touched mine and now she turned her head towards me and waited for me to do the same. I was trying to work out some way of retreat from the situation when Julie tossed my phone to the end of the bed and wrapped her arms around me. Pressed her face into the hollow of my neck. 'Can't we lie down for a bit?'

'You know very well we can't, Julie.' I neither moved nor responded to the embrace.

She lifted her face to mine. 'You smell of booze, Roy. Have you been drinking?'

'A bit. And so have you, I gather.'

'Then in that case we've both got an excuse,' she said and laughed.

I didn't reply.

She pushed me back, sat on top of me and pressed her heels against my thighs as though spurring on a horse. I could easily have bounced her off, but I didn't. She sat there and looked down at me. 'I've got you now,' she said in a low voice.

I still didn't reply. But I could feel myself getting hard again. And I knew she could feel it too. She started moving, carefully. I didn't stop her, just watched her as her gaze clouded over and her breathing grew heavier. Then I closed my eyes and imagined the other one. Felt Julie's hands pressing my wrists against the mattress, her bubblegum breath in my face.

I rolled her off towards the wall and stood up.

'What?' Julie called after me as I walked over to the worktop. I filled a glass of water from the tap, drank it, filled it again.

'You better go,' I said.

'But you want to!' she protested.

'Yes,' I said. 'And that's why you should go.'

'But no one need know. They think I've gone home, and at home they think I'm staying over at Alex's.'

'I can't, Julie.'

'Why not?'

'You're seventeen years old . . .'

'Eighteen. I'll be eighteen in two days.'

'. . . I'm your boss . . .'

'I can finish tomorrow!'

'. . . and . . .' I stopped.

'And?' she yelled. 'And?'

'And I like someone else.'

'Like?'

'Love. I'm in love with someone else.'

In the silence that ensued I heard the dying echo of my own words. Because I had said them to myself. Said them aloud to hear if they sounded true. And they did. Of course they did.

'Who then?' she hiccupped. 'The doctor?'

'What?'

'Dr Spind?'

I couldn't answer, just stood there, glass in hand, as she climbed off the bed and pulled on her jacket.

'I knew it!' she hissed as she pushed past me on her way out.

I followed, stood in the doorway and watched as she stamped across the forecourt as though she was trying to crack the asphalt. Then I locked the door, went back and lay on my bed. Plugged the headphones into my phone and pressed play. J. J. Cale. 'Crying Eyes'.

25

THE FOLLOWING MORNING A PORSCHE Cayenne
turned into the station forecourt. Two men and a
woman climbed out. One of the men filled up with
petrol while the other two stretched their legs. The
woman had blonde hair and was sensibly dressed in
the Norwegian way, but still she didn't strike me as one
of the cabin people. The man was wearing an im-
maculate woollen overcoat and scarf and had on a
pair of comically large sunglasses, the kind women
wear when they want you to know that they might
not be good-looking but they've still got something.
Active body language with much waving of the arms.
Pointed and explained things to the woman though

I was prepared to bet he'd never been here before. I would also have bet he wasn't Norwegian.

It was quiet, and I was bored, and travellers sometimes have interesting tales to tell. So I went out to them, gave the windscreen of the Porsche a wash and asked where they were headed.

'West country,' said the woman.

'Well, you can't miss that,' I said.

The woman laughed and translated into English for the guy in the sunglasses, who laughed too.

'We're scouting locations for my new film,' he said in English. 'This place looks interesting too.'

'Are you a director?' I asked.

'Director and actor,' he said and removed his sunglasses. He had a pair of extremely blue eyes in his well-looked-after face. I could see he was waiting for a reaction.

'This is Dennis Quarry,' the woman discreetly prompted me.

'Roy Calvin Opgard.' I smiled, dried off the windscreen and left them to give the other pumps a clean while I was at it. Well, OK, but **sometimes** they really do have interesting stories.

The Cadillac glided into the forecourt and Carl jumped out, unhooked one of the pump nozzles, caught sight of me and raised his eyebrows quizzically. He'd asked me the same question ten times in the two days that had passed since the football match and the dive. Have they taken the bait? I shook my head, and at the same time my heart skipped a beat when I saw Shannon in the passenger seat. And maybe her heart skipped a beat when she saw the American with the blue eyes, because she put a hand in front of her mouth, fumbled for pen and paper in her bag, got out and went over to him and I saw him smiling as he signed his autograph. His assistant walked over and sat in the SUV while Dennis Quarry stood there talking to Shannon. She was about to leave when he stopped her, took the pen and paper back and scribbled something else down.

I went over to Carl. His face was grey.

'Worried?' I asked.

'Some,' he said.

'He's a film star.'

Carl smiled wryly. 'Not about that.' He knew I was kidding. Carl never understood jealousy, which was one reason he had never managed to read the situations right at the dances at Årtun until it was too late. 'It's the official start.' He sighed. 'Gilbert called and said he can't dig the first shovelful after all, something came up. He wouldn't say what but it's obviously Kurt Olsen. Fuck him!'

'Easy now.'

'Easy? We've invited journalists from all over the place. This is a crisis.' Carl wiped his free hand over his face but managed to say 'hi' and smile at a guy I think works in the bank. 'Can't you just see the head-lines?' Carl went on once the guy was out of earshot. **'Hotel construction delayed owing to murder investigation. Entrepreneur himself chief suspect.'**

'In the first place they've no grounds for writing about either murder or suspects, and in the second the official start is still two days away. Things could well have changed before that.'

'It needs to happen **now,** Roy. If we're going to cancel the opening it'll have to be this afternoon.'

'A fishing net that's set out in the evening usually gets taken up the next morning,' I said.

'You're saying something's gone wrong?'

'I'm saying it's **possible** the owner is letting it hang there a while longer.'

'But you said that if they leave the net there for too long the catch gets eaten by the other fish down there.'

'Exactly,' I said, and wondered when it was I had started saying 'exactly'. 'So that net was probably pulled up this morning. Or maybe the owner is just slow to report it. Stay cool now.'

The SUV carrying the film people swung out onto the main highway as Shannon approached us, her face radiant, a hand held to her chest as though to keep her heart in place.

'You in love?' asked Carl.

'Not at all,' said Shannon, and Carl roared with laughter as though he'd already put our conversation behind him.

An hour later another familiar vehicle pulled in at the forecourt by the diesel pump and I thought how this day was just getting more and more interesting. I came out from the station as Kurt Olsen climbed out of his Land Rover, and when I saw the angry look on his face I thought **at last,** here comes an interesting story.

I dipped the sponge in the bucket and pulled up his windscreen wipers.

'Not necessary,' he protested, but I'd already splashed soapy water all over the windscreen.

'You can never have too much visibility,' I said. 'Especially now with autumn on the way.'

'I think I see well enough without your help, Roy.'

'Don't say that,' I said, spreading the dirty water across the glass. 'Carl called in. He's going to have to cancel the official opening at some point today.'

'Today?' said Kurt Olsen and looked up.

'Yeah. Damn shame. The school brass band is going to be really disappointed, they've been practising. And we bought fifty Norwegian flags – there isn't a single one left. Absolutely no chance of a last-minute reprieve for the condemned man?'

Kurt Olsen looked down. Spat on the ground.

'Tell your brother he can go ahead with the opening.'

'Oh?'

'Yes,' Olsen said in a low voice.

'Have there been developments in the case?' Apart from my choice of words I was trying not to sound ironic. I splashed on more soapy water.

Olsen straightened up. Coughed. 'I got a phone call from Åge Fredriksen this morning. He lives out near our cabin and sets his fishing net right outside our boathouse. He's done it for years.'

'You don't say?' I said, dropping the sponge into the bucket and picking up the squeegee, pretending not to notice Kurt's penetrating stare.

'And this morning he caught a queer fish all right. My father's mobile phone.'

'Jesus,' I said. The rubber emitted a low squeal as I drew the squeegee over the glass.

'Fredriksen thinks the phone's been lying there in the same place for sixteen years, covered by sludge so the divers who went down looking for Dad that time found nothing. Every time he's set out his net, it's brushed over the phone. And when he pulled up the net this morning the bottom rungs of the net just happened to glide in under the clip on the holder so the phone came up with the net.'

'Quite something,' I said, tearing a strip off the paper roll and wiping the blade of the squeegee.

'Quite something is an understatement,' he said. 'Sixteen years putting out that net, and the phone gets caught up in it now.'

'Isn't that the essence of what they call chaos theory? That sooner or later everything happens, including the most unlikely things?'

'I'll accept that. What I'm not buying is the timing. It's a bit too good to be true.'

He might as well have said: **too good for you and Carl.**

'And it doesn't fit in with the timeline from back then,' he said. He looked at me and waited.

I knew what he wanted. For me to argue. Say that

witnesses can't always be relied on. Or that the movements of a man in such deep despair that he takes his own life maybe aren't always the most logical. Or even that base stations themselves can be mistaken. But I resisted the temptation. I held my chin between my index finger and thumb. And nodded slowly. Very slowly. And said: 'Sure sounds like it. Diesel?'

He looked as if he wanted to hit me.

'Well,' I said, 'at least now you can see the road.'

He slammed the door hard behind him and revved the engine. But then eased off on the pedal, made a calm U-turn and rolled slowly out onto the highway. I knew he was watching me in the mirror and I had to struggle to stop myself giving him a wave.

26

IT WAS A CURIOUS SIGHT.

A harsh wind was blowing from the north-west and it was raining cats and rabbits, as people say round here. And yet some hundred shivering souls in rain gear were up there on the mountain watching a be-suited Carl as he posed with Voss Gilbert wearing his chain of office and his best politician's smile, both holding spades. The local paper and other press photographers were clicking away and in the background you could just about hear the Årtun school brass band playing 'Mellom Bakkar og Berg' between the gusts of wind. With a touch of humour Gilbert was introduced as 'the new chairman', although he hardly resented it, all the chairmen since Jo Aas had been referred to in that way. I had nothing special against Voss Gilbert, but he had that bald patch at the **front** of his head and a second name for his first name, so there was definitely something suspicious about him. But not definite enough to stop him being Os county council chairman. Obviously, though, any future expansion in the size of the county would lead to tougher competition for the hammer of office, and with that hairstyle Gilbert would definitely be struggling.

Carl signalled to Gilbert that he should make the first mark with his spade, since the one he was holding had been decorated for the occasion with ribbons and flowers. So Gilbert did so, smiling to the photographers, evidently unaware that his wet lug of hair now lay plastered across his bald spot in a sort of inadvertent comb-over. Gilbert shouted out some witticism which no one heard but which those around him dutifully laughed at. Everyone clapped and Gilbert hurried over to an assistant holding his inside-out umbrella, and we all marched down the mountainside to the buses that stood parked by the road ready to take us to Fritt Fall where the occasion would be celebrated.

The black-feathered Giovanni strutted nervously between the guests and the legs of the tables as I fetched my drink from the bar where Erik stood scowling at me. I thought of joining Carl who was talking to Willumsen, Jo Aas and Dan Krane, but instead walked over to where Shannon was standing at the betting table with Stanley, Gilbert and Simon Nergard. I gathered they were talking about Bowie and Ziggy Stardust, probably because 'Starman' was blasting from the loudspeakers.

'Course the guy was a pervert, he dressed up like a woman,' said Simon, already slightly drunk and aggressive.

'If by pervert you mean homosexual, well, you also get heterosexual men who'd rather look like women,' said Stanley.

'Fucking sick if you ask me,' said Simon, looking at the new chairman. 'It's not natural.'

'Not necessarily,' said Stanley. 'Animals cross-dress too. You, Roy, with your interest in birds, you probably know that in certain species of bird the male imitates the female. They camouflage themselves as females by using the same feathering.'

The others looked at me and I felt myself turning red.

'And not just on special occasions,' Stanley continued. 'They carry this female phenotype throughout their lives, don't they?'

'Not any of the mountain birds I'm familiar with,' I said.

'See?' said Simon, and Stanley gave me a quick look as much as to say I'd let him down. 'Nature's practical, so what the hell would be the point of dressing up like a woman?'

'It's quite simple,' said Shannon. 'The disguised males avoid the attention of the alpha males who want to fight off possible competitors in the sexual market. While the alpha males are fighting it out, the cross-dressers are mating on the quiet, so to speak.'

Chairman Gilbert laughed good-naturedly. 'Not a bad strategy.'

Stanley laid a hand on Shannon's arm. 'Here, at last, we have someone who understands the complexities of the game of love.'

'Well, it isn't exactly rocket science,' said Shannon, smiling. 'We're all looking for the most comfortable survival strategy. And if we find ourselves in a situation, personal or social, in which it no longer works, then we try another one that's necessary, although possibly a little less comfortable.'

'What do you mean, the most comfortable strategy?' asked Voss Gilbert.

'The one that follows the rules of society, so that we don't risk sanctions. Also known as morality, Mr Chairman. If that doesn't work, then we break the rules.'

Gilbert raised one of his heavy brows. 'Many people behave in a moral way even though it isn't necessarily the most comfortable.'

'The reason for that is just that for some people the idea of being thought of as immoral is so unpleasant that this becomes an important part of the decision. But if we were invisible and had nothing to lose we wouldn't care at all. We're all of us at heart opportunists with survival and the furtherance of our own genetic heritage as the overriding goal in life. That's why we're all willing to sell our souls. It's just that some of us ask a different price from others.'

'Amen to that,' said Stanley.

Gilbert chuckled and shook his head. 'That there is big-city talk. It goes way over our heads. Or am I right, Simon?'

'Also known as bollocks,' said Simon, emptying his glass and looking round for a refill.

'Now now, Simon,' said the chairman. 'But you should remember, fru Opgard, that we come from a part of the country in which people sacrificed their lives for the right moral values during the Second World War.'

'He means the twelve men in that heavy water sabo- tage action we keep making films about,' said Stanley. 'The rest of the population more or less let the Nazis do what they wanted.'

'You shut your mouth,' said Simon, his eyelids drooping halfway over his pupils.

'Those twelve men hardly sacrificed their lives for moral values,' said Shannon. 'They did it for their country. Their village. Their families. If Hitler had been born in Norway where the economic and political situation was the same as in Germany, he would have come to power here just the same. And your saboteurs would have been fighting for Hitler instead.'

'What the fuck!' Simon snarled, and I took a step forward in case he had to be stopped.

Shannon, however, couldn't be stopped. 'Or do you believe that the Germans who lived in the thirties and forties were a generation of out-and-out immoralists, while Norwegians of the time were lucky enough not to be?'

'Those are pretty strong claims, fru Opgard.'

'Strong? I can see that they're provocative and perhaps offensive to Norwegians with a deep emotional attachment to their history. All I'm trying to say is that morality as a motivating force is overrated in us humans. And that our loyalty to our flock is underestimated. We shape morality so that it suits our purposes when we feel our group is under threat. Family vendettas and genocides throughout history are not the work of monsters but of human beings like us who believed they were acting in a way that was morally correct. Our loyalty is primarily to our own and secondarily to the changing morality that at any given time serves the needs of our group. My great-uncle took part in the Cuban revolution, and even today there are still two diametrically opposed but morally equally dogmatic ways of looking at Fidel Castro. And what determines your view of him is not whether you are politically on the right or the left but the degree to which Castro affected the history of your close family, the extent to which they ended up part of the government in Havana or refugees in Miami. Everything else is secondary.'

I felt someone tugging at my jacket sleeve and turned. It was Grete.

'Can I have a word with you?' she whispered.

'Hi, Grete. We're just in the middle of a conversation about—'

'Mating on the quiet,' said Grete. 'I heard that.'

Something in the way she said it made me look more closely at her. And those words, they resonated with a hunch I'd had, something I'd already thought.

'A word then,' I said, and as we headed towards the bar I could feel both Stanley's and Shannon's eyes on my back.

'There's something I want you to pass on to Carl's wife,' said Grete once we were out of earshot.

'Why is that?' I asked 'why' instead of 'what' because I already knew the 'what'. Saw it in her murky eyes.

'Because she'll believe you.'

'Why should she believe it if it's something I'm just passing on?'

'Because you'll tell her as though it comes directly from you.'

'And why should I do that?'

'Because you want the same thing as me, Roy,'

'And that is?'

'For them to split up.'

I wasn't shocked. Not even surprised. Just fascinated.

'Come on, Roy, we both know that Carl and that southern girl don't belong together. We're only doing what's best for them. And it'll save her the slow torment of finding it out herself, poor girl.'

I tried to moisten my throat. Wanted to turn and go but couldn't. 'Find out what?'

'That Carl's having it away with Mari again.'

I looked at her. The perm stood out around her pale face like a halo. It's always surprised me that people fall for shampoo adverts that say it revitalises the hair. Hair has never had any life in it that can be **re**vitalised. Hair's dead, a cuticle of keratin growing out of a follicle. It's got as much of life and you in it as the excrement you squeeze out. Hair is history, it's what you've been, eaten and done. And you can't go back. Grete's perm was a mummified past, a permafrost, frightening as death itself.

'They do it at the Aas's cabin.'

I didn't answer.

'I've seen it with my own eyes,' said Grete. 'They park in the woods so you can't see the cars from the road and then they meet in the cabin.'

I wanted to ask how much of her time she spent shadowing Carl but didn't.

'But it's no wonder Carl fucks around,' she said.

She obviously wanted me to ask what she meant by that. But something – the look on her face, the certainty of something, reminded me of when Mum read 'Little Red Riding Hood' to us – persuaded me not to. Because as a child I had never understood why Red Riding Hood has to ask the disguised wolf that final question, why it has such big teeth, when she already has a suspicion that it is the wolf. Didn't she understand that once the wolf realises he's been unmasked he would grab her and eat her up? What I learned from it was: stop after 'why do you have such big ears?' Say you're going to fetch more wood from the woodshed, and then get the hell out of there. But I just stood there. And like any fucking

Little Red Riding Hood I asked: 'What do you mean by that?'

'That he fucks around? Because they usually do, the ones who were sexually abused when they were kids.'

I had stopped breathing. Couldn't move a muscle. And my voice was hoarse when I spoke. 'What the hell makes you think Carl was abused?'

'He said so himself. When he was drunk, after he fucked me in the woods at Årtun. Sobbed, said he regretted it, but he couldn't help it, that he'd read somewhere that people like him became promiscuous.'

I moved my tongue around in my mouth looking for saliva, but it was dry as the inside of a hay barn.

'Promiscuous,' was all I could manage to whisper, but she didn't seem to hear.

'And he said you blamed yourself for him being abused. That that was why you always looked out for him. That you sort of owed him.'

I got a little more sound from my vocal cords. 'You've been lying for so long you believe it yourself.'

Grete smiled as she shook her head in pretended regret. 'Carl was so drunk that he's bound to have forgotten he said it, but he did. I asked him why you blamed yourself when it wasn't you but his own father who was abusing him. Carl said he thought it was because you were his big brother. That you thought it was your job to look after him. And that was why in the end you rescued him.'

'So you think you can remember him saying that?' I tried, but I could see it had no effect on her.

'That's what he said,' she nodded. 'But when I asked he wouldn't tell me **how** you rescued him.'

I was finished. I saw those wormlike lips moving. 'So I'm asking you now: what did you do, Roy?'

I raised my head and looked into her eyes. Expectant. Gleeful. Mouth half open, all that was left was to pop the fork in. I felt a bubbling in my chest, a smile coming, I just couldn't stop it.

'Eh?' said Grete, and the look on her face turned to surprise as I burst out laughing.

I was . . . actually, what was I? Happy? Relieved? The way exposed murderers feel liberated because the waiting is over and finally they are no longer alone with their terrible secret. Or was I just crazy? Because surely you must be crazy if you prefer people to believe you've been abusing your little brother rather than know that it was your father who did it and that you, the big brother, didn't do a thing about it. Or maybe it isn't madness, maybe it's as simple as that you can tolerate the disgust of a whole village which is rooted in lies and false rumours, but not if there's the tiniest element of truth in it. And the truth about what happened at Opgard wasn't just about a father who was an abuser, it was also about a cowardly, crawling big brother who could have intervened but didn't dare to, who knew but kept his mouth shut, who was ashamed of himself but kept his head down so low he could hardly bear the sight of his own reflection in the mirror. And now the worst that could happen had happened. When Grete Smitt knew something and talked about it then the whole hair salon found out about it followed by the whole village, that's how straightforward it was. So then why did I laugh? Because the worst that could happen had just happened, and it was already several seconds in the past. Now everything could go to hell in a handcart, and I was free.

'Well?' said Carl brightly. 'What do people do for kicks around here?' He put one arm across my shoulder, laid the other round Grete's. Breathed champagne breath on me.

'Hm,' I said. 'What do you say, Grete?'

'Trotting,' said Grete.

'Trotting?' Carl laughed loudly and took a glass of champagne from the tray on the counter. He was getting very drunk, no question about that. 'I didn't know Roy followed the gee-gees.'

'I'm trying to get him interested,' said Grete.

'And what's your **pitch**?'

'My pitch?'

'Your sales pitch.'

'If you don't play, you can't win. And I think Roy knows that.'

Carl turned to me. 'Do you?'

I shrugged.

'Roy's more the type that thinks if you don't play, you can't lose,' said Carl.

'It's just a question of finding a game where everyone's a winner,' said Grete. 'Just like with your hotel, Carl. No losers, only winners and a happy ending.'

'Let's drink to that!' said Carl. He and Grete clinked their glasses together and then Carl turned to me, his glass still raised.

I realised I was still wearing that idiotic smile.

'Left my glass over there,' I said, nodding towards the Bowie colloquy, and then walked away, with no plans to return.

As I walked back towards them my heart was singing. Paradoxical, carefree, and almost mockingly, like the wheatear that sat on a gravestone and sang his zip-tuk song as the priest tossed the earth down onto my parents' coffins. There are no happy endings, but there are moments of meaningless happiness, and each one of those moments might be the last, so why not sing at the top of your voice? Tell the world. And then let life – or death – knock you down another day.

As I approached Stanley turned his head towards me as though he had known I was coming. He didn't smile, just sought out my eyes. A warmth flowed through my body. I didn't know why, all I knew was that the time had come. The time when I would drive into Geitesvingen and **not** come out of the turn. I would drive off the road and out in free fall, secure in the knowledge that the only prize awaiting me was those few seconds of freedom, understanding, truth and all of that stuff. And then I would come to the end, crushed against the ground in a place where the wreck could never be recovered, where I could rot in a blessed loneliness, peace and quiet.

I don't know why I chose that particular moment.

Maybe because that one glass of champagne had given me just enough courage. Maybe because I knew I had straight away to crush the little hope Grete had given me before I could pursue it and let it grow. Because I did not want the prize she was offering, it would be worse than all the loneliness a life could offer.

I passed Stanley, picked up the champagne glass beside the trotting coupons and stood behind Shannon, who was listening to the new chairman as he spoke enthusiastically about what the hotel would mean for the village, although what he probably meant was for the coming council election. I touched Shannon's shoulder lightly, leaned towards her ear, so close I could pick up the smell of her, so unlike the smell of any woman I had known or made love to, and yet so familiar, as though it could have been my own.

'I'm sorry,' I whispered. 'But there's nothing I can do about it. I love you.'

She didn't turn to me. Didn't ask me to repeat what I had just said. She just carried on looking at Gilbert with the same unchanged expression on her face, as though I had whispered a translation of something he was saying. But for an instant I could feel the smell of her grow stronger, the same warmth that flowed through me flowing through her too, lifting the scent molecules from her skin as it rose up towards me.

I carried on towards the door, stopped by the old payazzo machine, downed the rest of the champagne and placed the glass up on the wooden frame. Noticed that Giovanni was standing there looking at

349

me with his sharp and censorious rooster look before he – almost in contempt – turned away with a cock-a-doodle-doo that made his little red Hitler-quiff jump.

I went out. Closed my eyes and inhaled the air, washed clean by the rain, as sharp as the blade of an open razor against the cheek. Oh yes, winter would be coming early this year.

When I reached the station I called head office and asked to be put through to the personnel manager.

'This is Roy Opgard. I was wondering if that position as manager of the station in Sørlandet is still open?'

PART FOUR

27

THEY SAY I'M THE ONE who's most like Dad.

Silent and steady. Kind and practical. An average, hard-working type with no obvious talent for anything in particular but will always get by, perhaps mostly because he never asks too much of life. Bit of a loner but sociable when necessary, with enough empathy to know when someone's in trouble, but enough sense of shame not to interfere in other people's lives. The way Dad didn't let others interfere in his. They said he was proud without being arrogant, and the respect he showed others was reciprocated, though he was never the village bellwether. He left that to the more literary, the more eloquent, the more pushy, the more charismatic and visionary, the Aases and the Carls. Those with less shame.

Because he did feel shame. And that quality is something I very definitely inherited from him.

He felt ashamed of what he was and what he did. I felt ashamed of what I was and what I **didn't** do.

Dad liked me. I loved him. And he loved Carl.

As the older son I was given a thorough grounding in how to run a mountain farm with thirty goats. The goat population of Norway had been five times greater in my grandfather's day, and the number of goat farmers had fallen by half just over the last ten years, and my father probably realised that in the future it wouldn't be possible to make a living from goat farming on such a small scale at Opgard. But as he said: there's always the chance that one day the power would go, the world be hurled into a chaos in which it was every man for himself. And people like me will still get by.

And people like Carl will go under.

And maybe that's why he loved Carl more.

Or maybe it was because Carl didn't worship him the way I did.

I don't know if that's what it was, a mixture of Dad's protective instincts and a need to be loved by his son. Or that Carl was so like my mother when she and my dad first met. Alike in the way they talked, laughed, thought and moved, and even in the photos of Mum from back then. Carl was as good-looking as Elvis, Dad used to say. Maybe that's what he fell for in Mum. Her Elvis looks. A blonde Elvis, but with the same Latino or Indian features: almond-shaped eyes, smooth, glowing skin, prominent eyebrows. The smile and the laughter that seemed always to be just below the surface. Maybe my father fell in love all over again with Mum. And then with Carl.

I don't know.

All I know is that Dad took over the bedtime reading in the boys' room and that he spent longer and longer doing it. That he carried on long after I had fallen asleep in the upper bunk, and that I knew nothing about it until one night I was woken by Carl's crying and Dad trying to hush him up. I peered over the edge of the bunk and saw that Dad's chair was empty, that he must have sneaked into bed beside Carl.

'What's the matter?' I asked.

There was no answer from down below, so I repeated the question.

'Carl was just having a bad dream,' said my father. 'Go back to sleep, Roy.'

And I went back to sleep. I slept the guilty sleep of the innocent. And I went on doing so until one night Carl was crying again, and this time Dad had left, so my little brother was alone with no one to comfort him. So I climbed down to his bunk, wrapped my arms around him and told him to tell me what he had dreamed, because then the monsters would all disappear.

And Carl sniffed and said the monsters had said he wasn't to tell anybody, because then they would come and take me and Mum too, take us down into Huken and eat us.

'But not Dad?' I asked.

Carl didn't reply, and I don't know if I understood and repressed it right there, or if I only understood later, **wanted** to understand it: that the monster was our father. Dad. And I don't know either if Mum wanted to understand it but that in her case the will was lacking, because it was happening right in front of our eyes and ears. And that made her as guilty as me in looking the other way and not trying to stop it.

When I finally did it I was seventeen years old and Dad and I were alone in the barn. I was footing the ladder as he shifted light bulbs up under the ridge. Barns on mountain farms aren't all that high, but still I felt I was a risk for him, standing there a few metres below him.

'You're not to do what you do to Carl.'

'All right then,' said Dad quietly, and finished changing the light bulbs.

Then he climbed down the ladder, with me holding it as steady as I could. He put the used bulbs down before attacking me. He didn't hit me in the face, only on the body, in all the soft places where it hurt the most. As I lay in the hay, unable to breathe, he leaned over me and whispered in a thick, hoarse voice: 'Don't you accuse your father of something like that or I'll kill you, Roy. There's only one way to stop a father and that's by keeping your mouth shut, wait for your chance and then kill him. You understand?'

Of course I understood. That was what Little Red Riding Hood should have done. But I couldn't speak, couldn't even nod, just raised my head very slightly and saw that he had tears in his eyes.

Dad helped me to my feet, we ate supper, and that night he was with Carl in the lower bunk again.

Next day he took me into the barn where he'd suspended the big punchbag that came over with him from Minnesota to Norway. For a time he'd wanted Carl and me to box, but we hadn't been interested, not even when he told us about the famous boxing brothers Mike and Tommy Gibbons from Minnesota. Tommy Gibbons was Dad's favourite – he'd shown us pictures of him, said how Carl looked like the tall, blond heavyweight Tommy. I was more like Mike, the big brother who was nevertheless smaller, and whose career wasn't so successful. Anyway, neither of them had been champions, Tommy came closest in 1923, when he went fifteen rounds and lost on points to the great Jack Dempsey. It was in the little town of Shelby, a crossing on the Great Northern Railway which the railway director Peter Shelby – the place was named after him – called 'a godforsaken mudhole'. The town had been promised that the fight would put them on the map in the USA and they invested all they had and more in it. A big stadium was built, but only seven thousand turned up to watch, plus a handful that sneaked in without paying, and the whole town – including four banks – went bankrupt. Tommy Gibbons left a town in ruins, without a title, without a cent in his pocket, with nothing but the knowledge that he had at least tried.

'How's your body feeling?' asked Dad.

'Fine,' I said, though I still ached all over.

Dad showed me how to stand and the basic punches, then he tied his worn-out old boxing gloves on me.

'What about the **guard**?' I asked, recalling a news-reel I had seen from the Dempsey–Gibbons fight.

'You hit hard and you hit first, so you don't need that,' he said, and positioned himself behind the bag. 'This is the enemy. Tell yourself you've got to kill him before he kills you.'

And I killed. He kept a firm hold on the bag to stop it swinging too much, but now and then he peered out from behind it, as though to show me who it was I was training to kill.

'Not bad,' he said as I stood there bent double, drip-ping sweat, my hands on my knees. 'Now we'll tape your wrists and do it again without gloves.'

Within three weeks I had punched holes in the bag and the cloth had to be sewn up with thick twine. I bloodied my knuckles hitting those stitches, let them heal for two days and then bloodied them again. It felt better that way, the pain deadened the pain, dead-ened the shame I felt just standing there and punch-ing, unable to do anything else.

Because it went on.

Not as often as before, maybe, I don't remember.

Remember only that he no longer cared if I was

asleep or not, didn't care if Mum was asleep, cared only to show that he was master in his own house, and that a master does as he pleases. And that he had turned me into his physically equal opponent, as though to show us that he controlled us spiritually, not physically. Because what is physical is evanescent and fades, while spirit is eternal.

And I felt shame. Shame as my thoughts tried to flee from the sounds down below, from the swaying and creaking frame of the bunk beds, from that house. And after he'd gone I climbed down to Carl, held him until his crying stopped, whispered in his ear that one day, one day we'd go somewhere far away. I'd stop him. Stop that fucking mirror image of me. Empty words that only made my shame the greater.

We grew old enough to go to parties. Carl drank more than he should. And wound up in trouble more often than he should. And I was glad of it, because it opened up a place where I could do what I could never do at home: protect my little brother. It was simple, I just did what Dad had taught me: hit first and hit hard. Hit faces as though they were punchbags with Dad's face on them.

But the day had to come.

And the day did come.

Carl came and told me he'd been to the doctor's. That they'd examined him and asked him a lot of questions. That they had their suspicions. I asked what was wrong with him and he pulled down his trousers and showed me. I felt so angry I began to cry.

Before going to bed that night I went to the porch and took down the hunting knife. I put it under my pillow and waited.

On the fourth night he came in. As usual I was woken by the little creak from the door. He'd turned off the light in the corridor so all I saw was the outline in the doorway. I put my hand under the pillow and gripped round the handle of the knife. I had asked Uncle Bernard, who had read all about the saboteurs in Os during the war, and he said that silent killing was something you did by sticking your knife into the enemy's back at the level of the kidneys. That cutting someone's throat was much more difficult than it looks in films, that a lot of them ended up cutting their own thumb that was holding the enemy. I didn't know exactly how high up the kidneys were, but my plan anyway was to stab lots of times, so one of them would probably hit. If not, then I'd have to go for his throat and my thumb, I didn't give a fuck.

The figure in the doorway swayed slightly, maybe he'd drunk a few more beers than usual. He just stood there, as though wondering if he'd taken the wrong turning. As indeed he had. For years. But this would be the last time.

I heard a sound, as though he was drawing breath. Or sniffing the air.

The door closed, pitch darkness descended and I

got ready. My heart was pounding so hard I could feel it literally pressing against my ribs. Then I heard his footsteps on the stairs and realised he had changed his mind.

I heard the front door open.

Had he sensed something? I had read somewhere that adrenaline has a distinctive smell that our brain – consciously or unconsciously – registers, and puts us on the alert automatically. Or had he come to a decision there in the doorway? Not just to walk away from it tonight, but that it was over. That it would never happen again.

As I lay there I could feel my body start to shake. And when a rasping sound came from my throat as I drew breath I realised I had been holding it from the moment I heard the door creak.

After a while I heard the sound of someone crying quietly. I held my breath again, but it wasn't coming from Carl, he was breathing regularly again. It was coming through the stovepipe.

I crept out of bed, pulled on some clothes and went downstairs.

Mum was sitting in the half-dark in the kitchen by the worktop. She was wearing her red dressing gown that looked like a quilted coat, and staring out the window towards the barn, where the lights were on. She was holding a glass, and on the table stood the bottle of bourbon that for years had remained un-opened in the cupboard in the dining room.

I sat down.

Looked in the same direction as her, towards the barn.

She emptied her glass and filled it up again. It was the first time since that evening at the Grand Hotel that I had seen her drinking when it wasn't Christmas Eve.

When at last she spoke her voice was hoarse and trembling.

'You know, Roy, that I love your father so much I can't live without him.'

It sounded like the conclusion of a long, silent discussion she'd been having with herself.

I said nothing, just stared across at the barn. Waiting to hear something from over there.

'But he can live without me,' she said. 'You know, there were complications when Carl was born. I had lost a lot of blood and was unconscious, and the doctor had to let your father take the decision. There were two ways of doing it, one that was a risk for the foetus, and one that was a risk for the mother. Your father chose the one that was dangerous for me, Roy. Afterwards he said that of course I would have made the same choice, and he was right about that. But I wasn't the one that chose, Roy. It was him.'

What was I expecting to hear from the barn? I know what it was. A shot. The door to the porch had been open when I came down the stairs. And the shotgun that usually hung high up on the wall was gone.

'But if I had had to choose between saving your life and Carl's, then I would have chosen him, Roy.

362

So now you know. That's all the mother I've been to you.' She raised the glass to her mouth.

I had never heard her talk that way before, and yet I didn't care. All I could think about was what was happening in the barn.

I got up and walked out. It was late summer, and the night air was cool against my hot cheeks. I didn't rush. Walked at a measured tread, almost like a grown man. In the light from the open barn door I saw the shotgun, leaning up against the door jamb. As I came closer I saw the ladder leaning against one of the roof beams, and a rope slung over it.

I heard the dull thud of punches against the plastic covering of the punchbag.

I stopped before I reached the door, but close enough to be able to see him. He was punching and jabbing the bag. Did he know the face I had drawn on it was his? Probably.

Was that shotgun leaning there because he hadn't managed to finish what he had started? Or was it an invitation to me?

My cheeks were no longer hot. Abruptly, along with the rest of my body, they had turned ice cold, and the slight night breeze blew right through me as though I were a fucking ghost.

I stood there and watched my father. Of course I knew that he wanted me to stop him, stop what he was doing, stop his heart. Everything was arranged. He'd organised things so that it would look as though he'd done it himself, even that rope gave its own clear message. So all I needed to do was shoot at close range and lay the shotgun beside the body. I shook. I could no longer control my body, nothing obeyed, my limbs quivered and shook. I didn't feel anger or fear any longer, all I felt was impotence and shame. Because I couldn't do it. **He** wanted to die, **I** wanted him to die, and yet I still could not fucking do it. Because he was me. And I hated him and I needed him, as I hated and needed myself. As I turned and walked away I heard him groan and punch, swear and punch, sob and punch.

At breakfast next morning it was as though it hadn't happened. As though it was all just something I had dreamed. Dad peered out the kitchen window and passed some remark about the weather, and Mum hurried Carl along so he wouldn't be late for school.

28

A FEW MONTHS AFTER I'D left my father in the barn, fru Willumsen pulled up in front of the workshop and booked a service for her Saab Sonett '58 model, a roadster, and the only cabriolet in the village.

People in the village claimed that Willumsen's wife was obsessed with a Norwegian pop diva from the seventies and tried to copy her in every way: the car, the clothes, the make-up and her way of walking. She even went so far as to try to copy the diva's famous deep voice. I was too young to remember this pop star, but fru Willumsen was a diva all right, no question about it.

Uncle Bernard had a doctor's appointment so I had to go over the machine myself to see if there were any obvious problems.

'Nice lines,' I said, stroking a hand over one of the front fins. Fibreglass reinforced plastic. According to Uncle Bernard, Saab had produced fewer than ten of them, and it must have set Willumsen back more than he liked.

'Thanks,' she said.

I opened the bonnet and looked over the engine. Checked the leads and that the caps were on properly, copying someone else again, in this case Uncle Bernard.

'You look like you know how to handle the insides too,' she said. 'Even though you look so young.'

It was my turn to say thanks.

It was a hot day; I'd been working on a lorry and pulled down the top half of the overalls so my chest was bare when she arrived. I was boxing a lot up in the barn now, I had muscles where before there was just skin and bone, and her eyes glided over me as she told me what she wanted. And when I pulled on a T-shirt before checking over her car she had almost looked disappointed.

I closed the bonnet and turned to her. The high heels she was wearing meant she wasn't just taller than me, she towered over me.

'Well?' she said, and then continued after a pause that was much too long. 'Do you like what you see?'

'It seems fine but I ought to take a closer look,' I said with a fake self-assurance, as though it would be me and not Uncle Bernard who would be taking that look.

It occurred to me that she was older than she looked. The eyebrows looked as though they'd been shaved off and then drawn on again. There were small wrinkles in the skin above her upper lip. But all the same, fru Willumsen was what Uncle Bernard called a **full rigger.**

'And after that . . .' She put her head on one side and appraised me, as though she was in a butcher's shop and I was a piece of meat laid out on the slab. '. . . look?'

'Then we'll go over the engine and change anything that needs changing,' I said, 'within the limits of what's reasonable and acceptable, naturally.' Another line I'd nicked from Uncle Bernard. Apart from when I had to swallow in the middle of the sentence.

'Reasonable and acceptable.' She smiled, as though I'd just served up a witticism in the Oscar Wilde class. Apart from the fact that I'd never heard of Oscar Wilde at that time. But right about then it dawned on me that I wasn't the only one standing there and reading all sorts of hidden sex fantasies into the conversation. There could no longer be any doubt about it, fru Willumsen was flirting with me. Not that I kidded myself she wanted to take it any further, but she was definitely taking time for a little game with a seventeen-year-old, the way a grown cat will pat your dangling balls of wool before padding on its way. And just that was enough to make me feel proud and a little arrogant as I stood there.

'But I can tell you already that there isn't much here

that needs to be fixed,' I said, fishing up my silver box of snuff from the pocket of my overalls as I leaned against the bonnet. 'The car looks to be in excellent condition. For its age.'

Fru Willumsen laughed.

'Rita,' she said, extending a dazzlingly white hand with blood-red nails.

If I'd been more on the case I would probably have kissed it, but instead I put down my snuffbox, wiped my hand on the rag that was dangling from my back pocket and gave her a firm handshake. 'Roy.'

She gave me a thoughtful look. 'OK, Roy. But there's no need to squeeze so hard.'

'Eh?'

'Don't say "eh". Say "what". Or "excuse me". Try again.' She offered me her hand once more.

I took it again. Carefully this time. She pulled it towards her.

'I didn't tell you to treat it as though it were stolen property, Roy. I'm giving you my hand, and for these few brief moments it's yours. So use it, be good to it, treat it in such a way that you know you will be allowed to have it again.'

She offered me her hand for a third time.

And I put both of mine around it.

Stroked it. Pressed it against my cheek. No idea where I got the bottle from. Only knew that right now I had it, all that courage I had lacked as I stood outside the barn and saw the shotgun in the doorway.

Rita Willumsen laughed, looked around quickly

as though to confirm that we were still unobserved, let me keep her hand a little longer before slowly withdrawing it.

'You learn quickly,' she said. 'Quickly. And soon you'll be a man. I think you'll make someone very happy, Roy.'

A Mercedes pulled up in front of us. Willumsen jumped out and hardly had time to say hello to me he was so busy opening the car door for fru Willumsen. Who was now **Rita** Willumsen. He held her hand as she manoeuvred her way in, high heels, high hair, tight skirt. And when they drove off I felt a mixture of excitement and confusion at the thought of what now suddenly lay before me. The excitement came from having fru Willumsen's hand in mine, those long nails scraping against my palm. And the fact that she was the clearly much-treasured wife of Willumsen, the man who had cheated Dad over the purchase of the Cadillac and boasted of it afterwards. The confusion was caused by the engine compartment, in which everything seemed to be back to front. I mean, the gearbox was **in front of** the engine. Later Uncle Bernard explained to me that it was because of the special dispersal of the weight in a Sonett, that they had even turned the crankshaft so the engine on this car went the opposite way to all other cars. Saab Sonett. What a car. What a gorgeous, useless piece of outdated beauty.

I worked on the Saab until late at night, checking, tightening, changing. I possessed a new, furious energy and I didn't know quite where it came from.

Or actually, yes, I did. It came from Rita Willumsen. She had touched me. I had touched her. She had seen me as a man. Or at least as the man I **could** become. And that had changed something. At some point, as I stood there in the grease pit and ran my hand over the chassis of the car, I felt myself growing hard. I closed my eyes and imagined it. **Tried** to imagine it. A semi-naked Rita Willumsen on the bonnet of the Saab, beckoning to me with her index finger. That red nail varnish. Jesus.

I listened out to make sure I was alone in the workshop before I pulled down the zip on my overalls.

'Roy?' whispered Carl in the dark as I was about to creep up to the top bunk.

I was on the point of saying something about doing overtime at the workshop, that we should sleep now. But something in his voice stopped me. I turned on the light above his bed. His eyes were red-rimmed from crying and one of his cheeks was swollen. I felt my stomach tighten. After that time in the barn with the shotgun, Dad had kept away.

'Has he been here again?' I whispered.

Carl just nodded.

'Did he . . . did he **hit** you as well?'

'Yes. And I thought he was going to strangle me. He was furious. Asked where you were.'

'Shit,' I said.

'You've got to be here,' said Carl. 'He doesn't come if you're here.'

'I can't always be here, Carl.'

'Then I'll have to go away. I can't take it any more . . . I don't want to live any more with someone who . . .'

I put one arm around Carl, the other around the back of his head, pressed his head into my chest so that his sobbing wouldn't wake Mum and Dad.

'I'll fix it, Carl,' I whispered down into his fair hair. 'I swear. You won't have to run away from him. I'll fix this, d'you hear me?'

With the coming of the first pale light of morning my plan was complete.

Just to be thinking about it didn't put me under any obligation, but at the same time I knew I was ready now. I thought of what Rita Willumsen had said, that soon I would be a man. Well, this was soon. This time I wouldn't back off. I wouldn't walk away from that shotgun.

29

I HAD LEARNED A COUPLE of things during those hours I worked on the Saab Sonett. Not only was the engine mounted back to front, but the braking system was easier too. Modern cars have double braking systems so that if one of the brake hoses is cut, the brakes will still work, at least on two of the wheels. But on the Sonett all you have to do is cut one hose and hey presto, what you've got is a freewheeling wagon, a loose cannon on deck. And it struck me that this was generally true of most old cars – including Dad's 1979 Cadillac DeVille, although that does actually have two brake hoses.

When men in this part of the country don't die of some routine sickness, they die on a country lane in a car, or in a barn at the end of a rope or a shotgun barrel. I had failed the time Dad gave me the chance to use the shotgun, and maybe I understood too that he wouldn't be giving me a second chance. That now I had to do the thinking for myself. And once I'd thought it through, I knew I'd found the right solution. It wasn't about the skipper having to go down with his own ship or anything like that, it was purely practical. A car accident wouldn't be investigated in the same way as a man who'd been shot through the head, at least that's what I persuaded myself. And I didn't know how I was going to get Dad into the barn and shoot him without Mum at least knowing what had happened. And God knows whether she would lie to the police when the man she couldn't live without had been killed. **That's all the mother I've been to you.** But sabotaging the brakes on the Cadillac was a simple matter. And the consequences as easy to predict. Every morning Dad got up, saw to the goats, heated up his coffee and watched in silence as Carl and I ate breakfast. After me and Carl had cycled off – him to school, me to the workshop – Dad got in his Cadillac and drove down into the village to fetch the mail and buy a newspaper.

The Cadillac stood under the barn roof and I'd seen him do it countless times. Start the car, drive off and – unless there was snow and ice on the road – not touch the brakes or turn until he was heading into Geitesvingen.

We ate supper in the dining room and then I

said I was going out to the barn for a workout on the punchbag.

No one said anything. Mum and Carl scraped their plates, but Dad gave me a quizzical look. Maybe because he and I didn't usually announce what we were going to do, we just went ahead and did it.

I took my training bag containing the tool I'd brought home from the workshop. The job was a little more complicated than I had supposed, but after half an hour I'd got the set screw loose and the bolt holding the steering column to the rack, punched holes in both of the brake hoses and collected the brake fluid in a bucket. I changed into my workout gear and spent another thirty minutes on the punchbag, so when I entered the living room where Mum and Dad were sitting like some couple from a sixties advert, him with his newspaper, Mum with her knitting, I was dripping with sweat.

'You were late home last night,' said Dad without looking up from his paper.

'Overtime,' I said.

'You're allowed to tell us if you've met a girl,' said Mum. Smiled. As if that's exactly what we were, the average family in a fucking advert.

'Just overtime,' I said.

'Well,' said Dad, folding his newspaper, 'there might be more overtime from now on. They just rang from the hospital in Notodden. Bernard's been admitted. Apparently they saw something they didn't like when he was at the doctor's yesterday. He might have to have an operation.'

'Oh?' I said, and felt myself go cold.

'Yes, and his daughter's in Mallorca with her family and can't interrupt their holiday. So the hospital wants us to go.'

Carl came in. 'What's that?' he asked. His voice still sounded as if he'd been anaesthetised, and there was a nasty bruise on his cheek, although it was less swollen.

'We're going to Notodden,' said Dad, pushing himself up out of the chair. 'Get dressed.'

I felt panic, like the morning you open the front door and aren't prepared for the fact that the temperature's fallen to minus thirty, it's blowing a gale and you don't feel the cold, just a sudden and complete paralysis. I opened my mouth, closed it again. Because paralysis affects the brain too.

'I've got an important exam tomorrow,' said Carl, and I saw he was looking at me. 'And Roy's promised to test me.'

I hadn't heard anything about any exam. I don't know exactly what Carl had or hadn't understood, only that he realised I was desperately looking for a way out of going to Notodden.

'Well,' said Mum, with a look at Dad, 'they can probably—'

'Out of the question,' said Dad curtly. 'Family comes before everything.'

'Carl and I'll take the bus to Notodden after school tomorrow,' I said.

They all looked at me in surprise. Because I think we all heard it. That suddenly I sounded like him, like Dad when his mind was made up and there was nothing else to discuss, because that was the way things were going to be.

'Fine,' said Mum, sounding relieved.

Dad didn't say anything but kept his gaze fixed on me.

When Mum and Dad were ready to leave Carl and I followed them out into the yard.

Stood there in front of the car in the dusk, a family of four parting company after supper. 'Drive carefully,' I said.

Dad nodded. Slowly. Of course it's possible that I, like other people, make much too much out of famous last words. Or in Dad's case, the last silent nodding. But there was definitely something there that looked almost like a kind of recognition. Or was it acknowledgement? Acknowledgement that his son was turning into an adult.

He and Mum sat in the Cadillac and it started with a snarl. The snarl turned into a soft purring. And then away they drove in the direction of Geitesvingen.

We saw the brake lights on the Cadillac flare. They're connected to the pedal, so even if the brakes don't work the lights do. Their speed increased. Carl made a sound. I could see in my mind's eye Dad turning the wheel, hear a scraping noise from the steering column, feel the steering wheel turning and meeting no resistance, having no effect on the wheels. And I feel pretty sure he understood it then. I hope so. That he understood and accepted it. That he accepted it included Mum, and that the sums added up. She could live with what he did, but not without him.

It happened quietly and with a strange lack of drama. No desperate pounding on the horn, no scorching rubber, no screams. All I could hear was the crunching of the tyres, and then the car was just gone, and the golden plover sang of loneliness.

The crash from Huken sounded like the far-off rumble of delayed thunder. I didn't hear what Carl said or shouted, I just thought that from now on Carl and I were alone up here in the world. That the road ahead of us was empty, that all we could see right now in the dusk was the mountain in silhouette against a sky coloured orange in the west and pink in the north and south. And it seemed to me the loveliest thing I had ever seen, like a sunset and a sunrise both at the same time.

30

I REMEMBER ONLY SNATCHES OF the funeral.

Uncle Bernard was on his feet again, they had decided not to operate, and he and Carl were the only ones I saw crying. The church was full of people that – as far as I know – Mum and Dad had almost no connection with apart from what is absolutely unavoidable in a village like Os. Bernard said a few words and read out the condolences on the wreaths. The biggest was from Willumsen's Used Cars and Breaker's Yard, which probably meant he could charge it to customer services for tax purposes. Neither Carl nor I had expressed any wish to say anything, and the priest didn't press us, I think he appreciated the elbow room when he had such a large audience. But

I don't remember what he said, don't actually think I was listening. The condolences came afterwards, an endless row of pale, grief-stricken faces, like sitting in a car at a level crossing and watching the train pass by, faces staring out, seemingly at you, but actually on their way to quite other places.

Many people said they felt for me, but then of course I couldn't tell them that in that case they weren't feeling too bad.

I remember Carl and me standing in the dining room up at the farm the day before we were due to move down to Uncle Bernard's. We didn't know, of course, that it would only last a few days and that we would move back to Opgard. It was so bloody quiet in there.

'This is all ours now,' said Carl.

'Yeah,' I said. 'But is there anything you want?'

'That,' said Carl, pointing to the cupboard where Dad kept his crates of Budweiser and bottles of bourbon. I took the carton of tins of Berry's moist snuff, and that's how I began using the stuff. Not too often, because you never know when you're going to be able to get hold of Berry's next time, and you don't want to be using that Swedish shite, not once you've known the taste of properly fermented tobacco.

Even before the funeral we'd both been interrogated by the sheriff, though he referred to it as 'just a chat'. Sigmund Olsen wondered why there were no braking marks on Geitesvingen and asked if my father was depressed. But Carl and I stuck to our story that it had looked like an accident. Maybe driving a little too fast and a momentary lapse of attention as he glanced in the rear-view mirror to check that we were following. Something like that. And finally the sheriff appeared to be satisfied. But it struck me too that it was lucky for us these were the only two theories he had: accident or suicide. I knew that punching a couple of holes in the brake hoses and draining off enough brake fluid to significantly reduce the car's braking power would not in itself be enough to arouse suspicion if it was discovered. Air in the braking system is something you get all the time in old cars. It would be worse if they found out that the set screw holding the steering column had been loosened so the steering didn't work. The car had landed on its roof and not been the total wreck I'd been expecting. If they went over the car they might have come to the conclusion that anything that's fixed can also work loose, even set screws. But loose screws **as well as** holes in the brake hoses? And why no traces of leaking brake fluid on the ground beneath the car? As I say, we had been lucky. Or more accurately, **I** had been lucky. Of course I knew that Carl knew that somehow or other I had been behind the accident. He had instinctively realised that at any cost he and I must not ride in the Cadillac that evening. And then there was the promise I had given him, that I would fix things. But he never asked exactly how I'd done it. He probably realised it was the brakes, because he'd seen the brake lights go on without the Cadillac slowing down. And when he never asked, why would I tell him? You can't be punished for something you don't know about, and if I did get done for the murder of our parents I could take the fall alone, I didn't need to have Carl beside me, not the way Dad had had Mum. Because unlike them, Carl could easily live without me. Or so I thought.

31

CARL WAS BORN EARLY IN the autumn, I was born during the summer holidays. It meant that on his birthday he got presents from his classmates and even had a birthday party, whereas mine passed by without celebrations. Not that I ever really complained. That's why it took a couple of seconds before I realised that the words being sung were actually being sung for me.

'Happy eighteenth birthday!'

I was on a break and sitting out in the sun on a couple of pallets, my eyes closed and listening to Cream on my headphones. I looked up and pulled out the earbuds. Had to shade my eyes. Not that I didn't remember that voice. It was Rita Willumsen.

'Thanks,' I said, feeling my face and ears start to

glow as though I'd been caught doing something I shouldn't be doing. 'Who told you that?'

'Coming of age,' was all she said. 'The right to vote. Driving licence. And they can put you in jail.'

The Saab Sonett was parked behind her, just the way it had been all those months ago. But at the same time something felt different, as though she'd given me a promise back then and had come now to keep it. I felt my hand shaking slightly as I pushed the headphones into the back pocket. I was no longer completely unkissed and I'd fumbled a bit under a bra behind the village hall at Årtun, but I was very definitely still a virgin.

'There's funny sounds coming from the Sonett,' she said.

'What kind of sounds?' I asked.

'Maybe we should take a drive and you can hear them for yourself.'

'Sure thing. Just a moment.' I went into the office.

'I'll be away for a while,' I said.

'OK,' said Uncle Bernard without looking up from 'that damned paperwork', as he used to call it, and which now surrounded him in enormous piles after his stay in hospital. 'When are you back?'

'I don't know.'

He took off his reading glasses and looked at me. 'OK.' He said it like a question, like, was there something else I wanted to tell him? And if I didn't want to, fine by him, he trusted me.

I nodded and went back out into the sunlight.

'On a day like this we ought really to have had the roof back,' said Rita Willumsen as she drove the Sonett out onto the main highway.

I didn't ask why we didn't.

'What kind of sounds are you hearing?' I asked.

'People round here ask if I bought this car because the roof goes back. Here where the summer only lasts a month and a half, they're probably thinking. But do you know what the reason is, Roy?'

'The colour?'

'Quite the male chauvinist.' She laughed. 'It was the name. Sonett. Know what that is?'

'It's a Saab.'

'It's a verse form. A type of love poem with two quartets and two trios, fourteen lines in all. The master sonneteer was an Italian named Francesco Petrarch who was madly in love with a woman named Laura who was married to a count. Altogether he wrote 317 sonnets to her. Quite a lot, don't you think?'

'Pity she was married then.'

'Not at all. The key to passion is that you never wholly and completely get the one you love. We human beings are made rather impractically when it comes to things like that.'

'Oh yeah?'

'You've a lot to learn, I can hear that.'

'Maybe so. But I don't hear any strange noises from the car.'

She glanced in the mirror. 'It's there when I start it in the morning. It goes once the engine heats up.

We'll park for a while, give the engine a chance to cool down properly.'

She indicated and turned down a wooded track. She'd obviously driven here before, and after a while she turned down an even narrower track and stopped the car under some low-hanging pine-tree branches.

The sudden silence as she turned off the engine took me by surprise. I knew instinctively that silence had to be filled with something, because it was more charged than anything I could think of to say. I – who was already a killer – didn't dare to either move or look at her.

'So tell me, Roy. Have you met any girls since the last time we spoke?'

'A few,' I said.

'Anyone special?'

I shook my head. Glanced from the corner of my eye. She was wearing a red silk scarf and a loose-fitting blouse, but I could see the outlines of her breasts clearly. Her skirt had glided up and I could see her naked knees.

'Anyone you've . . . done it with, Roy?'

I felt a sweet surge in my stomach. I thought of lying, but what had I to gain by that?

'Not everything, no,' I said.

'Good,' she said and slowly pulled off the silk scarf. The three top buttons of her blouse were undone.

I was hard, felt it straining in my trousers and laid my hands in my lap to hide it. Because I knew my hormones were so disturbed right there and then that I couldn't be sure I hadn't misinterpreted the situation completely.

'Let's see if you're any better at holding a woman's hand,' she said and put her right hand on top of mine in my lap. It was as though the heat radiated straight down through the hand and down into my sex, and for a moment I was afraid I was going to come right there.

I let her take my hand, pull it towards her, saw her loosen her blouse slightly and draw my hand inside it, onto the bra over her left breast.

'You've waited a long time for this, Roy.' She gave a cooing laugh. 'Take firm hold of me, Roy. Squeeze the nipple a bit. Those of us who aren't young girls like it a **bit** harder. Easy, easy, that's a little too much. That's it. You know what, Roy, I think you're a natural.'

She leaned over towards me, held my chin between her thumb and forefinger and kissed me. Everything about Rita Willumsen was big, including the tongue as it coiled itself rough and strong like an eel round mine. And there was so much more taste to her than the two girls I had French-kissed with before. Not better, but more. Maybe even a bit too much – my senses were electrified, overloaded. She ended the kiss.

'We've still got some way to go there.' She smiled as she slid a hand under my T-shirt and stroked my chest. And even though I was so hard I could have broken stones with it I felt myself growing calmer. Because not much was being asked of me, she was the one at the wheel, she was in charge of the speed and where we were going.

'Let's take a walk,' she said.

I opened the door and stepped out into the intense shrill chirping of birds in the quivering summer heat. For the first time I noticed the blue trainers she was wearing.

We followed a track that curved upward over a hill. It was the summer holidays, fewer people in the village and on the roads, and up here the chances of meeting someone were minimal. All the same she asked me to stay fifty metres behind her so I could slip behind a tree if she gave a signal.

Near the top of the hill she stopped and beckoned to me.

She pointed down at the red-painted cabin below us.

'That's the sheriff's,' she said. 'And that one there . . .' She pointed up at a small summer farmhouse '. . . is ours.'

I wasn't sure whether by 'ours' she meant hers and mine, or hers and her husband's; but at least I knew that was where we were going.

She unlocked the door and we stepped inside a sun-warm and stuffy room. She closed the door behind me. Kicked off her trainers and put her hands on my shoulders. Even without shoes she was taller than me. We were both breathing heavily, we'd walked the last stretch quickly. So heavily we panted in each other's mouths when we kissed.

Her fingers unbuckled my belt as if that was all she'd

ever done, while I dreaded loosening the fastener on her bra, which I figured would be my job. But apparently it wasn't, because she led me into what had to be the main bedroom, where the curtains were drawn, pushed me down on the bed and let me watch as she undressed herself. Then she came to me and her skin was cold with dried sweat. She kissed me, rubbed herself against my naked body, and soon we were sweating again, slipping around each other like two wet seals. She smelled good and strong and moved my hands away when I was being too intimate. I veered between being too active and intolerably passive, and in the end she got hold of me and guided me in.

'Don't move,' she said, sitting motionless on top of me. 'Just feel it.'

And I felt it. And thought that now it's official. Roy Opgard is no longer a virgin.

'I thought it was tomorrow,' said Uncle Bernard when I got back that afternoon.

'What was?'

'That you were taking your driving test.'

'It **is** tomorrow.'

'You don't say? Judging by that grin on your face I thought you must've gone and taken it now.'

32

UNCLE BERNARD GAVE ME A Volvo 240 for my eighteenth birthday present.

I was speechless.

'Don't look at me like that, lad,' he said in embarrassment. 'It's second-hand, no big deal. And you and Carl need a car up there, you can't be riding your bikes all through the winter.'

The thing about the Volvo 240 is that it's the perfect car for tinkering about on, the parts are easy to come by even though they stopped production in '93, and if you look after it nicely you can keep it all your life. The bearings and the bushings on the front suspension were a little worn, as was the spider joint on the intermediate shaft, but the rest of it was in great condition, no trace of rust.

I sat behind the wheel, put my newly acquired driving licence in the glove compartment, turned on the ignition, and as I glided along the main road and passed the sign with Os on it I realised something. That the road went on. And on. That a whole world lay in front of that red bonnet.

It was a long, hot summer.

Every morning I drove Carl down to the Co-op where he had a summer job before heading on to the workshop.

And in the course of those weeks and months I became not just a useful driver but also, according to Rita Willumsen, a satisfactory if not expert lover.

We usually met in the late mornings. We each drove our own car, and I parked in a different farm track from her so that no one would connect us.

Rita Willumsen made just one condition.

'As long as you're with me, I don't want you going with other girls.'

There were three reasons for her condition.

The first was that she didn't want to catch any of the sexually transmitted diseases that she knew from working at the surgery were rife in the village, and the girls people like me have it away with are always tarts. Not that she was scared stiff of a dose of chlamydia or crabs, that could be quickly sorted out by a doctor in Notodden, but because now and then Willumsen still demanded his conjugal rights.

The second reason was that even tarts can fall in love, and analyse every word the boy says, take note of every evasion, ask questions about every undocumented trip to the woods, until they end up knowing things they shouldn't know, and suddenly you've got a full-blown scandal.

The third reason was that she wanted to hang on to me. Not because I was in any way unique, but because the risk of changing lovers in a little place such as Os was too great.

In simple terms, the condition was that Willumsen mustn't find out. And the reason was that Willumsen – like the canny businessman he was – had insisted on a prenup agreement, and fru Willumsen owned nothing beyond her physical attributes, as people say. She was dependent on her husband if she wanted to go on living the life she had become accustomed to. And that was fine by me, because suddenly I had a life that was worth living.

What fru Willumsen did have was culture, as she herself referred to it. She came from a good family over in the east of the country, but after her father squandered the family fortune she chose security over insecurity and married the charmless but wealthy and hard-working used-car salesman and for twenty years persuaded him that she wasn't using contraception and that there must be something wrong with his swimmers. And all the fine words, the useless knowledge of painting and the equally useless knowledge of literature that she didn't manage to force-feed him, got handed on to me instead. She showed me paintings by Cézanne and van Gogh. Read aloud from **Hamlet** and **Brand.** And from **Steppenwolf** and **The Doors of Perception,** which up until then I had thought were bands, not books. But best of all she liked to read Francisco Petrarch's sonnets to Laura. Usually in a refined New Norwegian translation, and usually with a slight quivering in her voice. We smoked hash, though Rita would never say where she got it from, and listen to Glenn Gould playing the Goldberg Variations. I could say that the school I went to during the time Rita Willumsen and I had those secret meetings up at her cabin gave me more than any university or academy would have done; although that would probably be a serious exaggeration. But it had the same effect on me as the Volvo 240 did that time I drove it out of the village; it opened my eyes to the fact that there was a whole other world out there. One that I could dream about making mine, if only I could learn the esoteric codes. But that would never happen, not to me, the dyslexic brother.

Not that Carl seemed to have any urge to travel the world either.

Rather the opposite. As summer turned to autumn and winter, he isolated himself more and more. When I asked what he was brooding about, if he wouldn't take a drive with me in the Volvo, he just looked at me with a vague, mild smile, almost as though I wasn't there.

'I have strange dreams,' he said one evening, completely out of the blue, as we sat in the winter garden. 'I dream that you're a killer. That you're dangerous. And I envy you for being dangerous.'

I knew of course that in some sense or other Carl knew that I had fixed things so the Cadillac would go over the edge at Geitesvingen that evening, but he'd never said a word about it, and I saw no reason to tell him and make him an accomplice as someone who'd heard a confession but not reported it. So I didn't respond, just said goodnight and left him there.

It was the closest to a happy time I had ever had. I had a job I loved, a car to take me wherever I wanted, and I was living out the sex dreams of every teenage boy. Not that I could boast of it to anyone, not even Carl, because Rita had said 'not a single soul', and I had sworn it on my brother's name.

And then one evening the inevitable happened. As usual Rita had left the cabin before me to avoid us being seen together. As usual I gave her twenty minutes, but that evening we were late, I'd been working hard at the workshop the night before and the whole day, and lying there in bed I was relaxing totally. Because even though the cabin had been bought and rebuilt with herr Willumsen's money, according to Rita he would never set foot there again, being too fat and sedate and the path there too long and steep. She'd told me he'd bought the place partly because it was bigger than Chairman Aas's cabin and he could look down on it, and partly as pure investment in the countryside wilderness at a time when oil was in the process of turning Norway into a wealthy nation – even back then Willumsen could smell the boom in mountain cabins that would come along many years later. That it came further up the highway was down to chance and certain councils that were quicker on the buzzer than ours, but it was still smart thinking by Willumsen. Anyway, lying there and waiting until I could leave, I fell asleep. When I woke up it was four o'clock in the morning.

Three-quarters of an hour later I was at Opgard.

Neither Carl nor I wanted to sleep in Mum and Dad's room, so I crept into the boys' room, not wanting to wake Carl. But as I was about to sneak into the upper bunk he gave a start and I was looking down at a pair of wide-open eyes shining in the dark.

'We're going to jail,' he whispered groggily.

'Eh?' I said.

He blinked twice before he sort of shrugged it off, and I realised he had been dreaming.

'Where have you been?' he asked.

'Fixing a car,' I said, swinging my leg over the railing.

'No.'

'No?'

'Uncle Bernard called by with some **lapskaus.** Asked where you were.'

I took a breath. 'I was with a woman.'

'A woman? Not a girl?'

'We'll talk about it tomorrow, Carl. We've got to get up in two hours.'

I lay there listening out to see if his breathing eased down. It didn't.

'What was that about jail?' I finally asked.

'I dreamed they were going to put us in jail for murder,' he said.

I took a breath. 'For murdering who?'

'That's the crazy thing about it,' he said. 'Each other.'

33

IT WAS EARLY IN THE morning. I was looking forward to a day with cars and simple mechanical problems to solve. Little did I know, as people say.

I was standing in the workshop as I'd done more or less every day for the past two years and was just about to start work on a car when Uncle Bernard came out and said there was a phone call for me. I followed him back into his office.

It was Sigmund Olsen, the sheriff. He wanted to have a word with me, he said. Hear how things were. Take me on a short fishing trip up near his cabin, it was just a few kilometres down the main road. He could pick me up in a few hours. And even though his voice had been soft as butter on the phone I could hear it wasn't an invitation but an order.

Which naturally gave me pause for thought. Why the hurry if it was just a harmless little chat?

I carried on working on the engine, and after lunch lay down on the car creeper and shoved myself under the car and away from this world. There is nothing more calming than working on an engine when you've got ants in your brain. I don't know how long I'd been lying there when I heard someone cough. I had a nasty premonition, which was maybe why I waited a bit before shoving myself out on the creeper.

'You're Roy,' said the man standing there looking down at me. 'You've got something that belonged to me.'

The man was Willum Willumsen. **Belonged.** Past tense.

I lay there beneath him, completely defenceless. 'And what might that be, Willumsen?'

'You know very well what it is.'

I swallowed. I wouldn't have time to do anything before he stamped the breath and the life out of me. I'd seen it done at Årtun, had some idea of how to do it, but not how to avoid it. I'd learned to hit first and hit hard, not how to keep up a guard. I shook my head.

'A wetsuit,' he said. 'Flippers, mask, diving cylinder, valve and a snorkel. Eight thousand five hundred and sixty kroner.'

He laughed loudly when he saw the look of relief

on my face, which he obviously interpreted as astonishment. 'I never forget a deal, Roy.'

'Oh no?' I said, getting to my feet and wiping my
fingers with a long rag. 'So not the one when my father bought the Cadillac either?'

'Nope.' Willumsen looked up into the air, chuck-
ling, as though it were a fond memory. 'He didn't like
haggling, your father. If I'd known how little he liked
it I might even have started a little lower.'

'Oh? You mean you've got a guilty conscience?'
Maybe I was hoping to get in before him if this was
what he'd come to ask me. Attack is the best form of
defence, people say. Not that I thought there was anything to defend, I wasn't ashamed. Not about that.
I was just a young lad that had got hit on by some
married woman, so what? That was something they
would have to sort out between themselves, I wasn't
going to get involved in a fight over territorial rights.
All the same, I had twisted the rag around the knuckles of my right.

'Always,' he said, smiling. 'But if there's one talent I
was born with, it's how to deal with a bad conscience.'

'Yeah?' I said. 'What do you do?'

He grinned until his eyes vanished in his fleshy face
and pointed to one of his shoulders. 'When the devil
on my right discusses things with the angel on my
left, I let the devil put his arguments first. And then
I put a stop to the discussion.' Willumsen laughed
again. The laughter was followed by a rasping sound,
the sound of a car being thrown into reverse while it's

moving forward. The sound of a man who is going to die at some unknown point in the future.

'I've come here because of Rita,' he said.

I weighed the situation up. Willumsen was bigger and heavier than me, but unless he pulled out a weapon he presented no physical threat. And what else could he threaten me with? I wasn't dependent on him economically or in any other way, and nor could he threaten either Carl or Uncle Bernard, as far as I knew.

But of course there was one person he could threaten. Rita.

'She says she's very pleased with you.'

I didn't respond. A car drove slowly by on the road outside, but we were alone in the workshop.

'She says the Sonett has never run better. So I've brought along a car I want you to check over and fix whatever absolutely has to be fixed. But no more than that.'

I glanced over his devil-shoulder and saw the blue Toyota Corolla parked outside. Tried not to look as relieved as I was feeling.

'The problem is, it has to be done by tomorrow,' said Willumsen. 'I've got a customer coming from a long way off who's more or less bought it over the phone. It'd be a pity for both of us if he ended up disappointed. Get my drift?'

'I get it,' I said. 'Sounds like overtime.'

'Ha, Bernard's probably glad to take any job that comes his way at hourly rates.'

'That's something you'll have to discuss with him.'

Willumsen nodded. 'Given Bernard's state of health it's probably just a question of time before it's you and me discussing hourly rates, Roy, so I want you to know even at this early stage who this workshop's most important customer is.' He handed the car keys to me, said it didn't look like rain today after all, and left.

I drove the car inside, opened the bonnet and groaned. I would be working into the night. And I couldn't even make a start on it now, as in another half-hour Sigmund Olsen would be picking me up. Suddenly I had a couple of things to think about. That was fine, this was still the happy time. But as things turned out, the last day of the happy time.

34

'WILLUMSEN WAS PISSED OFF HIS car wasn't ready,' said Uncle Bernard when I arrived late at the workshop the morning after the Fritz night.

'There was more to do than I thought,' I said.

Uncle Bernard put his large, square head on one side. It sat atop a small and equally square body. When we wanted to tease him Carl and I called him our Lego man. We really loved him. 'Like what for example?' he asked.

'Shagging,' I said as I opened the bonnet of the Corolla.

'Eh?'

'There was a bit of a double booking. I'd arranged to do some shagging yesterday too.'

Uncle Bernard gave a short, involuntary laugh. Struggled to resume his serious face. 'Work comes before shagging, Roy. Understood?'

'Understood.'

'What's the tractor doing outside?'

'No room for it in here, got three cars coming in later today. Cabin people.'

'OK. And why is the scoop up in the air?'

'Takes less room.'

'You think there's a shortage of space out there in the car park?'

'OK then, it's a celebration of the job I was working on last night. The one that wasn't the Corolla, that is.'

Uncle Bernard looked out at the tractor with its proudly raised elevating arms. Shook his head and left. But I could hear him laughing again inside his office.

I carried on working on the Corolla. It wasn't until late in the evening that rumours that Sheriff Sigmund Olsen was missing began to **circulate,** as people say.

When they found the boat with Sigmund Olsen's boots no one doubted that he had drowned himself, there wasn't even anything to discuss. Quite the opposite, people tried to outdo one another in saying how clearly they had seen the writing on the wall.

'Of course, Sigmund always had that dark edge behind the smile and the jokes, but people didn't notice it, they're blind to things like that.'

'Just the day before he said to me that it looked as though it was clouding over, but of course I thought he was talking about the weather.'

'Of course they have confidentiality at the surgery, but I heard they were prescribing those happy pills for Sigmund. Oh yes, a few years ago, when his cheeks were so firm and round, remember that? But just lately he was so hollow-cheeked. Stopped taking his pills.'

'You could see it on him. He had something on his mind. Something was bothering him and he couldn't work it out. And when we don't find the answer, when we can't find a meaning, can't find Jesus, well, that's the kind of thing that can happen.'

A woman sheriff came over from the neighbouring county and probably heard all this, but she still wanted to speak to those who had met Sigmund on the day he disappeared. Carl and I had discussed what Carl should say. I suggested it would be best to stay as close to the truth as possible and only leave out what was absolutely necessary. Say when Sigmund Olsen had visited him at the farm, roughly what time he left, that Carl hadn't noticed anything special about him. Carl had protested that he probably ought to say that Olsen had seemed down, but I'd explained that in the first place she would be talking to others who would say Olsen seemed his usual self that day. And in the second place, given that she suspected that someone else might be involved, what was it someone was trying to make her think?

'If you're too keen to convince them that Olsen has killed himself, it'll seem suspicious.'

Carl had nodded. 'Of course. Thanks, Roy.'

Two weeks later, and for the first time after the Fritz night, I was lying in bed in the cabin again.

I hadn't actually done anything different, but Rita Willumsen seemed to appreciate more than usual what had become our regular sessions of lovemaking.

Now she lay with her head resting in her hand, smoking a menthol cigarette as she studied me.

'You've changed,' she said.

'Really?' I said, a wedge of Berry's under my upper lip.

'You're more grown up.'

'Is that so surprising? It's been a while since you took my virtue, you know.'

She gave a slight start, I didn't usually speak to her like that.

'I mean since the last time we met,' she said. 'You're someone else.'

'Better or worse than the previous me?' I asked, fishing out the wad of tobacco with my index finger and laying it in the ashtray beside the bed. I turned towards her. Lay a hand on her thigh. She looked at it in a demonstrative way. One of the unwritten rules was that she was the one who decided when we made love and when we rested, not me.

'You know, Roy,' she said, and took a drag on her cigarette, 'I'd actually made up my mind to tell you today that it's time we rounded off this affair of ours.'

'Really?' I said.

'A friend of mine said that that hairdresser girl, Grete Smitt, has been spreading rumours about me having secret meetings with a young man.'

I nodded, but didn't tell her that I'd been thinking it might be time to stop too. I was simply getting tired of how repetitive it was getting. Drive over to the cabin, fuck, eat the home-made food she brought along, fuck, go home. But when I said the sentence aloud to myself, of course I didn't really know what it was I was getting tired of. And it wasn't as if I had some other fru Willumsen waiting for me.

'But after what you did to me today I'm thinking we can wait a while before we stop,' she said. She put her cigarette out in the ashtray and turned to me.

'Why is that?' I asked.

'Why?' She gave me a long, thoughtful look, as though she didn't have the answer. 'Maybe it's Sigmund Olsen's drowning. The thought that you can wake up dead one day. Because we sure can't postpone living, now can we?'

She caressed my chest and stomach.

'Olsen took his own life,' I said. 'He **wanted** to die.'

'Exactly.' She looked at her own hand with the red-painted fingernails as it continued on its way downward. 'And that can happen to any of us.'

'Maybe,' I said, picking up my watch from the bedside table. 'But I have to go now. Hope you don't mind me leaving first for once.'

At first she looked a bit surprised, but then she

composed herself, gave a thin smile and asked teasingly if I had a date with another girl.

In reply I gave an equally teasing smile, got up and began to dress.

'He's away this weekend,' she said, watching me from the bed with a slightly sulky expression on her face.

The name Willum Willumsen was never mentioned.

'You can come and visit me.'

I stopped dressing. 'Visit you **at home**?'

She leaned out over the side of the bed, dipped her hand into her bag, fished out a bunch of keys and began to work one of them loose.

'Come after dark, use the garden on the blind side of the house, where no neighbours can see you. This is to the basement door.'

She dangled the freed key in front of me. I was so surprised all I could do was stare at it.

'Take it, you idiot!' she hissed.

And I took it. Stuck it in my pocket and knew I wouldn't be using it. I'd taken it because for the first time I'd seen what looked like vulnerability in Rita Willumsen's expression. And with that anger in her voice she was trying to hide something I hadn't even thought about; that she might be afraid of rejection.

And walking down the path away from the cabin, I knew the balance between Rita Willumsen and me had changed.

Carl had changed too.

In some way he held himself more erect. And no

longer kept himself to himself but had started going out and seeing people. It had happened almost overnight. The Fritz night. Maybe he felt – like me – that the experience of the Fritz night was something that lifted us above the crowd. When Mum and Dad went over the edge into Huken, Carl had been a passive spectator, the victim who was being saved. But this time he'd been a participant, done what had to be done, things the people around us couldn't have imagined. We had crossed a line and crossed back over again, and you can't have been to the place we had been to without it changing you. Or to put it this way: maybe it was only now that Carl could be the person he had really been all along; maybe the Fritz night just tapped a hole in the cocoon that let this butterfly out. He had already grown taller than me, but in the course of the winter he had gone from being a fragile, shy young lad into a youth who understood he had nothing to be ashamed of. He'd always been well liked, now he became popular too. I began to notice that when he was hanging out with his friends it was him who was the leader, his comments people listened to, his jokes people laughed at, he was the one they looked at first when they were trying to impress or make the gang laugh. He was the one they imitated. And the girls noticed it too. It wasn't just that Carl's sweet, girlish prettiness had matured into strapping good looks, the way he acted had changed too. I noticed it when we were at the gatherings at Årtun, that he had acquired a natural self-assurance both in the way he spoke and the way he moved. He could be uninhibitedly playful, as though nothing was really serious, and then sit down with a mate who was having girl trouble, or a female friend with a broken heart, listen sympathetically to what they had to say and give them advice, as though he possessed experience and wisdom they hadn't yet acquired.

As for me, I guess I just became more of what I always had been. More self-assured, of course. Because I knew now that, when it really mattered, I was capable of doing what had to be done.

'Are **you** sitting here, reading?' Carl said one Saturday evening. It was gone midnight, he'd just come home, obviously a bit tipsy, and I was sitting in the winter garden with **An American Tragedy** open on my lap.

And in a flash it was as though I saw the two of us from outside. That I had taken his place now. Alone in a room without company. Only it wasn't his place. It was just him who had borrowed mine for a while.

'Where have you been?' I asked.

'At a party,' he said.

'Didn't you promise Uncle Bernard you would take it easy with the partying?

'Sure,' he said. There was laughter in his voice, but real regret too. 'I broke my promise.'

We laughed.

It was good to laugh with Carl.

'You have a good time?' I asked, closing the book.

'I danced with Mari Aas.'

'Oh yeah?'

'Yes. And I think I'm a little bit in love.'

I don't know why, but the words cut me like a knife.

'Mari Aas,' I said. 'The chairman's daughter and an Opgard boy?'

'Why not?' he said.

'Well, sure, there's no law against dreaming,' I said, and heard how ugly and mean my own laughter sounded.

'Guess you're right,' he said with a smile. 'I'll head up and dream a bit.'

One day a few weeks later I saw Mari Aas at the coffee shop.

She was very pretty. And apparently 'dangerously intelligent', as someone put it. One thing was for certain, she sure knew how to speak. According to the local newspaper she'd seen off aspiring politicians much older than herself when she represented AUF in a debate in Notodden before the local election. Mari Aas stood there, leaning forward slightly, chubby, blonde pigtails, breasts pressing against the Che Guevara T-shirt, and the cold, blue eyes of a wolf, and a gaze that passed over me there in the coffee shop as though I wasn't there, as though in search of something worth hunting for and I wasn't it. A gaze without fear, that's what I thought. The gaze of something at the very top of the food chain.

Summer returned and Rita Willumsen – who had been on a trip to America with **him,** her husband –

sent a text message saying she wanted to meet at the cabin. She wrote that she'd been missing me. She, who always made the decisions, had started to write stuff like that in her messages, especially since I never turned up at her home through the basement door that weekend she was alone.

When I got to the cabin she seemed unusually excited. She had presents for me, and I unwrapped a pair of silk underpants and a little bottle of so-called perfume-for-men, both bought in New York City itself, she said. But best of all were the two cartons of Berry's moist snuff, even though I wasn't allowed to take any of it home, it belonged to our world at the cabin, she said. So the snuff was stored in the fridge there. And I realised she thought of it as an extra incentive for me once I ran out at home.

'Take your clothes off,' I said.

She looked at me in astonishment for a moment. Then she did as I had told her.

Afterwards we lay in the bed, sweating, and slippery with bodily fluids. The room felt like a baker's oven, the summer sun roasting the roof, and I pulled myself free of Rita's literally damp embrace.

I picked up the book of Petrarch's sonnets from the bedside table, opened it at random and began reading aloud:

Clear, sweet fresh water where she, the only one who seemed woman to me.

I closed the book with a thump.

Rita Willumsen blinked uncomprehendingly.

'Water,' she said. 'Let's go for a swim. I'll bring some wine.'

We got dressed, she with a bathing costume underneath, and I followed her up to the mountain lake that lay behind some knolls above the cabin. There, beneath some overhanging birch trees, lay a little red dinghy that obviously belonged to the Willumsens. In the space of that short walk it had clouded over, but we were still warm and damp from the lovemaking and the steep climb, so we lifted the boat out onto the water, and I rowed until we were so far from land that we were sure no one passing by could identify us.

'Swim,' said Rita when we were halfway through the bottle of sparkling wine.

'Too cold,' I said.

'Softie' she said, and started taking off the clothes she was wearing over the swimming costume, which was tight in all the right places, as people say. And I remembered her explanation for her athletic body and broad shoulders, how in her youth she'd been a promising competitive swimmer. She stood on the thwart on one side, and I had to lean out the other side so the dinghy wouldn't capsize. The wind had risen and the surface of the water had turned a greyish white, like the coating of a blind eye. Small waves came in quick, rushing succession, actually more like ripples, and it occurred to me just as she bent her knees to dive off.

'Wait!' I shouted.

411

'Ha ha!' she said, and kicked off. Her body described an elegant parabola through the air. Because like so many swimmers, Rita Willumsen knew the art of diving. But she didn't know the art of gauging depth from the way the wind shapes the surface of water. Her body cut soundlessly down into the water before suddenly stopping. For a moment she looked like the diver on a Pink Floyd album cover Uncle Bernard had shown me, the one where the guy is standing on his hands underwater and his body seems to be growing out of the mirror-smooth surface of the water. Uncle Bernard told me it took the photographer several days just to get that one picture, and that the main problem was from the air bubbles ruining the surface when the diver breathed out air from the cylinder he was using. What ruined the picture here was that fru Willumsen's straight legs and the lower part of her upper body collapsed. It was like that footage you see on television showing the controlled demolition of a tower block, only without the control.

And when she stood up, a furious look on her face, greenish slime on her forehead and the water only reaching to her navel, I lay back, laughing so hard the dinghy almost capsized.

'Idiot!' she hissed.

I could have stopped there. I should have stopped there. Maybe blame it on the wine, say I wasn't used to it. But anyway, I grabbed the orange life jacket that lay under the thwart and tossed it out to her. It hit the water next to her and lay there and floated, and that was when I understood it was too late. Rita Willumsen, the woman who had towered over me at the workshop that first time, who had commanded me and guided me every step of the way we had taken, at that moment looked like a lost soul, an abandoned young girl dressed up as an older woman. Because now, in the merciless light of day, her make-up all washed off, I could see the wrinkles and years that lay between us. Her skin was white, with goose bumps from the cold, and it sagged around the edges of her swimsuit. I had stopped laughing, and maybe she read what I had seen in my face, because she crossed her arms in front of her, as though to protect herself from my gaze.

'Sorry,' I said. Maybe it was the only right thing to say, and maybe it was the worst thing. Maybe it would have made no difference what I said.

'I'm swimming back,' she said, and glided away below the surface, vanished from sight.

I didn't see Rita Willumsen again for a long time.

She swam faster than I rowed, and when I reached the shore I saw only the wet prints of her naked feet. I pulled the dinghy out of the water, emptied what was left of the wine, and picked up her clothes. And by the time I reached the cabin she had already left. I lay down on the bed, took a wad of Berry's from the silver snuffbox and checked the clock to see how long was left of the prescribed half-hour. Felt the burn of that fermented tobacco against the inside of my upper lip, and the shame on the inside of my heart. Shame at having caused her to feel shame. Why was that so much worse than the shame at my own inadequacy? Why was it worse to have laughed a little too heartily at a woman who had chosen you, just a kid, as her lover, than it was to have killed your own mother and dismembered a sheriff? I don't know. It just was.

I waited twenty minutes. Then I drove home. Even though I knew I wouldn't be coming back, I resisted the temptation to take the carton of Berry's with me.

35

IT WAS A SUNDAY, TOWARDS the end of the summer. As arranged Uncle Bernard arrived at Opgard with a casserole of **lapskaus** which I heated up while he sat at the kitchen table and talked about everything except his health. He was by now so thin it was a topic we both avoided.

'Carl?'

'He'll be along,' I said.

'How's he doing?'

'Fine,' I said. 'Doing well at school.'

'Does he drink?'

I chewed on it a moment before shaking my head. Knew Uncle Bernard was thinking of Dad's thirst.

'Your father would be proud of you,' he said.

'Yeah?' was all I said.

'He wouldn't have said so in so many words, but believe me.'

'Well, if you say so.'

Uncle Bernard sighed and looked out the window. 'And **I** am certainly proud of you. Here comes your little brother, by the way. Got company.'

I hadn't time to look out the window before Carl and his company had disappeared round the northern side of the house. Then I heard footsteps in the hallway and low, almost intimate voices, one of them female. Then the kitchen door opened.

'This is Mari,' said Carl. 'Is there enough **lapskaus**?'

I got to my feet and just stared at my now big, erect kid brother and the tall blonde with the wolf's eyes. My hand mechanically stirred the spoon around in the bubbling casserole.

Had I seen it coming or hadn't I?

On the one hand this was straight out of a fairy tale; the orphaned son of a mountain farmer who'd won the king's daughter, the princess whom no one could silence. On the other hand there was something almost inevitable about it, they were quite simply the logical couple, the way the moon and the stars shone down over Os just then. All the same I stared at him. To think that he, my kid brother, the one I'd held my arms around, the one who couldn't put Dog out of his misery, who panicked and called me for help on the Fritz night, that he had dared to do something I would never have dared. To approach a girl like Mari

Aas, talk to her, introduce himself. Believe himself worthy of her attention.

And I stared at her. She looked quite different now from the last time, down at the Kaffistova. Now she smiled at me, and that cold, hunter's gaze had been replaced by something open, inviting, almost warm. I realised of course that it wasn't me personally, it was the situation that brought out that smile, but right there and then it felt almost as though she was raising me too, the big brother from the little farm, up into her own sphere.

'Well?' said Uncle Bernard. 'Serious or just good friends?'

Mari gave a high, trilling laugh that was just a touch nervous. 'Oh, well, I guess we'd say—'

'Serious,' Carl interrupted her.

She swayed slightly away from him and looked at him with raised eyebrows. Slipped her hand in beneath his arm.

'Well, then let's say that,' she said.

Summer ended and the autumn was long and wet.

Rita rang once in October and once in November. I saw the R on the screen but didn't take the call.

Uncle Bernard was hospitalised again. With each passing week he grew sicker, weaker and smaller. I worked too much and ate too little. Drove to the hospital in Notodden two or three times a week. Not because I thought I had to, but because I enjoyed the minimalist conversations I had with Uncle Bernard, and the long drives alone up and down the highway listening to J. J. Cale.

Carl came with me sometimes, but he had a lot to do. He and Mari had become the village's glamorous couple. There were always things going on around them socially, and when I had the time I joined them. For some reason or other Carl liked me to come along, and on top of that it dawned on me I had no friends of my own. Not that I'd been lonely, or not had anyone to talk to, it was just something I didn't do. Would have found it boring, preferred to spell my way through one of the books Rita had recommended and which I usually found in the library at Notodden. Since I read so slowly I couldn't borrow too many at once, but what I did read I read thoroughly. **On the Road. Lord of the Flies. The Virgin Suicides. The Sun Also Rises. The Wasp Factory.** And I read out loud to Uncle Bernard from one called **Post Office** by Charles Bukowski, which made him – who had never read a book all the way through in his life – laugh so much he ended up having a coughing fit. Afterwards he looked tired. He said thanks for coming, but now it was best if I went.

And then came the day when he told me he was going to die. And followed that up with a Volkswagen joke.

And his daughter came and took the keys to the house.

I had expected Carl to start blubbing when I gave him the news about Uncle Bernard, but he seemed prepared for it, at least he shook his head sorrowfully for a while, as though it was something you could shake off. The way he seemed to have shaken off the Fritz night. Sometimes it seemed almost as though he had forgotten what had happened. We never spoke of it, as though we both understood that if we packed it in enough layers of silence and time it might one day become an echo from the past, like those flashbacks of old nightmares that for a fraction of a second seemed to have really happened, before you remember, and your pulse drops back down to normal again.

I told Carl I thought he should move into Mum and Dad's bedroom, on the grounds that he was eight centimetres taller than me and needed a longer bed. But really it was because I slept so badly there in the boys' room. Carl no longer heard the screams from Huken. Now I was the one hearing them.

Carl gave a long and wonderful eulogy for Uncle Bernard at the funeral, about how fine and genuine and funny he was. Maybe some people thought it was odd that Carl and not me, who was the older brother, spoke for us both, but I had asked him to do it, being afraid I would simply break down and cry. Carl said yes and got the material from me, all the anecdotes and thoughts, since I had been closer to Bernard than him. Carl had taken notes, written, rewritten, added his own lines, rehearsed in front of the mirror and really given the task his all. I had never realised he had so many refined thoughts in him, but then that's how things are: you think you know someone like the back of your own hand, and then suddenly they show you sides of themselves you had no idea about. But the truth is that trouser pockets – even your own – are just a darkness you fumble about in. Now and then you find a ten-øre coin, a lottery ticket or a foil-wrapped aspirin in the lining. Or you can be so hopelessly in love with a girl that you're on the verge of topping yourself, even though you don't really know her. So you start wondering is that ten øre maybe just from yesterday, that love just something you've made up, that she's just an excuse, a reason to go somewhere you long to go: anywhere that's away from here? But I never drove further than the county line when I just wanted to think, or to Notodden, if I wanted to borrow books. Never thought about driving into the mountain by the tunnel opening at the end of that long, straight stretch, or doing a repeat of what happened up at Huken. I always came back. Ticked off one day and waited for the next. One where I would see Mari, or I wouldn't see Mari.

It was around this time I started hitting people.

36

THE PERIOD AFTER UNCLE BERNARD'S death was a bleak time. I had taken over the workshop and was working all hours, and I think that was what saved me. That, and the fighting at Årtun.

The only relief were those Saturday-evening dances, with Carl getting drunk and flirting and me waiting for some poor jealous bastard to lose control so I could plant my fist in my own, pathetic mirror-image, punch it to the ground over and over again, week in and week out.

It was often the early hours of the morning before we got home from those Saturday night dances. Carl would collapse on the lower bunk, hung-over, farting and giggling. And once we had finished going through the night's adventures he might exclaim:

'God but it's good to have a big brother!'

And that warmed my heart, even though it was a lie. Because we both knew that by now it was him who was the big brother.

Not once did it occur to me to tell him I was in love with his girlfriend. I hadn't told Uncle Bernard either, or given any sign at all to Mari, obviously. The shame I felt was something I had to bear alone. I could hardly even endure my own reflection in the mirror. Was that something Dad had felt too? Had he thought that a man who lusts after his own son doesn't deserve to fucking well live, and left that shotgun outside the barn in the hope that I would do it for him? I believe I understood more of him now, and it scared all kinds of hell out of me, and didn't exactly do anything to lessen my self-contempt.

I can't remember much of what I thought or said when Carl told me he wanted to study. It was actually pretty obvious, not just because of the good marks he used to get at school, or the fact that he wasn't especially practical, but because Mari was equally obviously destined to be a student. And of course they would be students in the same city. I'd imagined the two of them sharing a little flat in Oslo or Bergen, coming back home to the village together in the holidays and hanging out with the old crowd. And I'd be hanging out with them too.

But then came that business with Grete and Carl at Årtun, Grete telling all to Mari, and suddenly everything was turned upside down.

And when Carl disappeared to Minnesota I was left with the feeling that he'd run out on the whole business. From the little village scandal and Mari Aas. From his responsibilities on the farm. From me, who had become more dependent on him than he was on me. And for all I know, maybe he'd started hearing them again, those screams from Huken.

At least it was quiet after he left.

Damn quiet.

The oil company bought the workshop and the land and suddenly I – a lad in his early twenties – was running a service station. I don't know if they noticed something I'd never noticed myself, but anyway I worked round the clock. It wasn't because I was particularly ambitious, that came later. But because I found it harder than expected to deal with being up there on the farm, listening to Huken and to the golden plover's song of loneliness. A bird on the lookout for company. Not a friend, necessarily, just company. All of that could be dealt with by being at work, having people around me, having sounds, things to do, having my thoughts somewhere they could be put to use, and not just grinding round and round the same old crap.

I'd got Mari out of my system, like a tumour after a successful operation. I realised of course that it was no coincidence it happened at the same time as the break between her and Carl, but I tried not to think about it too much. It was probably complicated, and I had just read Kafka's **Metamorphosis** – about a guy who wakes up one day to find he's turned into a disgusting insect – and had realised that, if I started grubbing around in my subconscious and all that, the chances of finding something I didn't like were pretty high.

Naturally I bumped into Rita Willumsen now and then. She looked good, the years didn't seem to have taken their toll on her. But she was always with someone, or there were people around us, so all I got was the general friendly smile between two villagers, and a question about how the station was doing, or Carl over there in the States.

One day I saw her outside by the pumps. She was talking to Markus who was filling her Sonett with petrol. Usually it was Willumsen himself who filled the petrol in their cars, but Markus is a nice-looking lad, quiet and gentle, and for a moment I wondered if Markus was her new project. It was strange, but it didn't seem to bother me at all, I just wished them both well. When Markus had replaced the petrol cap, as Rita was about to get into the car, she looked over towards the station shop. I doubt she could see, but anyway she lifted her hand almost like she was waving. And I waved back. When Markus came back in he said Willum Willumsen had got cancer but that he was expected to make a full recovery.

The next time I saw Rita was at the annual celebration of Constitution Day on 17 May at Årtun. She looked wonderful in her national costume. And was walking hand in hand with her husband. That was something I'd never seen before. Willumsen was thin, or at least less fat, and if you ask me it didn't suit him. The skin under his chin dangled and swung about like a lizard. But when he and Rita spoke together, the one leaned in towards the other and listened, as though wanting to catch every word. Smiling, nodding, looking each other in the eyes. Maybe the cancer had been an **epiphany,** a revelation. Maybe she had discovered that she had learned to love this man who adored her. And who knows, maybe Willumsen hadn't been as blind as I thought either. Anyway, I realised that that wave from the petrol pump had been a final goodbye. And that was fine, we had meant something to each other at a time when we both needed it. From what I've seen, very few affairs have a happy ending, but when I saw the two of them together it seemed to me that, in a way, Rita Willumsen and I were two of the lucky ones. And maybe Willum Willumsen a third.

So I was the golden plover again.

But just one year later I met the woman who would be my secret lover for the next five years. At the dinner following a meeting at head office in Oslo I met Pia Syse. She was the personnel manager and sat on my left, and as such she was not my formal dinner partner, but after a while she turned to me and asked if I would rescue her from the cavalier sitting on her left, a man who had been talking about petrol for the preceding hour, and there really isn't that much to say about petrol. I'd drunk a couple of glasses of wine and asked if it wasn't a type of chauvinism – in one direction or the other – to place on a man a greater responsibility to entertain a woman than the other way round. She agreed, so I gave her three minutes to say something that I found interesting, made me laugh, or provoked me. If she couldn't then she'd have to forgive me if I returned to the formal dinner partner on my right, a bespectacled brunette from Kongsberg who had said her name was Unni, and not much else. And respect to Pia Syse, she met all three challenges, and in well under three minutes.

We danced afterwards, and she said I was the worst dance partner she had ever had.

In the lift on the way up to our rooms we started making out, and she told me I couldn't kiss either.

And when we woke up in her hotel bed – as personnel manager she'd been allotted one of the suites – she said straight out that the sex was well below average.

But that she had rarely laughed as much as she had done over the last twelve hours.

I told her one out of four was above average for me, and she laughed again. And I spent the next hour trying to do something about that first impression. At least I hope I did. At any rate Pia Syse said she'd be summoning me to head office at some point during the next fourteen days, and that the agenda would be 'loose'.

Standing in the queue to check out at reception, Unni, my formal dinner partner, asked if I was driving to Os, and if so could she have a lift as far as Kongsberg.

426

We didn't talk much on the drive.

She asked about the car, and I said it was a present from my uncle and had sentimental value for me. I could have told her that even if every damn part on it had been replaced at least once, the 240 was a mechanical marvel. That it had for example none of the problems associated with the posher V 70 which often had trouble with the tie rod and the steering arm. And that one day I hoped to be buried in the chassis of my 240. But instead of jabbering on about uninteresting things, I asked about uninteresting things, and she told me she worked in accounts, had two kids and that her husband was headmaster at a secondary school in Kongsberg. She worked from home two days a week, commuted to Oslo, and took every Friday off.

'What do you do then?' I asked.

'Nothing,' she said.

'Isn't that difficult?' I asked. 'Doing nothing?'

'No,' she said.

And that was the full extent of our conversation.

I turned on J. J. Cale and felt a deep peace stealing over me. It was probably from lack of sleep, Cale's laid-back minimalism, and realising that Unni's default mode was silence, same as mine.

When I woke, with a start, staring out at the cars coming towards us, their lights scattered across the windscreen by the rain, my brain reached the conclusion that I had a) fallen asleep at the wheel, b) must have been asleep for more than a couple of seconds since I couldn't remember the rain or turning on the windscreen wipers, and c) should have stopped for a break long ago. Automatically I raised my hand and put it on the wheel. But instead of the wheel it closed around another warm hand that was already steering.

'I think you fell asleep,' said Unni.

'Kind of you not to wake me,' I said.

She didn't laugh. I glanced across at her. There was perhaps the hint of a smile at the corner of her mouth. In time I would learn it was about as far as that face would go when it came to expressing things. And only now did I see for the first time that she was pretty. Not classically beautiful like Mari Aas, or dazzling like Rita Willumsen in the pictures she had shown me of herself when young. Actually, to tell the truth, I don't know if Unni Holm-Jensen was pretty by any other standards than her own, because what I'm trying to say is that she was – at that moment, in that light, from that angle – prettier than I had seen her looking so far. Not the kind of pretty to fall in love with, I was never in love with Unni Holm-Jensen, and over five years she never fell in love with me either. But just right now she was pretty in the kind of way that makes you want to go on looking at her. And of course I could have done so, she was keeping her eyes on the road, hadn't let go the wheel, and I realised that here is someone you can actually count on.

It wasn't until after we'd met a couple of times half-way between us, which is to say at Notodden, and drunk coffee together, and the third time booked in at the Brattrein Hotel, that she told me she'd already made up her mind during the dinner in Oslo.

'You and Pia liked each other,' she said.

'Yes,' I said.

'But I liked you better. And I knew you would like me better.'

'Why is that?'

'Because you and I are alike, and you and Pia aren't. And because it isn't as far to Notodden.'

I laughed. 'You think I like **you** better because it isn't as **far** to Notodden as to Oslo?'

'As a rule our sympathies are practical.'

I laughed again and she smiled. Slightly.

Unni wasn't actually unhappy in her marriage, she said.

'He's a fine man and a good father,' she said. 'But he never touches me.' Her body was thin and hard, like a skinny young boy. She worked out a bit, jogging, pumping iron. 'We all need to be touched,' she said.

She wasn't too worried about him finding out she was having an affair. She thought he would understand. It was the kids she was worried about.

'They have a good, secure home. I can't let anything destroy that for them. My children will always come first, ahead of that type of happiness. I really like these hours with you, but I'll give it all up like a shot if it risks the slightest unhappiness or insecurity for my children. Do you understand?'

The question was delivered with a sudden intensity,

like when you download a fun app and suddenly a very serious, almost threatening form appears that you have to complete, filled with conditions you have to accept before the fun can begin.

One day I asked her if she, faced with a hypothetical crisis, would be willing to shoot me and her husband if doing so increased the likelihood of her children surviving by forty per cent. That accountant's brain of hers needed a few seconds before replying.

'Yes.'

'Thirty per cent?'

'Yes.'

'Twenty?'

'No.'

What I liked about Unni was that I knew exactly what I was dealing with.

37

CARL SENT ME EMAILS AND pics from his university. It looked and sounded like he was doing fine. White smile and friends who looked as though they'd known Carl all his life. He always was adaptable. 'Chuck that boy in the water and he'll grow gills before he's even wet,' Mum used to say. I remember that towards the end of that summer when he hung out with that pretty cabin visitor I was jealous of, Carl had learned to speak with an Oslo accent. And now American expressions began to crop up more and more in his emails, more than Dad ever used. It was as though his Norwegian was slowly but surely withering away. And maybe that was what he wanted. Pack everything that had happened here in layers of forgetfulness and distance. When Stanley Spind, the new doctor, heard me refer to the boot of the car as the 'trunk', he told me something about forgetting.

'In Vest-Agder where I grew up, whole villages emigrated to America. Some of them came back. And it turned out that the ones who had forgotten their Norwegian had forgotten almost everything about their old home country. It's as though language preserves the memories.'

In the days that followed I toyed with the idea of learning a new language, of never speaking Norwegian again, to see if it helped. Because now it wasn't just screams I heard from Huken. When the silence fell I could hear a low murmuring, as though the dead were talking to each other down there. Planning something. Fucking conspiring.

Carl was hard up, he wrote. He had failed a couple of exams and lost his stipend. I sent money. It was no problem, I had my wage, my outgoings were minimal, I'd even managed to put a little bit aside.

The year after that the college fees went up and he needed more. That winter I equipped a room down in the disused workshop that meant I saved on electricity and petrol. I tried to rent out the farm but there were no takers. When I suggested to Unni that we change our meeting place from the Brattrein to the Notodden Hotel, which was cheaper, she asked if I was short of money. And suggested we could share the cost of the room as she had insisted on doing for a while. I said no, and in the end we carried on meeting at the Brattrein, but the next time we met Unni told me she'd checked the accounts and seen that I was getting a lower wage than station managers with smaller stations than mine.

I rang head office and after a bit of toing and froing was put through to someone I was told could take decisions about pay rises.

The voice that took the call was bright: 'Pia Syse.'

I hung up.

Before the final semester – at least, he claimed it was the final semester – Carl called in the middle of the night and told me he was short twenty-one thousand dollars, two hundred thousand Norwegian kroner. He'd been banking on the award of a stipend from the Norwegian Society in Minneapolis, but he'd just found out he hadn't got it, and he needed the school fees before 0900 the next day, or he'd be excluded and not allowed to take his final exams. And without them his whole education was wasted, he said.

'**Business administration** is not about what you know but what people **think** you know, Roy. And what they believe in are exams and diplomas.'

'Have the school fees really doubled since you started there?' I asked.

'It's really . . . **unfortunate,**' said Carl, slipping into English. 'I'm sorry to have to ask, but the chairman of the Norwegian Society told me two months ago that there shouldn't be any problem.'

I was waiting outside the bank when it opened. The

bank manager listened as I suggested a loan of two hundred thousand, with the farm as security.

'You and Carl own the farm and land together, so for that we'll need both your signature and your brother's,' said the bank manager, a man with a bow tie and eyes like a St Bernard. 'And the processing and documentation take a couple of days. But of course I realise you need this today, and I've been authorised by head office to give you a hundred thousand on account of your honest face.'

'Without security?'

'We trust people here in the village, Roy.'

'I need two hundred thousand.'

'But not that much.' He smiled, and his eyes grew even more mournful.

'Carl's going to be barred at nine o'clock. Four o'clock Norwegian time.'

'I've never heard of universities operating with regimes as strict as that,' said the bank manager, scratching the back of his hand. 'But if you say so, then . . .' He scratched and scratched away at the back of his hand.

'Well . . . ?' I asked impatiently, glancing at my watch. Six and a half hours left.

'Well, you didn't hear this from me, but maybe you should have a word with Willumsen.'

I looked at the bank manager. So it really was true what people said, that Willumsen loaned money to people. With no security and at extortionate rates of interest. No security, that is, other than the certainty that Willumsen, somehow or other, sometime or other, would call in his debt. And if there was any trouble, rumour had it that he brought in that enforcer from Denmark to get the job done. I actually knew that Erik Nerell had borrowed from Willumsen when he bought the Fritt Fall bar, but there was no talk there of strong-arm stuff. On the contrary, Erik said that Willumsen had been patient and waited, and when he asked for an extension, Willumsen had answered: 'As long as there's interest coming in, I'll do nothing, Nerell. Because compound interest, that's heaven on earth.'

I drove down to Willumsen's Used Cars and Breaker's Yard. Knew Rita wouldn't be there, she hated the place. Willumsen saw me in his office. Above his desk was a stag's head that looked as if it had butted its way through the wall and was looking in astonishment at the sight that met its eyes. Willumsen sat beneath it and leaned back in his chair, his double chin flopping over his shirt collar, his small, pudgy fingers folded across his chest. Just raised the right hand now and then to flick off ash from his cigar. Put his head on one side and studied me thoughtfully. A process known as credit rating, I realised.

'Interest rate two per cent,' he said after I had described my problem and the time limit. 'Payable monthly. I can call the bank and transfer the money now.'

I took out my snuffbox and pushed a wedge in under my lip as I worked it out in my head.

'That's more than twenty-five per cent a year.'

Willumsen removed his cigar. 'The boy can do his sums. You get that from your dad.'

'And this time you've worked on the assumption that I don't haggle either?'

Willumsen laughed. 'Yup, that's the lowest I can offer you. Take it or leave it. The clock is ticking.'

'Where do I sign?'

'Oh, this'll be plenty good enough,' said Willumsen, holding out his hand to me over the desk. It looked like a bunch of bulging sausages. I suppressed a shudder and took it.

'Have you ever been in love?' asked Unni. We were walking in the big gardens of the Brattrein Hotel. Clouds raced across the sky and Lake Heddal, the colours changing with the light. I've heard it said that most couples talk less as the years go by. In our case it was the other way round. Neither of us was the talkative type, and the first few times I was the one who had to do most of the talking. We'd been meeting about once a month for five years now, and although Unni was more forthcoming now than when we had first met, it was unusual for her to broach a theme like this with no preamble.

'Once,' I said. 'How about you?'

'Never,' she said. 'And what do you think?'

'About being in love?'

'Yes.'

'Not something to hanker for,' I said, turning up the collar of my jacket to the gusting wind.

I glanced at her, saw that almost invisible hint of a smile. Wondered where she was headed with this.

'I read that you can only fall properly in love twice in your life,' she said. 'That the first time is action, and the second reaction. Those are the two earthquakes. The rest are just emotional aftershocks.'

'OK,' I said. 'So that means there's still a chance for you, then.'

'But I don't want any earthquake,' she said. 'I've got children.'

'I understand. But earthquakes happen, whether you want them or not.'

'Yes,' she said. 'And when you say it's nothing to hanker for, that's because the love didn't go both ways, am I right?'

'That was probably it.'

'So the safest thing is to get out of anywhere that's prone to earthquakes,' she said.

I nodded slowly. It began to dawn on me what she was talking about.

'I think I'm beginning to fall in love with you, Roy.' She stopped walking. 'And I don't think the house back home could withstand such a quake.'

'So . . .' I said.

She sighed. 'So I'm going to have to get away . . .'

'. . . from anywhere earthquake-prone,' I concluded for her.

'Yes.'

'On a permanent basis?'

'Yes.'

We stood there in silence.

'Aren't you going to . . . ?' she said.

'No,' I said. 'You've decided for me. And I'm probably like my father.'

'Your father?'

'No good at haggling.'

We spent our last hours together in the room. I had booked the suite and from the bed we had a view over the lake. The sky had cleared by sunset, and Unni said it made her think of that Deep Purple song, the one about the hotel by Lake Geneva in Switzerland. The hotel burns down in that song, I said.

'Yes,' said Unni.

We checked out before midnight, gave each other a farewell kiss in the car park and left Notodden, each driving in our own direction. We never saw each other again.

Carl called me on Christmas Eve that same year. I could hear party voices and Mariah Carey singing 'All I Want for Christmas is You' in the background. As for me I was sitting alone in my room at the workshop with an aquavit and a plate of Fjordland's ready-made lamb ribs with **vossa** sausage and mashed swede.

'Is it lonely?' he asked.

I hesitated. 'A bit.'

'A bit?'

'Quite. And you?'

'There's a Christmas dinner here at the office. Punch. We've closed the switchboard and—'

'Carl! Carl, come and dance!' The female voice, half whining, half snuffling that interrupted us, came straight out of the speaker. It sounded as if she was sitting in his lap.

'Listen, Roy, I've got to go now. But I've sent you a little Christmas present.'

'Oh?'

'Yes. Check your bank account.'

He hung up.

I did as he said. Logged in and saw there was a transfer from an American bank. In the comment field it said: **Thanks for the loan, dear brother. And Happy Christmas!** Six hundred thousand kroner. Far more than I had sent for college fees, even allowing for the interest, and the compound interest.

I was so happy I broke out into a grin. Not because of the money, I was managing. But because of Carl, that **he** was managing. Of course I could have asked questions about how he'd managed to earn such a large amount of money in just a few short months on starting salary at a property company. But I knew what I was going to do with the money. Proper insulation and a bathroom up at the farm. No fucking way was I going to spend another Christmas Eve down here at the workshop.

Here in the village – same as in the city – the only time heathens like me ever visit the church is at Christmas. Not on Christmas Eve the way they do in the city, but on Christmas Day.

On the way out after the service Stanley Spind came over and invited me over for Boxing Day breakfast – he'd asked several others too. It was a little surprising, and at such short notice that I realised something must have just told him that that Roy Opgard, he's alone at his workshop this Christmas, poor sod. A good man, Stanley, but I told him I was working all Christmas and had given the other staff time off, which was the truth. He put his hand on my shoulder and said that **I** was a good man. So he's no people expert, Stanley Spind. Because now I excused myself, hurried along and overtook Willumsen and Rita who were headed for the car park. Willumsen had swelled back up to his natural size again. Rita was looking good too, rosy-cheeked and probably warm inside that fur coat. And me, the lecher who had just been told he was a good man, took Willumsen's bunch of sausages – which was fortunately gloved – and wished them a very merry Christmas.

'Happy Christmas,' said Rita.

I remembered of course that she had told me that in refined circles one says 'Merry Christmas' up until Christmas Eve, but that from Christmas Day onwards until New Year's Eve it's '**Happy** Christmas'. But if Willumsen realised a country bumpkin like me was familiar with such niceties it might make him suspicious, so I nodded as though I hadn't registered the correction. Good man my arse.

'I just want to thank you for the loan.' I handed Willumsen a single white envelope.

'Oh?' he said, weighing it in his hand and looking at me.

'I transferred the money to your account last night,' I said. 'That there is the printout.'

'Interest until the first working day,' he said. 'That's another three days away, Roy.'

'I've taken account of that, yes. Plus a little extra.'

He nodded slowly. 'It feels good, doesn't it? To clear a debt.'

I did and didn't understand what he meant. I mean, I understood the words, of course, but not the way he said them.

But I would before the calendar year was over.

38

DURING THAT ENCOUNTER WITH WILLUMSEN and his wife outside church on Christmas Day Rita hadn't given away a thing with her body language and her facial expressions. She was good. But the meeting clearly set something going inside her. Enough for her to forget what ought to stay forgotten and remember what was worth remembering. Her text message came three days later, on the first working day after the break.

The cabin day after tomorrow 12.00.

It was so recognisably short and businesslike that I felt something like a shiver pass through my body and the saliva begin to run like one of Pavlov's dogs. **Conditioned reaction,** that's what they call it.

I had a brief and turbulent discussion with myself about whether to go. Commonsense Roy lost, in spades. And I had forgotten why it felt so like a liberation once we stopped meeting, but recalled all the rest in richly sensual detail.

At five to twelve I had reached that clearing in the woods from where you can see the cabin. I'd walked the whole way with the erection I got every time I saw the Saab Sonett parked along the gravel track. The snow had been late in coming that year, but there was a black frost, the sun only seen in glimpses, and the air sharp and good to breathe. Smoke rose from the chimney, and the curtains at the living-room window were closed. She didn't usually do that, and the thought that she had planned a surprise, that she was perhaps lying there all ready and waiting for me in front of the open fire in some way that required subdued lighting sent shockwaves through my body. I crossed the patch of open terrain and went up to the door. It was ajar. Before it had usually been closed when I arrived, sometimes even locked, so that I had to reach up and take down the extra key from the top of the door jamb. I suspected she liked the feeling that I was an intruder, literally a thief in the night. I knew that was why she had given me the key to the basement that time, a key I still had and that I now and then fantasised about using. I pushed the door open all the way and walked into the semi-darkness.

And sensed immediately that something was wrong.

It **smelled** wrong.

Unless Rita Willumsen had started smoking cigars.

And even before my eyes had adapted to the darkness, I knew who that figure was sitting in the armchair in the middle of the living-room floor, facing me.

'Glad you could come,' said Willumsen in a voice so friendly it made my back go cold.

He was wearing a fur coat and hat and looked like a bear. And in his hands he was holding a shotgun that was pointed at me.

'Shut the door behind you,' he said.

I did as he told me.

'Come three steps closer, slowly. And kneel.'

I took three steps closer.

'Kneel,' he repeated.

I hesitated.

He sighed. 'Now listen. Every year I pay a lot of money to travel to some foreign country and shoot an animal I've never shot before.' He raised his hand and make a ticking gesture in the air. 'I've got one of most species, but not a Roy Opgard. So **kneel**!'

I knelt. I noticed for the first time that plastic covering of the kind you use when you're decorating had been rolled out between the front door and the armchair.

'Where did you park your car?' he asked.

I told him. He nodded in satisfaction.

'The snuffbox,' he said.

I didn't respond. My head was full of questions, not answers.

'You're wondering how I found out, Opgard. The

answer is the snuffbox. The doctor told me the best thing I could do for my health after the cancer was to start eating more healthily and exercise more. So I started going for walks. Including up here, where I hadn't been for years. And I found a couple of these in the fridge.'

He tossed a silver Berry tin onto the plastic in front of me.

'You can't buy those in Norway. Or certainly not in this village. I asked Rita and she said they were probably left behind by the Polish workers who were here refurbishing the cabin the year before. And I believed her. Up until the point at which I saw you pull out the same box when you came to my office asking for a loan. I put two and two together. Moist snuff. The repair job on the Saab Sonett. The cabin. And a Rita who overnight turned into the sweetest and most agreeable of all Ritas, which she never is unless there's something behind it. So I checked her phone. And there, under the name of Agnete, I found an old message she hadn't deleted. The cabin, the day, the hour, that was all. I checked with directory enquiries and sure enough, Agnete's number was registered to you, Roy Opgard. And so – day before yesterday – I borrowed Rita's phone again and sent the same message to you all over again, just changed the hour.'

The kneeling had meant that I had to look upwards at him, but now my neck was getting tired and I bowed my head. 'If you found this all out months ago,' I said, 'why wait until now to do something?'

'That should be obvious to someone who's as good at mental arithmetic as you are, Roy.'

I shook my head.

'You'd borrowed money from me. If I'd blown your head off then, who would clear your debt?'

My heart wasn't beating faster, it was beating slower. This was unbefuckinglievable. Patient as the hunter he was, he had waited until his prey was in the right place, waited for me to clear my debt. Waited until I had paid the compound interest, until the cow had been milked dry. And now he was going to clear his debt. That was what he'd meant with that question he'd asked me outside the church; about how good it must feel to clear a debt. He was intending to shoot me. That was what this was about. Not scare me or threaten me but fucking well kill me. He knew I'd told no one where I was off to, that I'd made sure no one saw me walking up here, and that I'd parked the car so far away that no one would think of looking for me round here. He was just going to put a bullet through my forehead and then bury me somewhere nearby. The plan was so simple and straightforward I had to smile.

'Wipe that grin off your face,' said Willumsen.

'I haven't met your wife for years,' I said. 'Didn't you see the date on that message?'

'It should have been deleted, but there it was, and it tells me you two were at it for a long time,' he said. 'But not any more. Pray your last prayer.' Willumsen raised the rifle to his cheek.

'Aw, I already prayed that,' I said. My heart was still slowing down. Resting pulse. Psychopath's pulse, as people say.

'So you have, have you?' Willumsen breathed, the skin of his cheek flopping up onto the rifle butt.

I nodded and bowed my head again. 'So just go ahead, you'll be doing me a favour, Willumsen.'

A dry laugh. 'Are you trying to convince me you **want** to die, Opgard?'

'No. But I **shall** die.'

'That's true of us all.'

'Yes, but not within two months.'

I heard him fidgeting with the trigger. 'Says who?'

'Says Stanley Spind. Maybe you saw, I spoke to him at church. He's just received the most recent pictures of my brain tumour. I've had it for over a year, but now it's growing fast. If you aim just here . . .' I put my index finger to my forehead on the right-hand side, just above where the hair starts, 'then maybe I'll get rid of it at the same time.'

I could almost hear the used-car salesman's calculator ticking and whirring.

'You're desperate, of course, so you're lying,' he said.

'If you're so sure of that then go ahead and shoot,' I said. Because I knew what his brain was telling him. That **if** it was true, then the Roy Opgard problem would soon disappear by itself, and without any risk at all to him. But if I was lying, it would mean he had squandered a perfect chance that he would probably never get again. That's to say, the chance would be

there, but I would be ready, it would be more difficult. Risk contra profit. Cost against income. Debit
and credit.

'You can call Stanley,' I said. 'I'll just have to tell
him first he's released from his vow of confidentiality.'

In the pause that followed the only thing that could
be heard was Willumsen's breathing. This dilemma
demanded an increased supply of oxygen to the brain.
I said a prayer, not for my soul, but that the stress
might give him a stroke right here and now.

'Two months,' he said suddenly. 'If you're not
dead in two months, starting today, then I'll be back.
You won't know where, or when or how. Or who.
But it could be the last words you'll ever hear will be
Danish. This is not a threat, it's a promise. OK?'

I stood up. 'Two months at the most,' I said. 'This
tumour is a powerful bastard, Willumsen, it won't let
you down. And one other thing . . .'

Willumsen was still aiming the rifle at me, but with
a lowering and raising of the eyelid signalled for me
to continue.

'Is it OK if I take my tins of snuff from the fridge?'

Of course I knew I was pushing it, but I was supposed to be a dying man who didn't much care how
it happened.

'I don't use the stuff, so do what you want.'

I took my tins of snuff and left. Jogged down
through the trees with daylight already fading.
Headed west in an arc and then, hidden from view
behind the rocks, up towards the lake where I had

seen Rita that last time; naked, humiliated, aged by daylight and a young man's gaze.

I headed back towards the cabin from the north. There were no windows on that side, only thick timber walls, human fortifications, because attack always came from the north.

I walked right up to the wall, sneaked round the corner to the door. Wrapped my scarf around my right hand and waited. When Willumsen emerged I kept it simple. A punch directly behind the ear, where the cranium gives the brain less protection, and two in the kidneys which, besides hurting so much you can't even scream, makes you amenable. He dropped to his knees, and I relieved him of the shotgun which was slung over one shoulder. Hit him on the temple and dragged him back inside.

He'd tidied away the roll of plastic and pushed the chair back into place by the wall next to the fireplace.

I let him get his breath back, let him look up and stare into the mouth of his own shotgun before starting to talk.

'As you can see, I lied,' I said. 'But only about the tumour. It's true that I haven't met Rita for years. And since it only took one text message for me to come bounding up here with my tail wagging you'll also understand that she was the one who ended it, not me. Don't get up!'

Willumsen cursed quietly but did as I told him.

'In other words, this could have been a story

about what you never know will never hurt you and how we all live happy ever after,' I said. 'But since you don't believe me and have expressed your intention to bump me off, you leave me with no choice but to bump you off. Believe me, it brings me no pleasure to do so, and I've no intention of taking the opportunity to resume the affair with the woman who will shortly be your widow. In other words it might seem extremely unfuckingnecessary to kill you, but unfortunately, from a practical point of view, it's the only solution.'

'I've no idea what you're talking about,' groaned Willumsen. 'But you'll never get away with murder, Opgard. A thing like that has to be planned.'

'Yes,' I said. 'And I've had the few minutes I needed to realise that your plan to kill me has provided me with the best chance in the world to kill **you.** We're here alone, at a place where no one saw us come or go, and do you know what the most common cause of death among men between the ages of thirty and sixty is, Willumsen?'

He nodded. 'Cancer.'

'No,' I said.

'Oh yes.'

'It's not cancer,' I said.

'Car crash then.'

'No.' But I made a mental note to google that when I got home. 'It's suicide.'

'Nonsense.'

'In our village at least we'll have made our contribution

450

to the statistic if we include my father along with Sheriff Olsen and you.'

'Me?'

'Christmas week. Man takes his shotgun and goes alone to his cabin without telling anyone, found in the living room with the shotgun lying next to him. That's about as classic as it gets, Willumsen. And oh yeah, black frost. So no trails leading to and from the cabin.'

I raised the shotgun. Saw him swallow. 'I've got cancer,' he said, his voice thick.

'You **had** cancer,' I said. 'Sorry, but you recovered.'

'Shit,' he said, a sob in his throat. I curled my finger around the trigger. The sweat broke out on his forehead. He began shaking uncontrollably.

'Pray your last prayer,' I whispered. Waited. He sobbed. A puddle swelled out from under his bearskin.

'But of course, there is one alternative,' I said.

Willumsen's mouth opened and closed.

I lowered the shotgun. 'And that is if we agree not to kill each other,' I said. 'And take a gamble on trusting each other.'

'Wh-what?'

'What I've now just proved is that I'm so certain you will realise there's no reason to kill me that I'm passing up a more or less perfect opportunity to kill you. That is what I call a **leap of trust,** Willumsen. See, trust is a benign, contagious sickness. So if you don't kill me, I won't kill you. What d'you say, Willumsen? Gonna take that leap with me? Have we got a deal?'

Willumsen wrinkled his brow. Gave a sort of hesitant nod.

'Good. Thanks for the loan.' I handed the shotgun back to him.

He blinked, staring at me in disbelief. He wouldn't take it, almost as though he suspected a trick. So instead I propped the shotgun up against the wall.

'You realise of course that I – I . . .' He coughed snot, tears and slime from his throat. '. . . I would have said yes to anything right now. I haven't made any jump, only you. So how can I get you to trust me?'

I thought it over for a moment.

'Oh, this'll be plenty good enough,' I said, and held out my hand.

39

IT SNOWED ON NEW YEAR'S Day and the snow lay until the end of April. At Easter there were more people than ever before heading for their cabins and the service station did record business. We'd also been given an award as the best service station in the county, so the mood in the shop was good.

Then came the report into the development of the road network that concluded a tunnel should be built, and the main highway be routed around Os.

'It's a long way off yet,' said Voss Gilbert, Aas's successor in the party. Maybe so, but it wasn't long until the next local elections, and his party would lose. Because it stands to reason, when a village can be wiped off the map of Norway with a stroke of the pen then someone in the village hasn't been doing his lobbying job.

I had a meeting with head office and we agreed just to keep on milking the cow as long as we had her. Following that: readjustment, scaling back, for which read – redundancies. Small stations are needed too. And if things didn't work out, I wasn't to worry, they told me.

'The door is always open to you, Roy,' said Pia Syse. 'If you want to try something new, all you have to do is call, you have my number.'

I stepped up a gear. Worked harder than ever. That was fine, I like working. And I'd given myself a goal. I was going to get my own station.

One day Dan Krane came in as I was cleaning the coffee machine. Asked if he could ask me a few questions for a story he was doing about Carl.

'We hear he's doing well over there,' said Dan Krane.

'Oh yeah?' I said and carried on cleaning. 'So this is going to be a positive article, is it?'

'Well, our job is to show both sides.'

'Not **all** sides?'

'See there, you put it better than the newspaper editor,' said Dan Krane with a thin smile.

I didn't like him. But then again, I don't like many people. When he first came to the village he'd reminded me of one of those English setters that cabin people have with them in their SUVs; thin and restless, but friendly enough. But it was a cool friendliness, deployed as the means towards a more distant goal, and after a while I began to realise that's what

Dan Krane really was, a marathon runner. A strategist who never loses patience in the field, who never pulls away but just patiently keeps on grinding because he knows that what he possesses is the kind of endurance that will, in the end, get him to the top. And this certainty showed itself in his body language, it could be heard in the way he formulated himself, it even shone from his eyes. That even if today he was no more than the humble editor of a local newspaper, he was going places. Was meant for greater things, as people say. He'd joined the same party as Aas, but even though the **Os Daily** was an open supporter of the Labour Party, the paper's own internal regulations stipulated that the editor was prohibited from any political position that might cast doubt on his or her political integrity. Krane was moreover a father with a young family and a lot on his plate, so he wouldn't be standing at the coming election, although perhaps at the one after that. Or the one after the one after that. Because it was just a matter of time before Dan Krane got those skinny hands of his around the chairman's gavel.

'Your brother was a risk-taker and made good money from that shopping mall investment while he was still a student.' Krane fished notepad and pen up from the pocket of his Jack Wolfskin jacket. 'Were you a part of that too?'

'No idea what you're talking about,' I said.

'No? I gather you provided the last two hundred thousand for the share purchase?'

I hoped he didn't see the jolt that passed through me.

'Who told you that?'

Again that thin smile, as though smiling caused him physical pain. 'Even in local newspapers we need to protect our sources, I'm afraid.'

Was it the bank manager? Or Willumsen? Or someone else in the bank? Someone who'd followed the money, as people say.

'No comment,' I said.

Krane laughed softly and made a note. 'You really want it to say that, Roy?'

'Say what?'

'No comment. That's what big-time politicians and celebs in the cities answer. When they're in trouble. It can create a rather strange impression.'

'I'm thinking it's more likely you're the one who creates the impression.'

Still smiling, Krane shook his head. Narrow, hard, smooth-haired. 'I only write what people say, Roy.'

'Then do it. Write this conversation, word for word. Including your **self-serving** advice about the no-comment comment.'

'Interviews have to be edited, you know. So we focus on what's important.'

'And you're the one who decides what's most important. So you're the one who creates the impression.'

Krane sighed. 'I gather from your dismissive attitude that you don't want it generally known that you and Carl were a part of this high-risk project.'

'Ask Carl,' I said, closed the front of the coffee machine and pressed the On switch. 'Coffee?'

'Yes thanks. So then you've no comment either to the fact that Carl has just moved his business to Canada following an investigation by the American Stock Exchange Supervisory Authority into what they believe to be market manipulation.'

'What I **do** have a comment on,' I said as I handed him the paper coffee cup, 'is that you're writing a story about your wife's ex-boyfriend. Do you want my comment?'

Krane sighed again, pushed the notebook back into his jacket pocket and sipped the coffee. 'If a local paper in a village like this couldn't write about someone they have some connection or other with then we wouldn't be able to write a single story.'

'I understand that, but you will include the information below the article, right? That this was written by the man who was served after Carl Opgard.'

I saw the marathon runner's eyes flash now. That his long-term strategy was under pressure, that he was close to saying or doing something that wouldn't serve his ultimate goal.

And after his brother, Roy, turned down the offer of service.

I didn't say it. Of course I didn't say it. Just played with the thought of how it might cause Dan Krane to lose his rhythm.

'Thanks for your time,' said Krane, pulling up the zip on his rain jacket.

'You're welcome,' I said. 'Twenty kroner.'

He looked up at me from his coffee cup. I tried to mimic his wafer-thin smile.

*

The newspaper ran a story about Carl Abel Opgard, our very own local lad made good on the other side of the pond. The byline was by one of Krane's financial journalists.

Back home after the conversation with Krane I went for a run up behind the farm, inspected a couple of nests I had found, went out to the barn and punched that old sandbag for half an hour. Then I went upstairs to the new bathroom and showered. Stood there with soap in my hair and thought about the money that had been enough to cover not just the bathroom and the insulation but new windows. I raised my face to the warm jets and let them wash the day away. A new one awaited. I'd found my rhythm. I had a goal and I had a strategy. I wasn't aiming to be council chairman, all I wanted was my own bloody service station. But all the same, I was turning into a marathon runner.

Then Carl called, and said he was moving home.

PART FIVE

40

INCREDIBLE SPEED. THE BEAST CHARGING towards the abyss. The black hunk of metal, chrome, leather, plastic, glass, rubber, smells, tastes, memories you thought would stay with you forever, the ones you loved you thought you could never lose, all of it rolling away from you. I was the one who started it moving, the one who started the train of events in this story. But at a certain point – and it's bloody difficult to say exactly when and where – the story itself begins to make the decisions, the weight of gravity is in the driving seat, the beast accelerates, becomes autonomous and now it's of no consequence for the result if I've changed my mind. Incredible speed.

Do I wish everything that happened had never happened? Fucking right I do.

And yet there's something fascinating about seeing the avalanches from Ottertind in March, seeing the snow smash the ice on Lake Budal, seeing a forest fire in July and knowing that the old GMC fire engine won't be able to make it up the hills. It **is** thrilling to see the first proper storm of the autumn again test the roofs of the barns down there in the village, and think that this year it'll succeed in tearing off at least one of them, and you'll see it bowling along on its sides like a giant fucking sawblade across the fields before it breaks apart. And then that's exactly what happens. And the next thought you have is, what if someone, some person, had been standing out there when the sawblade came. Of course you don't wish it, but you can't quite dismiss the thought; that it would have been quite a sight to see. No, you don't wish for it. So if I'd known the train of events I was setting in motion, I would probably have done things differently. But I didn't, so I can't really claim I would have done things differently if I'd had another chance but no new information.

And even if it was your will directing the blast of wind that took the barn roof off, what happens after that is out of your hands. The barn roof, now a wheel of razor-sharp corrugated iron, is heading for that solitary person out there in the field, and all you can do is watch with a mixture of horror, curiosity and regret that this was part of something you were hoping for. But the next thought is maybe something you weren't ready for: that you find yourself wishing you yourself were that person out there in the field.

41

ME AND PIA SYSE SIGNED a contract of employment that said that after two years in Sørlandet I was free to return to my job as station boss in Os.

The service station was outside Kristiansand, on the other side of the Europa highway that passes the zoo and amusement park. Naturally it was much bigger than the one in Os, with more employees, more pumps, a bigger shop stocking a bigger range and with a higher turnover. But the biggest difference was that because the previous boss had treated the staff like a brain-dead financial drain on the firm what I got there was a bunch of demoralised and moaning boss-haters who never did more than exactly what they were employed to do and sometimes not even that.

'All service stations are different,' said Gus Myre, the sales director at head office, in his lectures to us. 'The sign is the same, the petrol's the same, the logistics are the same, but in the final analysis our stations aren't about petrol, Peugeots and Pepsi, they're about **people.** The ones standing behind the counter, the ones in front of it, and the meeting between the two.'

He sang his message as though it was a tune he was growing a bit more tired of playing with each passing year, and yet was, in spite of everything, his hit. From the exaggeratedly playful alliteration of what must have been that self-composed **petrol, Peugeots and Pepsi,** to the equally exaggerated and – over time – ever more forced sincerity of **people,** which always put me in mind of those revivalist meetings at Årtun. Because, just like a preacher, it was Myre's job to get the gathering to believe in something that, deep down, everyone knew was just bollocks, but which they badly **wanted** to believe was true. Because belief makes life – and in the preacher's case: death – that much easier to deal with. If you really believe yourself to be unique, and every encounter therefore unique, you can maybe trick yourself into believing in a kind of purity, an everlasting and virgin innocence which stops you spitting in the customers' face and puking with boredom.

But I didn't feel myself to be unique. And the station was – the previously mentioned differences notwithstanding – not unique either. The chain observes strict franchise principles, meaning that you can move from a small station in one part of the country to a larger one in another part, and it's like changing sheets on the same bed. It took me two days from the moment I arrived to learn the technical details that distinguished this one from the one at Os, four days to talk to all members of staff, find out what their ambitions were, what changes they thought might turn the station into a better place for them to work, and a better place for the customer to be. Three weeks to have introduced ninety per cent of these changes.

I gave an envelope to the safety deputy and told her not to open it for eight weeks but to wait until the day of a staff meeting to evaluate the changes. We had hired a local cafe for the meeting. I welcomed everyone and then handed over to a staff member who gave the figures for sales and profits; another gave us the statistics for absence due to sickness; and a third announced the results of a simple customer satisfaction survey, along with a more informal assessment of the atmosphere among the employees. I just listened as the employees, after much arguing, then voted to drop eighty per cent of their own suggested changes. Afterwards I summarised which changes everyone thought had worked and which we would be continuing with, and announced that we would be eating now and the bar was open. One member of the staff, a real old sourpuss, raised his hand and asked if that was all I was in charge of, the bar.

'No,' I said. 'I'm in charge of the fact that for the last eight weeks you've been allowed to be your own

466

bosses. Lotte, will you open the envelope I gave you before we introduced the changes?'

She did so and read out my list of which changes I thought would work, and which wouldn't. There was a lot of murmuring as it gradually became apparent that my advance projections – with just two exceptions – agreed with what they had decided themselves after the results were known.

'The point here is not to convince you that I'm Mr Know-it-all,' I said. 'Look, I was wrong on two counts, the coffee cards, which I thought would work, and the offer of five day-old buns for the price of one, which I thought wouldn't. But since I was right about the other twelve it might look as though I know **something** about running a service station, right?'

I saw a few heads nodding in agreement. They nod in a different way here in the south. Even slower, in fact. As the nodding spread there were sounds of a low murmuring. Finally even the old sourpuss was nodding.

'We're second bottom of the list of the best stations in the county,' I said. 'I've spoken to head office and worked out a deal. If we're among the ten best at the next grading, they'll pay for a trip on the Danish ferry for the whole gang. If we're among the five best, a trip to London. And if we're best, you'll be given a budget and allowed to decide for yourselves what the prize should be.'

They just stared at me. Then the cheering began.

'This evening . . .' I shouted, and the racket

immediately died down. 'This evening we're the second worst in the county, so the bar is only going to be open for one hour. After that everyone will go home and charge their batteries ready for tomorrow, because it's tomorrow – and not the day after – that we start climbing up that list.'

I lived in Søm, a quiet residential area on the east side before you cross the bridges over to the town side. I rented a spacious three-roomed apartment, of which I only had furniture enough for two. I figured that by now the rumours about Carl having been abused by Dad were spreading like wildfire through Os. That the only one who hadn't heard them was Carl. And me. Though she had waited fifteen years, when Grete made up her mind to tell people what Carl had confided in her I was the first one she told, and by now she must be having one field day after another in her hair salon. If Carl found out, he would probably be able to handle it. And if he never heard anything that was probably OK too. In any event, the responsibility and the shame were above all mine. I couldn't take it. I was weak. But that wasn't the main reason I'd had to leave Os. It was her.

By night I dreamed of Shannon.

By day I dreamed of Shannon.

Eating, driving between work and home, serving customers, working out, washing clothes, sitting on the toilet, masturbating, listening to an audio book or watching TV, I dreamed of Shannon.

About that sleepy, sensual eye. An eye that expressed more feelings, more warmth and cold than other people's two eyes put together. Or about a voice that was almost as deep as Rita's, and yet completely different, so soft you felt you wanted to lie down in it like a warm bed. About kissing her, fucking her, washing her, holding her tight, setting her free. About the red hair that glowed in the sunlight, about the tense bow of her spine, laughter that contained an almost imperceptible predatory snarl, as well as a promise.

I tried to tell myself it was the same old story all over again, about Mari, about falling in love with my brother's girl. That it was some kind of fucking sickness or short circuit in my brain. Driving yourself crazy over what you can't have or shouldn't have. And that if by some miracle Shannon wanted me too, that would just be a repeat of what happened with Mari. That love would dissolve, the way the rainbow you see stretched above the mountain top disappears when you drive. Not because the love was delusory, but because rainbows need to be seen from a particular angle – from outside – and from a certain distance – not too close up. And if the rainbow should happen to be still there when you reach the top of the mountain, you'll discover there's no pot of gold at the end, just tragedy and shattered lives.

I told myself all of this, but it didn't help. It was like fucking malaria. And I thought that maybe it's true what people say, that it's the second time you catch jungle fever that it does you in. I tried to work it away, but it kept coming back. I tried to sleep and forget, but was woken by screams from the zoo, even though that was impossible, the place was almost ten kilometres away.

I tried going out, someone recommended a pub in Kristiansand, but I ended up sitting alone at the bar. Hadn't a clue how to approach people, and no desire to either, it was more a case of thinking I **ought** to. Because I don't get lonely. Or rather yes, I do, but it doesn't bother me, at least not to mention. What I was thinking was that maybe women would help, that they might be a remedy for the fever. But none of them looked at me for more than a second. If it'd been the Fritt Fall at least after a couple of beers someone would have asked who you were. But they probably saw it in that single second, that I was a country bumpkin out for a night on the town and not worth the bother, as people say. Maybe noticed the way my middle finger stuck out when I picked up my glass. So I gulped down the rest of the beer – a **pale lager,** Miller's, American dishwater – and took the bus home. Lay in bed and heard the apes and the giraffes screaming.

It was when Julie called with some technical questions about the stocktaking that I realised Grete had kept her mouth shut about Dad's abuse. After I'd explained the technicalities to her I asked her for the latest gossip. Which she provided, although somewhat surprised, I noticed, since I'd never shown any interest in that kind of stuff before. When it turned out to be uninteresting stuff I asked her straight out if there were any rumours involving our family, anything concerning Carl and Dad.

'No – why should there be?' she asked, and I could hear that she really had no idea what I was talking about.

'Just ring if there's anything else you want to know about the stocktaking,' I said.

We hung up.

I scratched my head.

Maybe it wasn't so strange that Grete hadn't been spreading the news about Carl and Dad. She'd kept her mouth shut for all these years. Because in all her craziness she was most of all crazy in love, just like me. She didn't want to hurt Carl, and for that reason she would continue to keep her mouth shut. But then why had Grete told me what she knew? I remembered her question about how had I saved Carl. **What did you do, Roy?** Was it a threat? Was she trying to tell me she had worked out who was to blame for Mum and Dad going over the edge into Huken? That I mustn't do anything that got in the way of her plans for Carl?

If so, then it was so crazy the mere thought of it made me shiver.

But what it did mean was that I had one reason less to stay away from Os.

I didn't go home at Christmas.

Nor Easter either.

Carl called and kept me updated on the hotel.

Winter had arrived earlier than expected and the snow had lain for a long time, so they were behind schedule. They'd also had to make some adjustments to the drawings after the council had said they wanted to see more timber and less concrete.

'Shannon's pissed off, she doesn't understand that if the council hadn't got those fucking timber walls of theirs then we wouldn't have got permission from the planning department. She tried arguing that timber isn't solid enough, but of course that's crap, all she cares about is the aesthetics of the place, that it'll have like her signature on it. But you always have these kinds of discussions with the architect.'

Maybe so, but I could hear in his voice that the quarrel had probably been a bit more violent than those one usually had with architects.

'Is she—' I coughed to interrupt myself when I realised I couldn't complete the question in a neutral tone of voice. Not neutral enough for Carl's ears, at least. But at least I understood she hadn't told him about that idiotic declaration of love I'd made during the launch party at Fritt Fall, or I would have heard it in his tone of voice, because that's a door that swings both ways. I could, for example, hear that he'd downed a few Budweisers.

'Is she settling down OK?'

'Yeah yeah,' he said. 'It takes time to adapt to something that's so different from what you know. For example, after you left she was very quiet and taciturn for a while. Of course, she wants kids, but it's not that easy, she has some kind of something, so it looks like the test tube is the only way.'

I felt the muscles of my stomach tighten.

'That's OK too, but it's a bit much right at the moment. Oh, and she's going to Toronto in the summer, got a couple of projects there to finish off.'

Did I hear a false note there? Or was that just something I wanted to hear? I could no longer even trust my own bloody judgement.

'Maybe you should take some holiday and come up here then?' said Carl. 'We'll have the whole house to ourselves. What d'you think? Party time. Like in the old days! Yeah!'

That old enthusiasm in his voice was still infectious, and I very nearly just said yes.

'I'll have to see. Summer is like the peak season with all the holidaymakers here down south.'

'Come on. You need a holiday too. Have you had even a single day off since you've been there?'

'Oh yes,' I said, counting them. 'When is she leaving?'

'Shannon? First week in June.'

I drove home the second week in June.

42

SOMETHING STRANGE HAPPENED AS I was driving over Banehaugen, passing the county sign for Os, Lake Budal calm as a millpond before me. I felt myself choking up, and the road began to float away, and I had to blink hard. It was like one of those times when from sheer boredom you're slumped in front of the TV watching some third-rate tearjerker and – because you're quite relaxed and unprepared – you suddenly find yourself having to swallow hard.

I'd taken four days off.

For four days Carl and I sat around on the farm and looked out at the summer. At a sun that seemed as though it would never set. Drinking beer after beer in the winter garden. Talking about the old days. About school, friends, parties, the dances at Årtun and the Aas cabin. He talked about the USA and Toronto. About the money pouring in through a red-hot property market. About the project where, finally, they had bitten off more than they could chew.

'What's hardest to take is that it **could've** worked out,' said Carl, adding his empty beer bottle to the row along the windowsill. His was three times longer than mine. 'It was just a question of timing. If we'd managed to keep the project afloat for another three months, we'd be filthy rich today.'

When it all went pear-shaped the other two partners had threatened to sue him, he said.

'I was the only one who hadn't lost absolutely everything, so they thought they could shake a bit of money out of me,' he said with a laugh and opened another bottle.

'Don't you have a ton of work you should be doing?' I asked.

We'd visited the building site and had a look around. Work had begun there, but it didn't exactly look like things were in full swing. A lot of machinery but not many people. And if you were to ask me, I'd have to say it didn't look as though all that much had happened in the nine months they'd been at it. Carl explained they were still working on below-ground stuff, and that it had taken time to organise the roads, the water supply and sewage disposal. But that once they started work on the actual hotel building things would really speed up.

'Actually the hotel is being built somewhere else even as we stand here. Module building is what they call it. Or element building. Over half the hotel will arrive here ready-made as large boxes that we then put in place.'

'On the foundations?'

Carl rolled his head. 'In a way.' He said it the way people say things when they either want to spare you the details because they're too complicated to explain, or want to hide the fact that they don't really know themselves. Carl went over to have a word with some of the guys working while I wandered around in the heather and looked for new birds' nests. I didn't find any. Maybe the noise and the traffic had frightened them, but they were probably brooding not far away.

Carl returned. Wiped the sweat from his brow. 'Want to go for a dive?'

I laughed.

'What?' Carl shouted.

'The gear is so old it would be almost suicide.'

'Swim then?'

'OK.'

But of course we'd just ended up back here in the winter garden again. Somewhere between his fifth or sixth bottle Carl suddenly asked: 'D'you know how Abel died?'

'He was murdered by his brother,' I said.

'I'm talking about the Abel Dad named me after, the secretary of state, Abel Parker Upshur. He was being given a guided tour of the USS **Princeton** on the Potomac River and they wanted to demonstrate the firepower of one of the cannons. It exploded, killing Abel and five others. It was in 1844. So he never saw the completion of his life's greatest achievement, the annexation of Texas in 1845. What d'you make of that?'

I shrugged. 'Sad?'

Carl laughed loudly. 'At least you live up to your own middle name. Did you hear about the woman that sat next to Calvin Coolidge . . . ?'

I only half listened, because of course I knew the anecdote, Dad loved to tell the story. The lady sitting next to Coolidge at a formal dinner had made a bet that she'd get more than a couple of words out of the famously taciturn president. Towards the end of the meal the president turned to her and said: 'You lose.'

'Which of us is most like Dad and which like Mum?' asked Carl.

'Are you kidding?' I said, diligently taking a couple of pulls of my Budweiser. 'You are Mum and I'm Dad.'

'I drink like Dad,' said Carl. 'You like Mum.'

'That's the only thing that doesn't add up,' I said.

'So **you're** the pervert?'

I didn't answer. Didn't know what to say. Even when it was happening we hadn't talked about it, not really, I would just comfort him as though he'd got a normal beating from Dad. And promised revenge without saying anything directly related to the subject. I have often wondered whether things might have been different if I'd talked openly about it, set the words free, turned them into something that could be heard, something real and not just something that happened inside our heads and could therefore be rejected as just imagination. Damned if I know.

'Do you think about it?' I asked.

'Yes,' said Carl. 'And no. It bothers me less than the ones I read about.'

'Read about?'

'Other victims of abuse. But it's probably mostly those who've been badly damaged who write about it and talk about it. I'm guessing there's a lot like me. Who put it behind them. It's a question of context.'

'Context?'

'Sexual assault is harmful mostly because of the social condemnation and shame that surrounds it. We're taught that we **will** be traumatised by it, so everything that goes wrong in our lives, we blame it on that. Take Jewish boys who get circumcised. It's a sexual mutilation. Torture. Much worse than being fiddled with. But there's not much to suggest that many of them suffer mental damage from circumcision. Because it takes place within a context that says this is OK, this is something you just have to put up with, it's a part of the culture. Maybe the worst damage is done not when the abuse takes place, but when we understand that it's beyond what's regarded as acceptable.'

I looked at him. Did he mean it? Was it his way of

rationalising it away? And if so, why not? **Whatever gets you through the night, it's all right.**

'How much does Shannon know?' I asked.

'Everything.' He put the bottle to his lips, turned it upwards instead of putting his head back. Clucking sound. Not like laughter, like crying.

'Well she knows that we covered it up when Olsen went over into Huken, but does she also know I fixed the brakes and the steering on the Cadillac when Mum and Dad died?'

He shook his head. 'I only tell her everything that concerns **me.**'

'Everything?' I asked, looked out, let the low evening sun dazzle me. Saw from the corner of my eye that he was looking enquiringly at me.

'Grete came up to me at the opening do last year, after the first spadeful was dug up there,' I said. 'She said you and Mari have secret meetings up at the Aas cabin.'

Carl said nothing for a few moments. 'Shit,' he said in a low voice.

'Yes,' I said.

In the silence out there I heard two quick cries from a raven. Warning calls. And then came the question: 'Why did Grete tell **you?**'

I had been waiting for it. It was the reason I hadn't told him before. To avoid the question and the need to lie, to keep secret what Grete thought she'd found out about me: that I wanted Shannon. Because if I just said the words, no matter how mad it sounded

479

and though we both knew how crazy Grete was, the possibility would have been planted in his mind. And then it would be too late, Carl would see the truth, as if it stood printed across my forehead in capital letters.

'Haven't a clue,' I said casually. Too casually, probably. 'She still wants you. And if you want to start a fire in paradise and get away with it then you creep in and start at the edge and hope the fire spreads. Something like that.'

I put the bottle to my mouth and knew that my explanation had been a little too poetic, the metaphor a bit too artificial to seem spontaneous. I had to put the ball back in his court. 'But is that true, about you and Mari?'

'Clearly you don't,' he said, placing the empty bottle on the windowsill.

'I don't what?'

'Have a clue. Or else you would have told me before. Warned me, like. Or at least confronted me with it.'

'Of course I didn't believe it,' I said. 'Grete had had a few and that makes her even crazier than usual. The whole thing just slipped my mind.'

'Then what made you remember it now?'

I shrugged. Nodded towards the barn. 'Could use another coat. Maybe you can get an estimate from one of the guys painting the hotel?'

'Yeah,' said Carl.

'We split it, then?'

'I mean yes to your other question.'

I looked at him.

'About Mari and me meeting each other,' he concluded, and belched.

'None of my business,' I said and took another swig of my beer which was beginning to taste flat.

'It was Mari who took the initiative. At the homecoming party she asked if we couldn't meet, just the two of us, and talk things over, clear the air. But she said all eyes were on us right then, so it was best we meet somewhere discreet, so there wouldn't be any tittle-tattle. She suggested we meet at the cabin. We each drove our own cars there, parked in different spots, and I arrived a while after her. Pretty smart, right?'

'Pretty smart,' I said.

'Mari thought of it because Grete told her Rita Willumsen once had a similar arrangement at her cabin with a young lover.'

'Jesus. She keeps herself pretty well informed, that Grete Smitt.' I could feel my voice was dry. I hadn't asked Carl if he remembered telling Grete about Dad that time he'd been drinking at Årtun.

'Something wrong, Roy?'

'No. Why d'you ask?'

'You've gone all pale.'

I shrugged. 'I can't tell you. I swore on your soul.'

'Did you say **mine**?'

'Yes.'

'Ah, that was lost a long time ago. Come on.'

I shrugged. I couldn't remember if I'd sworn to keep

silent for all eternity back then – after all I was only a teenager; or just to serve out a period of quarantine. 'That young lover of Rita Willumsen's,' I said. 'That was me.'

'You?' Carl stared at me, eyes wide open in astonishment. 'You're kidding.' He slapped his thigh and laughed loudly. Clinked his bottle against mine. 'Tell,' he ordered.

I told. In rough outline at least. Sometimes he laughed, and sometimes he was serious.

'And you've been keeping this secret from me ever since you were a teenager?' he said when I finished, his head shaking from side to side.

'Well, we've had plenty of practice at doing that in this family,' I said. 'Now your turn to tell me about Mari.'

Carl told me. At that very first reunion they'd ended up in the hay, as people say. 'I mean, she's had plenty of practice when it comes to seducing me,' he said with an almost melancholic smile. 'She knows what I like.'

'So you think you had no chance,' I said, and could hear it sounded more accusing than I had intended.

'I take my share of the blame, but it's obvious that's what her aim was.'

'To seduce you?'

'To prove both to herself and to me that she would always be my first choice. To show me I was prepared to risk everything. That Shannon and anyone like her were and always would be substitutes for Mari Aas.'

'**Betray** everything,' I said, taking out my snuffbox. 'Eh?'

'You said **risk** everything.' This time I really couldn't bring myself to even try to hide the accusatory tone.

'Whatever,' said Carl. 'We carried on seeing each other.'

I nodded. 'All those evenings you said you had meetings and Shannon and I waited at home.'

'Yeah,' he said. 'I'm no better than I should be.'

'And that time you said you were at Willumsen's, but you'd seen Erik Nerell and his wife out for an evening walk?'

'Yeah, I nearly gave myself away there. Of course, I was on my way back from the cabin. Maybe I **wanted** to give myself away. It's no fucking picnic walking around with a guilty conscience all the time.'

'But you managed to survive,' I said.

He acknowledged the barb, just lowered his head. 'After we'd met a few times, Mari probably felt that she'd made her point and dumped me. Again. But it was OK by me too. It was just . . . nostalgia. We haven't seen each other again since.'

'Well, you've seen each other in town.'

'Yes, it happens, of course. But she just smiles as if she's won at something.' Carl smirked contemptuously. 'Shows Shannon the kids in the pram which is of course being wheeled by her newspaper guy, he trips along behind her like a fucking coolie. I'm sure he suspects something. Behind that straight, snobbish mug of his I see a guy that wants to kill me.'

'Oh?'

'Yes. If you ask me he's definitely asked Mari, and she's – quite deliberately – given him an answer that leaves room for doubt.'

'Why would she do that?'

'Keep him on his toes. That's what they're like.'

'Who's they?'

'Oh, you know. The Mari Aases and Rita Willumsens. They suffer from queen syndrome. That's to say it's us, the male drones, who **suffer.** Of course even queens want their physical needs satisfied, but the most important thing is for them to be loved and worshipped by their subjects. So they manipulate us like puppets in their fucking schemes. You get so fucking tired of it.'

'Aren't you exaggerating a bit?'

'No!' Carl put his beer bottle down hard on the windowsill and two of the empties toppled over and fell to the floor. 'Real love doesn't exist between a man and a woman who aren't related, Roy. There has to be blood. The same blood. The only place you find real, selfless love is in the family. Between brothers and sisters and between parents and their children. Outside of that . . .' He gestured expansively, knocked over another bottle and I realised he was drunk. 'Forget it. It's jungle law. Every man is his own best friend.'

484

By now he was snuffling. 'You and me, Roy, we're all we've got. Nobody else.'

I wondered where that left Shannon, but I didn't ask.

Two days later I drove back south.

As I passed the county sign I glanced in the rear-view mirror. It looked as though it said OZ.

43

IN AUGUST I GOT A text message.

My heart almost stopped beating when I saw it was from Shannon.

I read it over and over again during the next few days before finally figuring out what it meant.

That she wanted to meet me.

Hi Roy, it's been a while. I'll be in Notodden, meeting a possible client, on 3 September. Can you recommend a hotel? Hugs, Shannon.

When I first read the message I thought it had to mean that she knew I used to go there and meet Unni at a hotel. But I had never told her about that, and I couldn't remember telling Carl about it either. Why hadn't I mentioned it to Carl? I don't know. It wasn't because I was ashamed of having an affair with a married woman. And hardly that the taciturn Cain in me had kept quiet about it. I don't know. Maybe it was just something I came to understand at a certain point. That Carl didn't tell me everything either.

Shannon probably just figured I would have some idea about good places to stay in the vicinity of Os, I thought. And studied that text message – even though of course I knew it off by heart – one more time. Told myself not to read things into a text that consisted of three everyfuckingday sentences.

But all the same.

Why get in touch with me after a year's silence and ask about **hotels** in Notodden? In reality there were two, at the most three hotels to choose between, and Tripadvisor had of course more relevant and up-to-date information than I could provide. I knew that, having checked online the day after receiving the text message. And why tell me the date when she was going to be there? And that she was meeting a potential client, which was another way of telling me she would be travelling alone. And as people say, last but not least: why spend the night there when it was just a two-hour drive home?

OK, so maybe she didn't fancy driving those roads in the pitch-dark. Maybe her and the client were having dinner together, and she wanted to be able to have a glass of wine. Or maybe it was simply that she looked forward to spending the night at a hotel as a change from staying on the farm. Maybe she even wanted a short break from Carl. Maybe that's what she was trying to tell me with that slightly laboured text message. No, no! It was just an ordinary text message, a slightly feeble opportunity to re-establish normal communications with her brother-in-law after he'd blown the whole thing by telling her he was in love with her.

I replied the same evening I received the message.

Hi – yes, long time. Brattrein's pretty good. Got great views. Hugs, Roy.

Every single bloody syllable had, of course, been carefully considered. I had to force myself not to send anything with a question mark, along the lines of **how are you?** Or anything else that seemed to beg for a continuation. An echo of her own message, nothing more, nothing less, that's what it had to be. I got a reply an hour later.

Thanks for the help. Big hug.

There was nothing you could read into that, and anyway, all she could do was relate to my own short and inhibited reply. So that sent me back to her initial message: was that an invitation to go to Notodden?

Over the next two days I tormented myself. Even counted the words and saw that she had sent 24, I had answered with 12, and then she had sent 6. Was this halving accidental, or should I now send 3 words and see if she replied with one and a half? Ha ha.

I was going crazy.

I wrote:

Enjoy the journey.

The reply came as I lay there trying to sleep.

Thanks. X

One and a half words. I knew of course that x was the symbol for a kiss, but what kind of kiss? I googled it the next morning. No one knew, but some thought the x stemmed from the days when letters were sealed with an x and a kiss on top of it. Others suggested that the x – as an ancient symbol of Christ – made it a religious kiss, like a kiss of blessing. But the explanation I liked best was that the x shows two pairs of lips meeting.

Two pairs of lips that meet.

Was that what she meant?

No, for chrissakes, she couldn't possibly have meant that.

I looked at the calendar and began counting the days to 3 September until I realised what I was doing.

Lotte popped her head in the door to say that the display on pump number 4 had gone out and asked what my calendar was doing on the floor.

At a bar in Kristiansand one evening, just as I was getting up to leave, a woman approached me.

'Going home already?'

'Maybe,' I said, and looked at her. It would be an overstatement to say she was pretty. Maybe one day she had been. No, not beautiful, but all the same one of the first girls in class who got the boys' attention. Because she was sassy, a bit cheeky, a lot of front. **Promising,** as people used to say. And maybe she'd kept her promise a little too quickly, given them what they wanted before they'd earned it. Thought she'd get something in return. A lot had happened since then, and most of it she wished hadn't, the things she'd done to herself, as well as the things that had been done to her.

Now she was a bit tipsy and looking hopefully for someone she knew deep down would disappoint her again. But if you abandon hope, what's left?

So I bought her a beer, told her my name, my marital status, where I worked and lived. Then I asked the questions and let her do the talking. Let her pour bile over all the men she'd met who'd ruined her life. Her name was Vigdis, she worked at a garden centre, at the moment she was off sick. Two children. Each with its respective father that week. Only a month ago she'd kicked a third man out of the house. I wondered whether it was during that eviction she'd got that bruise on the forehead. She said he drove around outside her house at night to check whether she was bringing anyone home with her so it was best if we went to my place.

I considered it. But her skin wasn't pale enough, and her body too big. Even if I closed my eyes, that metallic voice of hers – which I already knew wouldn't be silent for long – would destroy the illusion.

'Thanks, but I have to go to work tomorrow,' I said. 'Some other time.'

Her mouth twisted into an ugly grimace. 'You're no great catch yourself, if that's what you were thinking.'

'I wasn't thinking that,' I said, emptied my glass and left.

Out in the street I heard heels clacking against the asphalt behind me and knew that it was her. Vigdis linked arms with me and blew smoke from a freshly lit cigarette into my face.

'At least take me home in a taxi,' she said. 'I live in the same direction as you.'

I hailed a taxi and let her out after the first bridge, outside a house in Lund.

I had seen someone in one of the cars parked by the pavement, and as the taxi pulled away I turned and saw a man climb out of the car and walk quickly towards Vigdis.

'Stop,' I said to the driver.

The taxi slowed, and I saw Vigdis fall to the pavement.

'Back up,' I said.

If the driver had seen the same as me he probably wouldn't have done it. I jumped out of the taxi and felt in my pockets for something to wrap round my right hand as I walked towards the man who was standing over Vigdis and yelling something that was lost among the echoes from the blind, silent walls of the houses along the street. I guessed it must be curses, and it wasn't until I got up close I could hear the words:

'I love you! I love you! I love you!'

I walked up to him and lashed out as he turned his tearful face towards mine. I felt the skin of my knuckles tear. Fuck. Hit him again, in the nose, which is

491

softer, and didn't know if the blood that spurted out was his or mine. Hit him a third time. The idiot stood there swaying in front of me without trying to defend himself or avoid the punches, forcing himself to stay on his feet so that he could go on being hit, as though it was something he welcomed.

I hit him quickly and methodically, the same way I hit the punchbag. Not hard enough to do more damage to my knuckles, but enough to make him bleed and the fluid run under the skin of his face until gradually it began swelling up like a fucking lilo.

'I love you,' he said between two flurries of punches, not to me, but in a whisper, as though to himself.

His knees buckled, and then buckled again, and I had to aim gradually lower, he was like the Black Knight in that **Monty Python** sketch, the one who gets his legs cut off but refuses to give up, until he becomes a torso hopping round on the ground.

I drew my shoulder back to give him one last punch, but my arm got caught up in something. It was Vigdis. She was on my back.

'Don't!' that metallic voice of hers screeched in my ear. 'Don't! Don't hurt him, you bastard!'

I tried to shake her off, but she wouldn't let go. And on the tearful, swollen face of the man in front of me I saw an insane smile start to spread.

'He's mine!' she screamed. 'He's mine, you bastard!'

I looked at the man. He looked at me. I nodded. Turned and saw that the taxi had left and started to walk towards Søm. Vigdis clung on for ten or fifteen metres before she let go, and I heard the clacking of her shoes as she ran back, heard her words of comfort, and the sobbing of the man.

I carried on walking eastwards. Through sleeping streets, towards the E18. It began to rain. And for once it was proper rain. My shoes were squelching as I set off across the half-kilometre of the Varoddbro Bridge over to Søm. Halfway across it occurred to me that there was actually an alternative. And I was already soaking wet. I peered over the edge at the greeny-black waters down below. Thirty metres? But already I must have started to doubt, even before my head began telling me I would probably survive the drop, and the survival instinct would kick in and I would splash my way to shore, almost certainly with a few broken bones and damaged organs that wouldn't mean a shorter life, just an even more shitty life. And even if I was lucky enough to die in the water down there, was there really anything to be gained in being dead? Because I had just remembered something. The answer I gave when the former sheriff asked why we should go on living when we didn't enjoy it. 'Because being dead may be even worse.' And once I'd recalled that, I remembered what Uncle Bernard had said when he had been diagnosed with cancer: 'When you're up to your neck in shit, best not to hang your head.'

I laughed. Like a madman I stood there alone on the bridge and roared with laughter.

And then walked on towards Søm, my footsteps

493

lighter, and after a while I even began whistling that **Monty Python** song, the one where Eric Idle is hanging on the cross. When the Vigdises of this world manage to go on hoping, hoping for miracles, why shouldn't I?

On 3 September, at two o'clock in the afternoon, I rolled into Notodden.

44

A HIGH, MILKY-BLUE SKY. STILL some lingering summer warmth, the smell of pine trees and new-mown grass, but also a bite in the gusts of wind, a sharpness that was quite absent down in the soft south of the country. The drive from Kristiansand to Notodden had taken three and a half hours. I drove slowly. Changed my mind several times along the way. But in the end concluded that only one thing would be more pathetic than what I was now embarked upon, and that would be to drive halfway to Notodden and then turn back.

I parked in the town centre and began to trawl the streets looking for Shannon. When we were growing up, Notodden had seemed to us big, alien, almost threatening. Now – perhaps because I had spent so much time in Kristiansand – it seemed strangely small and provincial.

I kept an eye out for the Cadillac, though I guessed she would have hired a car from Willumsen. Glanced in at the cafes and restaurants I passed. I headed down towards the water, passed the cinema. Finally I entered a small cafe, ordered a black coffee, sat so that I had a view of the door and looked through the place's newspapers.

Notodden didn't have many cafes and bars and the perfect scenario was obviously if it was Shannon who found me and not the other way round. That she came in, I looked up, our eyes met, and in that gaze I could read that I wouldn't be needing the cover story I'd dreamed up, that I was here to take a look at a service station that was for sale. That I remembered she was going to be in Notodden, but not that it was today. That if she wasn't busy with her client the whole day, maybe we could meet for a drink after dinner? Or even meet for dinner if she didn't have other plans?

The door opened and I glanced up. A gang of kids in eager conversation. A few moments later the door opened again, another gang of kids, and I realised school was out for the day. The third time the door opened I saw her face. It had changed, was not at all the way I recalled it. This face looked open. She didn't see me, and I could study her unobserved from behind my newspaper. She sat and listened to the boy she had come in with. She neither smiled nor laughed, and you could still sense a certain watchfulness, that she was guarding a sensitive vulnerability. But I thought that I could also tell that she and this boy had something, a contact you don't get unless you let someone in close. Then her eyes glided round the room, and when they met mine they tensed for a moment.

I don't know if Natalie knew the reason why her father, Moe the roofer, had sent her to secondary school here in Notodden. Nor how he had explained the injuries he had come by at home in their kitchen. In all probability she didn't know I had anything to do with either situation. But if she did? If she came over here now, sat down and asked why I had done it, what should I answer? That I had intervened because of the shame I felt at not having been able to do the same for my brother? That I had nearly made an invalid of her father because he was a punchbag with my own father's face on it? That in reality it was all about me and my family, not hers?

Her gaze wandered on. Maybe she hadn't recognised me. But of course she had. Obviously. But even if she didn't know that I had threatened to kill her father, she might well want to pretend she didn't recognise the guy who'd sold her morning-after pills, especially now she had the chance to be another girl from that cowed and withdrawn person she had been back home in Os.

I could see she was having difficulty concentrating

on what the boy over there was saying, turning towards the window, turning her face away from me.

I stood up and left. Partly to leave her in peace. Partly because I didn't want anyone from Os as a witness if Shannon should turn up.

By five o'clock I had been to every cafe and bar and restaurant in Notodden, apart from the restaurant at the Brattrein, which I was guessing still didn't open until six.

As I walked across the car park towards the main entrance I felt for a moment the same expectant tickle in the stomach as when I was going to meet Unni. But that was probably just Pavlov's dogs who recognised a situation and began to salivate, because in the next moment it was driven out by anxiety. What the hell was I doing? Suicide from the bridge would have been better. If I jumped in the car now I could probably get there by sundown. But I kept going. Into the hotel reception, which looked exactly the same as when I had left it for the last time . . . years earlier.

She was sitting in the empty restaurant working on a laptop. Dark blue suit and white blouse. Her short red hair was parted at the side and held in place by grips. Stockinged knees and black high-heeled shoes pressed together below the table.

'Hi, Shannon.'

She looked up at me. Smiled without a trace of surprise but as though I'd finally turned up to a meeting we'd agreed upon. Took off the glasses that I'd never seen her wearing before. Her wide-open eye expressed the joy of reunion, a joy that might have been of the sisterly variety. Real enough, but with no undercurrent. The half-shut eye told a very different story. It made me think of a woman who has just turned towards you in bed with the reflected light of morning glinting in her iris, a look still drenched in sleep and lovemaking from the night before. I felt a jolt, something heavy, like sorrow. I had to swallow and sank into the chair opposite her.

'You're here,' she said. 'In Notodden.'

Her tone was enquiring. OK, so we were going to beat about the bush for a while after all.

I nodded. 'I'm looking at a service station I'm interested in.'

'Did you like it?'

'Very much,' I said, not taking my eyes off her. 'That's the problem.'

'Why is that a problem?'

'It's not for sale.'

'Well, you can always find another.'

I shook my head. 'I want this one.'

'And how are you going to manage that?'

'Persuade the owner that since he's losing money on it, that sooner or later he'll lose it anyway.'

'Maybe he's planning to change the way he runs it.'

'I'm sure he is planning to, he's promising to, probably even believes it himself. But after a while everything will go back to the same old same old again. The staff will desert him, the station will go bust, and he'll have thrown away even more years on a hopeless project.'

'So when you take the station from him, you'll be doing him a favour. Is that what you're saying?'

'I'll be doing us all a favour.'

She looked at me. Was that hesitation I read in her face?

'When is your meeting?' I asked.

'It was at twelve,' she said. 'We were finished before three.'

'Did you expect it to last longer?'

'No.'

'So then why book a hotel room?'

She looked at me and shrugged her shoulders. I felt my breathing stop. Could feel an erection coming on.

'Have you eaten?' I asked.

She shook her head.

'They don't open for another hour,' I said. 'Feel like a walk?'

She nodded down at her high-heeled shoes.

'Fine here too,' I said.

'Know who I saw here?' she asked.

'Me,' I said.

'Dennis Quarry. The film star. He was at the service station location-scouting, remember? I think he's staying here. I read somewhere that they're making that film now.'

'I love you,' I whispered, but at that precise moment she closed the lid of her laptop with unnecessary force so she could pretend she hadn't heard.

'Tell me what you've been up to lately,' she said.

'Thinking about you,' I said.

'I wish you hadn't.'

'Me too.'

Silence.

She sighed heavily. 'Maybe this was a mistake,' she said.

Was. Past tense. Had she said **is** a mistake it would have meant the wheels were still in motion but **was** meant that she had already made up her mind.

'Probably,' I said, waving dismissively to a waiter whom I recognised and guessed was on his way to offer something from the kitchen, even though it wasn't open yet.

'Faddah-head,' hissed Shannon, slapping her palm against her forehead. 'Roy?'

'Yes?'

She leaned forward across the table. Laid her small hand in mine and looked me in the eyes. 'Can we agree that this never happened?'

'Of course.'

'Goodbye.' She gave a quick smile, as though she had a pain somewhere, picked up the laptop and left. I closed my eyes. The clacking of those heels on the parquet behind me reminded me of Vigdis's footsteps behind me that night in Kristiansand, only those footsteps were approaching. I opened my eyes again. I hadn't moved my hand, which was still lying on the table. The sensation of the only touch between us since I had entered the room was still there, like prickling beneath the skin after a scalding hot shower.

I went out into reception where the tall, thin man

in the red suit jacket smiled at me. 'Good afternoon, herr Opgard. Nice to see you back again.'

'Hello, Ralf,' I said as I stood in front of the counter.

'I saw you on your way in, herr Opgard, so I took the liberty of reserving the last vacant room we have today for you.' He indicated the screen in front of him with a nod. 'So tiresome if someone else were to snap it up at the last moment.'

'Thanks, Ralf. But I was wondering which room Shannon Opgard was in. Or Shannon Alleyne.'

'333,' said Ralf, making a point of not even having to look at his screen.

'Thank you.'

Shannon had finished packing the bag which was on the bed, and was struggling to close the zip as I pushed open the door to Room 333. She loosed off a few curses that I guessed must be in Baja-English, squeezed the two sides of the bag, tried again. I left the door half open as I walked in and stood behind her. She gave up, her hands went to her face and her shoulders began to shake. I put my arms around her and felt her soundless crying transfer itself from her body and into mine.

We stood like that for a while.

Then I carefully turned her round, dried her tears with two fingers and kissed her.

And, still sobbing, she kissed me, her teeth biting into my lower lip so that I felt the sweet, metallic taste of my own blood mingle with the strong, spicy taste of her spittle and her tongue. I held back, ready to withdraw if she showed any sign of not wanting this. But she didn't, and slowly I let go of what was holding me back: common sense, the thought of what must come – or not come – afterwards. The image of me lying in the lower bunk with my arms around Carl, the only thing he has, the only thing that has not yet betrayed him. But it slips away, drifts away, and all that remains are her hands pulling up my shirt tails, the nails pressing my body against hers, the tongue like an anaconda round mine, her tears running down my cheek. Even in high-heeled shoes she's so small I have to bend my knees to pull up her tight skirt.

'No!' she groans and pulls herself free, and my first reaction is one of relief. That she has saved us. I take a step backwards, unsteady and still shaking a little, and push one of my shirt tails back under my belt.

Our breaths share the same gasping rhythm. I hear footsteps and a voice speaking on a phone out in the corridor. And as the steps and the voice move away we stand staring watchfully at each other. Not like a man and a woman, but like boxers, like two raging bucks ready for a fight. Because of course the fight isn't over, it's hardly even begun.

'Shut that bloody door,' hisses Shannon.

45

'I HIT MEN,' I ANSWERED, handed a piece of moist snuff to Shannon and wedged one under my lower lip.

'That's what you actually **do**?' she asked, raising her head so I could put my arm back on the pillow.

'Not all the time, but I've done a lot of fighting, yes.'

'You think it's in your genes?'

I studied the ceiling of Room 333. It was different from the one Unni and I used to spend our hours together in, but it looked exactly the same and the smell was the same, some mildly perfumed cleaning agent possibly. 'My father mostly hit a punchbag,' I said. 'But yes, I probably get the fighting from him.'

'We repeat the mistakes of our own parents,' she said.

'And our own too,' I said.

She pulled a face, took the wedge of snuff, put it on the bedside table.

'You have to get used to it,' I said, meaning the snuff.

She snuggled into me. The little body was even softer than I had imagined, the skin even smoother. The breasts were slight rises on snow-covered **viddas** of skin on which the nipples stood up like two burning beacons. She smelled of something, a sweet, strong spice, and her skin was shaded, darker under the armpits and around her sex. And she was glowing like an oven.

'Do you sometimes get the feeling you're going round in circles?' she asked.

I nodded.

'And when you find yourself walking in your own footsteps, isn't that a sign that you've lost your way?'

'Maybe,' I said. But right at that moment it didn't feel like that. Sure, the sex had been more like mating than loving, with more fight than tenderness, more anger and fear than joy and pleasure. At one point she pulled away, struck me in the face with the flat of her hand and told me to stop. So I stopped. Until she hit me once more and asked why the hell I had stopped. And when I started to laugh, she buried her face in the pillow and wept, and I stroked her hair, the tensed muscles of her back, kissed her neck. She stopped crying, began breathing heavily. Then I slipped my hand between the cheeks of her arse and bit her. And she cried out something in Baja-English, pushed me down the bed, lay on her stomach with her arse sticking up in the air. And I was so horny I didn't care at all that her screams when I took her were the same as those I heard from the bedroom when she was with Carl. God knows, maybe that's what I was thinking of when I came, distracting me so much that I withdrew a little too late, but in time to see the remainder of my load land on the skin of her back, like a mother-of-pearl chain, greyish white and glistening in the light from the lamp that had been turned on in the car park outside. I had fetched a towel and dried it off, tried also to dry off two dark flecks before I realised they were shading that wouldn't wipe off. And thought that this too, the things we had just done, was the same, dark patches that couldn't be wiped away.

But there would be more. And it would be different, I knew that. Lovemaking that wasn't fighting, not just a meeting between two bodies but two souls. I know it sounds corny, but I can't think of any other way to express it. Two fucking souls is what we were and I was home now. She was my footprint and I had found it. All I wanted was to be here and go round in circles, in a delirium, quite lost, just as long as it was with her.

'Will we regret this?' she asked.

'I don't know,' I said, but knew that I wouldn't. I simply didn't want to frighten her, something that was bound to happen if she realised that I loved her so much I didn't care a damn about anything else.

'We just have tonight,' she said.

We pulled the blackout curtains to prolong it and make the most of the hours we had.

I awoke to a shriek from Shannon.

'I've overslept!'

She slipped out of the bed before I could get hold of her, and the arm I threw out after her hit instead her mobile phone that was on the bedside table. It hit the floor some distance away from the bed. I jerked the curtains open to get what I knew could well be the last sight I would have of Shannon's naked body for a long time. Daylight flooded the room and I caught a glimpse of her back as she disappeared into the bathroom.

I stared down at the phone lying in the shadow of the bed. The screen had turned itself on. The glass was cracked. And from behind the prison bars of that shattered screen a smiling Carl looked up at me. I swallowed.

A single glimpse of her back.

But it was enough.

I lay back in the bed. The last time I had seen a woman so naked, so stripped bare by daylight, was when Rita Willumsen stood there in the mountain lake, humiliated in her swimming costume, her skin bluish in the icy cold. If I'd been in any doubt, it was now that I saw the writing on the wall, as people say.

I understood what Shannon had meant when she asked if hitting was in my genes.

46

CARL WAS MY BROTHER. THAT was what the problem was.

Or problems.

More specifically, **one** of the problems was that I loved him. The other that he had inherited the same genes as me. I don't know why I had once been so naive as to believe that Carl didn't have the same capacity for violence in him as me and Dad. Maybe because it was an accepted fact that Carl was like Mum. Mum and Carl who wouldn't hurt a fly. Only people.

I got up from the bed and crossed to the window, saw Shannon running over the car park towards the Cadillac.

Probably she regretted it. Probably she had no

appointment to keep, she had just woken up and knew that this was wrong, that she had to go.

She had showered, dressed in the bathroom, probably put on her make-up, and when she'd emerged given me a sisterly kiss on the forehead. She muttered something about a meeting in Os about the hotel, grabbed her bag and ran from the room. The brake lights on the Cadillac went on as she almost drove onto the road straight into a bin lorry.

The air in here was still dense from the sex, the perfume and the sleep of the night. I opened the window which I had closed at some point because she was shrieking so loudly I was afraid it might bring someone to the door, and because I knew we weren't finished for the night. And I had been right. Each time one of us woke even the most innocent touch had started a new session, like a hunger that could not be satisfied.

What I had seen once the curtains were opened was that what I had thought were dark patches on the skin were bruises. These were not like the red love-marks and the streaks which had also appeared on her white skin during the night, and which hopefully would disappear in a day or two. These were the marks left by heavy blows, the way they look for days and weeks afterwards. If Carl had hit her in the face too then he had held back just enough for her to be able to cover it up with a little make-up.

Hit her, the way I'd seen Mum hit Dad in the corridor of the Grand Hotel that time. That was the memory that flickered through my brain when Carl had tried to convince me it was an accident when Sigmund Olsen went over the edge and down into Huken. Mum. And Carl. You live with a person and think you know all there is to know about them, but what do you really know? Did it occur to Carl that I might be capable of having sex with his wife behind his back? Hardly. A long time ago I had realised that we are all strangers to each other. And of course it wasn't just those bruises on Shannon that made me realise Carl had violence in him. That my little brother was a murderer. It was the simple facts. Bruises and plumb lines.

47

FOR DAYS AFTER RETURNING TO Sørlandet I waited
for Shannon to ring, to send a message, an email,
anything. It was obvious that she would have to be
the one to take the initiative, she was the one who
had most to lose. Or so I thought.

But I heard nothing.

And there was no longer any room for doubt. She
regretted it, of course. It had been a fairy tale, a fantasy I had planted in her when I told her I loved her
and then went away, a fantasy that she, in peace and
quiet, and in the absence of any other stimulation,
had turned into something fantastic while she went
about her daily round in the village and bored herself.
So fantastic that the real me had been unable to live

up to it. But now she'd got it out of her system and could return to her normal life.

The question now was when would I be able to get it out of my system? I told myself that our night together had been the aim, something to cross off on my to-do list, and that now I had to move on. But all the same, the first thing I did every morning was to check the phone for a message from Shannon.

Nothing.

So I started sleeping with other women.

I don't know why it was, but it was as though they had suddenly discovered me, as though there was a secret society of women in which the news that I'd bedded my wife's brother began to circulate, and that had to mean I was hot stuff. A bad reputation is a good reputation, as people say. Or else it was just writ large on my forehead that I didn't care a damn. Maybe that was it. Maybe I had become the silent, sad-eyed man in the bar whom they'd heard could get anyone except the one he wanted, and for that reason didn't give a fuck. The man they all wanted to prove wrong, that there is hope, there is salvation, there is another, and it's them.

And yes, I played up to it. I played the part I had been allotted, told them the story, just left out the names and that it involved my brother, went home with them if they lived alone or to Søm if not. Woke up beside a stranger and turned to check my phone for messages.

But things improved, they did. On some days,

hours would go by without my thinking of her. I knew that malaria is a parasitic illness that never completely leaves your blood, but it can be neutralised. If I stayed away and didn't see her then I reckoned that the really hard part should be over within two years, three at the outside.

In December Pia Syse phoned and informed me that the station was now ranked sixth best in all Sørlandet. Naturally, I knew that it was the sales manager Gus Myre's job to make calls with that type of news, not the personnel manager's. That she probably had something else on her mind.

'We want you to continue to run the station after the contract runs out next year,' she said. 'The conditions will of course reflect the fact that we are very pleased. And that we believe you can move the station even further up the list.'

It suited my plans well. I looked out the window of my office. Flat landscape, big industrial buildings, motorway with circular entrance and exit roads that made me think of the racing-car track on the floor of the back room at Willumsen's Used Car and Breaker's Yard, where kids could play if their father was out front buying a car. I'm guessing quite a few used-car sales came about because of kids kicking up about wanting to go down there.

'Let me think about it,' I said and hung up.

I sat there looking at the mist over the woods by the zoo. Jesus, the leaves on the trees were still green.

I hadn't seen a snowflake since coming here fourteen months earlier. They say you never really get a winter down here in the south, just more of that pissrain that isn't really rain but just something wet in the air that can't decide whether to go up or down or just stay where it is. Same as the mercury in the thermometer that reads six degrees for day after day. I stared into that bank of fog that lay like a thick duvet across the landscape and rendered it even flatter and more shapeless. A winter in Sørlandet was a shower of rain frozen in time. It just was **there.** So when the phone rang again and I heard Carl's voice, for about two seconds I longed – yes, I longed! – for those ice-cold, freezing blasts, and that driving snow that whips against your face like grains of sand.

'How's things?' he asked.

'Can't complain,' I said. Sometimes Carl rang just because he wondered how I was doing. But today I could hear that was not the reason.

'Can't complain?'

'Sorry, it's just something they say down here in Sørlandet.' I hated the way they said 'can't complain'. It was like the winters, neither one thing nor the other. When people down here meet someone they know on the street they say 'now then', which I think is a cross between a question and a greeting, sort of like 'how are you', but sounding more like they've caught you red-handed at something.

'And you?'

'Fine,' said Carl.

I heard that it wasn't fine. Waited for the 'but'.

'Apart from going slightly over budget,' he said.

'How slightly?'

'Not much. What it actually is, there's a little disharmony in the cash flow. The invoices from the builders are due for payment earlier than expected. We don't need more cash putting into the project, we just need it a little earlier. I told the bank that we're a bit ahead of schedule now.'

'And are you?'

'We, Roy. We. You're a co-owner, or have you forgotten? And no, we aren't ahead. It's one hell of a conjuring trick when so many airheads have to be coordinated. The building business is a strange ragbag of subcontractors who are all school dropouts and ended up in jobs no one else wants. But because there's such a demand for the few of them there actually are, they can come and go as they please.'

'The last shall be first.'

'Do they say that down south as well?'

'All the time. They like everything that's slow. Compared to down here things in Os are all fast-forward.'

Carl laughed his warm laugh, and I felt happy and warm myself. Warmed by the sound of the murderer's laugh.

'The bank manager pointed out that one of the conditions of the loan is that certain milestones have to be reached before we can have access to further credit. He said they'd been up to have a look around the site and that what I said about progress up there wasn't accurate. So there was what you might call a crisis of confidence. Sure, I managed to patch things up, but now the bank is saying I have to inform the participants before they'll make further payments. It says in the participants' agreement that, since they have unlimited responsibility, they need an official resolution from the committee to the effect that the project needs more capital.'

'Then that's what you'll have to do.'

'Yeah yeah, so I guess I will. It's just that **that** may set up bad vibes, and in principle the committee can summon a general meeting and put a stop to the whole thing. Especially now that Dan has started digging and poking around.'

'Dan Krane?'

'He's been trying to dig up something to take me down all autumn. Calling round the contractors and asking about progress and budgets. He's looking for something that he can turn into a full-blown crisis, but he can't print a thing as long as he's got nothing definite to go on.'

'And not as long as a quarter of your readers and your father-in-law are involved in the hotel.'

'Exactly,' said Carl. 'You don't shit in your own nest.'

'Well, not unless you're a gentoo penguin,' I said. 'Then you shit in your own nest so as to make it your nest.'

'Really?' said Carl doubtfully.

'The shit attracts the sunlight, which melts the ice so you get a depression and – hey presto – there's your nest. It's the same method journalists use to attract a readership. The media lives off the attracting powers of shit.'

'An interesting image,' said Carl.

'Indeed,' I said.

'But for Krane this is personal, you do realise that?'

'And how do you propose to put a stop to it?'

'I've talked to the contractors and got them to promise to keep their mouths shut. Fortunately they know what's best for them. But yesterday I heard from a pal in Canada that Krane has started digging around into that business in Toronto.'

'What will he find there?'

'Not a lot. It's my word against theirs, and the whole thing is too complex for a Mickey Mouse journo like Krane to be able to understand.'

'Unless he's got the bit between his teeth,' I said.

'Shit, Roy, I'm ringing you to cheer me up here.'

'It'll all work out. And if it doesn't you can get Willumsen to set one of his enforcers on Krane.'

We laughed. It sounded as if he was relaxing a bit.

'How are things at home?' The query was so general it could hardly make my vocal cords quaver suspiciously.

'Well, you know, the place is still standing. And Shannon seems to have calmed down. Not when it comes to all her objections to the hotel, but at least she's stopped going on about us having kids. Probably realises the timing's off when we're in the middle of all this.'

I made a few appropriate noises that told him

this was information of interest, but nothing more than that.

'But what I'm really calling you about is that the Cadillac needs a bit of work doing on it.'

'Define **a bit of work.**'

'You're the expert, I haven't a clue, you know that. Shannon was driving it and she heard some funny noises. She grew up in a Buick from Cuba and says she has a feel for veteran American cars. She suggested you take a look down at the workshop when you're home for Christmas.'

I didn't answer.

'Because you **are** coming home for Christmas?' he said.

'A lot of people at the station want time off—'

'No! A lot of people at the station want **overtime.** And they live there, and you're coming home for Christmas! And you promised, remember? You've got family. Not a big family, but the family you have got are looking forward so damn much to seeing you again.'

'Carl, I . . .'

'**Pinnekjøtt,**' said Carl. 'She's taught herself to make **pinnekjøtt.** And mashed swede. I'm not kidding. She loves Norwegian Christmas food.'

I closed my eyes, but there she was, so I opened them again. Damn. Not damn. **Damn.** And why hadn't I worked out a proper excuse? After all, I knew the question about Christmas would come up.

'I'll see what I can work out, Carl.'

Right. That gave me time to think of something. Something he'd accept. Hopefully.

'You'll work it out,' Carl exulted. 'We'll arrange a proper family Christmas here, you won't have to worry about a thing! Just cruise on into the yard, smell that smell of **pinnekjøtt,** and be served an aquavit on the steps by your little brother. It won't be the same without you, you **must.** You hear me? You must!'

48

THE DAY BEFORE CHRISTMAS EVE. The Volvo was purring along nicely and the piled-up snow lay like massive lines of cocaine along the sides of the highway. 'Driving Home for Christmas' came on the radio, which was appropriate enough as far as it goes, but I slipped J. J. Cale's 'Cocaine' into the CD player anyway.

Speedometer needle under the speed limit. Pulse normal.

I sang along. Not that I sniff that stuff. Apart from the one time Carl sent it in one of his rare letters from Canada. I was already on a high anyway when I took it, which was maybe why I didn't really notice any difference. Or maybe it was because I was alone.

Alone and on a high, like now. There was the county sign by the roadside. High, and pulse normal. That must be what people mean when they say happy.

I hadn't managed to come up with an excuse not to come home for Christmas. And I could hardly not **ever** see my family again, now could I? So I ought to be able to manage three days of Christmas celebrations. Three days in the same house as Shannon. And after that straight back to solitary.

I parked in front of the house next to a brown Subaru Outback. There must be a name for that particular shade of brown, but I'm not much good at colours. The snow lay several metres deep, the sun was on its way down, and behind the rise in the west the silhouette of a crane was visible.

As I rounded the house Carl was already standing in the doorway. His face looked sort-of wide, like that time he had mumps.

'New motor?' I called as soon as I saw him.

'Old,' he said. 'We need a four-wheel drive for the winter, but Shannon wouldn't let me buy a new one. It's a 2007 model, got it for fifty big ones down at Willumsen's. One of the chippies who's got the same type says it was a steal.'

'Blimey, you mean you bargained with him?' I said.

'Opgards don't bargain.' He grinned. 'But ladies from Barbados do.'

Carl gave me a long and warm embrace out there on the steps. His body felt bigger than before. And he smelled of alcohol. Already started celebrating Christmas, he said. Needed to wind down after a tough week. It would be good to think about something else for a few days. During the holly days, as Carl used to think it was when he was a kid.

We entered the kitchen while Carl talked. About the hotel, where they had finally managed to get things moving. Carl had pressed the contractors to get the walls up and a roof so that they could get started on the indoor work and not have to wait for the spring.

There was no one else in the kitchen.

'Tradesmen give you a better price if they can work indoors during the winter months,' said Carl. At least I think that's what he said, I was listening out for other sounds. But all I heard was Carl's voice and the pounding of my own heart. Not exactly normal pulse now.

'Shannon's up at the building site,' he said, and now I listened attentively. 'She's so bloody concerned that it's got to be exactly like on the drawings.'

'That's good then.'

'It is and it isn't. Architects don't think of the cost, they only want to make sure they're reflected in the glory of their masterpiece.' Carl gave a sort of tolerant laugh, but I could hear the anger bubbling below it. 'Hungry?'

I shook my head. 'Maybe I'll take the Cadillac down to the workshop, get that out of the way.'

'Can't. Shannon's got it.'

'Up at the hotel site?'

'Yup. The road isn't that good yet, but it does go all the way up to the building site now.' He said it with a strange mixture of pride and pain. As though that road had cost him plenty. And if that was the case I wasn't surprised, it was steep and there was a lot of mountain to be blasted.

'With road conditions like this, why doesn't she take the Subaru?'

Carl shrugged. 'She doesn't like manual gears. Prefers the big Americans, that's what she grew up with.'

I carried my bag up to the boys' room, went back down.

'A beer?' said Carl, standing there with one in his hand.

'Nope. I'm going to drive down and say hello at the station and pick up a decent shirt at the workshop.'

'Then I'll call Shannon and she can take the Cadillac straight down to the workshop and get a lift back up with you. Sound OK?'

'Yeah, sure,' I said. Carl looked at me. At least I think he looked at me, I was busy examining a loose seam on one of my gloves.

Julie was on with Egil. She glowed and squealed with delight when she saw me. Customers were queuing up at the till but she ran round the counter and threw herself around my neck as though it was a family re-union. And that's exactly what it was. It wasn't there any more, that steamy undercurrent of something else, of longing and desire. And for a brief moment it was almost a disappointment, a recognition of the fact that I had lost her, or at least stopped being that teenage crush of hers. And though I never wanted to have it or respond to it, I knew that in lonesome times I would think about what might have been, what it was I had said no to.

'Much happening?' I asked when she finally released me and I had time to glance around. Looked like Markus had copied the Christmas decorations and choice of stock we'd done so well with in previous years. Smart kid.

'Yes,' Julie cried excitedly. 'Me and Alex are engaged.'

She held her hand up to me. And damned if there wasn't a ring on her finger.

'You lucky monkey.' I smiled, heading behind the counter to turn over a hamburger that was about to be incinerated. 'How are you, Egil?'

'Fine,' he said as he worked the till for a Christmas sheaf of oats for the birds and a battery shaver. 'Merry Christmas, Roy!'

'Same to you,' I said, and for a moment I observed the world from my old vantage point. From behind the counter of what should have been my own station.

Then I stepped out again into the cold and the winter darkness, said hello to people hurrying by puffing grey clouds before them. Saw a guy in a skinny-fit suit standing smoking by one of the petrol pumps and went over to him.

'You can't smoke here,' I said.

'Yes I can,' he said in a low, rasping voice that made

me think he might have damaged vocal cords. Three short words weren't enough for me to identify the accent, but it sounded guttural, like a Sørlandet accent.

'No,' I said.

Could be he smiled, because his eyes turned to narrow slits in his pitted face. 'Watch me,' he said in English.

And I did. I watched him. He wasn't tall, shorter than me, around fifty, but with pimples in his red, swollen-looking face. At a distance he'd looked chubby in his accountant's suit, but I saw now that it was other things that made it look a little too tight. Shoulders. Chest. Back. Biceps. A muscle mass you probably needed roids to maintain at his age. He raised his cigarette and took a long drag. The tip glowed. And suddenly my middle finger was itching.

'You're in the pump area of a fucking service station,' I said, pointing at the large SMOKING PROHIBITED sign.

I didn't see him move, but suddenly he was right up close to me, so close I wouldn't be able to put any power into a punch.

'And what do you propose to do about it?' he said, his voice even lower.

Not Sørlandet. Denmark. His speed worried me more than his muscles. That, and the aggression, the will, no, the **lust** to do harm that shone from his small eyes. It was like staring into the mouth of a fucking pit bull. It was like the time I tried cocaine. I did it once, and that sure didn't leave me wanting more either. I was scared. Yes, I was. And it struck me that this was how they must have felt, those boys and men at Årtun, in the second before they got hammered. They had known, as I knew now, that the man in front of them was stronger, faster and had a willingness to cross certain lines that I knew I didn't possess. It was staring into that willingness, and that madness, that made me back off.

'I don't propose to do anything at all,' I said, my voice as quiet as his. 'You have a merry Christmas in hell.'

He grinned and stepped back himself. Never took his eyes off me. I'm guessing he saw something of the same in me as I had seen in him, and showed his respect by not turning his back on me before he had to, in order to slip into the low, white, torpedo-shaped sports car. A Jaguar E-Type, a late-seventies model. Danish plates. Wide summer tyres.

'Roy!' The voice came from behind me. 'Roy!'

I turned. It was Stanley. He was on his way out of the door, loaded down with bags from which I could see Christmas wrapping paper sticking out. He staggered over to me. 'Good to see you back!' He offered me his cheek since his hands weren't free and I gave him a quick hug.

'Ha! Men buying Christmas presents on 23 December at a service station,' I said.

'Typical, isn't it?' Stanley laughed. 'I came here because there are queues in all the other shops. Dan Krane says in today's paper that there's a record turnover in Os, never before have so many spent so much on Christmas presents.' He wrinkled his brow. 'You look pale, nothing wrong I hope?'

'No no,' I said, and heard the low roar and then growling as it rolled away down the highway. 'Seen that car before?'

'Yes, I saw it driving off when I called in at Dan's office earlier today. Smart-looking beast. Seems like a lot of people have been getting themselves these smart-looking beasts recently. But not you. And not Dan. He was looking pale today too, as it happens. I hope it's not flu doing the rounds, because I'm counting on a quiet Christmas, you hear?'

The low white car slid away into the December darkness. Southwards. On its way home to the Amazon.

'How's that finger?'

I held up my right hand with the stiff middle finger. 'It's still fit for purpose.'

Stanley laughed obligingly at the stupid joke. 'Good. And how's Carl?'

'Everything as it should be, I think. I only came home today.'

Stanley seemed to be on the point of saying something else but changed his mind. 'We'll talk later, Roy. By the way, I'm having my annual open-house breakfast on Boxing Day. Like to come?'

'Thanks, but I'll be heading back early on Boxing Day, have to get back to work.'

'New Year's Eve then? I'm having a party. Mostly single people you know.'

I smiled. **'Lonely hearts club?'**

'In a way.' He smiled back at me. 'See you there?'

I shook my head. 'I got Christmas Eve off on condition I work New Year's Eve. But thanks.'

We wished each other a merry Christmas and I crossed the car park and unlocked the door to the workshop. That old familiar smell came rolling out as I opened it. Engine oil, car shampoo, scorched metal and oily rags. Not even **pinnekjøtt,** wood fires and sprigs of spruce smell as good as that cocktail there. I turned on the light. Everything was just as I had left it.

I went into the sleeping alcove and got a shirt from the cupboard. Entered the office, which was the smallest room and the quickest to heat up, turned the fan heater on full blast. Looked at my watch. She might arrive at any time. It was no longer that old, spotty-faced guy at the petrol pumps who was making my heart pound like a piston. Thud thud. I checked myself in the mirror, neatened my hair. Dry throat. Like when I was taking the theory exam. I straightened the licence plate from Basutoland, it had a tendency to slip round on its nail when the cold came and the walls compressed, same thing in the summer, only the other way.

I jerked so the office chair screeched when there was a sudden knock on the window.

I stared out into the darkness. Saw first just my own reflection, but then also her face. It was within mine, as though we were one and the same person.

I got to my feet and went to the door.

'Brr,' she said and slipped inside. 'It is cold! Good job I'm getting toughened up with the ice-bathing.'

'Ice-bathing,' I repeated, and my voice was all over the place, just air and thickness. I stood there bolt upright, my arms sticking out from my body, as naturally relaxed as a scarecrow.

'Yes, can you imagine? Rita Willumsen's an ice-bather and she persuaded me and a few other women to join her, three mornings a week, but now I'm the only one left still with her, she bores a hole in the ice and then plop, in we go.' She spoke quickly and breathlessly and I was glad it wasn't just me who was feeling tense.

And then she stopped and looked up at me. She had changed the simple, elegant architect's coat for a quilted jacket, black, as was the hat she wore pulled down over her ears. But it was her. It really was Shannon. A woman I had been with in a very concrete, physical sense, and yet it was as though she, here, now, had stepped out of a dream. A dream that had been recurring since 3 September. And now, here she stood, her eyes bright with joy, and a laughing mouth I had kissed goodnight 110 times since that day.

'I didn't hear the Cadillac,' I said. 'And yes, it's really good to see you.'

She put her head back and laughed. And that laughter loosened something inside me, like a snowdrift grown so heavy that even the slightest thaw caused it to collapse.

'I parked in the light, in front of the station,' said Shannon.

'And I still love you,' I said.

She opened her mouth to say something, then closed it again. I saw her swallow, her eyes glisten, and I didn't know it was tears until one fell onto her cheek and ran and ran.

And then we were in each other's arms.

When we got back to the farm two hours later, Carl sat snoring in Dad's armchair.

I said I was going up to bed and heard Shannon wake Carl as I climbed the stairs.

That night, for the first time in over a year, I didn't dream of Shannon.

Instead I dreamed of falling.

49

CHRISTMAS EVE FOR THREE.

I slept until twelve, had worked like a Trojan over the last few weeks and had a lot of catching up on sleep to do. Went downstairs, said Happy Christmas, heated up the coffee and browsed through an old Christmas magazine, explained some of the unique Norwegian Christmas traditions to Shannon, helped Carl mash the swedes. Carl and Shannon hardly exchanged a word. I cleared snow, even though it was obvious none had fallen over the last couple of days, changed the birds' Christmas sheaf, made porridge and took a bowl to the barn for the barn elf, hit the punchbag a few times. Put my skis on out in the yard. Skied the first few metres along some unusually broad tyre tracks left by summer tyres. Stumped up and over the snow piled alongside the road and then made my own tracks as I set off in the direction of the hotel building site.

For some reason the view of the building site up there on the bare mountain made me think of the moon landing. Emptiness, stillness, and the sense of something man-made that was out of place in the landscape. The large, prefabricated timber modules Carl had talked about were held up on the foundations by steel cables that would, according to the engineers, keep everything in place even in gusts of hurricane force. This being Christmas week and holidays, there were no lights on in the workmen's sheds. Darkness fell.

On the way back I heard a long, sad and familiar sound, but saw no bird.

I don't know how long we sat around the table, probably not more than an hour, but it felt like four. The **pinnekjøtt** was probably excellent, Carl at least was full of praise for it, and Shannon looked down at the food, smiled and said thank you, politely. Carl had charge of the bottle of aquavit, but he kept refilling my glass, so that had to mean I was knocking it back too. Carl described the big Santa Claus parade in Toronto where he and Shannon had met for the first time, when they joined the parade along with mutual friends who had made and decorated the sleigh they sat in. The temperature had been minus twenty-five and Carl had offered to keep her hands warm beneath the sheepskin rugs.

'She was shaking like a leaf, but said no thanks.' Carl laughed.

'I didn't know you,' said Shannon. 'And you were wearing a mask.'

'A Father Christmas mask,' said Carl, looking at me. 'Who are you going to trust if you don't trust Father Christmas?'

'It's OK, you've taken the mask off now,' said Shannon.

After the meal I helped Shannon clear the table. In the kitchen she rinsed the plates with warm water and I ran my hand over the small of her back.

'Don't,' she said in a quiet voice.

'Shannon . . .'

'Don't!' She turned towards me. There were tears in her eyes.

'We can't just carry on as though nothing has happened,' I said.

'We must.'

'Why must we?'

'You don't understand. We must, believe me. So just do as I tell you.'

'Which is?'

'Carry on as though nothing has happened. Jesus Christ, nothing **has** happened. It was . . . it was just . . .'

'No,' I said. 'It wasn't nothing. It was everything. I know it. And you know it too.'

'Please, Roy. I'm asking you.'

'OK,' I said. 'But what is it you're afraid of? That he'll hit you again? Because if he so much as touches you . . .'

She uttered a sound, part-laughter, part-sob. 'It's not me who's in danger, Roy.'

'Me? You're afraid Carl might beat me up?' I smiled. I didn't want to, but I did.

'Not beat you up,' she said. She folded her arms across her chest as though she were cold, and she must have been, because the outside temperature had fallen rapidly, and the walls had started to creak.

'Presents!' cried Carl from the living room. 'Some-one's put presents under a bloody spruce tree in here!'

Shannon went to bed early, complaining of a head-ache. Carl wanted to smoke and insisted that we wrap up warmly and sit out in the winter garden, which is obviously a highly fucking misleading name when the thermometer falls below fifteen minus.

Carl pulled out two cigars from his jacket pocket. Held one of them out to me. I shook my head and held up my snuffbox.

'Come on,' said Carl. 'Got to get in training for when you and me light the victory cigars, don't you know.'

'An optimist again?'

'Always the optimist, that's me.'

'Last time we spoke there were a couple of prob-lems,' I said.

'There were?'

'Cash flow. And Dan Krane poking about.'

'Problems are there to be solved,' said Carl, puffing out a mixture of condensed air and cigar smoke.

'And how did you solve those?'

'The important thing is, they were solved.'

'Maybe the solution to both problems is connected to Willumsen in some way?'

'Willumsen? What makes you think that?'

'Only that the cigar you've got there is the same brand as he hands out to people he's doing deals with.'

Carl removed the cigar and looked at the red band. 'Is it?'

'Yes. So they aren't particularly exclusive.'

'No? You could've have fooled me.'

'So what sort of deal have you done with Willumsen?'

Carl sucked on the cigar. 'What do you think?'

'I think you've borrowed money from him.'

'Cripes. And some people think I'm the brainy one.'

'Have you? Have you sold your soul to Willumsen, Carl?'

'My soul?' Carl emptied the last drop of aquavit into the absurdly small glass. 'Didn't know you believed in souls, Roy.'

'Come on.'

'It's always a buyer's market when it comes to souls, Roy, and looked at in that light he gave me a good price for mine. Plus, his business can't afford to let this village go under. And by now he's so heavily into the hotel that if I fall, then he falls too. If you're going to borrow from someone, Roy, it's important to borrow a **lot.** That way you've got as much hold

535

on them as they have on you.' He raised his glass to me.

I had neither glass nor response. 'What did he get in security?' I asked.

'What security does Willumsen usually ask for?'

I nodded. Just your word. Your soul. But in that case the loan couldn't really be all that big.

'But let's talk about something else besides money, it's so boring. Willumsen has invited Shannon and me to his New Year party.'

'Congratulations,' I said curtly. Willumsen's New Year party was where everybody who was somebody in the village gathered. Old and current council chairmen, landowners selling off their land for cabins, those with money, and those with farms big enough to **pretend** they had. Everyone on the inside of an invisible divide here in the village, the existence of which everyone who was inside it denied, of course.

'Anyway,' said Carl. 'So what was the problem with my lovely little Cadillac?'

I coughed. 'Minor stuff. It's no wonder, it's done a lot of kilometres and been driven hard. Lot of steep hills here in Os.'

'So nothing that can't be repaired?'

I shrugged. 'Sure I can do a temporary repair, but it might be time to think about getting rid of that jalopy. Get yourself a new car.'

Carl looked at me. 'Why is that?'

'Cadillacs are complicated. When small parts start to go it's a warning there's bigger trouble on the way.

And you're no grease monkey when it comes to cars, are you?'

Carl wrinkled his brow. 'Maybe not, but that's the only car I want. Can you repair it or can't you?'

I shrugged. 'You're the boss.'

'Good,' he said and sucked on his cigar. Took it out and looked at it. 'In a way it's a shame they never got to see what you and I achieved in life, Roy.'

'Mum and Dad, you mean?'

'Yes. What d'you think Dad would be doing now if he was alive?'

'Scratching on the inside of his coffin lid,' I said.

Carl looked at me. Then he started to laugh. I shuddered. Looked at my watch and forced a yawn.

That night I dreamed about falling again. I was standing on the edge of Huken and heard Mum and Dad calling to me down there, calling me to join them. I leaned over the edge, the way Carl had described the old sheriff doing before he fell. I couldn't see the front of the car that was closest to the rock face, and at the back, on top of the boot, two huge ravens were sitting. They took off and came flying up towards me and as they got closer I saw they had Carl and Shannon's faces. As they passed me I heard Shannon cry out twice, and I woke with a start. I stared out into the darkness and held my breath, but not a sound came from the bedroom.

On Christmas Day I lay in bed for as long as I could stand it. By the time I got up Carl and Shannon had left for the church service. I'd seen them from the window, middle class, subtly dressed up. They drove off in the Subaru. I hung around the house and the barn, repaired a couple of things. Heard the crisp ringing of the church bells wafting all the way up from the village on the cold air. Then I drove down to the workshop and started on the Cadillac. There was enough there to keep me busy until far into the evening. At nine I called Carl, told him the car was ready and suggested he come down and fetch it.

'I'm in no fit state to drive,' he said. As though I hadn't reckoned on that.

'Send Shannon then,' I said.

I heard his hesitation. 'Then the Subaru will have to stay down at your place,' he said. And two meaningless thoughts flitted across my brain. That by **your place** he meant the workshop, which meant that he thought of the farm as his place.

'I'll drive the Subaru and Shannon the Cadillac,' I said.

'That leaves the Volvo behind.'

'OK,' I said. 'Then I'll drive the Cadillac up and Shannon can drive me back down to pick up the Volvo.'

'Goats and oats,' said Carl.

I held my breath. Had he really just said that? That leaving Shannon and I alone at the same place was like leaving the goat alone with the sack of oats? How long had he known? What was going to happen now?

'You still there?' said Carl.

'Yes,' I said, strangely calm. And I felt it now, I felt

538

the relief. Yes. It was going to be brutal, but at least now I could stop slinking around like a fucking cheat. 'Come again, Carl,' I said. 'What was that about goats and oats?'

'The goat,' Carl said patiently. 'That has to stay in the rowing boat both ways, right? Oh, it's too complicated. Just **leave** the Cadillac outside the workshop and come back here, and Shannon or I can fetch it later. Thanks for the work, bro. Now come up and have a drink with me.'

I could feel myself clutching the phone so hard that my damaged middle finger was throbbing. Carl had been talking about logistics, the solution to that old fairy-tale riddle about the goat in the rowing boat and the sack of oats. I started breathing again.

'OK,' I said.

We ended the call.

I stared at the phone. He had been referring to the logistics, hadn't he? Of course he had. Maybe we Opgard men didn't always say everything that was on our minds, but we didn't talk in riddles.

When I got back to the farm Carl was sitting in the living room and offered me a drink. Shannon had gone to bed. I said I didn't really feel like a drink, I was tired myself and would be going straight to work as soon as I was back in Kristiansand.

In the bunk bed I tossed and turned in a sleepless dreaming state until seven o'clock and then got up.

It was dark in the kitchen and I jumped when I

539

heard the whispered voice from over by the window. 'Don't switch on the light.'

I knew my way blindfold around that kitchen, took a mug from the cupboard and poured coffee from the warm pot. I didn't see the swelling until I crossed to the window and that side of her face was lit by the snow outside.

'What happened?'

She shrugged. 'It was my own fault.'

'Oh yeah? Did you cross him?'

She sighed. 'Go home now, Roy, don't think about it any more.'

'Home is here,' I whispered. I lifted my hand and laid it carefully on the swelling. She didn't stop me. 'And I can't stop thinking. I think about you all the time, Shannon. It isn't possible to stop. We can't stop. The brakes are gone, they're past repair.'

I had raised my voice while speaking, and she glanced automatically up at the stovepipe and the hole in the ceiling.

'And the road we're on now leads straight over the edge,' she whispered. 'You're right, the brakes don't work, so we need to take another road, one that doesn't take us closer to the edge. **You** need to take another road, Roy.' She took my hand and pressed it against her lips. 'Roy, Roy. Get away while there's still time.'

'Beloved,' I said.

'Don't say that,' she said.

'But it's true.'

'I know it is, but it hurts so much to hear it.'

'Why?'

She made a face, a scowl that abruptly banished all the beauty from her face, and made me want to kiss it, kiss her, I had to.

'Because I don't love you, Roy. I want you, yes, but it's Carl I love.'

'You're lying,' I said.

'We all lie,' she said. 'Even when we think we're telling the truth. What we call true is just the lie that serves us best. And there are no limits to our ability to believe in necessary lies.'

'But you know yourself that isn't true!'

She laid a finger against my lips.

'It **must** be true, Roy. So leave now.'

It was still pitch-dark as the Volvo and I passed the county sign.

Three days later I called Stanley and asked if I was still invited on New Year's Eve.

50

'SO PLEASED YOU COULD COME,' said Stanley, squeezing my hand and giving me a glass containing some sort of yellowy-green slush.

'Merry Christmas,' I said.

'Finally – someone who knows when to say "merry" and when to say "happy"!' he said with a wink. I followed him into the room where the other guests had already arrived.

It would be going too far to say that Stanley's house was luxurious, since there were no such houses in Os, with the possible exception of the Willumsens' and the Aases'. But while the Aas house was furnished with a mixture of peasant common sense and the self-assured discretion of old money, Stanley's villa was a confusing mix of rococo and modern art.

In the living room, above the calf-legged chairs and round table, hung a large crudely painted picture that resembled the cover of a book with the title **Death, What's in It for Me?**

'Harland Miller,' said Stanley, who had followed my gaze. 'Cost me a fortune.'

'You like it that much?'

'I think so. But OK, there may have been a touch of mimetic desire involved. I mean, who doesn't want a Miller?'

'Mimetic desire?'

'Sorry. René Girard. Philosopher. He called it that when we automatically desire the same things as people we admire. If your hero falls in love with a woman, your unconscious goal becomes to win that same woman.'

'I see. Then which one are you actually in love with, the man or the woman?'

'You tell me.'

I looked around. 'Dan Krane's here. I thought he was a regular at Willumsen's New Year's Eve party.'

'Right now he's got better friends here than there,' said Stanley. 'Excuse me, Roy, I need to fix a couple of things in the kitchen.'

I circulated. Twelve familiar faces, twelve familiar names. Simon Nergard, Kurt Olsen. Grete Smitt. I stood there, rocking on my heels like a sailor, and listened to the conversations. Turning the glass in my hand and trying not to look at the clock. They talked about Christmas, the highway, the weather, climate change and the forecast storm that was already drifting the snow outside.

'Extreme weather,' someone said.

'The regular New Year's Eve storm,' said another. 'Just check in the almanac, it comes every five years.'

I stifled a yawn.

Dan Krane stood by the window. It was the first time I had seen the controlled and always correct newspaper man like that. He spoke to no one, just watched us with a curious wildness in his gaze as he downed glass after glass of the strong yellow slush.

I didn't want to, but I went over to him.

'And how are you?' I asked.

He looked at me, seemingly surprised that anyone at all should address him.

'Good evening, Opgard. Are you familiar with the komodo dragon?'

'You mean those giant lizards?'

'Precisely. They're found on only a couple of small Asian islands, one of them is Komodo. About the size of Os county. And they really aren't that big, not as big as people believe anyway. They weigh about the same as a grown man. They move slowly, you and I would be able to run from it. So for that reason it has to use ambush, yes, cowardly ambush. But it doesn't kill you there and then, oh no. It just bites you. Anywhere. Perhaps just an innocent nibble on the leg. And you get away and think you're saved, right? But the truth is, they injected you with poison. And it's a weak, slow-acting poison. I'll return to the subject of why it's weak, here I'll mention only that it costs the animal an enormous amount of energy to produce the poison. The stronger the poison, the more energy. The poison of the Komodo dragon prevents the blood from coagulating. So you've suddenly become a bleeder, the wound in your leg won't heal, nor the inner bleeding from the bite either. So no matter where you run to on that little Asiatic island, the Komodo dragon's long, olfactory tongue picks up the scent of blood and comes slowly waddling after you. The days go by, you grow weaker and weaker. Soon you can't run any faster than the dragon, and it's able to give you another bite. And another one. Your whole body is bleeding and bleeding, the blood won't stop, decilitre by decilitre you're being emptied. And you can't get away of course, because you're trapped on this little island and your scent is everywhere.'

'So how does this end?' I asked.

Dan Krane stopped and stared at me. He looked offended. Perhaps he interpreted the question as a desire to get his lecture over with.

'Venomous creatures that live in small places from which prey, for practical or other reasons, cannot escape, don't need to produce precious, quick-acting poison. They can practise this form of evil slow torture. It's evolution in practice. Or am I wrong, Opgard?'

Opgard didn't have much to say. I realised, of

course, that he was talking about a human version of the venomous animal; but did he mean the enforcer? Or Willumsen? Or somebody else?

'According to the forecast the wind is going to drop during the night,' I said.

Krane rolled his eyes, turned away, stared out of the window.

Not until we were seated at table did the conversation turn to the subject of the hotel. Of the twelve sitting there, eight were involved in the project.

'Anyway, I hope the building's securely moored,' said Simon, with a glance towards the large picture window that was creaking as the wind gusted.

'Oh it is,' a voice said with great certainty. 'My cabin'll blow away before that hotel does, and that cabin's been standing for fifty years.'

I couldn't contain myself any longer and looked at my watch.

In our village there was a traditional gathering in the square just before midnight. There were no speeches, no countdowns or other formalities, it was just an opportunity for people to come together, wait for the rockets and then – in an atmosphere of carnival chaos and social anarchy – use the big community embrace at midnight to press bodies and cheeks against the person or persons who would, in the remaining nine thousand hours of the year, otherwise be off-limits. Even the New Year party at Willumsen's would break up so that guests could mingle with the hoi polloi.

Somebody said something about it being a boom time for the village.

'The credit must go to Carl Opgard,' Dan Krane interrupted. People were used to hearing him speak in a slightly nasal, quiet voice. Now his voice sounded hard, and angry. 'Or blame. All depending.'

'Depending on what?' someone asked.

'Oh yes, that revivalist speech on capitalism he gave up at Årtun, that got everyone dancing round the golden calf. Which, by the way, should be the name of the hotel. The Golden Calf Spa. Although . . .' Krane's wild gaze spun round the table. 'Actually Os Spa is pretty appropriate anyway. Ospa is the Polish word for smallpox, the sickness that wiped out whole villages as late as the twentieth century.'

I heard Grete laugh. Krane's words were maybe what people were used to hearing from him – intelligent, witty – but delivered now with an aggression and chill that silenced the table.

Registering the mood, Stanley raised his glass with a smile. 'Very amusing, Dan. But you're exaggerating, aren't you?'

'Am I?' Dan Krane smiled coldly and fixed his gaze on a spot on the wall somewhere above our heads. 'This business where everyone and anyone can invest without having the money for it is an exact replica of what happened in the crash of October 1929. Those bankers jumping from the tops of skyscrapers along Wall Street – that was just the tip of the iceberg. The real tragedy involved the little people, the millions of small investors who trusted the stock-brokers when they talked in tongues about an everlasting boom and borrowed way over their heads to buy shares.'

'OK,' said Stanley. 'But take a look around, there's optimism everywhere. To be blunt, I don't exactly see any big warning signals.'

'But that is precisely the nature of a crash,' said Krane, his voice getting louder and louder. 'You see nothing until suddenly you see everything. The unsinkable **Titanic** sank seventeen years earlier, but people learned nothing. As late as September 1929 the stock exchange was at its highest ever. People think the wisdom of the majority is unimpeachable. That the market is right, and when everyone wants to buy, buy, of course no one cries wolf. We're gregarious animals, who delude ourselves that it's safer in the flock, in the crowd . . .'

'And so it is too,' I said quietly. But a silence descended so quickly that even though I didn't raise my eyes from my plate, I knew everyone was looking at me.

'That's why fish form shoals and sheep flocks. That's why we form limited companies and consortiums. Because it really is safer to operate as a flock. Not a hundred per cent safe, a whale could come along at any moment and swallow up the whole shoal, but **safer.** That's where evolution has tried and failed us.'

I lifted a loaded fork of gravlax to my face and chewed away, feeling those staring eyes on me. It was as though a deaf-mute had suddenly spoken.

'Let's drink to that!' cried Stanley, and when I finally looked up, I saw everyone with glasses raised in my direction. I tried to smile and raised my own, though it was empty. Quite empty.

Port was served after the dessert and I sat on the sofa opposite the Harland Miller painting.

Someone sat next to me. It was Grete. She had a straw in her glass of port. 'Death,' she said. 'What's in it for me?' she added in English.

'Are you just reading, or are you asking?'

'Both,' said Grete, looking around. Everybody else was engaged in conversation.

'You shouldn't have said no,' she said.

'To what?' I asked, though I knew what she was referring to, I was just hoping I could get her to understand by pretending not to understand that she would drop the subject.

'I had to do it alone,' she said.

I stared at her in disbelief. 'You mean that you've . . .'

She nodded gravely.

'You've been gossiping about Carl and Mari?'

'I have been spreading **information.**'

'You're lying!' It just slipped out, and I glanced round quickly to make sure no one else had heard my outburst.

'Oh yeah?' Grete smiled sardonically. 'Why do you think Dan Krane's here and Mari isn't? Or to be more precise, why do you think they aren't both at Willumsen's like they usually are? Babysitting? Yes, that's probably what they want people to think. When I told Dan he thanked me. He made me promise not to tell anyone else. That was the initial reaction, see? On the outside they act like nothing has happened. But on the inside, believe you me, the split is complete.'

My heart was pounding and I could feel the sweat that had broken out under my tight-fitting shirt. 'And Shannon, have you gossiped to her too?'

'This isn't gossip, Roy. It's information I think everyone has a right to if their partner is unfaithful. I told her at a dinner at Rita Willumsen's. She thanked me too. You see?'

'When was this?'

'When? Let me see. We'd stopped ice-bathing, so it must have been in the spring.'

My brain was working feverishly. The spring. Shannon had travelled to Toronto in the early summer, stayed away for some time. Come back. Contacted me. Fuck. Fuck fuck fuck. I was so angry the hand holding the glass had started to shake. I felt like I wanted to empty the port all over Grete's fucking perm, see if it worked like white spirit when I pushed her face down into the candles standing on a plate next to us. I clenched my teeth.

'Must have been a disappointment for you then that Carl and Shannon are still together.'

Grete shrugged. 'They're obviously unhappy, and that's always a comfort.'

'If they're unhappy, why are they together? They don't even have children.'

'Oh yes,' said Grete. 'The hotel is their child. That's going to be her masterpiece, and that makes Shannon dependent on him. In order to get something you want, you're dependent on someone you hate – sound familiar?'

Grete looked at me as she sucked at her port. Clenched cheeks, lips shaped as though kissing around the straw. I got up, couldn't sit there any longer, went out into the hall and put on my jacket.

'Are you going?' It was Stanley.

'Heading down to the square,' I said. 'My head needs airing.'

'There's still an hour to midnight.'

'I walk and think slowly,' I said. 'See you there.'

Walking down the highway I had to lean into the wind. It blew right through me, blew everything away. The clouds from the sky. The hope from the heart. The fog around everything that had happened. Shannon knew about Carl's infidelity. She'd got in touch with me prior to going to Notodden so that she could have her revenge. Just like Mari wanted. Of course. Replay. I'd crossed my own footsteps; it was the same fucking circle all over again. Impossible to break out of it. So why struggle? Why not just sit down and let yourself drift into a frozen sleep?

A car drove by. It was the new red Audi A1 that had been standing outside Stanley Spind's house. Meaning that the person in question must be driving under the influence, because I hadn't seen anyone there who wasn't drinking that yellow slush. I saw the brake lights as it turned off before the square, heading in the direction of Nergard's farm.

People had already started gathering in the square, mostly young, wandering around aimlessly in groups of four or five. And yet everything, the tiniest gesture or action, had a purpose, an aim, was part of the hunt. People came from every quarter. And even though the wind swept across the open square you could smell the adrenaline, like before a football match. Or a boxing match. Or a bullfight. Yes, that was it. Something was about to die. I was standing in the alleyway between the sports shop and Dals Clothes for Kids and from where I stood I could take in everything without being seen myself. I thought.

A girl broke from the group she was in, it looked like a division of cells, her walk was unsteady but she came more or less in my direction.

'Hi, Roy!' It was Julie. Her voice was hoarse and slurred from alcohol. She put a hand against my chest and pushed me further into the alleyway. Then she wrapped her arms tightly around me. 'Happy New Year,' she whispered, and before I had time to react she pressed her lips against mine. I felt her tongue against my teeth.

'Julie,' I groaned, my jaws clenched.

'Roy,' she groaned back, clearly misunderstanding.

'We can't,' I said.

'It's a New Year's kiss,' she said. 'Everybody—'

'What's going on here?'

The voice came from behind Julie. She turned, and there was Alex. Julie's boyfriend was in line to take over the farm at Ribu, and lads in line to take over the farm tend to be – with certain exceptions, such as me – big. He had the kind of thick, cropped hair that looks as though it's been painted on the head, with a parting, gel and stripes in it, like an Italian footballer. I weighed up the situation. Alex looked a bit unsteady on his feet too, and he still had his hands in his coat pockets. He'd have more to say before he hit out. He had an agenda. I pushed Julie away from me.

She turned and saw clearly what was brewing.

'No,' she shouted. 'No, Alex!'

'No, what?' asked Alex, pretending to be astounded. 'I just want to thank Opgard and his brother for what they've done for the village.' He held out his right hand.

OK, so no agenda. But the way he was standing – one foot in front of the other – showed plainly what he had in mind. The old handshake-to-nut-in-the-face trick. He was probably too young to know how many people I had beaten up. Or maybe he knew, but realised also that he had no choice, that he was a man and had to defend his territory. All I had to do was stand to one side of his line of sight, give him my hand, and jerk him off balance as he adjusted his footing. I took his hand. And at the same moment I saw the fear in his eyes. Was he afraid of me after all? Or was he afraid because he thought he was about to lose the one he loved, the one he had been hoping until now would be his. Well, soon he'd be flat on his back feeling the pain of yet another defeat, yet another humiliation, yet another reminder that he didn't count for much, and Julie's comfort would be like salt in his wounds. In short, a repeat of that night at Lund in Kristiansand. A repeat of that morning in the kitchen at the roofer's house. A repeat of every fucking Saturday night at Årtun when I was eighteen years old. I'd be leaving the spot with yet another scalp in my belt, and I'd still be the loser. I didn't want that any more. I had to get away, break out of the circle, disappear. So I let it happen.

He jerked me forward, butting me at the same time. I heard the crunch as his forehead met my nose. I took a backward step, and saw his right shoulder pulled back ready to swing. I could have easily side-stepped, instead I moved forward and walked straight into his punch. He yelled as his hand caught me directly below the eye. I steadied myself, ready for the next punch. His right wrist was hurting him, but after all, the lad had two hands. Instead he kicked out. Good choice. Caught me in the stomach and I doubled over. Then he elbowed me, catching me in the temple.

'Alex, stop!'

But Alex didn't stop. I felt the juddering in the cerebral cortex, the pain flashing like lightning in the dark before everything turned black.

*

Was there ever a moment when I would have welcomed the end? The net, the seine net that trapped me and drew me down under the water, the certainty that at last I would receive my punishment, for what I had done as well as for what I had not done? The sins of omission, as they call it. My father should be burning in hell because he didn't stop doing what he was doing to Carl. Because he could have done. And I could have. So I should burn too. I was dragged down to the bottom, where they waited for me.

'Roy?'

Life is, in essence, a simple matter. Its only goal is the maximising of pleasure. Even our much-lauded curiosity, our inclination to explore the universe and human nature, is a mere manifestation of the desire to accentuate and protract this pleasure. So when our sums end up on the minus side, when life offers us more pain than pleasure, and there's no longer any hope of things changing, we end it. We eat or drink ourselves to death, swim out to where the current is strong, smoke in bed, drive when drunk, put off seeing the doctor even though the lump on the throat is growing. Or quite simply hang ourselves in the barn. It's banal when you realise for the first time that this is actually a completely practical alternative; indeed, it doesn't even feel like the most important decision of your life. To build that house or get that education – these are bigger decisions than choosing to end your life sooner than it otherwise would have ended.

And this time I decided I wouldn't struggle. I would freeze to death.

'Roy.'

Freeze to death, I said.

'Roy.'

The voice calling to me was as deep as a man's but soft as a woman's, with no trace of an accent, and I loved to hear her say my name, the rolling, caressing way she pronounced the 'r'.

'Roy.'

The only problem was that the lad, Alex, risked a fine and possibly even a prison sentence that took no account of the situation that led up to the fight. In fact, it wasn't even a 'situation' but a quite reasonable response, given how he'd misunderstood things.

'You can't lie here, Roy.'

A hand shaking me. A small hand. I opened my eyes. And looked straight into Shannon's, brown and worried. I wasn't sure whether she was real, or I was dreaming, but that didn't matter.

'You can't lie here,' she repeated.

'No?' I said, raising my head slightly. We were alone in the alleyway, but from the square I could hear people chanting in unison. 'Have I taken someone's place?'

Shannon looked at me for a long time. 'Yes,' she said. 'You know that.'

'Shannon,' I said, my voice thick, 'I lo . . .'

The remainder was drowned in the noise as the heavens above her exploded in sizzling light and colour.

She took hold of my lapels and helped me to my feet, the landscape around me swimming, nausea blocking my throat. Shannon helped me out of the alleyway at the back of the sports shop. She led me along the highway, probably unseen, since everyone was gathered in the square and looking up as the fireworks blew this way and that in the gusting wind. A rocket whizzed low above the rooftops, as another – must have been one of Willumsen's powerful emergency flares – climbed into the sky where it described a white parabola as it headed towards the mountains at two hundred kilometres an hour.

'What are you doing here?' she asked, as we concentrated on putting one foot in front of the other.

'Julie kissed me and—'

'Yes, she told me, before her boyfriend dragged her away. I mean, what are you doing here, in Os?'

'Celebrating New Year's Eve,' I said. 'At Stanley's.'

'Carl told me that. But you're not answering my question.'

'Are you asking me if I came because of you?'

She didn't reply. So I answered myself.

'Yes. I came here to be with you.'

'You're crazy.'

'Yes,' I said. 'I am crazy for believing you wanted me. I should have understood. You were with me as revenge on Carl.'

There was a jerk in my arm, and I realised she had slipped and lost her balance for a moment.

'How do you know that?' she asked.

557

'Grete. She told me that she'd told you about Carl and Mari last spring.'

Shannon nodded slowly.

'So it's true?' I said. 'You and me, for you it was just revenge?'

'It's half true,' she said.

'Half?'

'Mari isn't the first woman Carl's been unfaithful with. But she's the first one I know he cared about. That's why it had to be you, Roy.'

'Oh?'

'For my revenge to be equal it had to be with someone I had feelings for.'

I had to laugh. It was brief, hard laughter. 'Bullshit.'

She sighed. 'Yes, it is bullshit.'

'There, you see.'

Suddenly Shannon let go my arm and stood in front of me. Behind the small figure the highway stretched like a white umbilical cord into the night.

'It is bullshit,' she said. 'Bullshit to fall in love with the brother of your husband because of the way he strokes the breast of a bird you're holding while he tells you about the bird. It's bullshit to fall in love with him because of the stories his brother has told about him.'

'Shannon, don't—'

'It's bullshit!' she shouted. 'Bullshit for you to fall in love with a heart that you know doesn't know the meaning of the word betrayal.'

She put her hands against my chest as I tried to walk by her.

'And it is bullshit,' she said quietly. 'Bullshit that you can't think of anything but this man because of a few hours in a hotel room in Notodden.'

I stood there, swaying.

'Shall we go?' I whispered.

The moment the workshop door closed behind us she pulled me in to her. I breathed in the smell of her. Dizzy and intoxicated I kissed those sweet lips, felt her bite my own until they bled, and we tasted once more the sweet, metallic taste of my blood as she unbuttoned my trousers and whispered a few angry words I seemed to recognise. Held me at the same time as she kicked and swept my legs from under me, so that I fell onto the stone floor. I lay there looking up at her as she danced round on one foot, pulling off her shoe and one of her stockings. Then she pulled up her dress and sat on me. She wasn't wet but grabbed my stiff cock and forced it into her, and it felt as though the skin of my prick was being ripped off. But fortunately she didn't move, she just sat there looking down at me like a queen.

'Is it good?' she asked.

'No,' I said.

We both began laughing at the same time.

The laughter made her sex contract around mine, and she must have felt it too, because she laughed even more.

'There's engine oil on the shelf up there,' I said, pointing.

She put her head on one side and gave me a loving look, as though I were a child who should be going to sleep. Then she closed her eyes, still not moving, but I could feel her sex growing warm and wet.

'Wait,' she whispered. 'Wait.'

I thought of the midnight countdown in the square. That the circle had finally been broken. That we had come out the other side and I was free.

She began to move.

And when she came it was with an angry, triumphal cry, as though she too had just managed to kick open the door that had been keeping her imprisoned.

We lay entwined in the bed and listened. The wind had dropped, and now and then we heard the burst of a late rocket. And then I asked the question I had been asking myself ever since that day Carl and Shannon had swung into the yard at Opgard.

'Why did the two of you come to Os?'

'Did Carl never say?'

'Only that business about putting the village on the map. Is he on the run from something?'

'He didn't tell you?'

'Just something about a legal wrangle concerning some property project in Canada.'

Shannon sighed. 'It was a project in Canmore that had to be scrapped because of soaring costs and the finances running out. And there's no wrangling. Not any more.'

'What do you mean?'

'The case is closed. Carl was ordered to pay restitution to his partners.'

'And?'

'And he couldn't. So he ran off. Came here.'

I raised myself up on one elbow. 'You mean Carl is . . . on the run?'

'In principle, yes.'

'Is that what the spa hotel is about? A way for him to pay off this debt in Toronto?'

She smiled vaguely. 'He's not planning on going back to Canada.'

I tried to take all this in. So Carl's homecoming was nothing more than the flight of a common-or-garden swindler?

'And you? Why did you come here with him?'

'Because I did the drawings for the Canmore project.'

'And?'

'It was my magnum opus. My IBM building. I didn't get it built in Canmore, but Carl promised me another chance.'

It became clear to me. 'The spa hotel. You've designed it before.'

'With a few modifications, yes. The landscapes round Canmore in the Rocky Mountains and round here aren't very different. We had no money left and no one who was willing to invest in our project. So Carl suggested Os. He said it was a place where people trusted him, where they regarded him as a local wonder-boy made good.'

'So you came here. Without a krone in your pockets. But in a Cadillac.'

'Carl said appearances are everything when you're trying to sell a project like this.'

I thought of Armand, the travelling preacher. When it emerged one day that he'd been lining his pockets with money taken from gullible people who were hoping for a cure, at the same time as he stopped them getting the medical help they needed, he'd had to flee north. But when they caught up with him there it turned out he'd started a sect, built himself a church of miracle healing, and had three 'wives'. He was arrested for non-payment of income taxes and fraud, and when he was asked in court why he had carried on swindling after he'd got away he had replied:

'Because that's what I do.'

'Why didn't the two of you tell me all this?' I asked.

Shannon smiled to herself.

'Eh?' I said.

'He said it wouldn't be good for you. I'm just trying to remember exactly how he put it. That's right: he said that even though you aren't sensitive and you don't know much about empathy, you're a moralist. Unlike himself, who is a sensitive and sympathetic cynic.'

I felt like cursing out loud, but instead I had to laugh. Damn him, he had a knack for describing things. He didn't just correct the orthography in my school essays, sometimes he tacked on a sentence

562

or two. Sort of lifted it a bit, gave wings to the crap. Giving wings to crap. Yeah, that was what his talent was.

'But you're wrong if you don't think Carl's intentions are good,' said Shannon. 'He wishes everybody well. But of course, he wishes himself a bit more well. And look, he actually manages it.'

'There are probably a few submerged rocks to look out for. Dan Krane, for example, is planning an article.'

Shannon shook her head. 'Carl says that problem has been solved. And things are going much better now. The project is back on schedule. In two weeks he's signing a contract with a Swedish hotelier who's going to run the place.'

'So Carl Opgard saves the village. Gets to erect a permanent monument to himself. And gets rich. Which of those do you think matters most to him?'

'I think our motives are so complex that we don't even understand them completely ourselves.'

I stroked the bruise beneath her cheekbone.

'And his motives for beating you, are they complex too?'

She shrugged. 'Before I left him and went to Toronto last summer he'd never laid so much as a finger on me. But when I came back something had changed. **He** had changed. He drank all the time. And he started to hit me. He was so distraught after the first time that I convinced myself it was a one-off. But then it turned into a pattern, like a form of compulsive behaviour, something he **had** to do. Sometimes he would be crying even before he began.'

I thought of the crying down below in the bunk bed, that time I realised it wasn't Carl but Dad.

'Why didn't you leave then?' I asked. 'Why come back from Toronto at all? Did you love him so much?'

She shook her head. 'I'd stopped loving him.'

'Did you come because of me?'

'No,' she said, and stroked my cheek.

'You came because of the hotel,' I said.

She nodded.

'You love that hotel.'

'No,' she said. 'I hate the hotel. But it's my prison, it won't let me go.'

'And yet still you love it,' I said.

'The way a mother loves the child that holds her hostage,' she said, and I thought of what Grete had said.

Shannon turned.

'When you've created something that has cost you so much time, pain and love, as I've put into the creation of that building, it becomes a part of you. No, not a part, it's bigger than you, more important. The child, the building, the work of art, it's your only shot at immortality, right? More important than anything else you might love. Do you understand?'

'So then, it's also your own personal monument?'

'No! I don't design monuments. I've designed a simple and useful and beautiful building. Because we, the people, need beauty. And the beauty of my designs for the hotel lies in their simplicity, their self-evident logic. There's nothing monumental about my drawings.'

'Why do you say the drawings and not the hotel? I mean, it's almost finished.'

'Because they're destroying it. These compromises with the council regarding the facade. The cheap materials Carl has agreed to use to stay within the budget. The entire lobby and the restaurant that were altered while I was in Toronto.'

'So you came back to save your child.'

'But I came too late,' she said. 'And the man I thought I loved tried to beat me into submission.'

'Then if you've already lost the battle, why are you still here?'

She smiled bitterly. 'You tell me. I guess maybe a mother feels compelled to be present at the funeral of her own child.'

I swallowed. 'Is there nothing else keeping you here?'

She gave me a long look. Then she closed her eyes and nodded slowly.

I took a deep breath. 'I need to hear you say it, Shannon.'

'Please. Don't ask me to do that.'

'Why not?'

I saw her eyes fill with tears. 'Because it's an **open sesame,** Roy. And that's why you're asking me.'

'What do you mean?'

'If I hear myself say it, my heart opens up, and then I'm weak. And until everything's finished here, I need to stay strong.'

'I need to stay strong too,' I said. 'And to stay strong enough I need to hear you say it. Say it low so that I'm the only one that hears it.' And I cupped my hands over her small, white, shell-like ears.

She looked at me. Took a breath. Stopped. Started again. And then she whispered the magic words, more powerful than any password, any declaration of faith, any oath of allegiance: 'I love you.'

'And I love you too,' I whispered in return.

I kissed her.

She kissed me.

'God damn you,' she said.

'When this is over,' I said, 'when the hotel is up, will you be free then?'

She nodded.

'I can wait,' I said. 'But then we'll pack up and leave.'

'Where?' she asked.

'Barcelona. Or Cape Town. Or Sydney.'

'Barcelona,' she said. 'Gaudí.'

'Deal.'

As though to seal the deal we looked into each other's eyes. From out of the darkness came a sound. A golden plover? What had caused him to come all the way down here from his mountain? The rockets?

Something showed in her face. Anxiety.

'What is it?' I asked.

'Listen,' she said. 'It isn't a good sound.'

I listened. It wasn't a plover. This note rose and fell.

'It's the bloody fire engine,' I said.

As though at a signal we jumped up out of bed

and ran into the workshop. I opened the door, just in time to see the old fire engine disappear in the direction of the village. I'd done repair work on it; it was a GMC. The council had bought it from the armed forces, who'd been using it at an airport. The sales argument was that the price was reasonable and came with a water tank with a capacity of 1,500 litres. One year later the sales argument was that the heavy vehicle was so slow in the steep terrain that if a fire broke out in the hills there would be nothing for those fifteen hundred litres of water to put out by the time it got there. But there were no takers for the monster and it was still here.

'In weather like this they shouldn't allow fireworks in the middle of the village,' I said.

'The fire isn't in the middle of the village,' said Shannon.

I followed her gaze. Up the mountain, up in the direction of Opgard. The sky above was a dirty yellow.

'Ah shit,' I whispered.

I turned the Volvo into the yard. Shannon was right behind me in the Subaru.

There was Opgard, sloping, shining, leaning a little eastward in the moonlight. Intact. We got out of the cars; I headed towards the barn and Shannon towards the main house.

Inside I saw that Carl had already been there and picked up his skis. I took my own and the ski poles and ran to the house where Shannon stood in the doorway holding out my ski boots. I fastened my skis and set off at double pace through the trees, towards that dirty yellow sky. The wind had dropped so much that Carl's tracks hadn't been covered over and I was able to use them to speed along. I would guess that the wind was down to a strong breeze by now, and now I could hear the shouts and the crackle of fire before I came up on the ridge. For that reason I was surprised and relieved when at last I arrived and looked down at the hotel, the framework and the modules. Smoke, but no flames – they must have managed to put it out. But then I noticed the glow in the snow on the far side of the building, on the red bodywork of the fire truck, and on the expressionless faces of those standing there, turned towards me. And when the wind dropped for a moment I saw those yellow, licking tongues everywhere, and realised that it was just that the wind had temporarily blown the flames out on the lee side. And I realised too the problem facing those trying to put them out. The road only went as far as the front of the hotel, and the fire truck had to park some distance away because the snow hadn't been cleared from the area in front. It meant that even with the hose fully unrolled it wasn't long enough for them to get round to the rear of the hotel and direct the jet of water with the wind behind them. Now, even though they must have had the hose turned on full, the jet dissipated in the facing wind and blew back across them as rain.

I was standing less than a hundred metres away and could feel no heat from the fire. But when I picked out Carl's face among the crowd, wet with sweat or maybe water from the hose, I saw that it was hopeless. All was lost.

51

THE GREY LIGHT OF THE first day of the year dawned.

It made the landscape look flat and featureless, and when I drove from the workshop up to the hotel site for a moment I had the feeling that I had lost my way, that this wasn't a landscape I knew like the back of my hand but somewhere strange, some strange planet.

When I got there I saw Carl standing with three men next to the smouldering blackened ruins of what was to have been the pride of the village. Which still could be that, of course, though hardly this year. Black, charred pieces of wood pointed to the sky like warning fingers, telling us, them, anyone, that you do not build a bloody spa hotel on the bare mountain, it's against nature, it awakens the spirits.

As I got out of the car and walked towards them I saw that the three other men were the sheriff Kurt Olsen, the council chairman Voss Gilbert, and the fire chief, a man named Adler who worked as an engineer for the council when he wasn't on duty at the fire station. I don't know whether they clammed up because I arrived or they'd just finished exchanging theories.

'Well?' I said. 'Any theories?'

'They found the remains of a New Year's Eve rocket,' Carl said so quietly I could only just hear him. His gaze was focused on something far, far away.

'That's right,' said Kurt Olsen, cigarette held into his palm between index finger and thumb, like a soldier on night watch. 'Obviously, it could have been carried up from the village by the wind and set fire to the timbers.'

Obviously and obviously. From the way he stressed the **could** it was evident he didn't have much faith in the theory himself.

'But?' I said.

Kurt Olsen shrugged. '**But** the fire chief here says that when they got here, they saw two sets of footprints half covered by snow leading towards the hotel. With a wind like that they can't have been made much before the fire truck arrived.'

'It wasn't possible to tell whether the footprints were two people who went in, or one person who went in and then came out again,' said the fire chief. 'We had to operate on a worst-case scenario and send men in to check whether there was anyone in the modules. But they were already alight and it was too hot.'

'There are no bodies here,' said Olsen. 'But it does look as though someone was here during the night. So obviously we can't rule out arson.'

'Arson?' I almost shouted.

Olsen perhaps thought I sounded a little too conspicuously surprised; at any rate he gave me that scrutinising sheriff's look of his.

'Who would have anything to gain by that?' I asked.

'Yes, who might that be, Roy?' said Kurt Olsen, and I did not like the fucking way he said my name.

'Well,' said the council chairman, with a nod down towards the village that lay half hidden beneath a layer of fog that had drifted in across the ice on Lake Budal, 'This is one helluva a hangover for them to wake up to.'

'Well,' said I, 'when you're up to your neck in shit the only thing to do is start the rebuilding.'

The others looked at me as though I'd said something in Latin.

'Maybe, but it'll take some doing to get a hotel up this year,' said Gilbert. 'And that means people can't be selling off land for cabin-building for a while.'

'Really?' I glanced over at Carl. He said nothing, didn't even seem to have heard us, just stared vacantly at the site of the fire with a look on his face that reminded me of newly set cement.

'Those are the terms of the agreement with the council.' Gilbert sighed in such a way that I realised he was repeating something he'd just said. 'First the hotel, then the cabins. Unfortunately quite a few in the village have been counting their chickens before they're hatched and bought themselves more expensive cars than they should have.'

'Good job the hotel was fully insured against fire,' said Kurt Olsen with a glance at Carl.

Gilbert and the fire chief managed little smiles, as much as to say that yes, true enough, but right now that was small comfort.

'Right, well,' said the council chairman and stuck his hands into his coat pockets as a sign that he wanted to leave. 'Happy New Year.'

Olsen and the fire chief trudged along behind him in the snow.

'Is it?' I asked quietly once they were out of earshot.

'A happy new year?' Carl asked with a voice like a sleepwalker's.

'Fully insured?'

Carl turned his whole body to face me, as though he really were cast in cement. 'Why in the world wouldn't it be fully insured?' He spoke so slowly, so quietly. This wasn't alcohol. Had he been taking pills of some kind?

'But is it **more** than fully insured?'

'What do you mean?'

I felt the anger beginning to bubble up in me, but knew I had to keep my voice down until they were inside their cars. 'I mean Kurt Olsen is more or less implying that the fire was started deliberately and that the hotel is overinsured. He's accusing you of an insurance fraud. Or didn't you realise that?'

'That I started the fire?'

'Did you, Carl?'

'Why would I do that?'

'The hotel was pretty much shot to hell, the spending way over budget, but so far you've managed to keep it hidden. Maybe this was the only way out, for your neighbours in the village to avoid paying the bill and you to avoid the shame. Now you can make a fresh start, from scratch, build the hotel the way it should be built, with proper materials and a fresh injection of insurance money. See, you can still erect that monument to Carl Opgard.'

Carl looked at me with a kind of fascination, as though I had changed shape in front of his very eyes. 'Do you, my own brother, really believe that I am capable of something like that?' Then he put his head slightly to one side. 'Yes, you do believe it. So then answer me this: why am I standing here and feeling like I want to commit hara-kiri? Why aren't I at home breaking out the champagne?'

I held his gaze. And it began to dawn on me. Carl could lie, but not act grief in a way that could fool me. No way.

'No,' I whispered. 'Not that, Carl.'

'Not what?'

'I know you were desperate and cutting costs. But not that.'

'What?' he roared, suddenly furious.

'The insurance. You didn't stop making the insurance payments on the hotel?'

574

He looked away, and the fury seemed to have passed. Had to be pills.

'Yes, that would have been stupid,' he whispered. 'To stop making the insurance payments just before the fire. Because then . . .' Slowly a smile spread across his face, the kind of smile I imagine the acid tripper on a balcony gives just before he demonstrates he can fly. 'Yeah, because what actually happens then, Roy?'

52

IN MOUNTAIN LANDSCAPES SUCH AS ours, darkness
doesn't fall, it rises. It rises from the valleys, from the
forests and the lake down there, and for a time we can
see that evening has come to the village and the fields
while up here it's still day. But that day, the first of the
year, was different. Maybe it was because of the cloud
that lay so thick above us, colouring everything grey,
maybe it was the blackened site of the fire that seemed
to suck all the light from the mountainside, or maybe
it was the despair that hung over Opgard, or the cold
from space. Whatever it was, daylight just disappeared as though it had burned out.

Carl, Shannon and I ate dinner in silence and listened to the sounds as the temperature fell in the walls.

When I was finished I grabbed a serviette, wiped the cod and the fat from my mouth and then opened it.

'On the **Os Daily** website Dan Krane says the fire just means a delay.'

'Yes,' said Carl. 'He called and I told him we'll start the rebuilding next week.'

'So he doesn't know the place wasn't insured against fire?'

Carl put his elbows either side of his plate. 'The only people who know, Roy, are those of us sitting round this table. And let's keep it that way.'

'You'd've thought that, with him being a journalist, he would have looked more closely at the insurance situation. After all, what's at stake is the future of the village.'

'No need to worry. I'll sort this out, you hear me?'

'I hear you.'

Carl ate more cod. Glanced over at me. Stopped, drank more water. 'If Dan had any suspicion the hotel wasn't covered for fire, he wouldn't have written that everything was under control. You do see that, right?'

'Well, OK, if you say so.'

Carl put down his fork. 'What is it you're actually trying to say, Roy?'

And for an instant I saw him. His imperious body language, his quiet but commanding voice, his penetrating gaze. For an instant it was as though Carl had become him, become Dad.

I shrugged. 'What I'm probably saying is that it might look like someone has told Dan Krane not to write anything negative about the hotel. And that it was well before the fire.'

'Like who for example?'

'A Danish enforcer who was here in town. Someone saw his Jaguar parked outside the offices of the **Os Daily** just before Christmas. And afterwards people said Dan Krane looked pale and ill.'

Carl grinned. 'Willumsen's enforcer? The guy we talked about when we were kids?'

'I didn't believe in him back then. I do now.'

'OK. And why would Willumsen want to shut Dan Krane up?'

'Not shut him up. Just guide his pen. When Dan Krane was talking about the hotel at Stanley's party yesterday he wasn't exactly complimentary about it.'

When I said that something blinked through Carl's eyes. Something I'd never seen there before. It was hard and dark, like the blade of an axe.

'Dan Krane doesn't write what he thinks,' I said. 'Willumsen censors him. So I'm asking **you** why?'

Carl grabbed his serviette, wiped around his mouth. 'Oh, Willumsen might well have a million good reasons for stopping Dan.'

'He's worried about the loan he's made to you?'

'Could be. But why do you ask me?'

'Because on Christmas Eve I saw tyre tracks in the snow outside here. Wide tracks, from summer tyres.'

Carl's face became curiously long. It was almost as though I was looking at him inside a Hall of Mirrors at a funfair.

'It snowed two days before Christmas,' I said. 'Those tyre tracks must have been from the same day or the day before.'

There was no need for me to say any more. No one else in the village still uses summer tyres in December. Carl cast what was supposed to be a casual look in Shannon's direction. She looked back at him, and there was something hard in her eyes too, something I'd also never seen before.

'Are we done?' she asked.

'Yes,' said Carl. 'That's all we need to say about this.'

'I meant the food; have we finished eating?'

'Yes,' said Carl, and I nodded.

She stood up, gathered the plates and the cutlery and went out to the kitchen. We heard her turn on the tap.

'It's not like you think it is,' said Carl.

'How do I think it is?'

'You think it was me who put that enforcer on Dan Krane.'

'But you didn't?'

Carl shook his head. 'That loan from Willumsen is obviously confidential and isn't part of the account-ing where it looks as though we're drawing on credit we don't have. But in terms of cash flow, the loan enabled us to carry out the final phase of the build-ing and now things were back on track, we'd cut costs dramatically and still managed to catch up on almost the entire delay from the spring. So it was quite a sur-prise when that enforcer turned up . . .' Carl leaned forward and hissed between clenched teeth. 'Here, to my own house, Roy! Came here to tell me what'll happen if I don't pay what I owe. As though I needed reminding.' Carl closed his eyes tight, sat back in his chair again and sighed heavily. 'Anyway, it turned out that the reason for the reminder was that Willumsen was starting to get worried.'

'Why, if everything was back on track?'

'Because a while ago Dan called Willumsen to interview him as one of the most prominent participants in the village, and to ask him how he felt about the project, and about me. In the course of the interview Willumsen realised that Dan finally had enough material for a highly critical article, one that would impact on the participants' belief in the project and in the indulgence of the council. About the accounts, or rather the lack of accounts. And Dan had talked to people in Toronto who'd told him I'd run off from a bankruptcy, and that there were a number of similarities between that case and the Os Spa and Mountain Hotel project. So Willumsen gets worried that I'm going to do a bunk again, and Dan's going to ruin the whole project with this article about fraud and swindling. So he called up his enforcer to carry out two jobs.'

'To stop Dan's article, and frighten you off any plans you might have for defaulting on your debt.'

'Yes.'

I looked at Carl. No doubt about it, he was telling the truth now.

'And now the whole fucking lot has burned down, what are you going to do?'

'Sleep on it,' said Carl. 'Nice if you'd sleep up here too.'

I looked at him. It wasn't just a courtesy. When a crisis comes some people try to sort things out on their own. Others, such as Carl, need people around them.

'Sure,' I said. 'I can take a couple of days off and stay here. Could be you'll need help.'

'Will you?' he said, giving me a grateful look.

Just then Shannon came in with the coffee cups. 'Good news, Shannon, Roy's staying.'

'That's nice,' said Shannon with what sounded like genuine enthusiasm, smiling at me like I was her dear brother-in-law. I wasn't sure if I liked her acting talent, but right now I appreciated it.

'It's good to know you've got family you can rely on,' said Carl, pushing his chair back, the legs making coughing sounds against the rough floorboards. 'I'll give the coffee a miss, I haven't slept for the last day and a half, so I'm off to bed now.'

Carl left, and Shannon sat in his chair. We drank coffee in silence until we heard the toilet flush up there and the bedroom door shut.

'Well?' I said quietly. 'How does it feel?'

'How does what feel?' Her voice was flat, her face expressionless.

'Your hotel burned down.'

She shook her head. 'It wasn't my hotel. As you know, that disappeared somewhere along the line.'

'OK, but Os Spa and Mountain Hotel SL will be declared bankrupt when it emerges the hotel wasn't insured. No hotel means no plots for sale for cabins, and in that case the market value of the land goes back to somewhere around zero. It's over for everyone now. Us, Willumsen, the village.'

She didn't reply.

'I've been doing a bit of research on Barcelona,' I said. 'I'm no city person, I like the mountains. And there are a lot of mountains just outside Barcelona. Houses are cheaper too.'

She still said nothing, just stared down into her coffee cup.

'There's a mountain called Sant Llorenç that looks really great,' I said. 'Forty minutes from Barcelona.'

'Roy . . .'

'And it must be possible to buy a service station there. I've got some money put aside, enough to—'

'Roy!' She raised her eyes from the coffee cup and looked at me. 'This is my chance,' she said. 'Don't you understand that?'

'Your chance?'

'Now that that abortion has burned down. This is my chance to get my building up. The way it **should** be.'

'But—'

I shut up when her fingernails dug into my underarm. She leaned forward. 'My baby, Roy. Don't you understand? It's risen from the dead.'

'Shannon, there's no money.'

'Roads, water, sewage, the site, everything's in place.'

'You don't get it. Maybe in five or ten years someone will build something there, but no one is going to build **your** hotel, Shannon.'

'**You**'re the one who doesn't get it.' There was a strange, feverish glow in her eyes that I had not seen before. 'Willumsen, he's got too much to lose. I know men like that. They **have** to win; they don't accept defeat. Willumsen will do anything not to lose the money he's owed and the profit on the cabin plots.'

I thought of Willumsen and Rita. Shannon had a point.

'You think Willumsen will take one more chance,' I said. 'Double or quits, like?'

'He **has to.** And I have to stay here until I've got my hotel up. Oh, you must think I'm mad,' she exclaimed in desperation, and laid her forehead against my arm. 'But that building is the building I was born to build, you must see. But once it's up, then you and I can go to Barcelona. I promise.' She pressed her lips to my hand. Then she stood up.

I was about to stand up too and put my arms around her, but she forced me back down into the chair.

'We've got to keep cool heads and cool hearts now,' she whispered. 'Think. We have to think, Roy. So that later we can be unthinking. Goodnight.'

She kissed me on the forehead and left me.

I lay in the bunk bed and thought about what Shannon had said.

It was true that Willumsen hated to lose. But he was also a man who knew when he had to take a hit in order to limit his losses. Did she believe what she said because she wanted it so badly? Because she loved that hotel, and love makes you blind? And was that why I let her convince me to believe it too? I didn't know which of the two opposing forces, greed and fear, would win when Willumsen found out that the hotel wasn't insured; but Shannon was probably right to say that he was the only one who could save the project.

I leaned out of the bed and looked at the thermometer outside the window. Minus twenty-five. Not a living soul out there today. But then I heard the warning cry of the raven. So there was something. Something was on its way. Living or dead.

I listened. Not a sound in the house. And suddenly I was a child again, telling myself there are no such things as monsters. Lying to myself that monsters don't exist.

Because next day it came.

PART SIX

53

WHEN I WOKE I COULD tell straight away that the **sprengkulda** had come. It wasn't so much the feel of the temperature on the skin as certain other sensory impressions. In the extreme cold sounds carried better. I was more sensitive to light, and the air I breathed, now that the molecules were more compressed, somehow made me feel more alive.

I could tell, for example, from the crunching in the snow outside the house that it was Carl who was up early and going about some business. I opened the curtains and saw the Cadillac driving slowly and carefully across the ice on Geitesvingen, although we had gritted the road and it was cold, 'sandpaper' ice. I went into Shannon's bedroom.

She was sleepy-warm and smelling more intently than usual of the deliciously spicy smell that was Shannon.

I kissed her awake and said that even if Carl had just gone to buy a paper, we had at least half an hour alone.

'Roy, I said we have to keep cool hearts and think!' she hissed. 'Get out!'

I got up. She pulled me back.

It was like emerging shivering from Lake Budal and lying down on a sun-warmed rock. Hard and soft at the same time, and a sense of well-being so powerful it made the body sing.

I heard her breathe in my ear, whispered obsceni-ties in a jumble of Baja, English and Norwegian. She came, loudly and with her whole body arched in a bow. And when I came I buried my face in the pillow so as not to shout directly into her ear and picked up the smell of Carl. Unmistakably Carl. But there was something else too. A sound. It came from the door behind us. I tensed.

'What is it?' Shannon asked breathlessly.

I turned towards the door. It was ajar, but it was me who hadn't closed it, wasn't it? Of course. I held my breath, heard Shannon do the same.

Silence.

Could I possibly not have heard the Cadillac com-ing? Too fucking right I could, we hadn't exactly been keeping our noise down. I looked at my wristwatch, which I had kept on. It was only twenty-two minutes since he'd left.

'No danger,' I said, and turned over on my back. She snuggled into me.

'Barbados,' she whispered into my ear.

'Eh?'

'We said Barcelona. But what about Barbados?'

'Do they have petrol-driven cars there?'

'Sure they do.'

'Deal.'

She kissed me. Her tongue was smooth and strong. Searching and showing. Giving and taking. Jesus was I hooked. I was about to enter her again when I heard the hum of the engine. The Cadillac. Her eyes and her hands were on me as I slid out of the bed, pulled on my underpants and walked across the cold floorboards to the boys' room. Lay in the bunk bed and listened.

The car stopped outside and the outer door opened.

Carl stamped the snow from his shoes in the hallway, and through the hole I heard him entering the kitchen.

'I saw your car outside,' I heard Carl say. 'Did you just let yourself in?'

I felt my body turn to ice as I lay there.

'The door was open,' said a second voice. Low and rasping. As though he'd damaged his vocal cords.

I raised up on my elbows and pulled the curtains aside. The Jaguar was parked over by the barn, where the snow had been cleared.

'What can I do for you?' Carl said. Controlled, but tense.

'You can pay my client.'

'So he sent for you because the hotel burned down? Thirty hours. Not a bad response time.'

'He wants his money now.'

'I'll pay him as soon as I get the insurance money.'

'You won't be getting any insurance money. The hotel wasn't insured.'

'Says who?'

'My client has his sources. The conditions for the loan have not been upheld. That means it falls due with immediate effect. You're aware of that, herr Opgard? Good. You've got two days. That's to say forty-eight hours from . . . now.'

'Now listen—'

'Last time I was here you got a warning. This isn't a three-acter, herr Opgard; so this is the hammer.'

'The hammer?'

'The end. Death.'

Silence down there. I saw them in my mind's eye. The Dane with his angry red pimples, seated at the table. Relaxed body language, which only made him all the more threatening. Carl sweating, even though he'd just come in from minus thirty.

'Why the panic?' asked Carl. 'Willumsen's got security.'

'Which he says ain't worth much without a hotel.'

'But what would be the point of killing me?' Carl's voice was no longer so controlled. Now it sounded more like the whining of a vacuum cleaner. 'If I'm dead then Willumsen's definitely not going to get his money.'

'You're not the one who's going to die, Opgard. At least not in the first instance.'

I already knew what was coming next, but I doubted if Carl did.

'It's your wife, Opgard.'

'Sh . . .' Carl swallowed the 'a'. '. . . nnon?'

'Nice name.'

'But that's . . . murder.'

'The reaction reflects the amount owing.'

'But **two days.** How do you and Willumsen suppose I'm going to get hold of that kind of money in such a short time?'

'I can imagine you'll have to do something pretty drastic, maybe even something desperate. Beyond that I have no opinion, herr Opgard.'

'And if I don't manage it . . . ?'

'Then you're a widower, and you'll have a further two days.'

'But Jesus, I mean . . .'

I was on my feet already, trying not to make a sound as I pulled on my trousers and pullover. I didn't hear in detail what would happen after four days, but I didn't need to either.

I sneaked down the stairs. I might possibly – **possibly** – have managed to handle the Dane with the element of surprise on my side. But I doubted it. I recalled the speed of his movements outside the service station, and from the acoustics I had realised he was sitting facing the door and would see me the moment I came in.

I slipped into my shoes and out the door. The cold was like a pressure forcing against the temples. I could have taken a detour, run in an arc towards the barn out of sight of the kitchen, but I figured I only had a few seconds so I banked on being right and that the Dane was sitting with his back to the window. The dry snow squeaked under my running steps. The enforcer's primary task is to frighten, so I reckoned the Dane would be elaborating on his threat. On the other hand, there were probably limits to how much there was to say.

I raced into the barn, turned on the taps and placed two zinc buckets below them. They were full in less than ten seconds. I grabbed the handles, ran out and down towards Geitesvingen. The water sploshed about and my trousers got wet. On the bend I put one of the buckets down on the ice and emptied the other in an arc in front of me. The water ran over the hard ice, over the sand strewn across it that looked like black peppercorns where it had bored its way into the ice. The water evened out irregularities and small holes and ran off towards the edge of the precipice. I did the same with the other bucket. It was too cold, of course, for the water to melt the ice, so it lay in a thin layer on top of it and started to penetrate down into the layer below. I was still standing there observing the ice when I heard the Jaguar start. And – almost as though they were synchronised – I heard the distant, crisp sound of church bells starting up from down in the village. I looked up towards the house and saw the enforcer's white car come driving along. Carefully, slowly. Maybe he'd been surprised at how easily he'd managed to climb the icy hills on his summer tyres. But most Danes don't really know much about ice, they don't know that the surface becomes like sandpaper if it gets cold enough.

But that when heated, for example, to around minus seven degrees, it turns into an ice-hockey rink.

I didn't move, stood there with the buckets dangling at my sides. The Dane stared at me from behind the front windscreen, the small slits of his eyes that I remembered from that time by the pumps now covered by a pair of sunglasses. The car approached and passed, and our heads revolved like a planet around its own axis. Maybe he had some vague memory of my face, maybe not. And maybe he'd come up with some plausible explanation for why this guy was standing there with two buckets, maybe not. And perhaps he understood when he suddenly lost his grip on the road, and he instinctively pushed down harder on the brake pedal, perhaps not. And now the car too was a planet as it slowly spun round on the ice to the music of the church bells, like a figure skater. I saw him desperately spinning the steering wheel, saw the front wheels with their broad summer tyres twist back and forth as though trying to escape what held them, but the Jaguar was trapped and out of

593

control. And when the car had spun 180 degrees and was sailing backwards towards the edge of the curve, I saw him again, I was looking straight into his face, a red planet with tiny, active volcanoes. The sunglasses had slipped down his face as with flailing elbows he fought the steering wheel. Then he caught sight of me and stopped his flapping. Because he knew now. Knew what the buckets had been for, knew that if he had understood immediately he might possibly have had a chance to jump out of the car straight away. Knew now that it was too late.

I'm guessing he was acting on instinct when he pulled his gun. The automatic response of an enforcer, a soldier, to attack. And I was probably acting in response to another instinct when I raised one hand, with a bucket, in a farewell gesture. I just about heard the crack inside the car as he fired, then a whipping sound as the bullet passed through the zinc bucket right next to my ear. I just had time to see the bullet hole, like a frost-rose in the windscreen, and then the Jaguar disappeared down into Huken.

I held my breath.

The zinc bucket in my raised hand still swayed from the hit.

The church bells rang faster and faster.

And then at last it came, a muted thud.

I stood there, still not moving. It must be a funeral. The church bells continued for a while longer, but with the silence between each peal ever longer. I looked out across the village, the mountains and

Lake Budal as the sun finally broke free of the peak of Ausdaltinden.

Then the church bells stopped completely, and I thought, Jesus Christ, how lovely it is round here.

I guess that's the kind of thing you think when you're in love.

54

'YOU POURED WATER OVER THE ice?' Carl asked in disbelief.

'It raises the temperature,' I said.

'It turns it into a skating rink,' said Shannon, bringing the coffee pot over from the stove. She poured coffees for us.

Saw Carl was looking up at her.

'Toronto Maple Leafs!' she cried, as though there was an accusation in his look. 'Did you never notice how they watered the rink during the breaks?'

Carl turned back to me. 'So there's another body in Huken.'

'Let's hope so,' I said, blowing across my coffee.

'What do we do? Report it to Kurt Olsen?'

'No,' I said.

'No? And if they find him?'

'Then it's got nothing to do with us. We never saw the car drive off the road and we never heard it either, that's why we never reported anything.'

Carl looked at me. 'My brother,' he said. The white teeth shone in his face. 'I **knew** you'd come up with a plan.'

'Listen,' I said. 'If no one knows or suspects that the enforcer was up here, then we don't have a problem and we keep our mouths shut. It might be a hundred years before anyone discovers the wreck in Huken. But if anyone finds out he was up here or discovers the Jaguar, then this is our story . . .'

Carl and Shannon came closer, as though I was going to whisper in our own kitchen.

'It's generally best to stick as close to the truth as possible, so we tell it like it was, that the enforcer was here to press us for the money Carl owes Willumsen. We say that none of us watched the enforcer as he drove off, but that it was pretty fucking slippery on Geitesvingen. So when the police get down into Huken and see the summer tyres on the Jaguar, they'll work the rest out for themselves.'

'The church bells,' said Carl. 'We can say we never heard the crash because of the church bells.'

'No,' I said. 'No church bells. There were no church bells the day he was up here.'

They looked quizzically at me.

'Why not?' asked Carl.

'The plan isn't a hundred per cent complete yet,' I said. 'But this didn't happen today, the Dane lived a little longer.'

'Why?'

'Don't worry about the Dane,' I said. 'I reckon an enforcer keeps it to himself where and when he's on the job, so we're probably the only ones who know he was here today. So if he is found dead then it's our story that gives the time of death. Our problem now is Willumsen.'

'Yes, because he's bound to know his enforcer was here,' said Carl. 'And he could tell the police.'

'I don't think so,' I said.

There was a short silence.

'Exactly,' said Shannon. 'Because then he would have to tell the police he was the one who hired the enforcer.'

'Of course,' said Carl. 'Right, Roy?'

I didn't answer. Took a long, noisy slurp of my coffee. Put the mug down.

'Forget the Dane,' I said. 'Willumsen is the problem because **of course** he won't stop trying to get back what you owe him just because the Dane is gone.'

Shannon made a face. 'And he's willing to kill. Do you think his enforcer really **meant** that, Roy?'

'I only heard it through the stovepipe hole,' I said. 'Ask Carl who was sitting right in front of him.'

'I . . . I think so,' said Carl. 'But I was so shit-scared I would've believed anything. Roy's the one of the three of us who understands how a . . . how the brain works.'

598

He so nearly said it. **A killer's brain.**

Again it was me they looked to.

'Yes, he would have killed you,' I said, and looked at Shannon.

Her pupils expanded and she nodded her head slowly, Os-style.

'And then it would've been your turn, Carl,' I said.

Carl looked down at his hands. 'I think I need a drink,' he said.

'No!' I said. Took a breath and calmed myself. 'I need you sober. And I need a towing rope and a driver who's done this before. Shannon, can you go down and spread more sand on the corner?'

'Yes.' She reached out a hand towards me and I stiffened because for a moment I thought she was going to stroke my cheek; but she just rested it on my shoulder. 'Thank you.'

Carl, sitting there, suddenly seemed to wake up. 'Yes, of course, thank you! Thank you!' He leaned across the table and grabbed my hand. 'You saved Shannon and me, and here I am moaning and complaining as though this was your problem.'

'It **is** my problem,' I said. And wasn't far off saying something very high-flown, like we were a family, and we were in a war together; but decided that could wait. After all, no more than half an hour ago I'd been in bed fucking my sister-in-law.

'Dan's really banging on the big bass drum in his editorial today,' said Carl from the kitchen as I stood in the hallway getting dressed and wondering what kind of boots would be best if there was ice on the rock face. 'He thinks Voss Gilbert and the council are populist and spineless. That the tradition was established during the time when Jo Aas was chairman, only it was a bit less obvious back then.'

'He wants to get beaten up,' I said, choosing Dad's old Norwegian welt boots.

'Does anybody **want** to get beaten up?' said Carl, but by that time I was already halfway out the door.

I crossed to the barn where Shannon was shovelling sand into one of the zinc buckets.

'Do you and Rita Willumsen still go ice-bathing three days a week?' I asked.

'Yes.'

'And there's just you two?'

'Yes.'

'Can anyone see you?'

'It's seven o'clock in the morning, and dark, so . . . no.'

'When is the next time?'

'Tomorrow.'

I scratched my chin.

'What are you thinking?' she asked.

I watched the sand trickling though the bullet hole in the bucket. 'I'm thinking about how you can kill her.'

Later that evening, after I'd gone through the plan with Carl and Shannon for the sixth time, and Carl had nodded and we had both looked at Shannon, she set her conditions.

'If I'm to be part of this, and if we succeed, then the hotel has to be rebuilt using my original drawings,' she said. 'Down to the smallest detail.'

'Fine,' said Carl after a few moments' thought. 'I'll do the best I can.'

'You won't have to,' said Shannon. 'Because I'll be in charge of the building, not you.'

'Now listen—'

'This isn't a gambit, it's an ultimatum,' she said.

Carl could probably see as well as I could that she meant it. He turned to me. I shrugged, as if to say I couldn't help him here.

He sighed. 'Fine, Opgard men don't bargain. If this works out well the job is yours, but I hope I can contribute.'

'Oh, I'm sure we'll keep you busy,' said Shannon.

'Fine,' I said. 'Then let's run through the plan one more time.'

55

IT WAS SEVEN O'CLOCK IN the morning and still dark out.

I crept through the darkened bedroom, listening to the steady breathing from the double bed. Stopped when the floor creaked. Stood still and listened. No interruption to the rhythm. The only light came from the moon through a gap in the curtains. I carried on, put my knees against the mattress and slid carefully towards the one sleeping. This side of the bed was still warm from the other who had been lying here. And I couldn't help myself, I pressed my face against the sheet and inhaled the scent of woman, and at once – as though from a film projector – the images of me and her were there. Naked and sweating from lovemaking, but hungry for more, always.

'Good morning, darling,' I whispered.

And rested the barrel of the gun on the sleeper's temple.

The breathing stopped. There were a couple of loud, angry snores. And then he opened his eyes.

'You sleep quietly for such a fat man,' I said.

Willum Willumsen blinked a couple of times in the semi-darkness as though to make sure he wasn't still dreaming.

'What's this?' he asked, his voice hoarse.

'It's the hammer,' I said. 'The end. Death.'

'What are you doing, Roy? How did you get in?'

'Basement door,' I said.

'That's locked,' he said.

'Yes,' was all I said.

He sat upright in the bed. 'Roy, Roy, Roy. I don't want to harm you. Get the hell out and I swear I'll forget this.'

I hit him on the bridge of the nose with the barrel of the pistol. The skin broke and he began to bleed.

'Don't move your hands from the duvet,' I said. 'Let the blood run.'

Willumsen swallowed. 'Is that thing there a pistol?'

'Correct.'

'I get it. So this is a kind of repeat of what happened last time?'

'Yes. The difference being that we parted company alive back then.'

'And now?'

'Now I wouldn't be too sure about that. You threatened to kill my family.'

'That's a consequence of defaulting on a debt that big, Roy.'

'Yes, and this is the consequence of setting in motion the consequence of defaulting on a debt that big.'

'You think I should allow my creditors to ruin me without doing anything? D'you really think so?' There was more indignation than fear in his voice, and I really had to admire Willum Willumsen for the speed with which he was able to grasp the reality of the situation, as people say.

'I don't have any particular thoughts on that, Willumsen. You do what you have to do, I do what I have to do.'

'If you think this is the way to save Carl then you're mistaken. Poul will get the job done no matter what, the contract can't be cancelled because I have no way of getting in touch with him now.'

'No, you haven't,' I said, and heard how like some half-remembered quote from the history of pop music it sounded when I said: 'Poul is dead.'

Willumsen's octopus eyes opened wide. Now he saw the pistol. And clearly recognised it.

'I had to go back down into Huken again,' I said. 'The Jaguar is lying on top of the Cadillac, both of them roof-down. Both squashed flat, looks like a fucking veteran-car sandwich. And what's left of the Dane is oozing out of the seat belt, like a fucking pork sausage.'

Willumsen swallowed.

I waved the gun. 'I found it trapped between the gearstick and the roof, had to kick it loose.'

'What do you want, Roy?'

'I want you not to kill anyone in my family, including in-laws.'

'Deal.'

'And I want us to cancel Carl's debt to you. Plus, you agree to make us a new loan of the same amount.'

'I can't do that, Roy.'

'I've seen Carl's copy of the loan contract that the two of you signed. We tear up yours and his here and now and sign the agreement for a new loan.'

'It won't work, Roy, the contract is at my lawyer's office. And as I'm sure Carl told you, it was signed there in the presence of witnesses, so it won't disappear just like that.'

'When I say "tear up" I'm speaking figuratively. Here's a loan contract that replaces the previous one.'

I lit the bedside lamp with my free hand, pulled out two sheets of A4 paper from my inside pocket and laid them on the duvet in front of Willumsen. 'It says here that the loan is to be written down from thirty million to a much lower sum. In fact, two kroner. It also says that the background to the writing down of the loan is that you personally advised Carl to cut out the insurance costs for the hotel, and that you therefore consider yourself equally to blame for the situation in which Carl finds himself. In short, his misfortune is your misfortune. In addition you're making him a new loan of thirty million.'

Willumsen shook his head vigorously. 'You don't understand. I don't **have** that much money. I borrowed to be able to make the loan to Carl. It'll break me if I don't get it back.' He sounded almost tearful as he went on. 'Everyone thinks I'm raking it in now that the villagers are spending so much money. But they all go to Kongsberg and Notodden and buy **new** cars, Roy. They don't want to be seen in a used car bought from me.'

The double chins on the collar of the striped pyjama jacket quivered lightly.

'But all the same, you're going to sign,' I said, handing him the pen I'd brought with me.

I saw his gaze drift down the page. Then he looked enquiringly up at me.

'We'll take care of witnesses and dates after you've signed,' I said.

'No,' said Willumsen.

'No . . . to?'

'I'm not signing. I'm not afraid to die.'

'Maybe not. But you are afraid of going bankrupt?'

Willumsen nodded mutely. He gave a brief laugh. 'Remember the last time we were in this situation, Roy? And I said the cancer had come back? I lied. But now it is back. I have a limited amount of time left. That's why I can't write off such a large debt, and why I certainly can't lend any more. I want to leave a healthy business to my wife and my other heirs. That's all that matters now.'

I nodded slowly, and for a long time, so that he would realise that I had thought this all the way through. 'That's a shame,' I said. 'A real shame.'

'Yes, isn't it?' said Willumsen, handing the papers back to me, along with the addenda Carl had written during the night.

'Yes indeed,' I said, without taking the papers. Instead I took out my phone. 'Because in that case we're going to have to do something much worse.'

'Considering the treatment I've been through I'm afraid torture isn't going to have much effect on me, Roy.'

I didn't reply, tapped in 'Shannon' and opened FaceTime.

'Kill me?' Willumsen asked, his voice pointing out the obvious idiocy in killing a person you're trying to squeeze money out of.

'Not you,' I said, and looked at the display on the phone.

Shannon appeared on the screen. It was dark where she was, but light from the camera was reflected by the snow on frozen Lake Budal. She spoke, not to me but to someone behind the camera.

'OK if I take a video, Rita?'

'Of course,' I heard Rita say.

Shannon turned the phone and Rita appeared in the sharp light from the camera. She was wearing a fur coat and hat with a white bathing cap sticking out beneath it. Her breath clouded in front of her face as she jumped up and down on the spot in front of a square hole in the ice, just wide enough for someone to get into. There was an ice-saw next to the hole, and the section of ice they had cut away.

'Kill your wife,' I said, and held the screen up to Willumsen. 'I got the idea from Poul.'

I didn't doubt that Willumsen had cancer. And I saw the pain in his eyes when it dawned on him that he could lose something he thought he could never lose, that he loved perhaps even more than himself, and that his only comfort was that she would survive him, and live on for him. I felt for Willumsen right then, I really did.

'Drowning,' I said. 'An accident, of course. Your wife jumps in. Plop. And when she returns to the surface she finds the hole is no longer there. She'll feel that the ice above her is loose and realise it's the section they cut away and try to push it up. But all Shannon has to do is keep her foot on it, like a lid, because your wife has nothing to brace her feet against, just water. Cold water.'

Willumsen gave a low sob. Did it bring me pleasure? I hope not, because that would mean I'm a psychopath, and of course that's not something you want to be.

'We'll start with Rita,' I said. 'Then, if you don't sign, we go on to your other heirs. Shannon – who does not exclude the possibility that your wife was complicit in her death sentence – is highly motivated for the task.'

On the screen Rita Willumsen had undressed. She

608

was obviously freezing cold, and no wonder. Her pale skin was burled and bluish in the sharp light. I noticed she was wearing the same bathing suit as when we rowed out on the lake that summer. She didn't look older, but younger. As though time wasn't even circular but moving backwards.

I heard the scratching of pen on paper.

'There,' said Willumsen, tossing the papers and the pen onto the duvet in front of me. 'Now stop her!'

I saw Rita Willumsen move to the edge of the hole. Same pose as in the boat, as though she were about to dive.

'Not until you've signed both copies,' I said without taking my eyes from the screen. Heard Willumsen grab the papers again and write.

I checked the signatures. They looked right.

Willumsen yelled, and I looked at the screen. I hadn't heard anything like a splash. Rita was good. The loose section of ice filled the screen and we saw a small pale hand take hold of it and lift it.

'You can stop, Shannon. He's signed.'

For an instant it looked as though Shannon was going to drop the lid over the hole anyway. But then she put it down beside her, and a moment later Rita appeared in the dark water, like a seal, hair smooth and glistening around the laughing face, her breath puffing white smoke signals into the camera.

I ended the connection.

'Well then,' I said.

'Well then,' said Willumsen.

It was cold in the room, and I had gradually slipped down under the duvet. Not with my whole body, but enough of it that it wouldn't be completely wrong to say the two of us were sharing a bed.

'You're leaving now, presumably.'

'If only it were that easy,' I said.

'What do you mean?'

'It's pretty obvious what you're going to do as soon as I leave here. You'll call another enforcer or contract killer and try to wipe out the Opgard family before we deliver this document to your lawyer. Then once you realise you won't have time you'll report us to the police for blackmail and refute the validity of what you just signed. You will also, naturally, deny all knowledge of any enforcer.'

'Is that what you believe?'

'Yes it is, Willumsen. Unless you can persuade me to the contrary.'

'And if I can't?'

I shrugged. 'You could certainly try.'

Willumsen looked at me. 'Is that why you're wearing the gloves and the bathing cap?'

I didn't answer.

'So you don't leave behind any hairs or fingerprints?' he went on.

'Don't worry about that, Willumsen. Instead try to find a way for us to get this done.'

'Hm. Let's see.' Willumsen clasped his hands together at the top of his chest, where a forest of black hair peered out from his pyjamas. In the ensuing silence I could hear the traffic up on the highway. I had loved those early mornings at the service station, being there when a village awakens to a new day, when people emerge to take their appointed places in the machinery of our little society. To have the big view, to sense the invisible hand behind everything that went on, that made sure everything worked out more or less as it should.

Willumsen coughed. 'I won't be getting in touch with any other enforcer or the police because both of us have too much to lose if I do.'

'You've lost everything already,' I said. 'You've only got everything to gain. Come on, you're a used-car salesman. Persuade me.'

'Hm.'

There was silence in the room again.

'Time's running out for you, Willumsen.'

'Leap of faith,' he said in English.

'Now you're trying to sell the same dodgy car two times in a row,' I said. 'Come on. You managed to foist that Cadillac off on my father, you got Carl and me to pay what we later found out was twice what second-hand diving gear costs in Kongsberg.'

'I need more time to think of something,' said Willumsen. 'Come back in the afternoon.'

'Alas, we need to do this before I leave, and before it's light enough for people to see me leaving here.' I raised the pistol and touched it to his temple. 'I really do wish there was another way, Willumsen. I'm not a killer, and in a way I like you. Yes, I really do. But it'll

611

have to be you who shows me that other way, because I don't see it. You've got ten seconds.'

'This is so unreasonable,' said Willumsen.

'Nine,' I said. 'Is it unreasonable of me to give you the chance to argue for your own life, even though Shannon never got the chance to argue for hers? Is it unreasonable for me to deprive you of your few remaining months instead of the rest of your wife's natural life? Eight.'

'Perhaps not, but—'

'Seven.'

'I give up.'

'Six. Want me to wait till I've finished counting down, or . . . ?'

'Everyone wants to live as long as possible.'

'Five.'

'I feel like a cigar.'

'Four.'

'Let me have a cigar. Come on.'

'Three.'

'They're in the desk drawer over there, let me—'

The crack was so loud it felt as though someone had stuck a sharp object through my eardrums.

Of course, I've seen in films how shots to the head like that always result in blood cascading all over the wall. But, to tell the truth, I was surprised to see that that's actually what really does happen.

Willumsen slumped backwards in the bed with what looked like an injured expression on his face, perhaps because I had cheated him of two seconds of life. Moments later I felt the mattress underneath me getting wet, and then I smelled the shit. They don't make much out of that in films, the way all the dead person's orifices open up like sluice gates.

I pressed the pistol into Willumsen's hand and got up from the bed. When I worked at the service station in Os I used to read not just **Popular Science** but also **True Crime,** so as well as the bathing cap and gloves I'd taped my trouser legs to my socks and the sleeves of my jacket to the gloves so no bodily hairs would fall out and leave DNA traces for the police, if this ever got investigated as a murder.

I hurried down the stairs to the basement, grabbed a shovel I found down there, left the basement door unlocked and walked backwards through the garden, turning over the footprints in the snow behind me. I took the lane that slopes down towards Lake Budal, there weren't many houses there. Tossed the shovel into a waste container at the entrance to a newly built house, and only now noticing how cold my ears were and remembering the woollen hat I had in my pocket, pulled it on over the bathing cap and followed the lane to one of the small jetties. I had parked the Volvo behind the boathouses. I peered out over the ice. Standing out there were two of the three women in my life. And I'd killed the husband of one of them. Weird. The engine was still warm and the car started without difficulty. I drove to Opgard. It was seven thirty in the morning, and still pitch-dark.

*

That same afternoon the news was on national radio.

'A man was found dead in his home in Os county in Telemark. The police are treating the death as suspicious.'

The news of Willumsen's death hit the village like a sledgehammer. I think that's an appropriate image. I imagine the shock was greater than when the hotel burned down. It hit people hard now that mean, friendly, snobbish, folksy used-car salesman who had always been there was gone forever. It was bound to be something people talked about in every shop and cafe, on every street corner and within the four walls of every home. Even the ones I met who knew Willumsen's cancer had come back were ashen-faced with grief.

I slept badly the next two nights. Not because I had a guilty conscience. I'd really tried to help Willumsen save himself, but how can you, as a chess player, help your opponent once it's checkmate? It just isn't your move. No, there was another reason altogether. I had an uneasy feeling of having forgotten something. Something crucial I hadn't thought of when I planned the murder. I just couldn't put my finger on what that might be.

On the third day after Willumsen's death, two days before the funeral, I found out. Where it was I'd fucked up.

56

IT WAS ELEVEN O'CLOCK IN the morning when Kurt Olsen pulled up in front of the house.

Two other cars behind him. Oslo number plates.

'Damned slippery down on the corner there,' said Kurt, who stood grinding out a smoking cigarette with his foot when I opened the door to him. 'You making an ice rink or what?'

'No,' I said. 'We grit. It should be the council's job, but we do it.'

'We're not going to start talking about that again now,' said Kurt Olsen. 'This is Vera Martinsen and Jarle Sulesund from KRIPOS.' Behind him stood a policewoman in those black trousers and matching short jacket and a man who looked Pakistani or Indian. 'We've got a few questions for you, so let's go inside.'

'We're wondering if we might ask you some questions,' interrupted the woman, Martinsen. 'If it's convenient. And if you'll allow us to come in.' She looked at Kurt. And then at me. Smiled. Short, fair hair in a plait, broad-featured, wide shoulders. I was thinking handball or cross-country skiing. Not because you can tell by looking which sports people enjoy but because those are the most popular sports among women and you've got a better chance of getting things right if you take account of the actual statistics rather than your own overblown gut feeling. These were the kind of irrelevant wisps of thought flitting through my head as I stood there. And looking at Martinsen realised I was going to have to be at my sharpest unless I wanted to be her breakfast, as people say. But OK, we were ready too.

We entered the kitchen where Carl and Shannon were already sitting.

'We'd like to talk to all of you,' said Martinsen. 'But we'd prefer one at a time.'

'You can wait in our old room,' I said casually, with a look at Carl, realising he understood my thinking. That they would be able to hear the questions and answers, so we could be sure to be as synchronised as we had been when rehearsing the story in the event of interrogation by the police.

'Coffee?' I asked once Carl and Shannon had left.

'No thanks,' said Martinsen and Sulesund, talking over Kurt's 'yes'.

I poured a cup for Kurt.

'KRIPOS are assisting me in the investigation into Willumsen's murder,' said Kurt, and I caught Martinsen's slight roll of the eyes to Sulesund.

'Because this is hardly a suicide here, but murder.' Olsen's voice fell to a deep bass on the word 'murder'. He let it sort of linger in the air and do its job, looked at me as though to check for a reaction before continuing. 'A murder disguised as a suicide. The oldest trick in the book.'

I felt as though I'd read that very sentence in an article in **True Crime.**

'But the killer didn't fool us. Yes, Willumsen was holding the murder weapon, but he had no gunpowder residue on his hand.'

'Gunpowder residue,' I repeated, as though savouring the words.

Sulesund coughed. 'Actually a bit more than gunpowder residue. It's called GSR, short for gunshot residue. Tiny particles of barium, lead and a couple of other chemical substances from the ammunition and the weapon that attach themselves to almost everything within a half-metre radius when a shot is fired. It attaches itself to the skin and the clothes and is very difficult to get rid of. Fortunately.' He gave a quick laugh and adjusted his wire-framed spectacles. 'It's invisible, but we've brought equipment with us, fortunately.'

'Anyway,' Kurt interrupted, 'we found **nada** on Willumsen. Understand?'

'I understand,' I said.

'What's more, the basement door was open, and Rita was certain it had been locked. So our guess is that it's been jemmied. The killer also turned over the snow to hide his footprints in the garden when he left. We found the shovel – which Rita identified – in a waste container not far away.'

'Blimey,' I said.

'Yes,' said Kurt. 'And we have our suspicions as to who the perpetrator must be.'

I didn't answer.

'Aren't you curious to know?' Kurt looked at me with his idiotic X-ray-type stare.

'Of course, but you're bound by professional secrecy, aren't you?'

Kurt turned to the two KRIPOS people and gave a short laugh. 'This is a murder investigation, Roy. We divulge and withhold information in accordance with how it helps our inquiries.'

'Ah, I see.'

'Dealing with a murder as professionally executed as the one we're dealing with here, our focus of interest has become a car. More precisely a fairly old, Danish-registered Jaguar that has been observed in the area, and which I suspect belongs to a professional enforcer.'

The one we're dealing with here. Our focus of interest. Christ, he made it sound like he was up

618

to his neck in murder cases. And that suspicion involving the enforcer was obviously not his own, it was something the villagers had been talking about for years.

'So we've been in touch with the Danish police and sent them the weapon and the projectile. They've found a match with a nine-year-old murder in Århus. That case was never solved, but one of the suspects was the owner of a vintage white E-Type Jaguar. His name is Poul Hansen, and it's an established fact that he operates as an enforcer.' Kurt turned to the KRIPOS investigators. 'He owns a Jaguar, but he's too tight-fisted to get rid of the murder weapon. How Danish is that?' he said with a grin.

'Would have thought that was more typically Swedish,' said Martinsen expressionlessly.

'Or Icelandic,' said Sulesund.

Kurt turned back to me. 'Have you seen this Jaguar around lately, Roy?' he said it casually. Too casually. So casually I realised it was a trick; this was where he was hoping to lure me out onto thin ice, get me to make a mistake. They knew more than they were letting on. But not so much more that they had to try to trick me, ergo they were missing something. Obviously, I wanted most of all to tell them I hadn't seen the car, hear them say thanks and leave; but that would leave us trapped. Because there was a reason they were here. And that reason was the Jaguar. I would have to watch myself now, and the one I instinctively knew I had to be most wary of was the woman, Martinsen.

'I saw that Jaguar,' I said. 'It was here.'

'Here?' said Martinsen quietly and placed her phone on the table in front of me. 'Do you mind if we record this, Opgard? Just to make sure we don't forget anything you tell us.'

'By all means,' I said. Her courteous way of speaking was infectious.

'So,' said Kurt, putting his elbows on the table and leaning closer. 'What was Poul Hansen doing here?'

'He was trying to get money out of Carl.'

'Oh?' said Kurt, staring at me. But I saw Martinsen's gaze had started to flit around the room, as though she were looking for something. Something other than what was happening right in front of them, and which anyway they had on tape. Her gaze fastened on the stovepipe.

'He said that this time he wasn't in Os to extort money for Willumsen but **from** Willumsen,' I said. 'He seemed pretty angry, to put it mildly. Apparently Willumsen owed him money for several jobs. And now Willumsen told him he was flat broke.'

'Willumsen **flat broke**?'

'When the hotel burned down, Willumsen decided to cancel Carl's debt from the loan he'd given him. It was a lot of money, but Willumsen felt he was partially to blame for the decisions that were taken that led to Carl's losses being even greater once the hotel burned down.'

I had to tread carefully here. Those of us at Opgard were still the only ones in the village who knew that the hotel hadn't been insured for fire. The only ones living, at any rate. But I was telling the truth all right. The documents regarding the cancellation of the first loan and the provision for a new loan were now with Willumsen's lawyer, and they would hold up in court.

'In addition,' I said, 'Willumsen had cancer and didn't have long left. So he probably wanted his legacy to be that he generously contributed to the building of the hotel and didn't let financial complications arising out of the fire stop him.'

'Wait,' said Kurt. 'Was it Carl or the company that owns the hotel who owed Willumsen money?'

'That's complicated,' I said. 'You'll have to take it up with Carl.'

'We aren't Economic and Environment Crime, so please continue,' said Martinsen. 'Poul Hansen demanded that Carl pay him the money Willumsen owed him?'

'Yes. But of course we had no money, only the cancelled debt. And we still hadn't received the new loan – that won't be until another two weeks from now.'

'Jesus,' said Kurt flatly.

'So then what did Poul Hansen do?' asked Martinsen.

'He gave up and drove away.'

'When was this?' Her questions were delivered rapidly and were intended to speed up the tempo of the answers too, we're easily conditioned that way. I wet my lips.

'Was it before or after Willumsen's murder?' Kurt blurted out, losing patience. And when Martinsen turned to Kurt, I saw for the first time something else beside the calm and the smile in her face. If looks could kill, Kurt would've been dead. Because now I knew what they were after. I'd been shown where the dog's body was buried, as people say. The time-line. They knew something about Poul Hansen's visit up here.

In the story we'd worked out, Poul Hansen hadn't come up to Opgard the day before the murder, as he had in reality, but directly **after** the murder, to demand from Carl the money he hadn't managed to shake out of Willumsen. Because only a sequence of events like that could explain that Poul Hansen had both killed Willumsen **and** ended up along with his Jaguar in Huken. But Kurt's outburst had been the raven's call I needed. I made a decision and hoped that Carl and Shannon were listening hard at the stovepipe hole up-stairs and hearing how I had changed our story.

'That was the day before Willumsen was killed,' I said.

Martinsen and Kurt exchanged looks.

'That more or less fits with the time when Simon Nergard told us he saw an E-Type Jaguar pass his farm on the road that leads up here, and only up here,' said Martinsen.

'And to the hotel site,' I said.

'But he came here?'

'Yes.'

'Then it's odd that Simon Nergard says he never saw the Jaguar come down again.'

I shrugged.

'But of course, the Jaguar is white, and there's a lot of snow,' said Martinsen. 'Right?'

'Could be,' I said.

'Help us out, you who know about cars; why did Simon Nergard neither see nor hear it?'

She was good. And she didn't give up.

'A sports job like that is easily heard when it's climbing hills in low gear, isn't it? But not when it's coming back down, not if he lets the car freewheel. Think that's what Hansen did? Rolled past Nergard in silence?'

'No,' I said. 'You have to brake too much on the corners, and the Jaguar is heavy. And people who drive cars like that don't coast, they aren't the types to worry about petrol. On the contrary, they **like** to hear their engines. So if I have to suggest something, it would be that Simon Nergard was having a shit in his toilet.'

I employed the ensuing silence to scratch my ear.

Then Martinsen gave me an almost imperceptible nod, like one boxer to another who has seen through a feint. The feint was to get me to be a little too keen to help explain why Simon hadn't seen the Jaguar, and in doing so reveal how important it was for me that they believe the Jaguar had driven by Nergard and back down into the village. But why? Martinsen checked that her phone was still recording like it should be, and Kurt quickly interjected:

'When you found out Willumsen was dead, why didn't you say anything about the enforcer?'

'Because everybody said it was suicide,' I said.

'And you didn't find it strange that it happened at exactly the same time as you knew his life was being threatened?'

'The enforcer didn't say anything about threatening anyone's life. Willumsen had cancer, and the alternative was maybe months of pain. I saw my uncle Bernard die of cancer, so no, I didn't think it was so strange.'

Kurt took a breath and was about to continue, but Martinsen indicated with her hand that he'd said enough, and he kept his mouth shut.

'And Poul Hansen hasn't been here since?' asked Martinsen.

'No,' I said.

I saw how her gaze followed mine, over to the stovepipe.

'Sure?'

'Yes.'

They had more, but what? What? I saw Kurt unconsciously fiddling with the leather mobile phone case attached to his belt. It even looked like the same type his father had used. The mobile phone. There it was again. The thing that had kept me awake, that I had forgotten, the flaw I didn't see.

'Because—' Martinsen began, and at that moment I knew.

'Actually, no,' I interrupted, and gave her what I hoped looked like an embarrassed smile. 'On the morning of Willumsen's death, I actually woke to the sound of a Jaguar. The car, that is. Not the creature.'

Martinsen stopped speaking and looked at me expressionlessly. 'Continue,' she said.

'It has a very distinctive sound in the low gears. It snarls, like one of the big cats, like a . . . well, a Jaguar, I guess.'

Martinsen looked impatient, but I took my time. I knew that in this minefield, the slightest false step would be punished without mercy.

'But by the time I was properly awake, the sound had gone. I pulled the curtain open and half expected to see the Jaguar. It was still dark out, but there was no car there, I could see that. So I thought I'd dreamt it.'

Again Martinsen and Kurt exchanged glances. The Sulesund guy clearly didn't take part in this aspect of the investigation. He was what they call a crime-scene technician, so what he was doing here I still didn't know. But I had a feeling that I would soon find out. Well, at least I'd given them a story that held water even **if** they found the Jaguar down in Huken. Then it would look as though Poul Hansen had driven up here the morning after the murder, maybe to make another attempt to extort money from us, his summer tyres had lost their grip on Geitesvingen and he'd slid over the edge and down into Huken unnoticed by anybody. I took a breath. Wondered whether to get up for more coffee, felt I needed it, but stayed seated.

'The reason we're asking is that we spent some time tracing a mobile phone number for Hansen,' said

625

Martinsen. 'Presumably on account of his occupation, he didn't have a phone registered in his own name. But we checked the base stations round here and they had registered signals from only one phone with this Danish number over the last few days. When we looked at which base stations had received signals from this Danish number, they coincided with witness observations of the Jaguar. What's odd is that if we look at the period around the time of the murder, that is, from roughly the point at which he visited you, the phone has remained within the same, very limited base-station area. **This one.**' Martinsen described a circle in the air with her index finger. 'And there is no one else but you Opgards living up here. How do you explain that?'

626

57

THE KRIPOS WOMAN — SHE PROBABLY HAD a more formal title – had finally come to the point. The mobile phone. Of course the Dane had a mobile phone. I had quite simply neglected to think about it when we made the plan, and now Martinsen had traced his phone to a small area in the vicinity of our farm. Just like the time with Sigmund Olsen's phone. How the hell could I have made the same mistake twice? Now they had established the enforcer's phone had been somewhere near Opgard before, during and following the murder of Willum Willumsen.

'Well,' said Martinsen and repeated herself: 'How do you explain that?'

It was like one of those video games where a load

627

of objects come flying towards you at different speeds and in different patterns, and you **know** it's just a question of time before you crash into at least one of them and then it's game over. It takes quite a bit to get me worried, but now my back was sweating. I shrugged my shoulders and tried desperately to look relaxed: 'How do **you** explain it?'

Martinsen seemed to take my question as rhetorical, as people say, ignored it and for the first time leaned forward in her chair. 'Did Poul Hansen never leave here after he came? Did he spend the night here? Because no one else we've spoken to has put him up, no boarding house or anyone else, and the heater in that old Jaguar isn't much good, so it would have been too cold to sleep in his car that night.'

'Then he probably booked in at the hotel,' I said.

'The hotel?'

'A joke. I mean, he drove up to the ruins and let himself into one of the workers' cabins, because of course they're unoccupied at the moment. If he's so good at jemmying locks he'd manage that easy enough.'

'But the mobile phone shows—'

'The hotel site is just over the hill here,' I said. 'In the same base-station area as us, isn't that right, Kurt? Because you once came up here looking for a mobile phone.'

Kurt Olsen sucked his moustache with something that looked like hatred in his eyes. Turned to the two KRIPOS investigators and gave a quick nod.

'What that means then,' said Martinsen without

628

taking her eyes off me, 'is that he left his phone behind in this workers' cabin when he left to kill Willumsen. And that it's still up there. Can you call up some reserves, Olsen? Looks as though we might need a search warrant for these cabins, and this sounds like a lot of searching.'

'Good luck,' I said, and stood up.

'Oh, we're not quite finished yet,' said Kurt.

'All right then,' I said, and sat down again.

Kurt wriggled in his chair, as though to show he was sort of making himself even more comfortable. 'When we asked Rita if Poul Hansen might conceivably have had a key to the basement door she said no. But then I saw her face twitch, and I've been a policeman long enough to be able to read faces **just a little bit,** so I pressed her on it, and she admitted that at one time you had been given such a key, Roy.'

'OK,' was all I said. I was tired.

Kurt was forwards on his elbows again. 'So the question is, did you give that key to Poul Hansen? Or if you let yourself in at Willumsen's the morning he died.'

I had to stifle a yawn. Not because I was tired, but because the brain needed more oxygen I suppose. 'What in the world makes you think something like that?'

'We're just asking.'

'Why would I kill Willumsen?'

Kurt sucked on his moustache and looked at Martinsen, who gave him the OK to continue.

'Grete Smitt once told me that you and Rita

Willumsen had a thing going up at the Willumsen cabin. And when I confronted Rita Willumsen with this after she'd told me about the basement key she admitted it.'

'So what?'

'So what? Sex and jealousy. Those are the two most common motives for murder in every developed nation in the world.'

That was straight out of **True Crime** too unless I was very much mistaken. I could no longer stifle that yawn. 'No,' I said, my trap wide open. 'Of course I didn't kill Willumsen.'

'No,' said Kurt. 'Because, of course, you've just told us you were snoring away in bed up here at the time at which Willumsen was killed, meaning between six thirty and seven thirty in the morning?'

Kurt fiddled with his mobile phone holder again. It was like having a prompt. And now I got it; they'd checked the movements on my mobile phone too.

'No, I got up,' I said. 'Then I drove down to one of the jetties on Lake Budal.'

'Yes, we have a witness who thinks they saw a Volvo like yours come driving from up that way just before eight o'clock. What were you doing there?'

'I went to spy on the bathing nymphs.'

'Sorry?'

'After I woke up and thought I'd heard the Jaguar I remembered that Shannon and Rita were going ice-bathing, but I didn't know exactly where. So I guessed it would be somewhere on a straight line between Willumsen's house and the lake. Parked at one of the boathouses and looked for them, but it was too dark and I couldn't locate them.'

I saw Kurt's face sort of implode, like when the air goes out of a beach ball.

'Is there anything else?' I asked.

'Just to be on the safe side we're going to check your hand for GSR,' said Martinsen, still pretty much expressionless, although her body language had changed. She'd turned off that air of tense, hyper-sensitive awareness, something you maybe need to have done martial arts or street-fighting to notice. Perhaps she didn't even realise it herself, but some-where inside she had concluded that I was not the enemy, and now she eased off almost imperceptibly.

Enter the crime-scene technician who opened his bag. He took out a laptop and something that looked like a hairdryer. 'XRF analyser,' he said and opened the laptop. 'I just need to scan your skin and we'll get the result immediately. First I just need to connect it to the analysis software.'

'OK. In the meantime shall I pop upstairs and fetch Carl and Shannon, so you can talk to them too?'

'So you can scrub your hands first?' asked Kurt Olsen.

'Thanks, but we don't need to talk to them,' said Martinsen. 'We've got what we need for the time being.'

'I'm ready now,' said Sulesund.

I rolled up my shirtsleeves, held my hands up in front of him and he scanned me as though I was an item from my service station shop.

Sulesund connected the hairdryer to the laptop with a USB cable and typed. I saw that Kurt was tensely scrutinising the technician's face. I felt Martinsen's gaze on my own as I let it glide out the window and thought it was a good thing I'd burned the gloves and the rest of the clothes I'd been wearing that morning. And that I should remember to wash the blood-stained shirt I'd been wearing on New Year's Eve so that I could wear it at the funeral tomorrow.

'He's clean,' said Sulesund.

I seemed to hear Kurt Olsen's silent curse.

'Well,' said Martinsen as she stood up. 'Thanks for your cooperation, Opgard. I hope you didn't find this too unpleasant. But we need to be a little tougher in cases of murder, you know.'

'You're just doing your job,' I said, and rolled down my shirtsleeve. 'And that's all there is to it. And . . .' I pushed in a wedge of moist snuff, looked at Kurt Olsen and added, quite truthfully: '. . . I really do hope you find Poul Hansen.'

58

IN A STRANGE WAY WILLUM Willumsen's funeral felt like the funeral of the Os Spa and Mountain Hotel.

It began with Jo Aas's valedictory speech.

'Lead us not into temptation, but deliver us from evil,' he said. And went on to say how, one brick at a time, the departed had built up a company that prospered because it played a natural role in local society. It was and remained a response to a real need felt by those of us living here, said Aas.

'We all knew Willum Willumsen as a hard but fair businessman. He made money where there was money to be made, and never made a deal he didn't think would end up being to his advantage. But he kept to the deals he made, even when the wind changed and profit turned to loss. Always. And that is the kind of blind integrity that defines a man, that is the ultimate proof he has backbone.'

At this point Jo Aas's gaze was fastened on Carl, who was sitting next to me on the second bench of a packed Os church.

'Unfortunately, it seems to me that not all of to-day's businessmen here in the village live up to Willum's standards.'

I didn't look at Carl, but it was as though I could feel the heat from the blush of shame burning in his face.

I'm guessing that Jo Aas chose that particular oc-casion for the character assassination of my little brother because he knew it was the best platform for what he wanted to say. And he wanted to say it be-cause the same thing still drove him: he wanted to set the agenda. A couple of days earlier, Dan Krane had written a leader on current and former council leaders in which he had described Jo Aas as a politi-cian whose outstanding talent was to have an ear to the ground and understand what he heard, and then adapt his responses in such a way as to make them seem in some magical way like a compromise of the views of all involved parties. It meant his sugges-tions were always accepted, which in turn created the impression of someone who was a powerful leader. Whereas in reality he had either simply adapted to his audience, or else merely gone with the flow. 'Is it the dog wagging its tail, or the tail wagging the dog?' wrote Dan Krane.

Of course, a lively discussion had ensued. Because how dare that cocky newcomer attack his own father-in-law, their beloved old council chairman? There were numerous responses both in print and online, to which Dan Krane replied that he had not been criticising Jo Aas. Because wasn't it the democratic ideal that the people should be represented, and could there be a more genuinely democratic representative than a politician who gauged the mood of the people, and adapted his responses accordingly? And, in a way, Krane's point was now being illustrated, because what we heard from the pulpit wasn't Jo Aas but an echo from the whole village, communicated via the man who always interpreted and then communicated what they, the majority, thought. Because even for those directly concerned, that's to say us, up at Opgard, it had been impossible not to know that people were beginning to talk. Maybe news had leaked that Carl had lost control of the hotel project after he had fired the main contractors. That Carl was struggling with the financing, that he had taken out personal loans in secret, and that the accounts did not reveal the true story. That the fire **might** have been a deathblow. For the time being it might be the case that there was nothing concrete to go on, but it was the sum of small things known by certain persons here and there which together made up a picture no one was happy with. But then Carl had been so optimistic in the autumn, loudly proclaiming that things were back on track, and that was of course what the villagers **wanted** to hear, now that they had already invested in the project.

And now Willum Willumsen had been killed by an enforcer, if the journalists who had invaded the village were to be believed, and what did that mean? Some thought he must have owed someone a great deal of money. According to rumour, Willumsen had been into the hotel more heavily than all the rest of them, that he'd handed out big loans. So was this killing the first crack in the foundations, a warning that the whole thing was about to go to hell? Had Carl Opgard, that slick, preacher-tongued charmer, come back home and led them all a merry dance with his castle in the air?

As we left the church, I saw Mari Aas – the usual warm, dark glow of her face now pale against the black coat – arm in arm with her father.

Dan Krane was nowhere to be seen.

The coffin, carried out by relatives wearing suits too big for them, was loaded into the hearse and driven off as we stood there, sort of devout-looking, and watched it.

'They're not cremating him now,' said a voice quietly. It was Grete Smitt who suddenly appeared at my side. 'The police want to hang on to the body as long as possible in case something crops up they need to check. They've just lent the body for the funeral. Now it's going straight back to the freezer.'

I continued to watch the hearse, driving so slowly it looked as though it was standing still, as the white smoke billowed from the exhaust. When at last it vanished round the corner I turned to where Grete had been standing. She was gone.

The queue of those wishing to offer their condolences to Rita Willumsen was long, and I wasn't at all sure my face was something she wanted to see right then, so I walked off and got into the driver's seat of the Cadillac and waited.

A besuited Anton Moe and wife passed in front of the car. Neither one looked up.

'Jesus Christ,' said Carl once he and Shannon were seated and I started the car. 'Know what Rita Willumsen just did?'

'What?' I said as we drove out of the car park.

'As I was offering my condolences she pulled me towards her and I thought she was going to give me a hug, and then she whispered "murderer" in my ear.'

'Murderer? Are you sure you heard right?'

'Yes. She smiled. Grin and bear it, all that stuff. But, I mean to say . . .'

'Murderer.'

'Yes.'

'She's probably been told by her lawyer that her husband wrote off thirty million in debt and gave you another thirty just before he died,' said Shannon.

'Does that make me a **murderer**?' Carl shouted indignantly. I knew he was upset, not because he was innocent but because the accusations were unreasonable, given how little Rita Willumsen could know. That was how Carl's brain worked. He felt Rita

Willumsen had judged him on the basis of who he was, not the facts, and that hurt him.

'It's no wonder she's suspicious,' said Shannon. 'If she knew about the debt, then she probably thinks it's strange her husband didn't tell her he'd written off such a large sum. And if she didn't know about it, then she probably thinks it stinks, that her lawyer receives the document after the murder, but signed and dated several days before it.'

In reply Carl just grunted. He obviously felt that not even such logical reasoning was any excuse for Rita's behaviour.

I looked up at the sky ahead. The forecast had been for fine weather, but now dark clouds were driving in from the west. Things change quickly in the mountains, as people say.

59

I OPENED MY EYES. IT was burning. The bunk beds and the walls around me were aflame, the fire raging at me. I jumped down onto the floor and saw long, yellow flames flaring up from the mattress. So how come I felt nothing? I looked down at myself and saw it. Saw that I was on fire too. I heard Carl's and Shannon's voices from their bedroom and ran to the door, but it was locked. I raced to the window and ripped aside the burning curtains. The glass was gone, replaced by iron bars. And there, in the snow outside, stood three figures. Pale, unmoving, just staring at me. Anton Moe. Grete Smitt. And Rita Willumsen. The fire truck came crawling from the darkness down by Geitesvingen. No siren, no lights. Dropping

639

down and down through the gears, the engine roaring louder and louder, the truck going slower and slower. And then it stopped completely and began sliding back down into the darkness from which it had emerged. A bow-legged man came rolling out of the barn. Kurt Olsen. He was wearing Dad's boxing gloves.

I opened my eyes. The room was dark, there was no fire. But the roaring was there. No, not a roar, but an engine revving furiously. It was the ghost of the Jaguar on its way up out of Huken. Then, as I grew more wide awake, I could hear it was the tractor-like sound of a Land Rover.

I pulled on my trousers and went downstairs.

'Did I wake you?'

Kurt Olsen stood on the steps, cigarette between his lips, his thumbs hooked in his belt.

'It's early,' I said. I hadn't checked the time but saw no sign of the sunrise when I turned and looked east.

'I couldn't sleep,' he said. 'We finished searching the workmen's cabins at the hotel site yesterday, and we found neither Poul Hansen, nor his car, nor any sign that they had been there. And now the base station has stopped getting signals from his phone, so either the battery's flat or he's turned off his phone. But then something occurred to me last night, and I wanted to check it as quickly as possible.'

I tried to collect my thoughts. 'Are you alone?'

'You thinking of Martinsen?' said Olsen. He gave me a grin. I had no idea what it was supposed to mean. 'Didn't see any reason to wake KRIPOS, this won't take long.'

Clattering from the steps behind me. 'What's up, Kurt?' It was Carl, drunk from sleep but irritatingly good-humoured as he always was in the morning. 'Dawn attack?'

'Good morning, Carl. Roy, last time we were here you said you were woken the morning Willumsen died by what you thought was a Jaguar. But that then the sound disappeared, and you thought it must have been a dream.'

'Yeah?'

'I remembered how slippery it was on Geitesvingen when we were here. And that it **might** – and this is just my brain that can't stop looking for possible solutions to this riddle – it **might** be the case that it wasn't a dream, that it was the Jaguar you heard, but that it just didn't manage that last bend, started to skid backwards, and then . . .'

Olsen paused deliberately as he tapped the ash off his cigarette.

'You think . . .' I tried to look astonished. 'You think that . . .'

'I'd like to check it anyway. Ninety per cent of all detective work . . .'

'. . . involves following leads that go nowhere,' I said. '**True Crime.** I read that article too. Fascinating stuff, isn't it? Have you taken a look down into Huken?'

Kurt Olsen spat to one side of the steps and looked

dissatisfied. 'I tried. But it's dark and steep, so I need someone to secure me so I can get far enough out to have a look.'

'Sure thing,' I said. 'D'you need a torch?'

'Got a torch,' he said, put the cigarette back in the corner of his mouth and held up something black that looked like a smoked sausage.

'I'll come with you,' said Carl, and shuffled back upstairs in his slippers to get dressed.

We walked down to Geitesvingen where Olsen's Land Rover stood with its headlights on and shining out across the edge. The change in the weather had brought a rise in temperature and it was only a few degrees below zero. Kurt Olsen got a rope from the back of the car and tied it around his waist.

'If one of you holds this,' he said, giving the end to Carl and making his way carefully forward to the edge of the road, where there were a couple of metres of steep, stony slope before the edge and where the rock face disappeared from view below. And while he was standing there, bending forward, his back to us, Carl leaned towards my ear.

'He'll find the body,' he said in a whispered hiss. 'And he'll realise something's wrong.' Carl's face glistened with sweat, and I could hear the panic in his voice. 'We need to . . .' Carl nodded towards Olsen's back.

'Think straight!' I hissed as quietly as I could. 'He **will** find the body, and there **is** nothing wrong.'

Just then Kurt Olsen turned towards us. In the dark his cigarette glowed like a brake light.

'Maybe best to fasten the end to the bumper bar,' he said. 'We could all find ourselves slipping here.'

I took the end from Carl, tied it in a bowline around the bumper, nodded to Kurt that it was secure and gave Carl a discreet warning look.

Kurt edged down the slope and leaned over as I held the rope taut. He switched on his torch and directed the beam downwards.

'See anything?' I asked.

'Oh yeah,' replied Kurt Olsen.

Low-lying steely-blue clouds filtered the flat light as the KRIPOS people lowered Sulesund and two colleagues down into Huken. Sulesund was wearing a quilted suit and had his hairdryer with him. Martinsen stood there with arms folded, observing the whole business.

'You got here quickly,' I said.

'They're forecasting snow,' she said. 'Crime scenes with a metre of snow on top are hard work.'

'You do know it's reckoned to be dangerous down there?'

'Olsen said so, but you don't often get loose rocks when it's below freezing,' she said. 'The water in the mountain expands when it freezes, forces open the space it needs, but acts like glue. It's when it melts the stones fall.'

She sounded like she knew what she was talking about.

'OK, we're down now,' said Sulesund's voice over her walkie-talkie. 'Over.'

'We await with excitement. Over.'

We waited.

'Isn't the walkie-talkie a bit Stone Age?' I asked. 'You could have just used your mobile phones.'

'How do you know you can get a signal down there?' she asked and looked at me.

Was she suggesting that I had just revealed I had been down there? Was there some last shred of suspicion still hanging there?

'Well,' I said, and wedged another pellet of snuff into place, 'if the base station was picking up signals from Poul Hansen after he ended up down there, surely that proves it.'

'First let's wait and see if him and his phone are there,' said Martinsen.

In response the walkie-talkie crackled. 'There's a body here,' said Sulesund. 'Squashed flat, but it's Poul Hansen. He's frozen stiff, we can forget about establishing an exact time of death.'

Martinsen spoke into the black box. 'Can you see his mobile phone there?'

'No,' said Sulesund. 'Or make that a yes, Ålgard just found it in his jacket pocket. Over.'

'Scan the body, get the mobile phone and come back up. Over.'

'Over. Over and out.'

'Is this your farm?' asked Martinsen as she fastened the walkie-talkie to her belt.

'My brother and I own it together,' I said.

'It's beautiful here.' Her gaze wandered over the

644

landscape the same way it had wandered over the kitchen the day before. I'm guessing she didn't miss much.

'You know much about how a farm is run?' I asked.

'No,' she said. 'Do you?'

'No.'

We laughed.

I pulled out my tin of snuff. Took out a pellet. Offered her the tin.

'No thanks,' she said.

'Packed it in?' I asked.

'Is it that obvious?'

'You had the look of a user when I opened the tin, yes.'

'OK, then give me one.'

'I don't want to be the person who—'

'Just one.'

I handed her the tin. 'Why isn't Kurt Olsen here?' I asked.

'Your sheriff is already at work solving new cases,' she said with a wry smile. With her index finger and extended middle finger she pressed the pellet in between the red, wet lips. 'Going through the workmen's cabins we found a Latvian, one of the builders working on the hotel.'

'I thought the cabins were closed until work started up again.'

'Yes they are, but the Latvian wanted to save money, so instead of going home for Christmas he was living illegally in the cabin. The first thing he said when the police knocked on the door was: "It wasn't me who

645

started the fire." Turns out he was down in the village to see the New Year's Eve rockets and when he was going back to the hotel site just after midnight a car had passed him coming the other way. And when he got there, the hotel was ablaze. It was him who phoned in and reported the fire. Anonymously, of course. And he didn't tell the police about the car, he said, because then it would emerge that he'd been living in the workmen's cabin all through Christmas and he would have lost his job. Anyway, he'd been so blinded by the car's headlights that he wouldn't have been able to tell the police what make it was or what colour. All he had noticed was that one of the brake lights wasn't working. Anyway, Olsen's talking to him now.'

'You think this has anything to do with Willumsen's murder?'

Martinsen shrugged. 'We don't exclude the possibility.'

'And the Latvian?'

'He's innocent,' she said. There was something different about her now, a calmness. The nicotine calm.

I nodded. 'In general you're fairly sure about who is guilty and who is innocent, aren't you?'

'Fairly,' she said. She was about to say something else, but at that moment Sulesund's face appeared above the edge of the precipice. He'd used a jumar to climb up the rope, and now he freed himself from the climbing harness and got into the passenger seat of the KRIPOS vehicle. He connected the hairdryer to the laptop and entered a command.

'GSR!' he shouted through the open door. 'No doubt about it, Poul had fired a weapon not long before he died. And so far it matches the weapon from the crime scene.'

'Can you tell that too?' I asked Martinsen.

'We can at least see if it's the same kind of ammunition and, if we're lucky, if the GSR traces on Poul Hansen could have come from that type of pistol. But the chain of events is pretty clear now.'

'And what is that?'

'Poul Hansen shot Willum Willumsen in his bedroom in the morning, and then drove up here to try to get the money Willumsen owed him from Carl, but then the Jaguar skidded on the ice on Geitesvingen, and —' Abruptly she stopped. Smiled. 'Your sheriff probably wouldn't like it if he knew how closely you were following our investigation, Opgard.'

'I promise not to tell.'

She laughed. 'All the same, for the good of our working relationship, I think it's best if I say you were inside the house for most of the time we were here.'

'Fair enough,' I said, zipping up my jacket. 'It sounds anyway as if the case is cleared.'

She pressed her lips together as though to say we don't answer questions like that, but at the same time blinked a 'yes' with both eyes.

'How about a coffee?' I asked.

I spotted a momentary confusion in her eyes.

'Because it **is** cold,' I said. 'I can bring a pot out for you.'

'Thanks, but we've got our own,' she said.

'Of course,' I said, turned, and left. I had the distinct feeling she was watching me. Not that she was necessarily interested, but of course you check out the arses you can. I thought of the hole in that zinc bucket and how close that bullet from the Dane had been to hitting me in the head. Professionally done, considering the car was in motion. And a good thing the drop had been so long there was no longer any front windscreen with a bullet hole in it to cause confusion about when and where Poul Hansen had fired that shot.

'Well?' said Carl, who was sitting at the kitchen table with Shannon.

'I'll say the same as Kurt Olsen,' I answered, heading for the stove. **'Oh yeah.'**

60

AT THREE O'CLOCK IT STARTED to snow.

'Look,' said Shannon, staring out through the thin glass windows in the winter garden. 'Everything is disappearing.'

Large, shaggy flakes of snow were drifting down to lie like a feathered quilt across the landscape, and she was right, a couple of hours later everything was gone.

'I'm driving to Kristiansand this evening,' I said. 'It seems the holiday took a few people down there by surprise, and the work's been piling up.'

'Keep in touch,' said Carl.

'Yes, keep in touch,' said Shannon.

Her foot touched mine beneath the chair.

*

It had temporarily stopped snowing as I left Opgard at seven o'clock. I thought I'd better fill up with petrol, turned in at the station and saw Julie disappearing through the new sliding doors. There was only one car parked on the old boy racer hangout, Alex's souped-up Ford Granada. I pulled up beneath the bright lights of the pumps, stepped out and started to fill up. The Granada was just a few metres away and with the light from a nearby street lamp falling on the golden-brown bonnet and windscreen we could see each other clearly. He was alone in the car, Julie had gone inside to buy something, a pizza maybe. Then they'd go home and watch a film, that was the usual thing to do around here when you started going steady. Removed from circulation, as people say. He pretended he hadn't seen me. Not until I hooked the pump nozzle inside the fuel cap opening and walked across. Then suddenly he was very busy, sitting up straight behind the wheel, pinched out a freshly lit cigarette so the sparks danced on the snow-free asphalt beneath the roof over the pumps. Started winding up his window. Maybe someone had told him he'd been lucky Roy Opgard hadn't been in the mood for a fight on New Year's Eve and mentioned a couple of stories from the old days at Årtun. His hand even crept up and locked the door on his side.

I stood next to his door and tapped on the glass with the knuckle of my index finger.

He wound the window down a couple of centimetres. 'Yes?'

'I've got a suggestion.'

'Oh?' said Alex and looked as if he reckoned what was coming was a suggestion for a rematch. And that would be a suggestion in which he had no interest at all.

'Julie's bound to have told you what happened before you came along on New Year's Eve, and that you should apologise to me. But that isn't so easy for a guy like you. I know, because I used to be that guy myself, and I'm not asking you to do this for my sake or for yours. But it's important for Julie. You're her fellah, and I'm the only boss she's had who's treated her decently.'

Alex gaped, and I realised that what I said was making sense to him.

'For this to look right I'm going to go over and finish fuelling, slowly. And when Julie comes back, you get out of the car and walk over to me, and you and I set things straight so she sees it.'

He stared at me, his mouth half open. I don't really know how smart Alex is, but when he did finally close his mouth I figured he'd realised that this would actually solve a couple of problems. In the first place, Julie would stop going on about how he wasn't man enough to dare to apologise to Roy Opgard. In the second place, it would mean he could stop looking over his shoulder and waiting for me to have my revenge.

He nodded.

'See you,' I said, and returned to the Volvo. I positioned myself behind the pump so Julie didn't see me

when she re-emerged a minute later. I heard her get
into the car, heard the door close. A few seconds later
a car door opening. And then Alex was standing in
front of me.

'Sorry,' he said, and held out his hand.

'These things happen,' I said. Over his shoulder I
saw Julie staring at us, wide-eyed, from inside the car.
'But, Alex?'

'Yeah?'

'Two things. Number one. Be kind to her. Number
two. Don't throw away lighted cigarettes when you're
parked this close to the pumps.'

He swallowed and nodded again. 'I'll pick it up,'
he said.

'No,' I said. 'I'll pick it up after you've gone. OK?'

'OK,' Alex said with his mouth. And then added a
'thanks' with his eyes.

Julie waved gaily to me as they drove by.

I got into my car and drove off. Slowly, the milder
weather had made the roads more treacherous. Passed
the county sign. I didn't look in the mirror.

PART SEVEN

61

IN THE SECOND WEEK OF January I received a summons to attend a company meeting of the Os Spa and Mountain Hotel SL. It was scheduled for the first week in February. The order of business was simple and consisted of one point: **Where do we go from here?**

The formulation opened up all sorts of possibilities. Should the hotel be scrapped? Or should it be sold to other interested parties and only the SL company be scrapped? Or should the project continue, only with a new timetable?

The meeting wasn't due to start until seven, and it was still only one as I pulled into the yard outside Opgard. A metallic white sun shone from a cloudless sky, and it was higher above the mountain peaks than it had been the last time I was home. As I stepped out of the car Shannon was standing there, so beautiful that it was painful.

'I've learned to walk on these,' she said, holding up a pair of skis in delight. I had to stop myself from taking her in my arms. Only four days earlier we had shared a bed in Notodden. I could still taste her on my tongue and feel the warmth of her skin.

'She's good!' said Carl as he emerged from the house with my ski boots in his hands. 'Let's take a trip over to the hotel.'

We fetched our skis from the barn, fastened them on and set off. I realised that Carl had of course exaggerated; Shannon managed to stay on her feet most of the way, but she wasn't **good.**

'I think it's the surfing I did as a child,' she said, obviously pleased with herself. 'It helps your balance, and—' She squealed as one ski reared up in front of her and down she went on her arse in the fresh snow. Carl and I doubled over with laughter, and after a failed attempt to look offended Shannon had to start laughing too. As we helped her up I felt Carl's hand on my back, felt it give my neck a little squeeze. And his blue gaze shone on me. He looked better than he had done at Christmas. A bit thinner, movements a little quicker, the whites of his eyes a little clearer, his diction clearer too.

'Well?' said Carl, leaning on his ski poles. 'Can you see?'

All I saw was the same burnt-out ruins of the previous month.

'Can't you see it? The new hotel?'

'No.'

Carl laughed. 'Just wait. Fourteen months. I've spoken to my people, and we're going to bloody well get it done in fourteen months. In a month's time we'll be cutting the ribbon down there for the start of the new building. And it's going to be bigger than the first launch. Anna Falla has agreed to come and cut the ribbon.'

I nodded. Elected member of the Storting, leader of the Committee for Business and Industry. It was pretty big.

'And afterwards, a party for the whole village at Årtun, just like the old days.'

'Nothing can be just like the old days, Carl.'

'Wait and see. I'm asking Rod to get the old band together for a reunion.'

'You're kidding!' I laughed. Rod. That was way bigger than anyone the Storting could send.

Carl turned. 'Shannon?'

She had struggled her way up the hill behind us. 'It's **bakglatt.** I kept slipping backwards,' she said with a smile, panting. 'Great Norwegian word. Easy to glide backwards, not so easy forwards.'

'Want to show Uncle Roy how you've learned to ski downhill?' Carl pointed to a sheltered slope. The fresh snow glistened like a carpet of diamonds.

Shannon made a face at him. 'I'm not proposing to entertain you two.'

'Just imagine you're surfing at Surfer's Point back home,' he said teasingly.

She swung out at him with a ski pole and almost lost her balance again. Carl laughed.

'You going to show her how to ski?' Carl asked me.

'No,' I said, and closed my eyes, which were smarting, even though I was wearing sunglasses. 'I don't want to spoil.'

'He means he doesn't want to spoil the fresh snow,' I heard Carl say to Shannon. 'It used to drive Dad nuts. We'd come to some perfect downhill slope with untouched, powdery snow, and he'd ask Roy to go down first, because Roy's the best of us on skis, and then Roy refuses. Says it's so lovely and he doesn't want to spoil it with ski tracks.'

'I can understand that,' said Shannon.

'Not Dad,' said Carl. 'He said if you don't spoil then you won't get anywhere.'

We took off our skis, sat down on them and divided an orange into three.

'Did you know that the orange tree came from Barbados?' said Carl, squinting his eyes at me.

'That's the grapefruit tree,' said Shannon. 'And not even that is by any means certain. But then . . .' She looked at me. 'It's all the things we don't know that make history true.'

Once the orange had disappeared, Shannon said she was going to head back, so she wouldn't have to worry about keeping us waiting.

Carl and I sat watching her until she disappeared over the rise.

Then Carl heaved a heavy sigh. 'That bloody fire . . .'

'Have they found out any more about how it happened?'

'Only that someone started it, and that a rocket was put there so it would look like that was what started it. That Lithuanian . . .'

'Latvian.'

'. . . couldn't even tell them the make of the car he'd seen, so they don't exclude the possibility that he started it himself.'

'Why would he do that?'

'Pyromaniac. Or else someone paid him to do it. There are a few jealous souls in this village who hate that hotel, Roy.'

'Hate us, you mean.'

'That too.'

There was a distant howl. A dog. Someone claimed to have seen wolf tracks up here on the mountain. And even bear tracks. Not impossible, of course, only pretty unlikely. Almost nothing is impossible. It's just a question of time, and then everything happens.

'I believe him,' I said.

'The Lithuanian?'

'Not even a pyromaniac would want to go on living on the same plot of land he's scorched himself. And if he was paid to do it, why complicate it by saying he'd seen a car with a defective brake light heading down from the site? He could have said it was already on fire when he got there; or that he was asleep in the cabin, that he knew nothing about it. And let the police find out if it was the rocket or something else.'

'Not everyone thinks as logically as you, Roy.'

I wedged in another snuff pellet. 'Maybe not. Who hates you enough to burn down your hotel?'

'Let's see now. Kurt Olsen, because he's still convinced we had something to do with his father's death. Erik Nerell, after we humiliated him with those naked pictures we got him to send. Simon Nergard, because he . . . because he lives at Nergard, you beat him up, and he's always hated us.'

'What about Dan Krane?'

'No. Him and Mari are part-owners of the hotel.'

'In whose name?'

'Mari's.'

'If I know Mari, they'll have a separate ownership agreement in that house.'

'Definitely. But then Dan would never do anything to harm Mari—'

'No? Consider a man whose wife has been unfaithful to him, and you're the man she did it with. Who's been threatened, censored, humiliated by an enforcer because he wants to write something about the hotel that is critical, but true. Who's lost his friends in high places and has to mingle with people like me on New Year's Eve. That marriage was already on the rocks, and on New Year's Eve he was planning to put the final nail in the coffin with a character assassination of her father in the leader column of his paper. Would a man like that **never** harm the cause of all his misery? If he could at the same time ruin you? At Stanley's party I met a Dan Krane who'd gone to the wall.'

'Gone to the wall?'

'Do you know how scary it is to have your life threatened by someone who knows exactly the right buttons to push?'

'Sort of,' said Carl with a sidelong glance at me.

'It eats away at your soul, as people say.'

'Yeah,' said Carl quietly.

'And what happens then?'

'In the end you just can't face being scared any more.'

'Yes,' I said. 'You don't give a fuck, you'd rather die. Destroy yourself or destroy the other. Burn down, murder. Anything, not to go on being afraid. That's what going to the wall means.'

'Yes,' said Carl. 'That's the wall. And it's better on the other side of the wall, no matter what.'

We sat in silence. I heard rapid wingbeats above, a shadow crossed the snow. Grouse, maybe. I didn't look up.

'She seems happy,' I said. 'Shannon.'

'Of course,' said Carl. 'She thinks she's going to get her hotel, the way she drew it.'

'Thinks?'

Carl nodded. He seemed to collapse imperceptibly and the smile, that bright smile, was gone.

'I haven't told her yet, but the news has somehow got out that the hotel wasn't insured against fire. That it's only Willumsen's money that's kept the project afloat until now. Dan Krane's probably the source.'

'Damn him!'

'People are worried about their money. Even the board members are muttering about getting out while the going's good. The meeting this evening could be the beginning of the end, Roy.'

'What do you intend to do?'

'I've got to somehow try to turn the mood around. But after that thunderous oration Aas gave at Willumsen's funeral, and what Dan wrote, and what he's been spreading through the village, I'm not exactly wading in confidence right now.'

'People here know you,' I said. 'In the final analysis that's more important than what some newcomer of a hack journalist scribbles and babbles about. And they'll have forgotten what Aas said once they see you standing tall again. When they realise the guy from Opgard doesn't give up, not even when he's been down for the count.'

Carl looked at me. 'D'you think so?'

I gave him a punch on the shoulder. 'You know what they say. **Everybody loves a comeback kid.** Anyway, the really rough work and the costliest investments on the site are behind you now, all that's left is the actual building. It would be idiotic to give up now. You can do this, brother.'

Carl rested a hand on my shoulder. 'Thanks, Roy. Thanks for believing in me.'

'The problem is getting everyone to agree to

Shannon's original drawings. The council probably still wants trolls and timber. You need to get the investors to sanction the extra cost of the more expensive materials and solutions Shannon wants to use.'

Carl straightened up. It looked as if I'd pumped a little optimism back into him. 'Shannon and I have been thinking about that. The problem when we showed the drawings at the first investors' meeting was that we hadn't done enough work on the visual aspect of the presentation, it looked too sad and bleak. Shannon's done some drawings and sketches with completely different lighting using completely different perspectives. The biggest difference is that these are in a summer landscape, not winter. The previous time, all the concrete merged into a monotonous, colourless winter landscape, the hotel looked like an extension of the winter people round here hate, right? Now we've got a colourful landscape that borrows light and colour from the concrete, the hotel stands out against the background, it doesn't look like a bunker trying to disappear into the landscape.

'Same shit, new wrapping?' I said in English.

'And not a soul will realise that's what it is. I promise you, they're going to be beside themselves in their enthusiasm.' He was back in the saddle now, sunlight flashing off his white teeth.

'Like natives being offered glass beads.' I smiled too.

'The pearls are real enough, only this time we're giving them a little polish before we offer them.'

'That's honest enough,' I said.

'Honest enough.'

'One simply does what one must do.'

'One does,' said Carl. He turned his gaze to the west.

I heard him take a breath. Shrink a little. Had he fallen off his horse again?

'Even when you know it's very, very wrong,' said Carl.

'True enough,' I said, though I knew he was talking about something else now. My eyes followed the tracks to where Shannon had vanished.

'And yet still we go on doing it,' he said slowly and with his new, clearer diction. 'Day after day. Night after night. Committing the same sin.'

I held my breath. Of course he could well be talking about Dad. Or about himself and Mari. But unless I was mistaken, this was about Shannon. Shannon and me.

'For example . . .' said Carl. His voice was tight, and he swallowed hard. I steeled myself. 'Like when Kurt Olsen stood there looking down into Huken for the Jaguar. And I freaked out and thought here we go again, now we're going to be exposed. Exactly the same as when his father stood in the same place and looked down to see if the wheels of the Cadillac had punctures.'

I didn't respond.

'But that time you weren't there to stop me. I pushed Sigmund Olsen over, Roy.'

My mouth was as dry as a bloody rusk, but at least I was breathing again.

'But you knew that all along,' he said.

I kept my gaze fastened on the ski tracks. Moved my head slightly. Nodded.

'So why did you never let me tell you?'

I shrugged.

'You didn't want to be made an accomplice to a murder,' he said.

'You think I'm afraid of that?' I said with a twisted smile.

'Willumsen and his enforcer are something else,' said Carl. 'This was an innocent sheriff.'

'You must have pushed him hard – he landed a long way out from the vertical.'

'I made him fly.' Carl closed his eyes, maybe the sunlight was too strong. Then he opened them again. 'You already knew when I called you at the workshop, that it wasn't an accident. But you didn't ask. Because it's always easier that way. To pretend that ugliness doesn't exist. Like when Dad came into our room at night and—'

'Shut up!'

Carl shut up. Rapid wingbeats. Sounded like the same bird on its way back.

'I don't want to know, Carl. I wanted to believe you were more of a human being than me. That you weren't capable of killing in cold blood. But you're still my brother. And when you pushed him, maybe you rescued me from being accused of the murder of Mum and Dad.'

Carl made a face. He put his sunglasses back on and tossed the orange peel into the snow.

'**Everybody loves a comeback kid.** Do people say that, or is that just something you made up?'

I didn't answer, looked at my watch instead. 'They're having problems with the stocktaking at the station and asked if I could help out. See you at Årtun at seven.'

'But you'll be spending the night with us?'

'Thanks, but I'll be driving straight home after the meeting. Got to be at work early tomorrow morning.'

Despite the fact that only the participants had a vote, the meeting at Årtun was advertised as being open to all. I had arrived early, taken a seat on the back row and watched as the hall gradually filled. But whereas there had been an atmosphere of excited anticipation at the first meeting eighteen months earlier, the mood this time was very different. Dark, sombre. A lynching mood, as people say. Everyone was there by the time the meeting began. On the front row Jo and Mari Aas sitting next to Voss Gilbert. A few rows behind them, Stanley next to Dan Krane. Grete Smitt was sitting next to Simon Nergard, leaning into him and whispering something in his ear, God knows when the two of them had become such friends. Anton Moe was there with his wife. Julie and Alex. Markus had taken time off from the station – I noticed him exchanging glances with Rita Willumsen sitting two rows behind him. Erik Nerell and his wife were next to Kurt Olsen, but when Erik tried to start a conversation it was obvious Kurt wasn't in the mood for it,

666

and Erik probably regretted sitting there but could hardly get up and move now.

At precisely seven o'clock Carl stepped out onto the stage. The room fell silent. Carl looked up. And I didn't like what I saw. Now, when it was so important for him to be at his very best, to turn that tide of negativity, to part the waters like a Moses, he seemed overwhelmed by the gravity of the occasion. He seemed tired even before he started.

'Fellow inhabitants of Os,' he began. His voice sounded impotent, his gaze flitting about from place to place as though seeking eye contact but being rejected everywhere. 'We are a mountain people. We live in a place where life has traditionally been hard. Where we have had to fend for ourselves.'

I'm guessing it was a pretty unusual way to open a partners' meeting, but then most of those in the room probably didn't know any more than me about the rituals involved in partners' meetings.

'In order to survive therefore, we have had to adopt the same maxim as the one my father taught my brother and me. Do what has to be done.' His gaze met mine. And stopped its flitting. He still looked tormented, but a slight smile crossed his lips. 'So that's what we do. Every day, every time. Not because we can, but because we have to. So each time we meet adversity, each time a flock wanders over the clifftop, a crop freezes, or the village is cut off by a landslide, we find a way back out to the world again. And when the route of the main highway is changed, and there is no longer a way **in** for the world out there, then we make one. We build a mountain hotel.' His voice was sounding a little livelier now and, almost imperceptibly, he stood up straighter. 'And when the hotel burns down, and everything lies in ruins, then we look upon the scene of destruction and we despair . . .' He held up his index finger and raised his voice. '. . . for one, single day.'

His gaze moved on from me and seemed to find other places to dwell, other invitations to accept.

'When we've laid our plan, and things don't work out as expected, then we do what we have to do. We make another. So things aren't exactly as we had imagined they would be. Fine. Then let's imagine something else.' Again his gaze found mine. 'For mountain people like us there is no place for useless sentimentality, no alternative in looking backwards. As our father used to say: **kill your darlings and babies.** Let us look forwards, my friends. Together.'

There was a long, deliberate pause. Was I mistaken, or did Jo Aas just move his head? Yes, that was a nod. And as though that had been the signal he had been waiting for, Carl continued.

'Because we **are** together, whether we like it or not. Like a family, you, me, all of us here this evening are together in a fateful union from which we cannot opt out. We, the mountain people of Os, will go down together. Or we will rise together.'

The mood turned. Slowly, but I could feel it. The lynching atmosphere was gone. Still a certain cool scepticism, of course. And as was only to be expected, an as yet unarticulated demand that Carl give his answers to certain vital questions. But they liked what they were hearing. Both what he said, and the *Os* way he said it. And I realised that the uncertain opening had been deliberate. That he had taken note of what I had said. **Everybody loves a comeback kid.**

But then, just as it seemed as though he had them hooked, Carl took a step backwards from the podium and showed the palms of his hands to the gathering.

'I can't guarantee anything. The future's too uncertain for that, and my powers of prophecy too feeble. The only thing I **can** guarantee is that, as solitary individuals, we are condemned to failure. We are as the sheep that has wandered from the flock and will be eaten up or freeze to death. But together, and only together, we have at least this one, unique **possibility** of getting out of the bind we undeniably find ourselves in, as a result of the fire.'

Again he paused, standing there in the semi-darkness beyond the podium. I just had to admire him. That last sentence was a bloody rhetorical masterpiece. In that one sentence he had done three things. One: appeared honest in admitting it was a setback but putting all the blame on the fire. Two: through a sort of inspired moralism preached solidarity, at the same time as handing responsibility for doing something about the situation onto everyone sitting in front of him. Three: appeared cautious, by stressing that a newly built hotel wasn't a guaranteed solution but only a **possibility,** at the same time as he implied that it was unique, and therefore the only one.

'But if we do this right, then we'll do more than just get out of a bind,' said Carl, still from the semi-darkness.

I'm pretty sure that one of the reasons he arrived early was in order to arrange the lighting. Because when he once again moved forward into the light falling on the podium, the visual effect was as striking as his words. The man who had seemed so worn out and troubled when he entered the stage was suddenly transformed into a bullish demagogue.

'We will make the village of Os blossom,' he boomed. 'And we will do it by building a hotel that is without compromises, that is without expensive tat like trolls and timber, because we believe that modern people, in search of an authentic experience, will find themselves entering the world of the Norwegian folk tale the moment they leave the city limits. The mountain is what they want, and that is without compromises too. So we'll build a hotel that submits to the mountain, that fits in, that obeys the mountain's own inexorable rules. Concrete is the material that comes closest to the mountain's own conglomerate. We'll build it like that not just because it's cheaper, but because concrete is beautiful.'

He looked out over the gathering as though challenging them, urging them to protest. But the silence was total.

'Concrete, this concrete, **our** concrete,' he almost

sang in the chanting, hypnotising rhythm of a salvationist preacher, at the same time as he beat out the same rhythm with his forefinger on the laptop standing on the lectern, 'is like us. It is simple, it can withstand the storms of autumn, of winter, defy avalanches, lightning and thunder, extreme weather, hurricanes and New Year rockets. In a word it is a material that, like us, survives. And because it is like us, my friends, that makes it beautiful!'

This was obviously the cue for someone in charge of the projector, because at that moment music came pouring through the loudspeakers. And the hotel – the same hotel that I had seen on Shannon's very first drawings – appeared on the illuminated screen. Green forests. Sunshine. A stream. Children playing, people strolling in summer clothing. And now the hotel didn't look at all sterile but like a calm, firm canvas for the life that was drawn all around it, something permanent, like the mountain itself. It looked, quite simply, every bit as fantastic as Carl had described it.

I could see he was holding his breath. Dammit, I was holding my breath too. And then the room erupted.

Carl let the applause ring out, milking it. Stepped forward to the podium and silenced them with raised hands.

'And since you clearly like it, how about a round of applause for the architect, Shannon Alleyne Opgard?'

She emerged from the wings and into the spotlight, and once again the room erupted.

She stopped after a few steps, smiled, waved to us, laughed happily, and remained there just long enough to show us that she appreciated the response but that she didn't want to distract their attention from the village's real hero.

After she'd left, and the applause died down, Carl coughed and gripped the sides of the lectern with both hands.

'Thank you, friends. Thank you. But this meeting is about more than the appearance of the hotel. It's also about future plans, a timetable, finances, accounting and the election of representatives for the owners.'

He had them in the palm of his hand now.

He was going to tell them that work on the resurrection of the hotel would begin in two months, in April, take just fourteen months, and that the cost would rise by only about twenty per cent. And that they had made a new deal with the Swedish operator who would be running the hotel.

Sixteen months.

In sixteen months from now, Shannon and I would be out of here.

Shannon sent a message she wouldn't be coming to Notodden as arranged, that from now and until the recommencement of building work in April she, as leader of the project, had to give it her full and complete attention.

I understood.

I suffered.

I counted the days.

In the middle of March, with the rain beating down on Søm and the Varodd Bridge in the evening dark outside my window, the doorbell rang. And there she stood. Rain dripping from the red hair that lay plastered to her head. I blinked. It looked like streaks of rust or blood running across the white skin of her neck. She had a bag in her hand. And a mixture of despair and determination in her eyes.

'Can I come in?'

I stepped aside.

I only found out the next day why she'd come.

To tell me the news.

And to ask me to kill again.

62

THE SUN HAD JUST RISEN, the earth was still wet with rain from the night before, and the birdsong deafening as Shannon and I walked arm in arm through the woods.

'These are birds of passage,' I said. 'They come back earlier here in the south of the country.'

'They sound happy,' said Shannon, and laid her head against my arm. 'They've probably been longing to come home. Who was which bird again?'

'Dad was the mountain lark, Mum the wheatear. Uncle Bernard was the bunting. Carl is—'

'Don't tell me! The meadow pipit.'

'Correct.'

'And I'm the dotterel. And you're the ring ouzel.'

I nodded.

We had hardly spoken that night.

'Can we talk about it tomorrow?' Shannon had asked after I'd let her in and helped her out of her wet coat, firing off one question after another. 'I need to sleep,' she said, wrapping her arms around my waist and pressing her chin against my chest, and I felt how my shirt was soaked through. 'But first I need you.'

I had to get up early, we were expecting a big goods delivery at the station in the morning and I had to be on site. She hadn't said anything about why she'd come over breakfast either, and I hadn't asked. It was as though once I knew why, nothing would ever be the same again. So now we closed our eyes and enjoyed the brief space of time we had, the free fall before we hit the ground.

I'd told her I had to stay at the station at least until lunch before I could get someone to cover for me, but that if she came to the station with me we could go for a walk after the delivery. She had nodded, we'd made the short drive and she had stayed waiting in the car while I checked and signed off for all the pallets.

We walked north. Behind us lay the motorway, with its Saturn-rings system of entry and exit roads, ahead of us the woods which already, this early in March, had a touch of green to them. We discovered a path that led deep into the woods. I asked if Os was still deep in winter.

'It's still winter in Opgard,' she said. 'In the village they already had two fake springs.'

I laughed and kissed her hair. We had reached a tall fence that barred any further progress and sat down on a large stone by the side of the path.

'And the hotel?' I asked with a glance at my watch. 'How is that coming along?'

'The official start-up will be in two weeks, as planned. So it's going well. In a manner of speaking.'

'OK,' I said. 'Tell me what **isn't** going well.'

She straightened her back. 'That's one of the things I've come to talk to you about. An unforeseen problem came up. The engineers discovered a weakness in the ground, in the mountain itself.'

'Discovered? But Carl knows the mountain is unstable, that's the reason for the rockfalls in Huken, that's why the highway tunnel wasn't built ages ago.' I could hear how irritated I sounded. Maybe it was at the thought that when she'd taken the trouble to drive all the way to Kristiansand, it wasn't for my sake but because of her hotel.

'Carl hasn't said anything about the stability of the rock to anyone,' she said. 'Because, as you well know, he prefers to suppress anything he thinks might be a problem.'

'And?' I said impatiently.

'It can be fixed, but that'll need more money, and Carl said we don't have it, and suggested we just keep quiet about it, that it would take at least twenty years before the building started looking a bit crooked. Of course, I wouldn't accept that and I did some checking of the financial situation on my own, to see if there was room to borrow a bit more from the bank. They told me that for that they would require more security, and when I said I would talk to you and Carl to see if you were willing to offer the bank all the outlying land around Opgard as security, they told me . . .' She stopped, swallowed before continuing. '. . . told me that according to the property register, Willumsen's estate already had security in all the outlying land around Opgard. And on top of that, Carl Opgard was the sole registered owner after he bought you out in the autumn.'

I stared at her. I had to cough to get my voice to work. 'But that's not correct. There must be some mistake.'

'That's what I said too. So they showed me a print-out from the property register with both Carl's and your signatures.' She held her mobile phone up to me. And there it was. My signature. That's to say, something that **looked like** my signature. Resembled it so closely that only one person could have done it, and that was the person who had learned to copy his brother's handwriting for his essays at school.

Something dawned on me. Something Carl had said to the enforcer while they were sitting in the kitchen. **But Willumsen's got security.** And the enforcer's response: **Which he says ain't worth much without a hotel.** Willumsen, who normally took a man at his word, had not trusted Carl and demanded the land as security.

'You know what Dad called that miserable little farm of ours?'

'What?'

'The kingdom. Opgard is our kingdom, he always used to say. As though he was worried Carl and I wouldn't take owning our own land seriously enough.'

Shannon said nothing.

I coughed. 'Carl's forged my signature. He knows I would have said no to using our land as security for a loan from Willumsen, so he transferred the property to himself behind my back.'

'And now Carl owns all the land.'

'On paper, yes. I'll get it back.'

'You think so? He's had plenty of time to discreetly hand it back to you after Willumsen cancelled the debt. Why hasn't he done so?'

'He's probably been too busy.'

'Wake up, Roy. Or do I know your brother better than you do? As long as it's his name on the property register, then he owns the land. We're talking about someone who didn't hesitate to swindle his partner and friends in Canada and then run off. When I was in Toronto in the summer I found out more about what happened that time. I talked to one of his partners who was also a friend of mine. He told me Carl threatened to kill him when he said he was going to warn the investors about the size of their losses on the project, so that it could be stopped before they lost even more.'

'Carl knows what to say.'

'He called round to see this friend of ours when he was at home on his own. Carl held a gun on him,

Roy. Said he would kill him and his family if he didn't keep his mouth shut.'

'He panicked.'

'And what do you think he's doing now?'

'Carl doesn't steal from me, Shannon. I'm his brother.' I felt her hand on my arm, wanted to pull it away, but didn't. 'And he doesn't kill people,' I said, and heard how my own voice was shaking. 'Not like that. Not because of money.'

'Maybe not,' she said. 'Not because of money.'

'What do you mean?'

'He won't let me go. At least, not now.'

'Not now? What's different between now and then?'

She looked me straight in the eye. There was a groan from the trees behind us. Then she put her arms around me.

'I wish I'd never met Carl,' she whispered in my ear. 'But then I wouldn't have met you either, so I don't know. But we need a miracle. We need God to do something, Roy.'

She rested her chin on my shoulder so that we were looking in different directions, her through the fence and into the dark forest, me towards the clearing and the motorway that led out, away, to other places.

There was another groan, a shadow fell over us, and the chorus of birdsong stopped abruptly, as though a conductor had raised his baton.

'Roy . . .' whispered Shannon. She raised her chin from my shoulder.

I looked at her, saw that she was staring upwards,

with one eye wide open and one almost closed. I turned and saw four legs directly behind the fence. I followed the legs upwards. And upwards. And there at last was a body, and above it a neck. That continued upwards, parallel with the tree trunks.

A wondrous thing to behold: a giraffe.

Chomping away and looking down on us without interest. Eyelashes like Malcolm McDowell in **A Clockwork Orange.**

'I forgot to tell you, this is a zoo,' I said.

'Yes,' said Shannon as the giraffe's lips and tongue pulled at one of the thin, bare branches, making the sunlight flicker across her upturned face. 'They forgot to tell us this is a zoo.'

After our walk in the woods, Shannon and I headed back to the station.

I said she could take the Volvo and that I would call her when I was finished so she could pick me up. I had accounts to go through, but I couldn't concentrate. Carl had sold me out. Swindled me, stolen my birthright, sold it to the highest bidder. He'd allowed me to go ahead and become a killer, let me kill Willumsen to save his own skin. As usual. And still kept quiet about how he had betrayed me. Yes, **he** had betrayed **me.**

I was so angry my whole body was trembling and would not fucking stop. Finally I had to go to the toilet and throw up. And afterwards I sat there whimpering and hoped no one heard me.

What the fuck should I do?

My eye fell on the poster in front of me. I'd pinned the same one up there as I had in the staff toilet at Os. DO WHAT HAS TO BE DONE. EVERYTHING DEPENDS ON YOU. DO IT NOW.

I think I made my decision there and then. I'm pretty sure about that. But of course, it could have been later that evening. When I heard the other thing Shannon had come to Kristiansand to tell me.

63

I SAT IN SILENCE AT the kitchen table Shannon and I had carried into the living room.

She'd been to the shopping centre and made cou cou, which she explained was the national dish of Barbados. It consisted of cornmeal, bananas, tomatoes, onions and peppers. Though she had to make do with cod instead of flying fish, she was pleased to have found okra and breadfruit.

'Is anything wrong?' asked Shannon.

I shook my head. 'It looks delicious.'

'Finally food shops with a bit of choice,' she said. 'You've got the highest standard of living in the world, but you eat as though you were paupers.'

'True,' I said.

'And I think the reason you all eat so quickly is that you aren't used to food that actually tastes of something.'

'True.' I poured wine into our glasses from the bottle of white Pia Syse and head office had sent me two weeks earlier, when it became clear that the station would take third place in the ranking list. Put the bottle down on the table but didn't touch my glass.

'You're still thinking about Carl,' she said.

'Yes,' I said.

'You're asking yourself how he could betray you like this?'

I shook my head. 'I'm asking myself how I could betray him like this.'

She sighed. 'You can't decide who you fall for, Roy. You told me you mountain people fall in love with someone it makes practical sense to fall in love with, but now you see that isn't true.'

'Maybe not,' I said. 'But maybe it isn't so completely random after all.'

'No?'

'Stanley told me about some French something-or-other who believes we desire the things other people desire. That we imitate.'

'Mimetic desire,' said Shannon. 'René Girard.'

'That was it.'

'He believes it's a romantic illusion that a person can follow their heart and their own inner desires, because beyond satisfying our most basic needs we don't have any inner desires of our own. We desire

683

what we see others around us desiring. Like dogs that are not interested in a toy bone suddenly **have to** have it when they see another dog wanting it.'

I nodded. 'And like when you feel a stronger desire to own your own service station once you know other people want to own it too.'

'And architects **have to** land the job when they know they're competing with the best.'

'And the ugly, stupid brother who has to have the woman that belongs to the smart, handsome brother.'

Shannon prodded at the food in front of her. 'Are you saying your feelings for me are really about Carl?'

'No,' I said. 'I'm not saying anything. Because I don't know anything. Maybe we're as much a riddle to ourselves as we are to others.'

Shannon touched her wine glass with her fingertips. 'Isn't it sad if we can only love what others love?'

'Uncle Bernard said a lot of things seem sad if you look at them too long and too closely,' I said. 'That we ought to be blind in one eye.'

'Maybe so.'

'Shall we try being blind?' I said. 'For one night, at least.'

'Yes,' she said, struggling to smile.

I raised my glass. She raised hers.

'I love you,' I whispered.

Her smile widened, her eyes glistened like Lake Budal on a calm summer's day, and for a moment I managed to forget all the rest, and hoped only that we could have this night, and then let the nuclear bomb drop. Yes, I **wanted** a nuclear bomb to drop. Because I had – I think I remember I already had – made up my mind. And I would have preferred a nuclear bomb.

As I put my glass down I saw that Shannon hadn't drunk from hers. She stood up, leaned over the table and blew out the candles.

'Time is tight,' she said. 'Too tight not to be lying naked beside you.'

The time was eight minutes to four when Shannon again collapsed on top of me. Her sweat mingled with mine, we smelled and tasted the same. I raised my head to look at the clock on the bedside table.

'We've got three hours,' said Shannon.

I dropped back onto the pillow and fumbled for the snuffbox next to the clock.

'I love you,' she said. She had said it every time she woke up, before we made love again. And before she went back to sleep again.

'I love you, dotterel,' I said, in the same tone as hers, as though the deep meaning of these words was now so familiar to us we didn't need to add emotion, or meaning or conviction to them, just to say them was enough, chant them like a mantra, a creed we knew off by heart.

'I cried today,' I said, wedging a pellet of snuff beneath my lip.

'You probably don't do that often,' said Shannon.

'No.'

'What were you crying for?'

'You know what for. For everything.'

'Yes, but exactly what? And why today?'

I thought about it. 'I was crying for what I lost today.'

'The family property,' she said.

I gave a brief laugh. 'No, not the farm.'

'Me,' she said.

'I've never had you,' I said. 'I was crying for Carl. I lost my little brother today.'

'Of course,' Shannon whispered. 'Sorry. Sorry for being so stupid.'

Then she laid a hand on my chest. And I could feel that this was different from the ostensibly innocent touching that we both knew was a prelude to a new bout of lovemaking. And I had a premonition when she placed her hand there. It was almost as though she were trying to take hold of my heart. Or no, not take hold of, but **feel.** She was trying to feel the beating of my heart, and how it would react now when she said what she was about to say.

'I said earlier today that the hotel was just one of the things I'd come here to tell you about.'

She took a breath, and I held mine.

'I am pregnant,' she said.

I still held my breath.

'By you. Notodden.'

Even though these six words held the answers to all the questions I might conceivably have had about what had happened, an avalanche of thoughts raced through my brain, and each one of them had a question mark attached.

'The endometriosis . . .' I started.

'That makes it difficult to get pregnant, not impossible,' she said. 'I took a pregnancy test and at first I didn't believe it, but now I've been to the doctor and had it confirmed.'

I started breathing again. Stared at the ceiling.

Shannon snuggled into me. 'I thought of getting rid of it, but I can't, I don't want to. Maybe this is the one time in my life when all the planets were aligned in just such a way as to enable this body to get pregnant. But I love you, and the child is as much yours as it is mine. What do you want?'

I lay there in silence, breathing into the dark and wondering whether my heart had given her hand the answers it wanted.

'I want you to have what you want,' I said.

'Are you afraid?' she asked.

'Yes.'

'Are you happy?'

Was I happy? 'Yes.'

I could tell from her breathing that she was on the verge of crying again.

'But of course, you're very confused, and wonder what we should do now,' she said. Her voice was trembling, and she spoke quickly, as though to finish before her crying started. 'And I don't know how to answer you, Roy. I have to stay in Os until the hotel is up. You think maybe that this child is more important than a building, but . . .'

'Hush,' I said, and stroked her soft lips with my

finger. 'I know. And you're wrong. I'm not confused. I know exactly what I have to do.'

In the darkness I saw the whites of her eyes almost turned on and off as she blinked.

DO WHAT HAS TO BE DONE, I thought. EVERYTHING DEPENDS ON YOU. DO IT NOW.

As I say, I'm not completely sure whether my mind was made up back there in the staff toilet, or later, in bed with Shannon after she had told me she was carrying my child. And maybe it doesn't matter too much, maybe the question is academic, as people say.

Anyway, I leaned close to Shannon's ear and in a whisper told her what had to be done.

She nodded.

I lay awake the rest of that night.

The restart was in fourteen days' time, the invitation advertising Rod at Årtun afterwards was pinned above the kitchen worktop.

I was already beginning to count down the hours.

I suffered.

The huge black beast was moving. Cruising slowly, almost reluctantly, the gravel crunching beneath its tyres. On the fins sticking out at the back two long, narrow red lights lit up. A Cadillac DeVille. The sun had set, but behind the bend a rim of orange framed Ottertind. And a 200-metre-deep crevice in the mountain, as though split by a blow from an axe.

'You and me, Roy, we're all we've got.' That was

what Carl used to say. 'All those others we think we love, the ones we think love us, they're mirages in a desert. But you and me, we're one. We're brothers. Two brothers in a desert. If one checks out, the other one checks out too.'

Yes. And death does not part us. It brings us together.

The beast was rolling faster now. On its way towards that hell for which we are all bound, all those of us with the heart for murder.

64

RESUMPTION OF WORK ON THE project wasn't due to kick off until seven o'clock in the evening.

Nevertheless I left Kristiansand at the crack of dawn, and morning sunlight glinted on the county signpost as I drove into Os.

Apart from the dirty grey remnants lining the road after the snowploughs had done their work, the snow was gone. The ice on Lake Budal looked rotten, like sorbet. Here and there I could see surface water.

I'd called Carl a couple of days earlier and told him I was coming, but that I would be busy all day until the opening because the station at Os had been asked to show the books for the preceding five years. Spot checks, routine stuff, I had lied, I was just going to help them go through the figures from my time as boss. I didn't know how long it would take, a few hours or a couple of days, but if necessary I would sleep down at the workshop. Carl replied that was fine, that anyway he and Shannon would be busy getting things ready for the opening ceremony and the party at Årtun afterwards.

'But there is something I wanted to talk to you about,' he said. 'I can meet you down there at the station if that's easier.'

'I'll let you know if there's a window and we can have a beer at Fritt Fall,' I said.

'Coffee,' he said. 'I've dropped alcohol completely. My New Year's resolution was to be boring, and according to Shannon it's looking good so far.'

He sounded in good spirits. Laughing and joking. A man with the worst behind him.

Unlike me.

I parked the car in front of the workshop and looked up towards Opgard. In the slanting morning sunlight it looked as though the mountain was painted in gold. The open slopes were bare, but snow still lay in the shadows.

On my way into the station I noticed rubbish in the pump areas. And sure enough, Egil was behind the till inside. He was dealing with a customer, and it took me a few seconds to recognise that stooping back. Moe. The roofer. I remained standing in the doorway. Egil hadn't noticed me, and now he reached up to the shelf behind him. The shelf where the EllaOne morning-after pills were. I held my breath.

'Was that all?' asked Egil, placing a packet in front of Moe.

'Yes thanks.' Moe paid, turned and came walking towards me.

I stared at the packet in his hand.

Paracetamol.

'Roy Opgard,' he said. Stopped in front of me with a broad smile. 'God bless you.'

I didn't know what to say. I kept an eye on his hands as he put the packet of headache pills into his coat pocket, but I can read the body language of people whose intention is to harm you, and Moe's wasn't talking that language now. My first reaction as he took my hand was to pull away; maybe his relaxed manner and the unhealthy and yet mild light shining in his eyes persuaded me not to. In an almost careful way he squeezed my hand between his own.

'Thanks to you, Roy Opgard, I am back in the flock.'

'Oh?' was all I could say.

'I was a prisoner of the devil, but you freed me. Me and my family. You thrashed the devil out of me, Roy Opgard.'

I turned and followed him with my eyes. Uncle Bernard said that now and then, when you couldn't find the solution to a mechanical problem, the best thing to do was take a hammer and hit as hard as you could and the problem would be solved. Now and then. Maybe that was what had happened.

Moe got into his Nissan Datsun pickup and drove off.

'Boss,' said Egil behind me, 'are you back?'

'As you can see,' I said, and turned towards him. 'How are the sausages selling?'

It took him a moment to suspect that maybe I was only joking, and he laughed hesitantly.

At the workshop I opened the bag I had brought from Kristiansand. It contained certain car parts obtained during more than a week of searching through breakers' yards and vehicle cemeteries. Most of these lay in a sparsely populated area west of the city where for a hundred years they had been worshipping everything American – and cars in particular – as intensely as they worshipped Jesus in their meeting houses.

'Those parts there are no good,' the last car breaker had said as he looked down at the rotten brake hoses and the frayed throttle cable I had unscrewed from two of his wrecks, a Chevy El Camino and a Cadillac Eldorado. Behind him hung a gaudy picture of a long-haired guy with a shepherd's crook and a lot of sheep milling round him.

'I guess that means I get them cheap,' I said.

He closed one eye, gave me a price that made me realise you get Willumsens in other places too besides Os. I consoled myself with the thought that most of the money probably went to charity, handed over the hundreds and confirmed that I didn't need any receipt.

I picked up the throttle cable and examined it. It wasn't from a Cadillac DeVille, but it was so similar it would do. And sure enough, it was defective. Frayed so that, when fitted in the right way, it would catch when the driver put his foot down, and even if he took his foot off the pedal his speed would just keep on increasing. If he was a car mechanic he might perhaps realise what was happening, and if in addition to that he was quick and kept a cool head maybe turn off the ignition or put the car in neutral. But Carl wasn't any of those things. He would, even supposing he had the time, simply try to brake.

I picked up the rotting, punctured brake hoses. I'd removed hoses like that before. Never fitted them. I put them down next to the throttle cable.

Any car mechanic examining the wreck afterwards would tell the police the parts hadn't been sabotaged but showed signs of ordinary wear and tear, and that it was likely water had got in under the plastic collar on the accelerator cable.

I chucked the tools I would be needing into the bag, closed it and stood there, breathing heavily. It felt as though my chest was wrapping itself around my lungs.

I checked the clock. 10.15. I had good time.

According to Shannon, Carl was meeting the organisers of the party at the building site at two. After that they would be going down to Årtun to decorate the place. That would take at least two hours, probably three. Good. At the most I would need an hour to switch the parts.

And since there was no audit that gave me plenty of time.

Way too much time.

I crossed to the bed and lay down. Put my hand to the mattress where Shannon and I had lain. Looked at that licence plate from Barbados on the wall above the kitchen alcove. I'd done a bit of reading. There were over a hundred thousand vehicles on the island, a surprising number for such a small population. And the standard of living was high, the third highest in North America, they had money to spend. And everyone spoke English. It should definitely be possible to run a service station there. Or a repair shop.

I closed my eyes and turned the clock forward two years. I saw myself and Shannon on a beach with a toddler eighteen months old beneath a parasol. All three of us pale, Shannon and me with sunburnt legs. **Redlegs.**

I wound backwards and now we were just fourteen months into the future. The suitcases ready in the hall. A child wailing from the bedroom upstairs and Shannon's comforting voice. Just details left now. Turn off the electricity and the water. Nail the shutters over the windows. Gathering up the last loose threads before leaving.

The loose threads.

I checked the time again.

It wasn't important any more, but I didn't like loose threads. Didn't like rubbish in the pump area.

I should let it go. The other thing was what I had to concentrate on now. **Keep your eyes on the prize,** as Dad always said in his American English.

Rubbish in the pump area.

At eleven o'clock I stood up and went out.

'Roy!' said Stanley, rising to his feet behind the small desk in his surgery. Walked round and gave me a hug. 'Did you have to wait long?' he asked, with a nod towards the waiting room.

'Only twenty minutes,' I said. 'Your receptionist slipped me in so I won't take up much of your time.'

'Sit down. Everything all right? How's that finger?'

'Everything's fine. I've really only come to ask you something.'

'Oh really?'

'On New Year's Eve, after I left for the village square, can you remember if Dan Krane left too? And if he had a car? And if maybe he didn't show up at the square until a little later?'

Stanley shook his head.

'What about Kurt Olsen?'

'Why are you wondering about this, Roy?'

'I'll explain afterwards.'

'OK. No, neither of them left. There was such a bloody wind and we were having such a good time that we carried on sitting there drinking and talking. Until we heard the fire engines.'

I nodded slowly. So much for that theory.

'The only ones who left before midnight were you, Simon and Grete.'

'But none of us were driving.'

'No, Grete was driving – she said she'd promised

her parents she'd be with them when the clock struck twelve.'

'I see. And what kind of car does she drive?'

Stanley laughed. 'You know me, Roy. I can't tell one make of car from another. I just know that it's fairly new and it's red. Yes, actually, it's an Audi I think.'

I nodded even more slowly.

Saw in my mind's eye that red Audi A1 turning up towards Nergard on New Year's Eve. Where the only other thing besides Nergard and Opgard is the hotel site.

'Speaking of new,' Stanley exclaimed. 'I completely forgot to offer my congratulations.'

'Congratulations?' Automatically I thought of that third place on the earnings list; but then realised, of course, that news from the world of service stations is really only for the specially interested.

'You're going to be an uncle,' he said.

A couple of seconds, and then Stanley laughed even louder.

'You really are brothers! Carl reacted in exactly the same way. Went white as a sheet.'

I wasn't aware that I had turned pale, but now it felt as though my heart had stopped beating too. I pulled myself together.

'You were the one who examined Shannon?'

'How many other doctors do you see here?' said Stanley, spreading his arms out wide.

'So you told Carl he was going to be a father?'

Stanley wrinkled his brow. 'No, I'm assuming it was

Shannon who did that. But Carl and I met in the shop and I congratulated him then and mentioned a couple of things Shannon should look out for as her pregnancy advances. And he turned pale, just like you are now. Understandable really, when people come up to you like that and remind you you're going to be a dad, and all that frightening responsibility overwhelms you again. Didn't know the same thing happened with uncles, but it looks like it does.' He laughed again.

'Have you told anyone else besides Carl and me?' I asked.

'No, I'm bound by professional confidentiality.' He stopped abruptly. Put three fingers to his forehead. 'Ouch. Maybe you didn't know Shannon was pregnant? I just assumed that . . . since you and Carl are so close.'

'They probably wanted to keep it to themselves until they feel fairly sure it's going well,' I said. 'Given Shannon's history of trying to get pregnant . . .'

'Yes, but it was very unprofessional of me,' said Stanley. He looked genuinely upset.

'Don't worry about it,' I said, getting to my feet. 'If you don't tell anyone, I won't either.'

I was out of the door before Stanley could remind me that I was going to tell him why I'd asked about New Year's Eve. Out of the surgery. Into the Volvo. Sat there, staring through the windscreen.

So Carl knew Shannon was pregnant. He knew, and he hadn't confronted Shannon with it. Hadn't told me either. Did that mean he knew he wasn't the father? Did he realise what was going on? That it was me and Shannon against him. I pulled out my phone. Hesitated. Among other things, Shannon and I had planned everything in such detail so as to avoid having more phone contact than would otherwise seem natural between a brother-in-law and sister-in-law. According to **True Crime,** that's the first thing the police check, who the victim's closest relatives or other potential suspects have been in phone contact with at the time immediately preceding the murder. I made up my mind, tapped in the number.

'Now?' said the voice at the other end.

'Yes,' I said. 'I've got some free time now.'

'Fine,' said Carl. 'Fritt Fall in twenty.'

65

FRITT FALL WAS OCCUPIED BY the usual early-afternoon gang of horse-racing enthusiasts and people who keep the social security system ticking over.

'A beer,' I said to Erik Nerell.

He gave me such a cold stare. I had had him on my list of people I suspected of torching the hotel, but today that list had been reduced to one.

Heading for an empty table by the window I saw Dan Krane sitting alone with his beer at another window table. He was staring out emptily. He looked – how shall I put it? – a bit scruffy. I left him alone, and reckoned he'd show me the same courtesy.

I was halfway through my beer when Carl trotted in.

He gave me a bear hug and bought a cup of coffee,

getting the same frosty treatment at the counter as I had. I saw Dan Krane register Carl's presence, finish his beer and leave the premises with demonstratively heavy footsteps.

'Yes, I saw Dan,' said Carl before I had a chance to ask him and sat down. 'Apparently he's no longer living at the Aas place.'

I nodded slowly. 'Anything else?'

'Oh yes . . .' said Carl and took a drink of coffee. 'Excited about the owners' meeting this evening, of course. And Shannon's taking more and more of the decisions at home. Today she decided she's going to use the Cadillac up until the meeting, so I'm driving the wifemobile.' He nodded towards the Subaru out on the car park.

'The most important thing is that you arrive for the ceremony in style,' I said.

'Of course, of course,' he said and took another sip. Waited. Almost dreading things, the way it looked. Two brothers sitting there, full of dread. Lying in bunk beds, dreading the sound of the door opening.

'I think I know who torched the hotel,' I said.

Carl looked up. 'Oh?'

I saw no reason to milk it and told him straight out. 'Grete Smitt.'

Carl gave a loud laugh. 'Grete's a bit touched, Roy, but not **that** touched. And she's quietened down now. It's done her good, hooking up with Simon.'

I stared at him. 'Simon? You mean, Simon **Nergard**?'

'You didn't know that?' Carl chuckled humourlessly.

'The rumour is that Simon got her to drive him home to Nergard on New Year's Eve and she stayed over. And ever since they've been like peanut butter and jelly.'

My brain was processing this as fast as it could. Could Grete and Simon have torched the hotel **together**? I mulled it over. It tasted funny. On the other hand, a lot of things had tasted funny recently. But that wasn't something I needed to take up with Carl. In fact, I didn't actually need to take it up with anyone, because what the fuck did it matter who had done it? I cleared my throat. 'There was something you wanted to talk to me about.'

Carl looked down into his coffee cup, nodded. Looked up, checked that the six other customers were sitting far enough away, leaned forward and said in a low voice: 'Shannon is pregnant.'

'Oh wow!' I smiled, trying not to overact. 'Congratulations, brother!'

'No,' said Carl, shaking his head.

'No? Something wrong?'

The shaking turned into nodding.

'With the kid?' I asked. Even though I was lying, the very thought of there being something wrong with the child Shannon was carrying, **our** child, made me feel ill.

Carl's head went back to shaking.

'Then what?' I asked.

'It isn't me who's the . . .'

'Who's the what?'

702

His head finally stopped and he gave me a defeated, broken look.

'Not the father?'

He nodded.

'How . . . ?'

'Shannon and I haven't had sex since she came home from Toronto. I haven't been allowed to touch her. And it wasn't her who told me she was pregnant, it was Stanley. Shannon doesn't even know that I know.'

'Fucking hell,' I said.

'Yeah, fucking hell.' His heavy gaze wouldn't let go of me. 'And you know what, Roy?'

He waited, but I didn't answer.

'I think I know who it is.'

I swallowed. 'Oh?'

'Yeah. Early last autumn Shannon suddenly had to go to Notodden, see. An interview about an architect job, she said. When she came back she was absolutely frantic, for days on end. Didn't eat, didn't sleep. I thought it was because obviously, nothing had come of the architect job. When I gathered from Stanley that Shannon was pregnant, I asked myself how in the world she'd managed to meet another man. I mean, Shannon and I, we live in each other's pockets. And so I began to think differently about that trip to Notodden. Shannon tells me everything, and what she doesn't tell me, I can easily read on her. But there's been something there I haven't quite managed to get hold of. Something she's been hiding. As if she had a guilty conscience about something. And when I think back, it happened after that night away she had in Notodden. And suddenly she's taking these day trips to Notodden, says she has to go shopping. You follow?'

I had to cough to get some volume into my voice. 'I think so.'

'So the other day I asked her where she stayed when she spent the night at Notodden, and she said the Brattrein Hotel, I called to check. Sure enough, the reception said a Shannon Alleyne Opgard had booked a room there on 3 September. But when I asked who with, he said she'd booked the room just for herself.'

'He told you all this? Just like that?'

'It's just **possible** I said my name was Kurt Olsen and I was calling from the sheriff's office in Os.'

'For God's sake,' I said, and could feel the back of my shirt getting wet.

'So I asked them to go through the guest register for that particular date. And then an interesting name cropped up, Roy.'

My mouth felt dry. What the fuck had happened? Had Ralf remembered I was there and given my name? Wait, now I remember, that's right: he said he'd reserved a room for me when he saw me going into the restaurant, he'd presumed I was going to be staying there. Had he put me down as a booking and then forgotten to delete it when it turned out I didn't need a room?

'An interesting and very **familiar** name,' said Carl. I steeled myself.

'Dennis Quarry.'

I stared at Carl. 'What?'

'Dennis Quarry. The actor. The director. The American who stopped by the service station. He was staying at the hotel.'

I didn't realise I'd stopped breathing until I inhaled again. 'So what?'

'So what? He gave his autograph to Shannon at the service station, don't you remember?'

'Sure. But . . .'

'Shannon showed me the piece of paper afterwards, in the car. She laughed because he'd written his phone number and email address there too. Said he reckoned on being in Norway for quite a while. Was going to be –' Carl made quotation marks in the air with his fingers – '**directing.** I thought no more about it, and I don't think she did either. Not until after what happened between Mari and me . . .'

'You think she met him to get her revenge?'

'Isn't it obvious?'

I shrugged. 'Maybe she loves him?'

'Shannon doesn't love anyone. The only thing she loves is that hotel of hers. She needs a good hiding.'

'And I guess someone's given her that.'

It just came out of me. Carl pounded his fist on the table, and his eyes looked as if they might explode out of his skull. 'Did that bitch say that?'

'Shush,' I said, and grabbed hold of my beer glass as though it were a lifebuoy. In the ensuing silence I noticed everyone in the place had turned to look at us. Carl and I stayed quiet until we heard the conversations resume, and saw Erik Nerell bent over his mobile again.

'I saw the bruises when I was at home at Christmas,' I said in a low voice. 'She came out of the bathroom.'

I saw Carl's brain was trying to cook up an explanation. Why the hell did I have to blurt that out just when I needed him to trust me?

'Carl, I . . .'

'It's OK,' he said in a hoarse voice. 'You're right. It happened a few times after she came back from Toronto.' He breathed in so heavily I saw his ribcage rise. 'I was so stressed out by all that hotel chaos, and she kept going on at me about what happened with Mari. And when I'd had a few bevvies, sometimes I . . . sometimes I snapped. But it hasn't happened since I stopped drinking. Thanks, Roy.'

'Thanks?'

'For confronting me with that. I've been meaning to talk to you about it for a long time. I was starting to get afraid I had the same thing as Dad. That you start doing stuff you don't really want to, and then you find you can't stop, right? But I did it. I changed.'

'You're back in the flock,' I said.

'Eh?'

'Are you sure you've changed?'

'Yes, you can bet on it.'

'Or you can do it for me. In fact, why not do it for both of us while you're at it?'

He just looked at me as though it was some stupid

word game he didn't understand. And I was coming out with a lot of stuff now I didn't even understand myself.

'Anyway,' he said, and drew a hand across his face, 'I just had to talk to someone about this kid. And that someone always turns out to be you. Sorry about that.'

'Think nothing of it,' I said, and turned the knife in myself. 'I'm your brother, after all.'

'Yes, you're the one who's always there when I need someone. God, I'm so glad I have you at least.'

Carl laid his hand on top of mine. His was bigger, softer, warmer than mine, which was ice-cold.

'Always,' I said hoarsely.

He looked at his watch. 'I'll have to sort out this business with Shannon later,' he said, getting to his feet. 'And this about me not being the father, that stays between us, OK?'

'Of course,' I said. Weirdly, I almost laughed.

'Start of the new building. We'll show 'em, Roy.' He clamped his jaws together and his eyes tight into a fighting face, shook a bunched fist at me. 'The Opgard boys are gonna win.'

I smiled and raised my glass, showed I intended to stay and finish my drink.

Watched Carl as he hurried towards the door. Saw through the window as he got into the Subaru. Shannon had arranged for her to use the Cadillac today. But Carl would be driving the Cadillac to the launch up at the hotel site. Or more accurately, driving **in that direction.**

A single brake light flared as the Subaru stopped for a trailer before swinging out onto the main road.

I ordered another beer. Drank it slowly as I thought.

I thought of Shannon. Of what it is that drives us human beings. And I thought about myself. About why I had practically asked to be exposed. Told Carl that I knew he beat Shannon. Hinted that I knew he had forged my signature. Asking to be exposed so that I didn't have to go through with it. Didn't have to go on filling Huken with cars and corpses.

66

AFTER FOUR BEERS AT FRITT Fall I left the place.

The time was only one thirty, time enough to get stone-cold sober again, but I knew those beers were a sign of weakness. A flight response. A single false step would be enough to screw up the whole plan, so why drink **now**? It was probably a sign that there was a part of me that perhaps didn't want to succeed. The reptile me. No, the reptile brain didn't have anything to do with this, see, I wasn't thinking straight, I was already getting my concepts mixed up. Anyway, the **me**-me was absolutely certain of what he wanted, and that was to get what was rightfully his, whatever was left of it. And get rid of those who stood in the way and threatened the people it was my duty to defend. Because I was no longer the big brother. I was her man. And father to the child. That was my family now.

All the same, there was something that didn't add up.

I left the Volvo at the workshop, and from the centre I walked south-east on the pedestrian and cycle track that ran alongside the main road. When I reached the workshop I stood and looked across the road, to the wall of the house with the poster advertising Grete's Hair and Sun Salon.

Checked my watch again.

I just about had time; but I should have let it rest, this wasn't the time to deal with it. Maybe no time was the time to deal with it.

So God knows why I suddenly found myself there on the other side of the road, peering into the garage, at the red Audi A1 standing there.

'Hi!' Grete called from the hairdressing chair. She had her head inside the pride of the place, the 1950s salon hairdryer. 'I didn't hear the phone or the doorbell.'

'I didn't ring,' I said, and established that we were alone. The fact that she was giving herself a perm indicated that she didn't have any imminent appointments. All the same, I locked the door behind me.

'I can do you in ten minutes,' she said. 'Just need to get my own hair into shape here first. Got to look presentable yourself when you're a hairdresser, right?'

She sounded nervous. Maybe because I had arrived

with no warning. Maybe because she noticed something about me. That I hadn't just come in for a trim. Or maybe because, deep down, she had been expecting me for a long time now.

'Nice car,' I said.

'What? I can't hear so well in here.'

'Nice car! I saw it outside Stanley's on New Year's Eve, but I didn't know it was yours.'

'Oh yeah. It's been a good year for the hairdressing business. Like it's been a good year for all the businesses here.'

'Same make and same colour that passed me just before midnight when I was on my way to the square. Not many red Audis in the village, so I imagine it was you, right? But then Stanley tells me you were going home to your parents to bring in the New Year with them, and that's in the opposite direction. Besides, the car turned off towards Nergard and the road up to the hotel. Not much there, apart from Nergard. Opgard. And the hotel. And that got me to thinking . . .'

I leaned forward and looked at the scissors lying on the worktop in front of the mirror. They all looked pretty similar to me, but I guessed it must be her famous Niigata 1000 scissors that lay in the open box, almost as if they were being exhibited.

'You said to me on New Year's Eve that Shannon hates Carl, but she needs him for her hotel. Did you think that if the hotel burned down and the project was abandoned then Shannon wouldn't need Carl any more, and then you could have him?'

711

Grete Smitt studied me calmly, all trace of nervousness gone. Her forearms lay motionless on the armrests of the large, heavy chair, her head swathed in a crown of plastic and filaments. She looked like a fucking queen on the throne.

'Of course that thought occurred to me,' she said, her voice lower now. 'And you have too, Roy. That's why I suspected you of starting the fire. You disappeared some time before midnight.'

'It wasn't me,' I said.

'Well, then there's only one other person it could be,' said Grete.

My mouth felt dry. It made no fucking difference who torched the fucking hotel. There was a vague buzzing sound; I couldn't tell if it was coming from inside the hair-drying helmet or my own head.

She stopped talking when she saw I had taken the scissors out of the box. And she must have seen something in my eyes, because she raised her arms up in front of her.

'Roy, you're not going to . . .'

And I don't know. I don't fucking know what I was going to. I only know that everything burst out of me. Everything that had happened, everything that shouldn't've happened, everything that was going to happen and mustn't happen, but that there was no longer a way round. It rose up in me like shit in a blocked toilet, had been doing so for a long time now, and now it had reached the rim and was overflowing. The scissors were sharp, all that remained was to stab them into that repulsive mouth of hers, cut open those white cheeks, cut out those ugly words.

And yet I stopped.

Stopped, looked at the scissors. Japanese steel. And Dad's words about hara-kiri flitted through my brain. Because wasn't I failing here? Wasn't it me, and not Grete, who had to be removed from the body of society like a malignant tumour?

No. Both. Both of us must be punished. Burned.

I grabbed the old black flex attached to the hairdryer, opened the scissors, and cut. The sharp blades cut straight through the insulation and when the steel made contact with the copper the electric jolt almost caused me to let go. But I was prepared and managed to sustain an even pressure on the scissors without cutting completely through the flex.

'What are you doing?' Grete shrieked. 'Those are Niigata 1000 scissors! And this is a vintage hairdryer from the 1950s—'

With my free hand I grabbed her hand and her mouth shut as the circuit closed and the current began to circulate. She tried to tear herself free, but I didn't let go. I saw her body shake, the eyes roll over backwards as the sparks crackled and flashed inside the helmet. A continuous scream, at first thin and pleading, then wild and demanding, rose up from her throat. My chest was pounding, I knew there was a limit to how long the heart can withstand two hundred milliamperes, but I never fucking let go. Because Grete Smitt was where we deserved to be now, united in a circle of pain. And now I saw blue flames rising from the helmet. And even though it took all my concentration to hold on, I still noticed the smell of burning hair. I closed my eyes, squeezed with both hands, muttering speechless words, the way I had seen the preacher do when he was healing or saving souls at Årtun. Grete's screams were deafening, so loud that I could only just hear the smoke alarm that began to howl.

Then I let go and opened my eyes.

Saw Grete tear off the helmet. Saw a mixture of melting rollers and burning hair before she rushed to the hair-washing basin, turned on the hand shower and started the work of extinguishing.

I walked over to the door. In the stairwell outside I heard tumbling footsteps on their way down. Seemed like the neuropath was taking a break. I turned and looked at Grete again. She was safe. Grey smoke drifted from what remained of her perm, which turned out to be not so permanent after all. Right now it looked like a blazing outdoor grill someone had emptied a bucket of water over.

I walked out into the corridor, waited until Grete's father was far enough down the stairs to see my face properly, saw him say something, my name, perhaps, though drowned out by the howling from the smoke alarm. Then I left the salon.

An hour passed. The time was quarter past three.

I sat in the workshop and stared at the bag.

Kurt Olsen hadn't arrived, arrested me and put an end to the whole thing.

There was no way out. Time to get started.

I grabbed the bag, walked out to the Volvo and drove up to Opgard.

67

I SLID OUT FROM BENEATH the Cadillac. Shannon stood looking down at me in that cold barn, shivering in her thin, black pullover, arms folded and a worried look on her face. I said nothing, just got to my feet and dusted off my overalls.

'Well?' she said impatiently.

'It's done,' I said, and started working the jack to get the car back down to the ground.

Afterwards Shannon helped me to push the car out and over to the winter garden with its front pointing down the road towards Geitesvingen.

I looked at my watch. Quarter past four. A little later than I'd expected. I headed quickly back to the barn to fetch the tools and was putting them into the bag on the workbench when Shannon came up behind me and put her arms around me.

'We've still got the option of pulling out,' she said, and laid her cheek against my back.

'Is that what you want?'

'No.' She stroked my chest. We hadn't touched each other, hardly even looked at each other since I arrived. I'd started work on the Cadillac straight away to be certain I had time to swap the working parts for the defective ones before Carl returned from the meeting, but that wasn't the only reason we hadn't touched. There was something else. Suddenly we had become strangers. Murderers as shocked by each other as by ourselves. But that would pass. DO WHAT HAS TO BE DONE. And DO IT NOW. That was all that mattered.

'Then we'll stick to our plan,' I said.

She nodded. 'The dotterel is back,' she said. 'I saw it yesterday.'

'Already?' I said, turned and held her, framing that lovely face of hers with my rough hands and stubby fingers. 'That's good.'

'No,' she said, and shook her head with a sad smile. 'It shouldn't've come. It was lying in the snow out-side the barn. It had frozen to death.' A tear in that half-closed eye.

I pulled her close.

'Tell me again why we're doing this,' she whispered.

'We're doing it because there are only two out-comes. Because I have taken what is his. Because we are both killers.'

She nodded. 'But are we certain this is the only way?'

'Everything else is too late for me and Carl now, I've explained that to you, Shannon.'

'Yes,' she snuffled into my shirtfront. 'When this is over . . .'

'Yes,' I said. 'When this is over.'

'I think it's a boy.'

I held her for some time. But then I heard the seconds ticking and chewing again, like a countdown, a countdown to the world losing its meaning. But that's not what was going to happen. It wouldn't end now, it would begin. New life. Meaning **my** new life.

I let go of her and put the overalls and Carl's brake hoses and throttle cable in the bag. Shannon watched me.

'What if it doesn't work?' she said.

'It's not **supposed** to work,' I said, though of course I knew what she meant, and maybe she heard the ir-ritation in my voice and wondered what lay behind it. Probably understood what lay behind it. Stress. Nerves. Fear. Regret? Did **she** feel regret? Definitely. But in Kristiansand, when we'd made the plan, we had talked about that too. That doubt would come sneak-ing and whisper to us, the way it whispers in the ears of bridal couples on their wedding day. Doubt that is like water, that always finds the hole in your ceil-ing, and was now dripping down on my head like the

Chinese water torture. What Grete had said about there being only **one** person who could have set fire to the hotel. That single brake light on the Subaru that didn't work. The car noticed by the Latvian near the building site on New Year's Eve.

'The plan will work,' I said. 'There's hardly any brake fluid left in the system, and the car weighs two tons. Colossal speed. There's only one possible result.'

'But what if he realises before the corner?'

'I've never seen Carl testing brakes before he needs them,' I said calmly, repeating something I had said many times before. 'The car is on flat ground. He accelerates, reaches the slope, takes his foot off the pedal, and because it's so steep he doesn't notice that the acceleration is also due to the fact that the throttle cable is stuck and making the heavy car go even faster. Two seconds later he is on the bend and realises that his speed is much higher than it usually is here. In panic he stamps down on the brake pedal. But there's no response. Maybe he manages to pump the pedal down one more time, manages to wrench the steering wheel round, but he's got no chance.' I licked my lips, I had made the point, could have stopped there. But I went on twisting the knife. In me, in her. 'His speed's too high, the car's too heavy, the turn too sharp, even if the surface was asphalt and not gravel it wouldn't help. And then the car is in the air and he's weight-less. Commander on a spaceship with a brain running at warp speed that has time to ask itself how. Who. And why. And maybe has time to answer before he—'

719

'Enough!' screamed Shannon. She put her hands over her ears and a shudder seemed to pass through her body.

'What if . . . what if anyway he discovers there's something wrong and doesn't drive the car?'

'Then he discovers something's wrong. Naturally he'll have the car checked and the mechanic will tell him the throttle cable is frayed, the brake hoses rotten, nothing more mysterious than that. And we have to make another plan, do it some other way. That's all there is to it.'

'And if the plan works, but the police are suspicious?'

'They examine the wreck and discover the worn parts. We've been through this, Shannon. It's a good plan, OK?'

With a sob Shannon threw herself at me.

I gently extricated myself from her embrace.

'I'm going now,' I said.

'No!' she sobbed. 'Stay!'

'I'll be watching from the workshop,' I said. 'I can see Geitesvingen from there. Call me if anything goes wrong, OK?'

'Roy!' She shouted it as though this was the last time she would see me alive, as though I was drifting away from her on an open sea, like a couple of newly-weds on a sailing boat who had drunk themselves into a lovely champagne high but were now abruptly sober.

'We'll see each other later,' I said. 'Remember to call the emergency services immediately. Remember how it happened, how the car behaved, and describe it to the police exactly as it happened.'

She nodded, pulled herself together, straightened her dress. 'What . . . what d'you think they'll do?'

'After that,' I said. 'I think they'll put up that crash barrier.'

68

THE TIME WAS 18.02 AND it was just starting to get dark.

I sat by the window in the office with my binoculars trained on Geitesvingen. I had worked out in my head that when the Cadillac went over the edge it would be visible for almost exactly three-tenths of a second, so I'd need to blink quickly.

I had thought I would be less nervous once I was finished with my own bit and the rest was in Shannon's hands, but it was the other way round. Sitting here idly now I had far too much time to think through everything that could go wrong. And I kept thinking of new things. Each one of them was more unlikely than the one before, but that didn't greatly help my peace of mind.

The plan was that when it was time to leave for the building site and the cutting of the ribbon Shannon was to complain that she wasn't feeling well and had to go upstairs and lie down, that Carl would have to go alone. That if he took the Cadillac and drove to the opening ceremony, she could take the Subaru to the party at Årtun if she felt better.

I looked at my watch again. 18.03. Three-tenths of a second. Raised the binoculars again. Swept over the Smitts' window where the curtains remained in the same position as earlier in the day, found the mountain behind, then Geitesvingen. It might have already happened. It **might** already be over.

I heard the sound of a car pulling up in front of the workshop and turned the binoculars on it, but they were out of focus. I took the binoculars away from my eyes and saw that it was Kurt Olsen's Land Rover.

The engine died and he climbed out. He couldn't see me, because I had turned off the light in the room, and yet he looked directly at me, as though he knew I was sitting there. He just stood there, bow-legged, his thumbs hooked in his belt, like a cowboy calling me out to a duel. Then he walked towards the workshop door, disappeared from sight. A few moments later I heard the bell.

I sighed, stood up and opened the door.

'Good evening, sheriff. What is it this time?'

'Hello, Roy. Can I come in?'

'Right now it's—'

He pushed me to one side and walked into the workshop. Looked around as though he'd never been there before. Walked over to the shelves on which several things were standing. Fritz heavy-duty cleaner, for example.

'I'm wondering what's been going on in here, Roy.'

I froze. Had he finally worked it out? That it was here his father's body had ended up? Vanished – quite literally – in Fritz's heavy-duty cleaner?

But then I noticed that he was tapping his index finger on his temple and realised he meant what was going on inside my head.

'. . . when you set fire to Grete Smitt.'

'Is that what Grete says?' I asked.

'Not Grete, no. Her father. He saw you leaving the place while Grete was still smouldering, as he put it.'

'And what does Grete say?'

'What d'you think, Roy? That something went wrong with the hairdryer. An overload or something. That you helped her. But I don't believe it, not for one fucking moment, because the flex was almost cut in half. So my question to you now is – and give this a good fucking think before you answer – what the hell did you threaten her with that's made her lie?'

Kurt Olsen awaited a reply, alternately sucking on his moustache and puffing his cheeks out like a bullfrog.

'Are you refusing to answer, Roy?'

'No.'

'Then what do you call this?'

'Doing what you said. Having a bloody good think.'

I saw something click behind Kurt Olsen's eyes and I knew he'd lost it. He took two steps towards me, pulled his right arm back and was about to hit out. I know it because I know what people who are about to hit out look like, like sharks whose eyes roll backwards as they bite. But he stopped, something stopped him. The thought of Roy Opgard at Årtun on a Saturday night. No broken jaws or noses, just nosebleeds and teeth knocked out, so nothing to bother Sigmund Olsen with. Roy Opgard, a man who never lost his head in a fight but in a cold and calculating way humiliated those who did. So instead of striking out, a warning forefinger poked up from Kurt Olsen's clenched fist.

'I know that Grete knows things. She knows things about you, Roy Opgard. What does she know?' He took another step closer and I felt the spray of spittle on my face. 'What does she know about Willum Willumsen?'

The phone rang in my pocket, but Kurt Olsen drowned it out.

'You think I'm stupid? That I think the guy who killed Willumsen **accidentally** skidded on the ice right outside your doorway? That Willumsen, without a word to anyone, wrote off millions of kroner in debt? Because he thought he **ought to**?'

725

Was that Shannon? I had to see who had rung, I **had to.**

'Come off it, Roy. As though Willum Willumsen ever wrote off a single krone anyone owed him.'

I fished out my phone. Looked at the display. Shit.

'Yes, I know you and your brother were involved. Just like when my father disappeared. Because you're a murderer, Roy Opgard. Are and always have been!'

I nodded to Kurt, and for a moment the torrent of words halted and he opened his eyes wide as though I'd just confirmed his accusations before realising it was a signal that I was going to take the call. Then he started up again.

'If you hadn't heard witnesses coming you would have killed Grete Smitt today. You would have . . .'

I half turned my back to Kurt Olsen, stuck a finger into one ear and pressed the phone against the other. 'Yes, Carl.'

'Roy? I need help!'

It was as though the lights went out and I was hurled back sixteen years in time.

Same place.

Same despair in my little brother's voice.

Same crime about to be committed, only this time it was him who was going to be the victim.

But he was alive. And he needed help.

'What is it?' I managed to say as the sheriff stood bellowing his refrain behind me.

Carl hesitated. 'Is that Kurt Olsen I can hear?'

'Yes. What is it?'

726

'The cutting of the ribbon is about to take place and it's sort of the point to arrive in the Cadillac,' he said. 'But there's something wrong with it. Bound to be some minor thing, but can you get up here and see if you can fix the problem?'

'I'll be there directly,' I said, ended the call and turned to Kurt Olsen.

'Nice talking to you, but unless you've got a warrant for my arrest then I'm off.'

His jaw was still hanging open as I left.

A minute later I was driving along the highway in the Volvo. I had the bag of tools on the seat beside me, the lights from Olsen's Land Rover in the mirror, and his departing promise to get both me and my brother still ringing in my ears. For a moment I wondered if he intended to pursue me all the way up to the farm, but when I took the turning for Nergard and Opgard he drove straight on.

Anyway, it wasn't Olsen that worried me most.

Something wrong with the Cadillac? What the hell could that be? Could Carl have got into the car and noticed the brakes and steering wheel weren't working properly **before** he started to drive? No, because in that case he must have had his suspicions about it. Or else someone had told him. Was that what had happened? Had Shannon been unable to go through with the plan? Had she cracked up and confessed the whole thing? Or even worse: had she changed sides and told Carl the truth? Or her version of the truth.

Yes, that was it. She'd told him the murder plan was mine and mine alone, told him I knew that Carl had forged my signature on the deeds, told him I'd raped her, got her pregnant and threatened to kill her, the child and Carl if she said anything. Because I was no timid, frightened ring ouzel, I was Dad, a mountain lark, a bird of prey with a black bandit's mask across his eyes. And then Shannon had told him what the two of them needed to do now. Lure me up to the farm and get rid of me the way me and Carl had got rid of Dad. Because of course she knew, she already knew the Opgard brothers were capable of murder, knew that she'd get what she wanted one way or the other.

I gasped for breath and managed to push these sick, unwelcome thoughts aside. I rounded a corner and a black tunnel opened up in front of me where no tunnel should have been. An impenetrable, dark stone wall it would have been hopeless to try to breach. And yet that was where the road led. Was this depression, the thing the old sheriff had talked to me about? Dad's dark mind finally rising up in me, not falling like the night but rising from the valley depths? Maybe. And the remarkable thing was that with each hairpin bend I rounded, climbing ever higher and higher, my breathing grew easier.

Because it was OK. If it ended here, if I was not to live for one more day, then that was OK. With any luck killing me would bring Carl and Shannon together. Carl was a pragmatist. He could live with raising a child that wasn't completely his and yet was still a member of his family. Yes, maybe my demise was the only chance of a happy ending in all this.

I rounded Geitesvingen and speeded up slightly, the gravel flying up behind the rear wheels. Below me lay the village, swathed in evening dark, and in what remained of the daylight I saw Carl standing in front of the Cadillac with arms folded, waiting for me.

And another thought struck me. Not another, but the first.

That that's all it was: something wrong with the car.

Something trivial that had nothing to do with the brake hoses or the throttle cable and could be easily fixed. That somewhere in the kitchen light, behind the curtains, Shannon was waiting for me to sort this out and after that the plan would be back on the rails.

I climbed out of the car, and Carl walked over and put his arms around me. He held me in such a way that I felt his whole body from head to toe, could feel he was trembling the way he used to after Dad had been to our room and I climbed down into his bed to comfort him.

He whispered a few words in my ear, and I understood.

Understood that the plan was **not** back on the rails.

69

WE SAT IN THE CADILLAC. Carl behind the wheel, me in the passenger seat.

Staring out past Geitesvingen, at the mountain peaks in the south framed in orange and pale blue.

'I said on the phone there was something wrong with the car because I knew Olsen was there,' Carl said tearfully.

'I understand,' I said, and tried to move my foot, which had fallen asleep. No, not asleep, but gone lame, as lame as the rest of me. 'Tell me in more detail what happened.' My voice felt and sounded as though it was someone else talking.

'Right,' said Carl. 'We were about to leave for the building site, were getting changed. Shannon's ready,

730

she looks like a million dollars. I'm in the kitchen ironing my shirt. And then suddenly she says she's not feeling well. I tell her we've got paracetamol, but she says she has to go upstairs and lie down, I should go to the opening on my own and she'll take the Subaru to the party if she feels any better. I'm shocked, tell her to pull herself together, this is important. But she refuses, says her health comes first and so on. And yeah, I'm really pissed off, it's all just bullshit, Shannon never gets so ill she can't manage to stay on her feet for a couple of hours, right? And this is, you know, it's her big moment every bit as much as mine. For a moment I lose control, and I just blurt it out . . .'

'You just blurt it out,' I said, and could feel the paralysis advancing into my tongue.

'I just blurt out that if she's feeling so ill it's probably because of that bastard kid she's got in the oven.'

'Bastard kid,' I repeated. It was so cold in the car. So fucking cold.

'Yeah, she asked about that too, like she didn't understand what I was talking about. Then I tell her that I know about her and that American actor. Dennis Quarry. And she repeats the name, and I can't even stand hearing the way she says it: **Denn-is Qu-arry.** And then she starts to laugh. To **laugh.** And I'm standing there with the iron in my hand, and something inside me just snaps.'

'Snaps.' Expressionless.

'I hit her,' he said.

'Hit her.' I'd turned into a fucking echo chamber.

'The iron hits her on the side of the head, she falls backwards and into the stovepipe so it breaks. There's a cloud of soot.'

I say nothing.

'So I'm leaning over her and holding that scalding hot iron right in front of her face and saying if she doesn't confess then I'll iron her as flat as my shirt. But she still goes on laughing. And lying there laughing away with the blood running down into her mouth so her teeth are red with blood she looks like a fucking witch and not all that fucking beautiful any more, see what I mean? And she confesses. Not just what I'm asking her about but she sticks the knife right in and confesses everything. She confesses the worst thing of all.'

I tried to swallow, but there was no saliva left.

'And what was the worst thing of all?'

'What do you think, Roy?'

'I don't know,' I said.

'The hotel,' he said. 'It was Shannon who set fire to the hotel.'

'Shannon? How . . . ?'

'As we were leaving Willumsen's party to go to the square to see the rockets Shannon said she was tired and wanted to go home and she took the car. I was still in the square when we heard the fire truck.' Carl closed his eyes. 'Shannon's sitting there by the stove and she says how she drove up to the building site and started the fire at a place where she knew it would spread, and left behind a dead rocket so it would look like that was the cause of the fire.'

I know what to ask. That I have to ask, even though I know the answer. Must ask in order not to reveal that I already know, that I know Shannon probably just as well as he does. So I do it. 'Why?'

'Because . . .' Carl swallows. 'Because she's God, creating in her own image. She couldn't live with that hotel, it had to be the way she had drawn it. That or nothing. She didn't know it wasn't insured and figured it wouldn't be a problem to start again from scratch and then, at the second attempt, she'd be able to insist we use her original drawings.'

'Is that what she said?'

'Yes. And when I asked if she didn't consider the rest of us, you, and me, and the people in the village who had worked and invested in it, she said no.'

'No?'

'**Fuck no,** was what she said. And laughed. And then I hit her again.'

'With the iron?'

'With the back of it. The cold side.'

'Hard?'

'Hard. I saw the light go out in her eyes.'

I had to concentrate in order to breathe. 'Was she . . .'

'I took her pulse, but I couldn't feel shit.'

'And then?'

'I carried her out here.'

'She's lying in the boot?'

'Yes.'

'Show me.'

We climbed out. As Carl opened the boot I raised my eyes and looked into the west. Above the mountain tops the orange was eating into the pale blue. And I thought that this was maybe the last time I would be able to think that something was beautiful. But for a fraction of a second, before looking down into the boot, I thought it had all been just a joke, that there wouldn't be anybody there.

But there she lay. A snow-white Sleeping Beauty. She slept the way she had done the two nights we had spent together in Kristiansand. On her side, with eyes closed. And I couldn't help thinking: in the same foetal position as the child inside her.

The wounds to her head left no room for doubt that she was dead. I laid my fingertips against that smashed forehead.

'This isn't just from one blow with the back of an iron,' I said.

'I . . .' Carl swallowed. 'She moved when I laid her beside the car to open the boot, and I . . . I panicked.'

Automatically I looked down at the ground, and there, in the interior light from the boot, I saw a flash from one of the big stones Dad had made us carry up to the wall of the house, to improve the drainage one autumn when it rained more than usual. There was blood on it.

Carl's sobbing whisper beside me sounded like porridge simmering. 'Can you help me out, Roy?'

My gaze went back to Shannon. Wanted to look

away but couldn't look away. He had killed her. No, he had **murdered** her. In cold blood. And now he was asking for help. I hated him. Hated, hated, and now I felt my heart start to pump again, and with the blood came pain, finally the pain came, and I bit down so hard it felt as though I would crush my own jaws. I drew a breath and freed up my jaw enough to say three words:

'Help you how?'

'We can drive her out to the woods. Leave her somewhere where they're bound to find her and leave the Cadillac next to her. Then I'll say she took the Cadillac and went out for a spin earlier in the day and still hadn't come back by the time I left for the opening ceremony. If we go now and leave her some-where, then I'll still have time to make it, and then I can report her missing when she doesn't show up at the party as arranged. Sound good?'

I punched him in the stomach.

He folded in the middle and stood there like a fuck-ing L, gasping for breath. I easily pushed him over onto the gravel, then sat on top of him so that his arms were trapped. He was going to die; he was going to die the same way she did. My right hand found the big stone, but it was sticky and slippery with blood and slipped out of my grasp. I was about to dry my hand on my shirt, but finally managed to think clearly enough to instead run my hand twice through the gravel and then picked up the stone again. Raised it above my head. Carl was still not breathing and lay with his eyes tight shut. I wanted him to see this, so I squeezed his nose with my left hand.

He opened his eyes.

He cried.

His eyes were on me, maybe he still hadn't seen the stone I was holding up above my head, or maybe he didn't understand what it meant. Or else he'd reached the same place as me and didn't give a fuck any more. I felt the pull of gravity on the stone, it wanted to fall, it wanted to crush, I wouldn't even have to use force, it was when I **stopped** using force, when I no longer kept it at arm's length from my brother that it would do the job for which it was intended. He had stopped crying, and already I could feel the burn of the lactic acid in my right arm. I gave up. Let it happen. But then I saw it. Like some fucking echo from childhood. That look in his eyes. That fucking humiliated, helpless little-brother look. And the lump in my throat. I was the one who was going to start crying. Again. I let the stone come, added speed to it, smashed it down so hard I could feel it all the way up my shoulder. Sat there panting like a fucking hound dog.

And after I'd got my breath back, I rolled off Carl who lay there, motionless. Silent at last. Eyes wide open, as though finally he had seen and understood everything. I sat there next to him and looked at Ottertind Mountain. Our silent witness.

'That was pretty damn close to my head,' Carl groaned.

'Not close enough,' I said.

'OK, so I fucked up,' he said. 'Have you got that out of your system now?'

I took the snuffbox from my trouser pocket.

'Speaking of stones to the head,' I said, and didn't care a shit if he could hear the shaking in my voice. 'When they find her in the woods, how do you think they're going to explain her head wounds? Eh?'

'Someone murdered her, I guess.'

'And who's the first person they're going to suspect?'

'The husband?'

'Who is the guilty party in eighty per cent of all cases, according to **True Crime** magazine? Particularly when he's got no alibi for the time of the murder.'

Carl raised himself up onto his elbows. 'OK then, big brother, so what do we do?'

We. Naturally.

'Give me a few seconds,' I said.

I looked around. What did I see?

Opgard. A small house, a barn, a few outlying fields. And what, actually, was that? A name in six letters, a family with two surviving members. Because, when you take away all the rest, what was a family? A story we told each other because family was a necessity. Because, over thousands of years, it had worked as a unit of cooperation? Yeah, why not? Or was there something beyond the merely practical, something in the blood that bound parents, brothers and sisters together? They say you can't live on just fresh air and love. But you can't fucking well live without them either. And if there's something we want, then it's to

737

live. I felt that now, perhaps even more strongly because death lay in the boot directly in front of us. That I wanted to live. And, for that reason, that we had to do what had to be done. That everything depended on me. That it had to be done now.

'First,' I said, 'when I checked the Cadillac last autumn I told Shannon you should replace the brake hoses and the throttle cable. Have you done that?'

'What?' Carl coughed and held a hand to his stomach. 'Shannon never said a word about that.'

'Good, then we're in luck,' I said. 'We move her into the driver's seat. Before you wash the kitchen and the boot, take what blood there is and smear it on the steering wheel, the seat and the dashboard. Got that?'

'Er, yes. But . . .'

'Shannon is going to be found in the Cadillac down in Huken and that will explain her head wounds.'

'But . . . that's the third car down in Huken. The police are bound to wonder what the fuck is going on.'

'Definitely. But once they find those worn parts I'm talking about, then they'll understand that this really was an accident.'

'You think so?'

'Certain of it,' I said.

A thin glow of orange light still lay around Ottertind as Carl and I started the heavy black beast moving. Shannon looked so tiny behind that big wheel. We let go of the car and it trundled slowly, almost reluctantly forward as the gravel crunched beneath its tyres. Uppermost on the fins sticking out at the back the two vertically mounted lights glowed red. It was a Cadillac DeVille. From the days when the Americans made cars like spaceships that could take you to the sky.

I followed the car with my eyes, the throttle cable must have got stuck because it just kept on accelerating and I thought this time it will happen, it'll take off for the sky.

She'd said she thought it was a boy. I had said nothing, but of course I couldn't help thinking about names. Not that I think she would have accepted Bernard, but that was the only one I could think of.

Carl put his arm around my shoulder. 'You're all I have, Roy,' he said.

And you're all I have, I thought. Two brothers in a desert.

70

'FOR A LOT OF US, we're back now where we started out,' said Carl.

He was on the stage at Årtun, in front of one of the microphone stands which would shortly be taken over by Rod and his band.

'And I'm not thinking about the first investors' meeting we had here, but when I, my brother and many of you who are here tonight used to meet at the local dances. And it was usually after a few drinks we would get up enough front to start boasting about all the great things we swore we were going to achieve. Or else we asked the one who had had the loudest mouth how things were coming along with that great plan of his, had he made a start yet? And then there would be mocking grins one way and curses the other and – if he happened to be the touchy type – a butt.'

Laughter from the audience standing in the hall.

'But when anyone asks us next year how things are going with that hotel us people from Os boast about so much, then we can tell them oh yes, we built that all right. Twice.'

Wild enthusiasm. I shifted from one foot to the other. Nausea gripped around my throat, a headache pounded rhythmically behind my eyes, the pain in my chest was excruciating, almost like I would imagine a heart attack feels. But I tried not to think, tried not to feel. For the moment it looked as though Carl was dealing with it better than me. As I should have known. He was the cold one of us. He was like Mum. A passive accessory. Cold.

He held his arms out wide, like a circus ringmaster, or an actor.

'Those of you who were present at the launch earlier this evening were able to see the drawings exhibited there, and you know how fantastic this is going to be. And actually our master builder, my wife Shannon Alleyne Opgard, should have been up here on the stage with me. She may be along later, but at the moment she's at home in bed because sometimes that's the way it is when a hotel isn't the only thing you're pregnant with . . .'

There was silence for a moment. Then the cheering started all over again, presently turning into foot-stamping applause.

I couldn't take any more, I hurried for the exit.

'And now, everyone, please give a warm welcome to . . .'

I elbowed my way out of the door and just managed to get round the corner of the building before my throat filled and the puke splashed down onto the ground in front of me. It came in contractions, something that had to come out, like a bloody birth. When at last it was over I sank to my knees, empty, done. From inside I heard the cowbell tap out the rhythm to the fast number Rod and his gang always opened with, 'Honky Tonk Women'. I pressed my forehead against the wall and started to cry. Snot, tears and puke-stinking slime poured out of me.

'Jesus,' I heard a voice say behind me. 'Did someone finally beat up Roy Opgard?'

'Don't, Simon!' said a woman's voice, and I felt a hand on my shoulder. 'Is everything all right, Roy?'

I half turned. Grete Smitt had a red headscarf wrapped around her head. And she actually looked quite good in it.

'Just some bad moonshine,' I said. 'But thanks anyway.'

The two of them walked on towards the car park, arms around each other.

I got to my feet and headed off in the direction of the birch wood, feet squelching on soft ground that swayed, heavy with meltwater. I cleared my nostrils one after the other, spat and breathed in. The evening air was still cold, but it tasted different, like a promise that things would change, into something new, and better. I couldn't comprehend what that might be.

I stood beneath a bare tree. The moon had risen and bathed Lake Budal in an eerie light. In a few days' time the ice would be gone. The current would take hold of the ice floes. Once things start to crack here, it doesn't take long for everything to go.

A figure appeared beside me.

'What does the ptarmigan do when the fox takes its eggs?' It was Carl.

'Lays new ones,' I said.

'Isn't it funny? When your parents say stuff like that when you're a kid you think it's just drivel. And then one day you suddenly understand what they meant.'

I shrugged.

'It's lovely, isn't it?' he said. 'When the spring finally reaches us too.'

'It is.'

'When are you coming back?'

'Back?'

'To Os.'

'For the funeral, I suppose.'

'There won't be any funeral here, I'm sending her in a coffin to Barbados. I mean, when are you moving back?'

'Never.'

Carl laughed as though I'd just made a joke. 'You maybe don't know it yourself yet, but you'll be back before the year is out, Roy Opgard.' And then he left.

I stood there for a long time. Finally I looked up at the moon. It should have been something bigger, like a planet, something that could really have set me and everybody else and our tragic and hurried lives in a proper perspective. I needed that now. Something that could tell me that all of us – Shannon, Carl and me, Mum and Dad, Uncle Bernard, Sigmund Olsen, Willumsen and the Danish enforcer – were here, gone and forgotten in the same instant, hardly more than a flash in the universe's vast ocean of time and space. That was the only comfort we had, that absolutely nothing had meaning. Not looking out across your own land. Not running your own service station. Not waking up beside the one you love. Not seeing your own child grow up.

That's what it was: unimportant.

But of course, the moon was too small to provide comfort for that.

71

'THANKS,' SAID MARTINSEN AS SHE took the cup of coffee I handed to her. She leaned against the kitchen worktop and looked out of the window. The KRIPOS car and Olsen's Land Rover were still down on Geitesvingen.

'So you didn't find anything?' I asked.

'Obviously not,' she said.

'Does it seem so obvious to you?'

Martinsen sighed and glanced round, as though to assure herself we were still alone in the kitchen. 'To be quite honest, under normal circumstances we would have rejected the request for assistance in a case which was so obviously an accident. When your sheriff contacted us, the faults on the car – which were obviously what caused it – had already been discovered. The extensive damages sustained by the dead person are what you would expect from such a long fall. The local doctor obviously couldn't say exactly when she died, given that it took a day and a half before he was able to get down to the car; but his estimate suggests she went off the road sometime between six o'clock and midnight.'

'So then why have you made the trip out here anyway?'

'Well, one reason is that your sheriff insisted on it. He was almost aggressive about it. He is convinced that your brother's wife was murdered, and he's read in what he calls a technical journal that in eighty per cent of cases the guilty party is the husband. And in KRIPOS we like to keep a good relationship with the sheriffs' offices round about.' She smiled. 'Good coffee, by the way.'

'Thanks. And what was the other reason?'

'The other?'

'You said Sheriff Olsen was one reason, so what was the other?'

Martinsen turned her blue eyes on me, and it was a look that was hard to judge. And I didn't meet her gaze. Didn't want to. I was quite simply not there. Moreover I knew that if I let her look me too directly and too long in the eye she might discover the wound.

'I appreciate your openness with me, Martinsen.'

'Vera.'

'But aren't you at least slightly sceptical when you

know that, in all, three cars have driven off the road and fallen down the same precipice, and that you are now talking to the brother of someone who was closely connected to all of those who have lost their lives here?'

Vera Martinsen nodded. 'I haven't forgotten that for one moment, Roy. And Olsen has reminded me of those road accidents over and over again. Now he has a theory that the first fatal accident might also have been murder and wants us to check whether the brake hoses on the Cadillac at the bottom were possibly sabotaged.'

'My father's,' I said, hoping my poker face was still in place. 'Did your people check?'

Martinsen laughed. 'In the first place the wreck lies squashed under two other cars down there. And if we **did** find something, the case is now eighteen years old and subject to the statute of limitations. Moreover I'm a great believer in what people call common sense and logic. Do you know how many cars go off the road in Norway each year? Around three thousand. And in how many different places? Less than two thousand. Almost half of all cars that go off the road do so in places where the same thing has happened earlier in the same year. For three cars to go off the road over a period of eighteen years at a place that should obviously have been better protected seems to me not merely reasonable, I think in fact it's strange there haven't been more accidents.'

I nodded. 'Perhaps you'd be kind enough to mention

that about better safety measures to the local authorities here?'

Martinsen smiled and put down her cup.

I followed her out into the hall.

'How is your brother doing?' she said as she buttoned up her jacket.

'Well, he's taking it hard. He's accompanied the coffin to Barbados. He's going to meet her relatives there. After that he says he's going to drown himself completely in work on the hotel.'

'And what about you?'

'It gets better,' I lied. 'Of course, it was a shock, but life goes on. For the eighteen months Shannon lived here I was mostly other places, so we never really knew each other well enough to . . . well, you know what I mean. It's not like losing someone from your own family.'

'I understand.'

'Hm, well,' I said, and opened the front door for her, since she hadn't done so herself. But she didn't move.

'Hear that?' she whispered. 'Wasn't that a plover?'

I nodded. Slowly. 'Are you interested in birds?'

'Very. I get it from my father. And you?'

'Yeah, pretty much.'

'You've got a lot of interesting specimens up in these parts, I expect?'

'Yes we do.'

'Maybe I can come up one day and you can show me?'

'That would've been nice,' I said. 'But I don't live here.'

And then I met her gaze anyway and let her see it. How damaged I was.

'OK,' she said. 'Let me know if you move back then. You'll find my number on the card I left under the coffee cup.'

I nodded.

Once she'd gone I went up to the bedroom, lay down on the double bed, pulled the pillow over my face and breathed in the last remnants of Shannon. A faint, spicy smell that in a few days' time would be gone. I opened the wardrobe on her side of the bed. It was empty. Carl had taken most of her things to Barbados with him and thrown away the rest. But in the dark recesses of the cupboard I saw something. Shannon must have found them somewhere in the house and stored them there. It was a pair of crocheted baby shoes, so comically small you had to smile. Grandma had crocheted them, and according to Mum they were mine first, and then later Carl's.

I went down into the kitchen.

From the window I could see the barn door was wide open. The glow of a cigarette. Kurt Olsen squatting on his haunches inside and examining something on the floor.

I took out the binoculars.

He ran his fingers over something. And I knew what it was. The marks from the jack on the soft planking. Kurt walked over to the punchbag, stared at the face painted on it. Gave it a tentative punch. Vera Martinsen had probably told him by now that KRIPOS were getting ready to pack up and leave. But Olsen wouldn't be giving up. I read somewhere that it takes the body seven years to change all its cells, including brain cells, and that after seven years we are in principle a new person. But our DNA, the programme the cells are based on, does not change. That if we cut our hair, our nails or a fingertip, what grows out again will be the same, a repetition. And that new brain cells are no different from old ones and take over many of the same memories and experiences. We don't change, we make the same choices, repeat the same mistakes. Like father like son. A hunter like Kurt Olsen will go on hunting, a killer will – if the circumstances are an exact repetition – again choose to kill. There's an eternal circle, like the predictable orbits of planets, and the regular progression of the seasons.

Kurt Olsen was on his way out of the barn when he stopped to look at something else. And now he lifted it up, held it up to the light. It was one of the zinc buckets. I focused the binoculars. He was studying the bullet holes. First on one side of the bucket, then on the other. After a while he put the bucket down, walked down to his car and drove off.

The house was empty. I was alone. More alone than I'd ever been before. Was this what it was like for Dad, even with all of us around him?

From the west came a low, threatening rumbling sound and I turned the binoculars to look.

It was an avalanche on the north face of Ottertind. Heavy, wet 'sugary' snow that couldn't stay up there any more, it had to get down and now thundered through the ice, making the water cascade high into the air on the far shore of Lake Budal.

Yes, merciless spring was on its way again.

Jo Nesbo is one of the world's bestselling crime writers, with multiple books including **The Son, Macbeth and Knife** topping the **Sunday Times** bestseller charts. He's an international number one bestseller and his books are published in 50 languages, selling over 45 million copies around the world.

Before becoming a crime writer, Nesbo played football for Norway's premier league team Molde, but his dream was dashed when he tore ligaments in his knee at the age of eighteen. After three years of military service he attended business school and formed the band Di Derre ('Them There'). They topped the charts in Norway, but Nesbo continued working as a financial analyst, crunching numbers during the day and gigging at night. When commissioned by a publisher to write a memoir about life on the road with his band, he instead came up with the plot for his first Harry Hole crime novel, **The Bat.**

Sign up to the Jo Nesbo newsletter for all the latest news: jonesbo.com/newsletter

Robert Ferguson has lived in Norway since 1983. His translations include **Norwegian Wood** by Lars Mytting, the four novels in Torkil Damhaug's Oslo Crime Fiction series, and **Tales of Love and Loss** by Knut Hamsun. He is the author of several biographies, a Viking history and, most recently, **The Cabin in the Mountains: A Norwegian Odyssey.**